FALLEN CREST FOREVER

THE 7TH IN THE FALLEN CREST SERIES

NYT & USA Bestselling Author
TIJAN

Edited by Jessica Royer Ocken
Proofread by: Paige Smith, Kara Hildebrand,
Holly Malagieri, Chris O'Neil Parece, and Amy English
Cover Design by Hang Le
Formatted by: Elaine York, Allusion Graphics, LLC/
Publishing & Book Formatting, www.allusiongraphics.com

DEDICATION

For everyone who fell in love with *Fallen Crest High*
and has continued to show their love and support for these guys.
This book is entirely for you.

CHAPTER ONE

"Will you marry me?"

I didn't know what to say.

I was Samantha Strattan. I'd been a nobody for so long, until Mason and Logan came into my life. Then I was Mason Kade's girlfriend, or Logan Kade's stepsister. I was *theirs*. It took a totally fucked-up summer for me to realize I lost who Samantha Strattan was somewhere along the way, and now my soul mate—the guy who was the air for my lungs—was asking me the question I recently realized was my nightmare.

"Mason." No other words would come out of my throat. "I . . ."

I couldn't breathe.

I couldn't move.

I couldn't look *at* him.

I couldn't look *away* from him.

He wasn't the nightmare. He was the dream.

The nightmare was my mother's marriage. It was Mason's parents' marriage. It was all the cheating, lying, and bitterness. I would die if that happened to Mason and me.

What the fuck? What the effing fuck? Oh my God. Those words were on repeat in my head. I was in a horror movie.

I watched in slow motion as Mason's eyebrows dipped when he realized I wasn't saying anything. Then he realized I *really* wasn't saying anything, and that said everything.

I felt myself falling backward, like someone pushed me off a cliff I didn't know was behind me. I was falling . . . falling . . . I reached out, trying to get ahold of something—anything to stop this fall. All I could find was air, and I was going to land soon.

I saw the wall first.

It slammed down behind his eyes, and he donned an unreadable mask. His jaw clenched, and he shifted backward on his knees until he could stand. Once he was up, he began turning off the tea lights that surrounded us, making the clearing twinkle. I could feel the physical and emotional distance between us.

Smack!

I hit rock bottom.

"Mason."

"No." He shook his head. He was so cold now. "Let's go." He gathered up the blanket and headed back for the Escalade. He was almost there. He reached for the door handle—

"Yes."

It came out as a whisper. I shocked myself.

Marriage: that word terrified me. But cheating wasn't me. It wasn't Mason. We wouldn't be liars. The bitterness would never come. I looked at him, watched as he froze and turned back to me. His back had been so rigid. He was still tense, but his eyes locked on mine.

I nodded, to him and for myself. Yes, I would marry him. Yes, I would love him forever. Yes, I would never let *us* be *them*.

"Sam?"

"Yes." My voice was coming back to me. I nodded again. "Yes! I'll marry you."

He started for me. "Are you sure?" His head dipped down, still holding my gaze.

I nodded. I was. I really was. I lifted my arms as he met me, then swept me up in a hug.

"Yes," I whispered again, burying my head in his shoulder.

He wasn't James. I wasn't Analise. We weren't going to repeat what we'd seen growing up.

I lifted my head to find his lips. "I love you." I kissed him with everything I had. I knew my hesitation had hurt him, and I needed to erase that. "Yes, I'll be your wife."

He held me tighter for a moment, then set me back on my feet. His hands fell to my waist, and he leaned back.

"Why the pause?" he asked.

He deserved the truth.

"Because I'm scared shitless about what our parents did. I'm scared of marriage. A part of me thinks it's a crock of shit, after seeing what my mom did to David and hearing what James did to your mom."

His face walled off again. My hands went to the tops of his arms, and I gripped tightly. I held him when he wanted to pull back. "But that's not you and me. I'm scared—I have to be honest—but we can change the cycle. We won't do what they did. What we will have, and do have, is already so much more sacred than what they *thought* they had."

Understanding edged out some of the guarded expression on his face. He nodded, just once, just slightly. "Are you sure, Sam? I've always thought we'd get married, but I wasn't planning on asking this early. It's just . . . seeing your mom coming down that aisle, I wanted it to be you."

Everything melted inside me.

My insecurities.

My worries.

My heart.

I was so humbled at that moment and wound my arms around him. What had I done to deserve this? Deserve him?

"I love you," I whispered, my lips pressing against his skin. "So goddamn much."

His hand came to the back of my head. "So goddamn much," he repeated.

His phone rang, and Mason groaned against my skin.

"Fucking hell," he cursed as he slipped his hand into his pocket.

When the phone appeared, we both glanced down. It was Logan, and we shared a look. He'd already called about the footage of the fight being leaked to Mason's football coach. If he was calling again so soon, it wasn't good news.

Mason hit the *Accept* button and put the phone to his ear. "Yeah?"

I started to untangle myself, but his arm just tightened around my back. He didn't want to let go and, falling a little more in love (if that was even possible), I relaxed against him. My head rested on his chest.

"Are you coming back to Cain tonight?" Logan asked through the phone. He sounded tense.

I frowned, but didn't lift my head. It felt too right to move.

"Uh . . ."

I looked up.

Mason lifted an eyebrow, wanting to know what I wanted to do.

We just got engaged. Time alone would be nice, though there was a huge crisis hanging over us. I wanted to stay in Fallen Crest, but I said, "We should go back. We won't relax otherwise."

He nodded, saying into the phone, "We're coming back."

"Good." Logan sounded relieved. "I know you're in deep shit because of the fighting, but I might need help with these guys that roughed up Taylor's friend."

"The same guy that we had to deal with a crime lord about?" Mason rolled his eyes.

"They beat the shit out of him because he's gay. They deserve something worse happening to them," Logan clipped out. "We can be inventive if you don't want to do a beatdown with me."

Mason's voice was strained. "Start brainstorming, because I can't do anything violent unless it's on the football field. They're going to watch me like a damned hawk, and that's *if* I'm still allowed to play."

"You'll be fine, but yeah, Nate and I will put our thinking hats on. See you when you get here."

"Yeah."

Logan suddenly called out, "Hi, Sam!"

I moved closer to the phone. "Don't get Mason in trouble, please."

He groaned. "I might start trouble, but he always delivers the knockout punch. There's a reason we work as brothers."

Anger glinted in Mason's eyes. His lips pressed together. "Okay. Be there in a few hours."

He hung up and looked down at me. "You didn't say anything."

"Neither did you."

"I was letting you make the decision."

I pressed a hand against his chest, feeling his heart beat just on the other side. "I know. Let's keep our engagement between us for a minute. Once we tell, it's no longer ours. It's everyone's to talk about—and give their opinions about everything." I tilted back to look up at him. "You know what I mean?"

His eyes darkened. I saw the love there. "I do." He cupped the back of my neck. "I love you." His lips found mine.

I closed my eyes, savoring this.

My man.

My other half.

My future husband.

So much lies ahead of us, but he was mine, completely mine, in this moment. My lips moved against his, deepening the kiss, and he tightened his hold on me.

CHAPTER TWO

Mason was driving, and I couldn't stop from looking over and studying him. He wasn't a boy anymore, not that he'd ever seemed like one. He was a man, and he was going to be my husband. It left me in awe. Forever. Though when had that word *not* been used to describe Mason and me? Never. But there was still a little voice in the back of my head that worried about repeating our parents' actions.

"What's wrong?" Mason asked.

"What?"

He gave me a half-grin, one hand on the steering wheel. "You seem like something's wrong. Is it the engagement stuff?"

"Yeah." I pressed a hand to my stomach. There were butterflies in there. "Does that bother you?"

"What? That my dad was a piss-poor husband or that your mom was psycho before?"

"Both." I turned in my seat, pulling up one of my legs so I could sit sideways with the seatbelt still in place. I rested my head against the seat, watching him fully now.

His lips were perfect. I loved brushing mine against his, feeling his body tighten under my touch. His jawline—oh holy fuck, his jawline. It was strong, and it had made me weak in the knees too many times to count. His eyes, beautiful green that could look right into me. He would turn, see my eyes, and slide inside where he could read my soul. It had been like that in the beginning. It still was.

I never wanted him to stop seeing me.

And his black hair, it was newly trimmed back into a crew cut, but there was just the smallest amount for me to grab hold of it. That only made me salivate more for him. When he held himself above me, his eyes darkening in lust, his shoulders rippling from my touch, I loved how every part of him was defined and cut like a sculpture. He did it for football, training so many hours each day, and the thought of that made my heart hurt.

Football.

Everything would work out.

The league would let him play. He was Mason Fucking Kade. He was a star wide receiver on Cain University's team, and he was mentioned on ESPN regularly. His draft was this year. Someone would take him. They'd be stupid if they didn't.

I reached over and placed my hand on his where it rested on his leg. "It'll get sorted out. You know it."

He didn't comment, just turned his palm upward and laced his fingers with mine.

I remembered what he'd said just before he proposed: that he was fucked. That the NFL doesn't do scandals, and a video of Mason Kade beating the shit out of someone was one of those. It wouldn't matter to them if he'd been protecting me, not once they opened up his record and started digging. There was a lot there. Mason and Logan had been fighting and setting cars on fire long before I came into their lives. They never bullied, but if they were hurt, they would hurt back. That was their rule. They reacted, rather than incited.

I knew they'd continue to do so, but there had to be a change. Mason tried before, and he learned to be smarter when he was defending himself. He slipped this summer and returned to the violence, but that was done.

They'd be smarter. They had to . . .

"Stop worrying," he said.

"Hmmm?" I'd been staring at him, lost in my own head.

"You're worrying. I can feel it." His hand squeezed mine. "I believe you."

My head lifted from the seat. "You do?"

"Yeah." He glanced sideways at me, grinning again.

God—that mouth.

"You said everything will get sorted," he added. "You're usually right. I believe you."

My heart pounded against my chest. "Good." My voice was breathless. I don't know why it affected me so much to have Mason believe in me. Mason always believed in me.

Whatever the reason, I was going to follow through. I knew Mason and Logan—even their father—would do anything necessary to ensure Mason's future in football, but so would I.

My throat was full so I could only whisper, "I love you." The feeling swept over me, leaving me renewed and invigorated.

He winked, his grin morphing into a smirk. "I know."

I pretended to hit his arm, and the smirk turned serious. "I love you too," he said.

———

Logan sent a couple text messages as we traveled, with the last one telling us to go right to Taylor's house. We passed the exit that would've taken us to our house, and it wasn't long before we pulled up at the large home where Taylor had grown up, but it wasn't Logan or Taylor who met us at the door.

Taylor's father, who was in his early forties, opened the door. He was a good-looking man with sandy brown hair. He kept himself trim, which made sense because he was also one of Mason's coaches.

The two regarded each other.

Mason readied himself, adopting an unreadable mask and lifting himself to his fullest height. He never cowered for anyone. He wasn't going to start now, but I knew he was tense. He respected Taylor's father, Coach Bruce, nicknamed Coach Broozer. And Coach Broozer wasn't looking very happy.

Finally, the coach moved back, and Mason and I stepped inside. He nodded to me as I passed, following Mason.

"Let's go to the kitchen." Coach Broozer led the way.

We walked through the small front entrance hallway and past the living room and stairs before turning in to the kitchen. I got the distinct impression no one else was home.

Broozer indicated the chairs in the dining room. "Take a seat."

"I thought my brother was here," Mason said.

"No." He gestured to the kitchen. "Either of you want water or something else to drink? I can make a pot of coffee, or we have Gatorade. Mason?"

Mason sat at the far end of the table. I sat next to him.

"Nothing for me," he said.

"Sam?"

I shook my head. I had a feeling we wouldn't be here long.

"Why'd Logan tell me to come here first?"

Taylor's father poured himself a glass of water and took his time settling into his chair. He took the far end, closest to the kitchen and opposite Mason and me. He leaned forward, resting his arms on the table, and paused another few seconds before taking a deep breath. His hands cupped his water glass, and he looked down, almost like he was going to talk to the table.

"It's not the greatest, Kade."

Mason's jaw clenched.

"Logan said your case was thrown out, and I called the FCPD," he continued. "They confirmed what he said, so I talked to the head coach, and he agreed. The whole department agreed. You're back in time to start practicing with the team, so you won't be suspended. Your case was dropped. There's no reason to punish you further, but I have to warn you . . ." His voice dropped ominously. "If word gets out about this video, or it gets leaked online and stirs up a fuss, we may have to handle it appropriately."

"I'm good as long as no one knows about it or gets upset about it?" Mason's jaw clenched. "Otherwise you'll have to punish me to save face. Is that what you're saying?"

Broozer's eyes twitched before he nodded. "Yes."

"That's bullshit."

"It's the hand you're dealt. You haven't helped. That video was horrifying to watch. I know your reputation, and if a reporter starts digging, you could be made into an example."

"An example of what?"

Broozer leaned forward, his eyes no-nonsense. "Of every other rich prick who gets away with murder."

"I was protecting my girlfriend."

"That's not what they're going to think." He pointed out the window. "All those people who hate the wealthy and privileged. They ain't going to see you as a guy who steps up and protects his loved ones. They'll see your pretty face, find out how rich your daddy is, and see your record of violence. You'll be slapped on the front of a magazine as the asshole who 'got off.' They won't take the time to be educated about the real issue."

Mason leaned back in his chair.

I eyed him. He didn't look upset, but he didn't show anything. He was closed off. Coach was being honest, and I knew Mason appreciated that, but I understood his frustration. It sucked. He couldn't relax, knowing Caldron and Adam were behind him. Both douchebags from the summer were still hanging over his head.

I touched his leg under the table, and he looked at me from the corner of his eye. His hands remained locked together on top of the table, but his leg angled closer to me.

We heard car doors slam outside, and all looked over. We couldn't see through the window from where we were, but Logan's voice quickly carried over the distance.

"Look." Coach Broozer straightened in his seat. He pointed toward the table and jabbed it twice. "I know what kind of kid my daughter is dating, and I know the lengths he'd go to for his brother. You can't say a word of this to him. This could all go away if we don't do a damned thing. You got it? If Logan knows, he'll do something. He won't be able to help it. He means well, but he could really fuck up your life if you don't handle him right."

Mason didn't have time to reply.

The door opened, and Logan's voice boomed through the house. "Mason! Sam! You guys beat us." He was trailing behind Taylor as they walked around the corner. His arms spread wide. "So, what's up my compadres?" He clapped a hand on Coach Broozer's shoulder. "What's up, Pop-n-Lock?"

"Pop-n-Lock?" Broozer echoed, his eyebrows drawing together. He turned toward Taylor. "Do I dare ask?"

She rolled her eyes, going to the fridge. "He started off calling you Pop-n-Law. That turned into Pop-n-Lock somewhere."

Logan barked out a laugh and smacked the table. "You guys are back. Broozer had good news for you, didn't he?" He rounded on his Pop-n-Lock. "What did you say to my brother? I thought he was off the hook."

Taylor's father opened his mouth, but Mason spoke first.

"I am, *if* no one makes a big deal out of it."

Broozer shot Mason a dark look. "There went that whole plan of keeping quiet."

Mason sent a look back just as quick. "Like I'm going to keep something from my brother."

"Wait." Logan frowned. He held a finger up, pausing as he looked from Pop-n-Lock to Mason and back again. "I'll ignore whatever that was about. No one? Like, *no one* no one?"

"The opposite of anyone," Mason said.

Logan gave his brother a look. "You know what I mean. We're fucked. Everyone gets pissed at us. What about partying tonight?"

"Here's a thought." Coach Broozer's tone turned sarcastic. "Why don't you try not to get in trouble?" He took his water over to the sink. As he passed his daughter, he ran a hand down her arm, and they exchanged loving smiles. "And on that note, I have football tapes calling my name." He clapped Mason on the shoulder. "Keep your head down. Don't listen to that idiot brother of yours—"

"Hey!" Logan called, but he didn't sound like he minded the statement.

"—And I'll see you at practice Monday morning."

Mason nodded. "Thanks, Coach."

"Anytime." He pointed at Logan. "Protect my girl. She's my soul."

Logan's chest puffed up. "Always."

Then Coach left us alone, disappearing back into the house.

Logan smirked, going right back to where he'd left off. "What about partying? Nate's ready to throw a rager. We were going to do one at home, but we're all up here now."

Mason stood, taking my hand in his. "We're going to have the party tonight, but whatever trouble your friend is in, I might have to sit this one out." He looked carefully from Taylor to Logan.

Logan's lips formed a flat line.

Taylor nodded. "That's *completely* and *understandably* fine," she said, looking at Logan. "This is about your future."

Mason nodded.

I felt relieved.

The only one who seemed to want to protest was Logan. His eyes found mine and narrowed. "You haven't said a word. What do you think?"

I frowned. "About what?"

"What I need help with. Those guys are assholes. They almost put Delray in the hospital."

"You're kind of exaggerating." Taylor bit her lip and looked at me. "But Jason was hurt bad. And I do think they'll do it again."

"Decision made. We go and fuck 'em up instead," Logan announced.

"Yeah, without me," Mason countered. "I can't fight. Probably never again."

"Come on. For real?"

"Yes," Mason ground out. His hand tightened over mine, and I looked up in concern. Logan was pushing him. Mason always wanted to be there to cover his brother's back, but he couldn't. He had to stay under the radar, and it was killing him.

I moved in front of him, pulling my hand free. I folded my arms over my chest and felt Mason's hands fall to my waist. "Stop it, Logan."

"Stop what?"

"Being a dumbass. You're looking for trouble because you're bored. You know it."

He bristled. "Delray was beat up. Taylor's mine, so that means he's mine. How can I—"

"There are other ways!" My patience snapped. "And fine, whatever. Go beat the shit out of them, but stop making Mason feel guilty about it. If you want his help, do it another way. If you don't, then respect his decision."

Taylor laughed. "I just got a glimpse into your guys' future. Logan trying to get shit going, Mason trying to be smart about it, and Samantha finally delivering the last word on it." She whistled under her breath, giving her boyfriend a wolfish grin. "You guys will never lead boring lives. Ever."

Logan shot a grin back, moving to the kitchen and scooping an arm around her waist. He pulled her against him, half lifting her in the air. "Only because you're going to be there right with us." He wrapped his other arm around her and buried his face in her neck.

She shrieked in laughter, hitting his arm. "You know that tickles. Stop it!"

Logan pulled back, a pleased look on his face, and grinned down at her. "Just wait till we get back to my place. I'll show you what tickles. I'll show you real deep how some things can tickle."

Then he glanced around, a teasing smile on his face. "Are we ready to party?"

We were ready to party.

CHAPTER THREE

The music pounded.

Cain University students, football players, and students from the other private college in town filled our house. The booze flowed, and everyone was having a great time.

Mason sat at the bonfire with Nate and some of his football teammates. Logan stood behind them, holding a beer and throwing horseshoes with Matteo as his partner. They were playing against two guys I didn't know, and there was a lot of shit-talking going back and forth.

I stood behind the outside bar, filling drinks. I saw some of my floormates from freshman year, but our friendships had faded last year. They'd gotten busy with their own lives, and I was with Mason and Logan. That should've been enough for me. Right?

I studied Mason as he listened to Nate. The bonfire lit up his face, but also cast such darkness over his chiseled features. My heart lurched, and I felt it start to move up to my throat. I tried pushing down whatever emotion was there, filling me up. It wasn't a good one; that I knew.

"Do you moonlight as a bartender now?"

Taylor slid onto one of the barstools and flashed me a grin. She was teasing, but our eyes caught and held as a shared memory passed between us. There'd been another party and another bar we'd hidden behind not long ago.

I laughed and pointed toward an empty jar. "Maybe I should put a sign in front of it for tips?"

She snorted, crossing her arms on the counter. "At this rate, you might get some. People are drunk—like, really drunk."

A girl shrieked, and we followed the sound. A guy chased her around the yard. She was half-naked—her breasts hanging out and her jeans undone. Her hair was messy and her lips smudged, but she followed that shriek with a laugh. She flew past the bar, and I wasn't the only one who stopped to watch her. Most of the guys took notice.

She shrieked again, the sound ending in a lust-filled groan when the guy caught up to her. He wrapped an arm around her waist and pressed her up against the house. His mouth was on hers, and she was soon clutching at his shoulders. Her legs climbed up to wrap around his waist.

Taylor sighed, watching them. "A part of me thinks she's an idiot, so maybe she should deal with the consequences." She pointed to a few guys who'd pulled out their phones to record the live porno. "But the other side of me knows we have to step in, especially if she's intoxicated."

A couple of girls came around the corner from the same direction the drunk and half-naked couple had come. Both were my height and slim. One had dark hair, and the other had curly, light-blond hair and a fairer complexion. The first girl seemed to be their leader. Her square jaw held a tight frown, and her hair was pulled back into a fierce braid. The lighter complexioned girl had more of a bounce to her walk, and probably a bit more pep in her personality. She also had a smile tugging at her lips, but when they both paused, seeing the two making out, the smile disappeared behind her hand. Her eyes widened in mortification.

The fierce braid girl turned to her friend. "What the fuck are we going to do? She's unhinged."

The second friend's shoulders shook as she tried to keep in her laugh. She couldn't. She doubled over, and her laughter rang out. "She's going to regret that," she managed with a snort. "So bad. It's so bad."

The first rolled her eyes. "Morons. That's who I'm friends with."

Taylor and I glanced at each other.

The second girl crumpled to the ground now, still laughing, with tears running down her face.

Fierce Braid just shook her head. Her hands found her hips, and she looked from the making-out friend to the one on the ground. "What the hell am I going to do?"

Taylor was holding back a laugh.

"You want a drink?" I called to the girl.

She looked over and blushed. "Tell me you didn't hear that."

I shrugged. "Sorry."

She glanced around, and I knew why she'd assumed no one could hear her—because no one cared to overhear. The music still blared, and except for the two guys recording the making out, everyone else was absorbed with their own group of friends. Logan and Matteo were still playing horseshoes. I didn't think Mason and the guys at the bonfire even knew about the half-naked couple, and there were a few other groups of girls, but they were watching the guys.

She shook her head and went back over to tap her still-laughing friend on the shoulder. "Grace, come on."

The girl staggered to her feet and then half-collapsed onto a stool two over from Taylor's. "Sorry. I'm—" Snort. "—Grace, and I'm completely—" Another laugh, followed with a hiccup. "—useless right now." She turned wide eyes to her friend. "Sorry, Court. I suck."

Court eyed the two guys with the phones. "I have to stop that. All of it. Nettie's going to be mortified."

"No, no." Taylor slid off her stool. "I'll get someone to deal with it. Trust me, he'll enjoy it."

Court and Grace, who was mostly hiccupping now, watched as Taylor headed through the crowd toward Logan. Their eyes widened.

"Is that Logan Kade?" one of them asked.

I looked over, but neither paid me any attention. The hiccups seemed to be gone, and Grace's mouth hung slightly open.

Taylor touched Logan's arm, and he bent his head toward her. A loving smile bloomed on his face, but then vanished as Taylor kept talking. His eyes narrowed, and he lifted his head toward us at the bar. I pointed to the couple, and he moved over so he could see them. He said something to Taylor, who started back to us as Logan then said something to Matteo.

Matteo passed along the message to Mason, gesturing to the recording guys. Mason stood, along with Nate, and the rest of the guys at the bonfire turned to watch.

Logan veered toward the bar, stepping behind it next to me.

He bent down, fitting the hose to the water supply and turning it on. I followed the hose to its end. Water streamed out where it lay next to the house—about five feet from the couple.

"You're going to hose 'em?" I asked.

He winked at me. "It'll be my pleasure."

As Logan walked over to pick up the end of the hose, Mason stepped in front of the two guys recording with their phones. Matteo and Nate joined him to block their view. They protested and started to move—until they looked up and saw who was standing in front of them. Both snapped to attention then, trying to turn off their phones.

Mason said something I couldn't hear and snatched their phones. The guys started to protest again, but soon realized half the football team was there and moving in. They'd back up Mason if they needed to.

Realizing they had no way to fight back, the two guys waited as Mason deleted the video from one phone. He'd handed the other to Nate, who seemed to be doing the same thing.

Logan now had the end of the hose in his hands, and he positioned himself with his feet set apart, holding the hose like a fireman might've. He jerked the end of the hose, pressed his thumb over the end, and blasted the porno couple.

The girl shrieked, and the guy yelled, his face twisted in anger. He whirled to find Logan with the hose and everyone else watching. The girl cowered against the house, her hands covering her breasts, and her bottom lip starting to tremble.

"Shit," Court mumbled as she moved toward her friend.

Grace remained behind, one eyebrow raised as she watched everything unfold. A serene calmness had settled over her features, and she seemed content to remain in place, watching the scene like it was a movie.

As Court put her arms around Nettie, hugging her and helping to shield her, the guy she'd been making out with started to walk away. Logan wasn't having it. He continued to spray him, laughing until anger darkened the guy's face. He shot a hand out, but Logan just aimed the hose there, and the water splashed up, soaking the guy's face.

I looked over. Mason was heading my way, the two phones in his hands. The phones' owners were escorted away by some of Mason's teammates.

"Are those two guys going to be a problem?" I asked.

Mason slid the phones over to me, ignoring the way Grace's mouth hung open again. "I told 'em to come back tomorrow to get their phones. I want to make sure they didn't upload that video somewhere."

I checked the screens. Only one was password protected, and I held it up. "Did you get the password?"

He nodded, glancing over at Logan, who was still hosing down the now-yelling guy. "You know that girl?"

I shook my head and gestured to Grace. "But she does."

He turned to her, his face unreadable. "Is that your friend?"

She lifted a hand to her chin and closed her mouth, then smiled at him. "Yep."

He studied her. "You're drunk?"

"Yep." She continued to beam at him. "You're Mason Kade."

He looked back toward the house. Court was bringing her half-naked friend over. "Do you have a staff shirt or anything behind that bar?" she called.

"Staff shirt?"

She frowned at me. "Yeah, you're working this party, aren't you?"

She thought I was the help.

Taylor joined us again, motioning toward Logan. "He's done fooling with the guy. They got his name and number, so if something happens, at least we know who he is."

Court looked at her gratefully. "Thank you for that. So much."

"She asked for a shirt," I told Taylor. "Want to—"

I was going to ask if she'd stand behind the bar so I could grab a shirt from my room, but Taylor held a hand up.

"I'm on it," she said. "Half my wardrobe's here anyway. Be right back."

"Oh, good." Court's shoulders dropped, visibly relieved. She nodded to me. "Thank you for helping, you and your friend." She grinned ruefully. "Who knew your friend would know Logan Kade personally."

An awkward silence settled over us.

I waited for her to realize Mason was here. Then again, maybe she didn't know who he was. After a few beats of silence, Court looked at Grace. Grace pointed at Mason, and only then did Court realize someone else stood with us at the bar. Her eyes widened as she looked up at him. The blood drained from her face, and her lips formed a small O.

This reaction wasn't that uncommon, but the surprised looks on people's faces when they realized who Mason was usually happened from a distance. He would be with his classmates, Logan, or me when people would notice his presence. The whispering came first, followed by a mix of reactions. Either people would respect his privacy and remain at a distance or they would come over to stare. Sometimes people would rush up for an autograph or to give him their number. It was usually girls who did the latter.

The funniest reactions were the people who looked at him like he was an alien. They'd just gawk. I once overheard a guy say to his friend, "That's not Kade. He's not big enough. Kade's a fucking legend."

His friend had shaken his head. "Huh-uh. I'm pretty sure that's Mason Kade. And he's not six four. Check out his stats. That's him, dude."

"Whatever. I could take him. He's not that big of a deal."

Mason might've overheard, but he didn't react then, and he didn't now. He generally ignored people.

He stared at Court. "That's your friend?"

"Uh." She tugged Nettie closer, almost using her for protection now. "Yeah . . . You're Mason Kade, aren't you?"

"Yeah," he clipped out. "How drunk is she?" He jerked his gaze to Nettie, half scowling. "How drunk are you? Was it consensual with that guy?"

It hit me like a lightning strike.

Consensual. He was worried. *Girl Sexually Assaulted at Mason Kade's Party* would be the headline, and soon people would think he'd sexually assaulted the girl.

Fuck.

I felt slapped in the face.

"What?" Nettie shivered in Court's arms. They switched positions so it was Court's back toward Mason now. I watched as Court closed her eyes and drew in a breath. She needed a moment. I could relate.

Mason was intense, especially when he was pissed. And he was livid right now.

He cast me a look, asking for help. I stepped forward just as Taylor came outside, but I motioned for her to head back in.

"Why don't we all go inside? We can talk in private."

Court and Nettie nodded, looking relieved. They started for the patio doors where Taylor waited.

I followed and turned around to see Mason coming behind me. I placed a hand on his chest. "Maybe you should stay?"

"Grace!" Court yelled. "Come on."

The third friend slid off her stool, a contented, serene look still on her face, now topped with a goofy grin. As she walked past, I saw how glazed over her eyes were. I wondered if she'd even remember this the next day. Of the three, Court was the most sober, with drenched, shivering Nettie a close second now.

They headed inside, and I looked back up at Mason. He hadn't moved.

"Do you know the attention that could put on me?" he asked.

I did. I was cringing that I hadn't considered it sooner. "I won't let anything happen to you. Okay? You guys protected her. That should count for something." I started to leave, but he caught my arm.

"Sam." I looked back up at him. "Thanks for taking care of this."

I hadn't done anything yet. "Thank me later in bed."

He relaxed, the lines around his mouth softening. He bent down for a kiss and murmured, "Trust me, I'll be thanking you for the rest of our lives."

A tingle shot through me.

I pressed my lips against his before heading inside. He'd watch the bar. I didn't need to worry about that, and I felt a smile tug at my lips. A little extra sensation warmed me.

I forgot our current trouble for the moment.

I was going to be his wife. I rubbed at my bare finger. Mason had been reaching into his pocket when he first started to propose, but then his phone rang, and the whole football and fight video thing took over. He'd gotten back around to asking me after that, but then my hesitancy had put another damper on things.

Since then, I'd been waiting for him to give me the ring, but he hadn't, and I would respect his wishes. Mason would give it to me when he decided it was time. I pushed my insecurities aside and let myself feel a little thrill at the secret we had.

No one knew. Not even Logan.

I couldn't wait until we told, but as I stepped inside and went to Logan's bedroom, I paused. I could hear the girls' voices, and I took a deep breath.

I had something else to deal with first.

CHAPTER FOUR

"What were you thinking, Nettie?" Court demanded, standing over her friend.

Nettie sat on the edge of Logan's bed with her elbows resting on her knees and her head pressed into her hands. Her black hair was matted and still drying, but she wore one of Logan's sweatshirts now. It hung on her, giving her a drowned-kitten look. She lifted her head and used the end of the sleeve to wipe her face.

She sniffled. "Court, don't rail on me. Okay? I'm pissed enough."

Grace was perched on Logan's couch at the opposite end of the room. She sat sideways, with one foot on the floor and the other pulled up next to her. Still looking glazed, she blinked over and over again.

"Come on, Courtney," she said, yawning. "Net met a boy." A dreamy look settled over her, and Nettie laughed a little. Grace winked at her. "She felt those special tingles only tequila gives us, and the two fell in love . . . with exhibitionism."

Nettie barked out a louder laugh.

Courtney folded her arms over her chest, frowning. "This isn't funny."

Grace rose from the couch. She gestured to Nettie with a wave. "Seriously, Courtney. Logan Freaking Kade—" She turned to Taylor, who stood just inside the door, next to me. "—Who it just clicked is probably your boyfriend. You're Taylor Bruce?"

Taylor nodded. "Yeah." Her hand rose in an awkward wave. "Hi."

Grace returned the nod before continuing. "I mean, seriously, Nettie, you're wearing Logan Kade's sweatshirt. You're in his bedroom. Your partner in public love got booted from the party."

I cleared my throat. This was my opening. "About that guy . . ." I paused. They all looked at me. "Who was he?"

Nettie grimaced before plopping her head back in her hands. "Just my biggest embarrassment. Ever," she groaned.

"He's a guy she's liked in our poly sci class. They hooked up at another party, and it continued here. I hope you get a bonus for helping us."

I paused. Blinked. Then it clicked. She *still* thought I was the help.

Taylor frowned at me.

I shook my head. I was enjoying this anonymity.

Stepping toward them, I crossed my arms over my chest. "But that was consensual, right?"

Nettie stared at me, a blank expression on her face. Then understanding dawned. Her eyes widened. "Oh, of course! I was just being stupid." She gave me a more pointed look. "Courtney said two guys were filming us? Is that true?"

Taylor spoke before I could. "Yeah, but Mason took care of it. I'm pretty sure I saw him deleting something on their phones."

Nettie's eyes widened even more, and a look of astonishment took over. "Mason *Kade*?"

"I told you. He was at the bar just now." Courtney's arms dropped. Her hands went into her pockets.

Grace sighed dreamily. "Now he's someone I'd let myself be filmed with. Good Lord, the guy is from another planet."

I fought against smiling.

Taylor bit her lip, her eyes twinkling. "Uh, so yeah. He got the videos, and all of the guys were booted from the party." She looked over the three friends. "Do you guys need a ride somewhere?"

Grace and Nettie both gestured to Courtney with haphazard waves. Courtney ran a hand through her hair. "Yeah, I drove. I'm the sober cab tonight."

"How'd Jonathan get home?"

I looked over at Nettie. She'd asked Taylor, but Taylor looked at me.

"That's the guy you were making out with?" I asked.

She nodded. "He came with us. I don't think he knew anyone here."

This girl was concerned about the guy who'd almost put her in a bad porno? For real? I shrugged. "I don't know how he got home, but I know he was kicked out."

"Oh." Her shoulders fell. "Okay."

She was pissed about that? I didn't know if she was being stupid or ungrateful, but she could fuck things up royally for Mason. My mouth remained shut.

"Thank you." She looked around the room. "I mean it. I know this was a hassle." She sounded sincere as she looked at Taylor. "You think I could thank your boyfriend and Mason?"

"Uh." Taylor's eyes darted to mine. I shook my head, the slightest of movement, and she looked back to Nettie. "I'll be honest, Logan probably won't know who you are, and Mason . . . I guarantee he'll be surrounded by all his teammates."

"Yeah." Nettie's head bobbed up and down. "You're right. Maybe later? I can say something if I see them on campus."

"Yeah." Taylor's smile relaxed at the corners. "It might just be best if you take it easy now. Go home, you know?"

Nettie stood, looking at her friends. Similar to the way Taylor and I were with Mason and Logan, the three of them moved as a unit. Grace led the way this time, and she and Court cast concerned looks at Nettie, who looked at the floor as they left the room and continued out of the house.

They all looked back at us from the sidewalk and offered a short wave before moving on to where they had parked.

Taylor stood next to me in the doorway, and as soon as they were out of eyesight, she punched me in the arm. It was a soft one, no heat to it, but she cursed. "Fuck you, Sam. They thought you were hired help. You left me to be the official Kade spokesperson."

I laughed. "It was kinda awesome. I won't lie."

She groaned, and I followed her back outside to the bar.

Mason and Logan were behind it, with Nate and Matteo on the bar stools. A couple other guys were standing nearby, and everyone looked over as we approached.

"Everything okay?" Mason asked.

I nodded, slipping behind the bar and against his side. His hand came to rest on my hip, anchoring me there. "All good," I added. "She was embarrassed, but it was consensual. They first hooked up at a different party, and he rode with them here."

"You serious?" Logan leaned back, his hands on Taylor's hips as she stood in front of him. "They brought that fucker here?"

"Yeah. The girl asked us how he got a ride home."

"Wait." Logan stood straighter, moving Taylor to the side. "You mean he didn't have a ride?"

"According to the girl he was mauling ten feet from here, no."

Logan looked at the two guys standing behind Nate and Matteo. "Did anyone pick him up or give him a ride somewhere?"

One shook his head. "We pointed down the street and told him to start walking." He shrugged. "He did."

Mason frowned at Logan. "What are you thinking?"

"She might not say anything, but he might. If he's pissed enough, he could really say something. And we live six miles out of town. You do the math."

I felt Mason's hand tighten, just a little bit. His jaw clenched. "That's a long walk to fume."

"Exactly." Logan looked at the guys. "We should go find him, give him a ride to his place. Then we'd know where he lives too."

Everyone looked at Mason.

He nodded, a short clip of the head. "Do it, but don't say anything." He turned to Logan. "You go with them."

Logan, the two guys, and Matteo all left.

Nate remained behind. "This can't fall back on you," he assured Mason. "Don't worry. We'll take care of it."

Mason nodded, but his hand still gripped my hip.

I lifted my hand to touch the side of his face. "It'll be fine."

He didn't reply. He just rested his forehead against mine.

CHAPTER FIVE

I wanted to run.

As soon as I opened my eyes, I was ready to go. I skipped yesterday. We spent all day Saturday cleaning up after the party, and then we spent the evening cuddling. Chef Logan had declared Saturday night to be Meat Rushmore, and he'd put together a whole display of grilled goodies—not just meat, but he made sure to point out the meat every chance he could . . . until Taylor got tired of it.

We hadn't gone to bed too late, but it was four in the morning now. I sat up, not hearing Mason's steady, deep breaths. He wasn't here. His side of the bed was empty.

I stood, went to the bathroom, and got dressed as quickly as possible. I'd laced my shoes and was uncoiling my earbuds' cord when I walked past the living room. I braked.

Mason wasn't there either, but I saw him through the front window. He was stretching outside on the front porch.

"You okay?" I asked as I stepped out to join him.

He pulled his foot up behind him, stretching the front of his quad. "I'm going with you."

It wasn't that we never ran together. It was just not usually at four in the morning.

"What?"

He laughed, letting his leg back down. "I have training tomorrow. Figured I should run with you this morning."

Uh . . .

His eyebrows furrowed. "What?"

I scratched behind my ear.

He grinned, his eyes amused. "You don't want me to run *with* you? Or to run in general?"

It wasn't that, but I lifted my shoulder, starting to walk down the driveway toward the road. Mason fell in step beside me, pulling his arm across his chest to stretch.

"I'm just— It's just—" God. What *was* my problem?

"Sam." He touched my elbow, stopping me. "What's going on?"

I shook my head, resting a hand against his chest because I wanted to touch him. I let out a frustrated sigh. "I'm sorry. I don't know what's going on with me. A few months ago, I would've been exhilarated that you wanted to run with me in the morning. But this summer . . ."

Things had started to change this summer. I'd started to change.

"What?" he asked.

I bit my lip. I didn't want him to run with me. It punched me hard in the chest. Even I wasn't ready for that one, but as soon as I realized it, I knew it wasn't the real issue here. I wanted space, that was the issue, but it wasn't. It was all confusing in my head. I didn't want to say what the real issue was, but I had to. Mason deserved the truth. He deserved that respect.

"Things changed when everyone started getting married."

His eyebrows lifted, but he didn't say anything.

I started to walk again. Mason stayed right next to me. I held my phone and earbuds in one hand, while the other clenched and unclenched. I didn't know what to do with it as I spoke.

"It didn't bother me when David and Malinda got married," I told him. "That wasn't in the cards for us—not yet anyway—but then I started thinking about Analise and James getting married. I had begun stressing when we went home for the summer, and I thought it was just because of my mom being there. But then one night I made a joke to Heather about her and Channing getting married, and she said Channing wanted to. That shocked me." I stopped walking.

Mason was still right with me. He was listening.

"It threw me because then I realized that *could* be you and me. I think it's early, but I know a lot of people get engaged their last year of college or right after. And that's where you are, so when I started thinking about that, all this shit came up inside of me. It was all about Analise, about how she and David were, about the stories you've told me about your dad."

My eyes found his. "And some of it's about hearing how angry you were at your dad," I said softly. "You still are angry. I know it's not as much, but it's there. He'll never be a normal dad to you. That relationship will never happen, and the same for Analise and me. She let me go, for real, and I like it. There's no weight or pressure from her anymore, but I'm sad too. I have a choice now, and I have to say goodbye to the kind of relationship I should've had with my mother. Does that make sense?"

He nodded. "And all that's connected to us getting married?"

"Because it's what I know. It's what I grew up in."

He touched my arm and rubbed back and forth with his thumb, soothing me. "You know Malinda and David. They're a good example of what we didn't know."

"I know." I'd tried telling myself that. Malinda and David were good. Analise and James were not. "Our parents might beat the odds and make something good with each other, but I'm waiting for the other shoe to drop. The jaded part of me knows Analise is going to start cheating in two years. And David and Malinda . . ." I pressed a hand to my forehead. The pressure was mounting there too. "Who knows? They're still early, but I *hope* they remain good."

"Sam." Mason's hand slid down my arm to catch my hand. "Do you want me to take it back? Do you want me to wait a couple years? Because I can do that."

Did I? I wasn't caught off-guard here, but I took a moment to really ask myself that question.

I liked being engaged.

But I was scared too.

I shook my head, squeezing his hand. "I'm not asking you to take it back. I'm asking you to be patient with me. I'm afraid of marriage, and I don't want to ever feel like that about anything that's connected to you."

He stepped closer, his forehead resting on mine. "You sure?" He grazed my bare finger, where the ring should've been. "I have something to put on here, you know." The corner of his mouth lifted. "I was waiting to surprise you at a better time. But I can wait and ask you all over again later. I have no problem waiting."

Warmth flooded me.

I felt myself grinning back at him, matching his smile. Some of the pressure lessened.

"I don't want you to take back the question, but maybe you could *still* ask again when you give me the ring?"

He was trying to read me, watching intently. "You're sure?"

I didn't have a clear-cut answer. But I liked knowing we were engaged, and I liked knowing that others didn't know. I also liked knowing he was going to be patient with me, and that he was going to ask again at some point. He wasn't taking it back. It was more a "making sure" sort of thing. That was all.

I shook my head, rolling my eyes. "I'm messed up."

"No. Your mother is messed up. You just got affected by some of it. It makes sense."

"You're not mad?"

He shook his head. "Never."

I expelled a deep breath, feeling tears behind my eyes. "Thank you, Mason."

His lips rested over mine, so softly, so tenderly, and he whispered right before he sealed our mouths together. "You never have to thank me. That's part of loving someone."

I kissed him, standing on my tiptoes. He wrapped his arms around my waist and lifted me as the kiss deepened.

Mason had proposed, and I didn't want to hurt him, but I wasn't being honest with myself either. Being nervous about marriage wasn't going to go away. I couldn't force it away. It was a part of me. I learned the bad shit as a child, and I couldn't mess up a life with the man I loved. I loved him more than myself. He was better than both our parents put together, and what we had was the best thing I would ever be a part of.

I never wanted to lose it.

But I couldn't let it be contaminated either.

We pulled apart, and I vowed to deal with my insecurities.

"You ready to run now?" He smiled down at me.

The need to go was back, and I nodded. "I'm going to go fast today. Think you can keep up?"

Mason barked out a laugh, taking off at a light jog. "Pretty sure I can handle myself."

I laughed, softly punching him in the arm as I caught up to jog with him. He might be some well-toned and trained athlete for the pros, but I was Samantha Fucking Stratton. I could outrun anyone and, nine miles later, I pulled into the lead.

An hour and a half after that, Mason started back for the house, but I had a few more miles in me. They were itching to get out, so I veered down a new running path and amped up my music.

A river wound around Cain, and a part of it wasn't far from the house. I'd been eyeing the path alongside it since last spring. Now that Mason and I were on sure footing again, nothing could weigh me down. I picked up my pace, swung my arms a little wider, and was almost sprinting within half a mile.

This run felt different. It wasn't bad. It wasn't good. It was just different, and I couldn't put my finger on why.

Then, after two miles, it hit me.

I braked suddenly.

Nothing was wrong. That was what was different. I hadn't felt like this since . . . ever.

I'd lost everything I had four years ago—a family, two best friends, a boyfriend. After one weekend, I lost all of them.

I barely survived the first year, but formed a different family with Mason and Logan.

Then I got David back.

I got a loyal friend.

I got a new stepmother.

I started an actual relationship with my real dad.

And the last thing: Analise finally set me free.

The last two things that had been bothering me were the future of Mason's football career and my concerns with marriage, but both seemed under control now. I'd gotten everything back that had been taken from me: a family, a soul mate, a loyal friend—and now Mason had offered me a future.

But even as I recounted all these good things, something that wasn't quite right rose to the surface.

I'd been so focused on keeping my new family, on never losing Mason and Logan, that these last four years had passed by without me doing something else important: finding myself.

I still didn't know my major, and I *still* didn't know who Samantha Strattan was—not completely.

I turned and began walking back to the house. After a few hours, I found a curb and called Mason.

He was showering, but Logan answered his phone and agreed to come. It wasn't long before the yellow Escalade pulled up in front of me, and when we got back home, Mason was dressed in comfortable sweats. He lounged at his desk, looking delectably refreshed.

Those old knots were back in my stomach.

Mason looked up, a smile gracing his features right away. "Hey. How was the rest of the run?"

I stepped inside our room and shut the door.

His smile faded. "I thought we were good when I started back. What's wrong?"

"Me."

His smile vanished completely. He sat up straight in his chair, rolling it back to face me. "What are you talking about?"

"When Analise and I moved in with you guys, I lost everything. And over the last four years, you guys became everything to me. I've only been focused on not losing you or Logan."

I sat at the edge of our bed, folding my hands on my lap. "I haven't really done my own thing. It was always about you guys. I took a job at Manny's to occupy my time when I wasn't with you two. I moved into a dorm, and I was going to find my own friends, but it became about you guys again. I got my roommate because of you. Then this last summer, I took that job at a freaking carnival because I had no idea what I was doing. Logan was gone, you were working, and I went along with Mark because that's what I've been doing the last four years. I've been just going along with things."

My throat hurt, and my lungs were constricting.

"Sam." Mason leaned forward. His voice was soft.

I closed my eyes for a beat. It was that voice I loved so much, and he was going to say what he always said. That'd be okay. That everything would be fine. That he would be there for me. This was part of why I loved him so much, because his love for me was pure.

I shook my head. "Don't say whatever you're going to say."

He frowned. "What do you want to do then?"

"I don't know, but I think this is another reason why I'm scared of marriage. I don't know me anymore. I'm a junior, and I should know what I want to do. I should have a major declared by now."

"Sam." He scooted his chair closer. "Logan just realized that himself. I think it's kind of normal. I only knew what I wanted to do because I've known since junior high it was business or football. I've always loved taking pieces of shit down on the field." His mouth twisted up in a rakish grin. "Or I'd be my own boss. No way is someone else going to give me orders. I've got some authority issues, just like Logan. I just show them in a different way."

I nodded. "I know, and I know Logan just figured out what he wants to do, but I still have no clue. How can I commit to a future if I don't know who I want to be in the future?"

"We talked about this. It's okay. We'll take our time. We don't have to do anything right now. Shit. We technically still have a month left of summer, too."

He made sense. I tried to tell myself that, but I didn't like this feeling. Now that I'd realized what was wrong, I wanted to fix it. I didn't want to be lost anymore.

"Sam." Mason scooted even closer, his knees touching mine now. He took my hand in his. "You can take all the time you want. I'm not going anywhere. Logan isn't either. You're not going to lose us, no matter what you do."

I laced our fingers together.

"I don't like not knowing myself," I admitted.

He squeezed my hand. "Then get to know yourself."

I laughed. "It's so simple to you. You've always known."

He shrugged. "You will too. It's just coming at a different pace."

"Thanks, Mason."

His eyes darkened and, then I was on his lap. His hands found my waist, and leaning back in his chair, he held me anchored over him.

"You never have to thank me, but if you really feel obligated . . ." He winked, and his teasing intention was clear as his hand slid under my shirt, and he sat up to find my lips.

We moved to the bed after a moment, and all talk ceased.

CHAPTER SIX

"Where exactly did you lose yourself? Maybe we could retrace our steps. You could find yourself where you last saw yourself?"

"Har har." I rolled my eyes.

Logan was walking me to the career center on campus. It was Monday morning, which would normally make the quad filled with students, except we were a month early. The only students around were those who'd stayed to take summer classes, or athletes, like Mason, who were starting their practices already.

I looked over the lush green lawns and sidewalks crisscrossing the quad. It was peaceful and eerie all at the same time.

"I'm going to talk to someone and probably take a test, because I have no idea what I want to do with my future."

He grinned, shoving his hands into his pockets. "Let me help you with that. I'm Logan Kade." He pointed to himself, then to me. "You're Samantha Strattan. You've been boning my brother for almost four years."

He held his hand out, and I ignored it. "Har har. So funny."

"I amuse myself."

"You make jokes, but you know what I mean. I was picking up trash at the local carnival this summer. If that isn't a cry for help, I don't know what is."

"Don't knock the carnies. They have deep pockets we may need someday."

And I really ignored that one. I could see the career center ahead on our right and picked up speed.

"I know you could've spent all day with Taylor," I told him. "So I appreciate you coming with me."

He shrugged. "Your guy's in football all day. My woman's hanging out with her posse. Seemed fitting that you and I spend the day together."

I reached for the door, but he grabbed it, holding it open for me.

"I'll admit, I didn't envision the career center when you asked if I'd go to campus with you. I thought we'd hit up the cafeteria—sneak in and get free food or something."

"We can do that later."

We were crossing through the lobby when I heard my name being called.

I looked up to find one of my track coaches coming down the stairs.

"Coach Carillo. Hey."

In his mid-forties, with dark black hair and a few specks of gray, he was dressed completely in Cain University apparel. A whistle hung from his neck.

He eyed Logan as he held out his hand. "Logan Kade, right?"

"Yes, sir." Logan shook his hand. "We've met once or twice over the years at Sam's meets."

"Mason Kade's brother."

"Right again."

He nodded, a look of approval on his face. His turned back to me and narrowed his eyes slightly. "What are you doing here?"

"I was going to see a career counselor."

"No, I mean, what are you doing in this building?" He pushed back his sleeve and looked at his watch. "Cross-country is starting today. Why aren't you there?"

"Oh."

I never joined the cross-country team because of the time commitment it would require. It was a fall sport, just like football, and finding time to spend with Mason was already challenging enough when he was playing. It'd be almost impossible if I joined a sports team with a season at the same time. Besides, track had been my forte since freshman year.

"I never joined," I confessed.

"What?" His eyes bulged, and he crossed his arms over his clipboard. "Are you kidding me? Why wouldn't you join? Your running times are amazing. You'd be one of the best on the team."

"I . . ."

I gave Logan a look. I didn't know what to say. I should explain to my coach that I chose not to join the team so I could spend time with my boyfriend? I didn't think he'd respect that.

I shrugged instead. "It's just a decision I made. I've been content with doing track only."

He shook his head. "You're here to see a career counselor, but, Sam, I really urge you to join the cross-country team. They could use a runner like you. You know what? Come to my office tomorrow. I'd like to talk about this some more with you." He lowered his head; his eyes still meeting mine. "Would you do that?"

"Uh . . . sure. Yeah."

He nodded. "Good." He seemed to relax and pressed the clipboard against his side. "I'll see you tomorrow then." Clapping Logan on the shoulder, he moved for the door. "It was nice meeting you again, Kade."

"You too." Logan waited until the door closed. "Why didn't you just tell him the truth? You didn't join because of Mason, right?"

"Because he wouldn't understand."

Logan snorted. "You're being *that* girl."

We'd started down the hallway toward the counselors' offices, but I stopped. "What does that mean?"

"You know. *That* girl." He grinned. "The chick who puts her boyfriend first."

"I'm not *that* girl."

"Yeah, you're exactly that girl." He gestured to me. "You don't want to admit it, but you're putting Mason first. It's cool, Sam. It's only half the year. The other half, you get to do your thing. Track."

I scowled. I hated the way he said that, like I was weak-willed and submissive.

But he was right.

During the fall, I did put Mason first.

It stung.

I blinked a couple times. "So you're saying I should join the cross-country team?"

"If you want. It's up to you. Has Mason ever asked you not to? Did he say he'd be mad if you did or something?"

I stiffened. "Are we talking about the same guy?"

Mason put me first. Always had, always would.

Logan's grin widened. He snapped his fingers and pointed at me. "Exactly. You know Mason won't care, so you can relax. You're not that girl. Your boyfriend didn't make you choose him over yourself. You made that decision all on your own."

My scowl was back. "Stop fucking with me."

"I'm not." He held his hands up. "Honestly. But I've always wondered why you didn't join. I just figured there was a good reason. I mean, I thought Mason probably factored into it, but I thought there was more to it too."

I thought for a moment. They had meets every weekend, and sometimes during the week. Mason had practices every day, and there were team activities off the field too. That wasn't including the games—those he had every week too.

There'd be no time. I would almost never see him.

The thought of it—no. I couldn't. I started forward again. "I can't do it. I'll never see him."

"Isn't that why you're here?"

I stopped again. A spark of anger lit in my stomach. I turned back around to him. "Stop it, Logan."

"Look." He rubbed the back of his neck. "I can't be hypocritical here. I love you, Sam. You're family, and I know Mason would want you to do what you want. You two are good. There's no vulnerability in your relationship, so what are you doing? Why are you choosing him over something I know you'd love? You loved it in high school. You love running, and that's all this team does—and not for a just a mile or two. It's literally everything you love doing. If the only reason you're not doing it is because of Mason, I know my brother would tell you to do it. Have you guys ever talked about it?"

He knew the answer. I refused to give it. I just stared.

He sighed, his hand dropping back down. "That's what I thought. Let me guess. He asked if you were going to join, and you said no. That was probably the entire conversation, wasn't it?"

"Not fully."

He snorted. "He probably asked if you were sure, and you said you were. Then he dropped it. Right?"

He was a bit closer this time. I gritted my teeth. "You're mad because he didn't push me? Is that it?"

"No, but the whole reason you're coming here today is because you don't know what you want to do. Maybe you should *do* something you want to do. Maybe that's the first step. Instead of taking some stupid test, actually go out there and join the team. Yes, you're sacrificing time with Mason, but it's only for a few months. It's not like you don't live with the guy. I'm foreseeing lots of midnight screwing happening."

I wavered. He was right, but it'd be hard.

"*If* I did this—" I shot a hand out when his grin morphed into a smirk. "—And that's a big if. But if I did this, you'd have to make me a promise."

"Sure. Anything."

"No. Don't say that. I mean it. You'd really have to make me a promise."

The smirk fell away, and he grew serious. "I promise." His head inclined toward mine. "I'll do whatever you want me to do."

"You can't get Mason in trouble."

His eyes widened. "What do you mean?"

"He's walking on eggshells. No drama can happen. Nothing. His name can't be linked to any kind of scandal."

He shook his head. "Do you not know who we are? We should've been named Mason and Logan Scandal, not Kade."

"Taylor's dad said that if anyone got wind of them looking the other way about the tape, there could be consequences. Like, if a lot of people got pissed about a wealthy guy not being punished, Mason would be off the team. He'd be suspended, or worse. You know that's not good for his career. He still has to get drafted."

"That's bullshit. That'd never happen."

I raised an eyebrow. He knew it could. He just didn't want to admit it.

Logan cursed, raking a hand over his jaw.

I nodded. "It just takes one person to find out, get pissed, and start talking."

"I know. I heard what Mase said in Taylor's kitchen. I just . . . don't like it."

"Don't get him in trouble. Be smart about things. I'll join the team, if you don't get Mason in trouble."

He stilled, eyeing me.

I held my hand out.

He looked at my hand. If he shook it, he'd honor our agreement. That meant no fighting, no pranks, nothing combustible.

The part of Logan that would make him a great lawyer was the part Mason didn't need in his life right now. He couldn't go and fuck things up.

He let out a surrendering sigh and shook my hand. "Deal."

CHAPTER SEVEN

Logan was right.

Mason was understanding and even encouraging when I told him about Coach Carillo and the deal I'd struck with Logan. He laughed a little at that, but I saw the relief in his eyes. It was small, but it was there. I understood it too, because no matter what was best for Mason's career, if Logan got into a spot, Mason would have his back. Damn the consequences.

This made him a little less worried about having to do that.

I, however, was all sorts of worried. I was going to have to do the unthinkable: I'd have to branch out. I couldn't stay back within what was comfortable to me.

Last night I spoke to Coach Carillo on the phone, and he promised he would call the cross-country coach and instructed me to show up early. And here I was. Bright and early.

I pulled up outside the coaching administration offices at seven in the morning. There was a small chill in the early morning breeze, but it felt nice. I wore running clothes, running tights under my sweatpants, and I'd skipped my four a.m. run, banking on running with the team later. But my body was ready to go now. I could feel the itch.

"Hey!"

I turned to notice another car had pulled into the parking lot and saw Taylor jogging over.

"What are you doing here?" I asked.

She was dressed similar to me, but I'd snagged one of Mason's Cain University sweatshirts. She had on a black hoodie instead.

"Logan said you were trying out for the cross-country team today." She shrugged. "I'm not in your league, but I'm no slouch. Figured I might try too."

"Are you sure?"

She rolled a shoulder again, glancing away for a moment. "Yeah. I mean, I've been adding to my mileage since I started dating Logan. I think I can hold my own, or try it." Her eyes widened. "Unless you don't want me to. Did you want this to be your own thing? I can go. I mean it. I just thought it'd be nice to have something in common with you that Logan and Mason weren't a part of. You know what I mean?"

I relaxed. She was doing this for me.

I squeezed her hand. "Thank you, and I'd love it if you ran with me."

"Oh. *Phew*." She laughed, pretending to wipe her brow. "I just thought, if it were me, I'd be nervous to join a team my junior year. I'd want a friend with me." She leaned closer, lowering her voice. "I'm shitting my pants about trying to catch up, but I really would like to try."

"No. Thank you. I appreciate it." I smiled at her. "Carillo said we need to find Coach Langdon's office."

More cars were arriving, and soon a few more girls headed our way. As Taylor and I started for the coaching staff building again, some of those girls dropped down on the grassy area just outside the doors. They began stretching, talking, and laughing with each other.

One looked our way, and then her eyes widened. She gasped, hitting her friend on the arm. I saw her say something, and she pointed in our direction.

That's when I recognized her. It was the drunk, naked chick from the party.

I groaned. "I don't know if this is good or not."

Taylor had reached for the door handle. She glanced back. "What?"

I nodded at Nettie, and the other girl looked over too. I recognized Grace. A third girl stretched on the other side of them. I was betting that was Courtney.

"Our best friends from the party this weekend. Look."

Taylor stiffened. "Oh no. They're coming over."

They moved toward us in a group, but Courtney didn't seem as enthused as the other two.

"Hey!" Grace waved and stopped just short of barreling into us. "Logan Kade's girlfriend."

More girls had arrived to stretch, and most looked over after Grace's exclamation. Even the ones still stretching seemed to be listening.

Taylor shared a look with me. If we'd hoped to remain anonymous, be known only as Taylor and Sam, that was over. It was only a matter of time before my secret was blown too.

"What are you doing here?" Nettie gushed.

She and Grace directed all their attention to Taylor. The only one looking at me was Courtney, and she wore a slight frown. Her eyes narrowed as she tilted her head to the right.

"Bartender girl, right?"

I coughed.

"Strattan!"

A fit-looking guy, strong jaw, older forties, came out the door behind us. The clipboard, whistle, athletic warm-up clothes, and the fact he had the same aura as Coach Carillo indicated immediately who he was.

I turned to him. "Coach Langdon?"

He nodded, looking me over. "Martin says you're worth my time." He gave Taylor the same cold appraisal. "He never said anything about an entourage."

"This is—"

Taylor held out her hand. "Taylor Bruce. I'm not in the same league as Sam, but I was wondering if I could try out too. I can do ten miles on a good day."

He didn't move to shake her hand. "Bruce?"

She withdrew her hand. "My dad is Coach Broozer."

"Whoa!" someone exclaimed.

We heard Nettie whisper behind us. And like a chain reaction, more whispering and conversation followed.

Taylor glanced over her shoulder, a worried look on her face. She was still adjusting, but this had become my norm over the years. People realized who we were connected to. They were excited. They'd give us lots of attention. They'd want to become our best friends. But that was only half of it. The other part was jealousy. Maybe they didn't like who we slept with, or who we were connected to. Logan. Mason. Coach Broozer. It didn't matter. If our star shone brighter than theirs, whoever they were, they weren't happy.

Also, there was usually a small group who was indifferent. They didn't know Mason, Logan, or now Coach Broozer, in Taylor's situation. And they didn't care to know. Those were the girls I usually sought out as class partners, or in this case, just a friend on the team.

I snuck a look over my shoulder too.

Some were scowling at us. Half had lit-up eyes and bright smiles, but there were two girls just doing their own thing.

My eyes skimmed over Courtney. Suspicion lurked in her gaze, mingling with something else I didn't normally encounter.

"Broozer's your dad?" Coach Langdon was saying.

He pulled me back to their conversation.

Taylor nodded, folding her hands in front of herself. "Yes, sir."

He paused, mulling it over. Then he nodded. "Okay. Fine. But if you can't keep up, you can't have a spot." He looked at me. His eyes hardened, like he was assessing me. "Martin told me your times. You do anything like what he says you can, you're on the team too."

I nodded. "Yes, sir."

I hadn't expected anything less, and I'd turned to go stretch when he called my name again.

I looked back. "Yes?"

"We run with the football team sometimes. Is that going to be a problem?"

My eyes rounded. I shook my head. "No, sir. Why would it?"

"I know about your relationship with Kade." He gestured to the girls stretching. "Is that going to be a problem?"

Shit. I swallowed a lump in my throat. "No, sir. I'll handle it."

"Okay. Finish stretching, and get ready. You guys take off in five minutes."

He went over to talk to one of the girls who seemed oblivious on the far side of the grassy area. Both took out their earbuds now to listen to him.

Courtney looked over to them. "That's Faith Shaw and Raelynn Quang. They're the stars of the team. Both princesses and spoiled by their rich daddies—and our coach too."

"Why are you telling me this?"

Nettie and Grace were still fawning over Taylor, so they weren't paying attention, but Courtney lowered her voice anyway. "Because you're Samantha Strattan, aren't you?"

"My name means something to you?"

She laughed, rolling her eyes. "I should've put two and two together. I was stupid to assume you were staff. You weren't dressed like someone hired to man the bar. You were just helping out, weren't you?" She didn't wait for an answer. "I'd started to wonder just now, but then Coach called you Strattan. In running circles, you're known. You're a big deal on the track team. I always wondered why you didn't join cross-country, but it was because of your boyfriend. Mason Kade, right?"

"Is that really your business?"

She laughed again. "No, but I couldn't help asking." She nodded toward Faith and Raelynn, who were now both looking in our direction. Correction: they were looking at me. There was no hostility or emotion in their eyes, but I felt an awareness in the air. Coach Langdon moved to the sidewalk, and the others began to stand up. It was almost time to run, but in that moment, everything faded to those two girls and myself.

They had competition, and they were now aware of it.

This could get interesting.

Courtney chuckled under her breath. "Nettie and Grace haven't figured out who you are, but expect them to freak. Their reaction will be nothing compared to how they're going crazy over Logan's girlfriend."

I gritted my teeth. I was Samantha Strattan. I wasn't going to be known as Mason Kade's girlfriend on this team. Not here. I was a runner, and I was good at it.

"Her name is Taylor," I snapped before I could help myself. "Learn to use it."

I broke away, grabbing Taylor by the arm and pulling her to our own section of grass. "We have to stretch quick. He's going to blow the whistle soon."

She dropped down with me, reaching for her toes. "How far will we go today?"

I shook my head. "I don't know." I turned to see Courtney, Nettie, and Grace talking together in a small huddle. Their heads were bent together. I didn't know what they were saying, but it didn't matter. My blood had started to boil. All these girls were going to be in my dust.

I needed to run.

Coach Langdon gave us a few minutes, but when we hopped up, he raised the whistle to his mouth. The girls knew, and everyone was ready. Earbuds went in. People shook out their arms, jumping in place.

Faith and Raelynn stood at one end of the group, as if they were their own unit. The rest of the team stood together, and Taylor and I were at the opposite end.

I asked the closest girl, "How far's the morning run?"

"We do five in the morning. Then you can run as far as you want for the afternoon practice."

Only five? I'd hoped for more.

"Strattan."

I looked over to Coach Langdon.

"Follow the girls. They know the route."

Which meant I had to keep pace with them. I couldn't go faster on my own. *This is the first run*, I reminded myself.

"Okay, Coach."

He nodded and blew his whistle.

We were off.

It was about how I'd expected it to be.

Faith and Raelynn took the lead, and the rest of the group seemed content to run as a pack behind them. I stayed with Taylor, who kept up with everyone just fine. She held steady at the back end of the group, and I ran slightly on the outside, waiting and biding my time.

Faith and Raelynn had glanced back at me as we first started, but when I remained back by Taylor, they seemed to settle in and lead the team. Both were slender, their hair pulled up in high buns, and they had a confidence to their gait. They were good, and they knew it.

The other girls paid attention to us at the beginning too, but by the end of mile four, they'd lost themselves in their own running. Taylor was still fine. She looked like she could do another five. As if reading my mind, she looked over and winked.

"You can go," she mouthed.

I nodded. That was all I needed, and I started to edge forward.

I recognized the feeling in my legs. I could tell when we'd started the fifth mile. The girls up front picked up their pace. A mile to them was just a jog home. It'd go fast, and as Raelynn and Faith pulled away, the gap closed between the team and them. The pack had picked up speed too.

I moved on the side until I neared the head of the pack. Some girls noticed, but I held back until we were at the half point of mile five. Then I surged ahead, still running on the side, but bridging the gap between the team and Faith and Raelynn. We were rounding the last quarter mile when they noticed me. I was right behind them, almost on their heels, and this time, I looked ahead.

If I were right, Coach Langdon would be there. And when we cleared a set of trees, I saw him waiting, consulting his stopwatch.

It was time.

I put my head down and moved around the last two girls.

They surged ahead, but I kept going.

I kicked it up to my normal pace, but Faith and Raelynn could handle their own, at least for this distance. They stuck next to me until we surged past the coach. Then they dropped to a walk, but I kept running in place. I wanted to do more.

He checked his watch as he walked over to me. "Well, you're definitely on the team. I don't think it's a coincidence that everyone had faster times than usual." He eyed me running in place. "You're still hoping to run?"

I nodded. "I didn't know the route." I smirked. "I do now."

He eyed me, cocking his head to the side. "Martin said you'd have good times. I expected that. I thought you'd keep with those two." He gestured to Faith and Raelynn, who were stretching as the rest of the team trickled in. "Did you hold back?"

I wasn't going to boast, so I shrugged. "Just let me do my thing. You won't regret it."

He seemed to mull it over before he nodded. "I'll send the girls in and wait. You do another five. Blow me away with your times, Strattan."

That was all I needed.

This time, I ran for myself.

CHAPTER EIGHT

The second run didn't take as long.

I soared past Coach Langdon, and he showed me my time, shaking his head. "What year are you?"

"Junior." I pulled my leg up behind me, stretching my quad.

Taylor waved from the curb. She'd showered and had two cups sitting next to her. I could smell the coffee from where I stood. Its aroma mingled with my sweat.

"Why are you joining this year? You wasted two years, Strattan."

I gulped, lowering my leg. "There were reasons."

He snorted, heading back to the building. "You're on the team. Your friend too. We run in the mornings and at three every day. Meet here by seven thirty and meet at the running track at three. Our first meet is in two weeks, but I have no worries about your performance. Hydrate. I'll have a meal plan for you later."

He nodded as he passed Taylor, who stood and brought over the coffee. "I made the team. Did you hear?" She offered me a cup.

Hearing the excitement in her voice, I grinned. "Did you really think you wouldn't make it?"

She lifted a shoulder, sipping from her cup. "I wasn't sure what I was getting into. But I'm happy. Logan will flip for me."

I laughed. "He's going to buy some kind of ATV and follow us. You know that, right?"

Her lip tugged up. "You're right. He'll blast music, and he'll have towels, water, and protein snacks for us."

I nodded. I expected more than that. "Nate will be with him too."

"And Jason."

"We're bringing our own fan club to the team. Now they'll really love us."

"Man." Her eyes lit up. She glanced over my shoulder, and I turned. Some of the girls were coming out of the building. All were showered, and some held their own coffees as they laughed together. I waited, but neither Faith nor Raelynn came out behind them.

"If you're looking for the two divas, you missed them," Taylor said. "Not that they threw a big scene, but when you took off, no one said a word. It was complete silence. I think everyone was waiting for an explosion, but then those two just stormed off. They were the first to leave, and they were pissed."

I wasn't that surprised, but I didn't get to say anything. Courtney, Grace, and Nettie were coming over. Courtney was grinning now, almost as wide as the other two.

Grace gushed first. "You're a bitch. You let us think you were the bartending staff at that party." She punched me lightly. "We had no idea you were Mason Kade's girlfriend, and oh my God—Faith and Rae are livid. We've been hearing about you, but you never joined the team. They thought they were clear to take the top two spots. Now they gotta fight like the rest of us."

Courtney touched my arm, jerking her head to the side.

I frowned, following her.

"Be careful," she said once we were a few steps away.

"What do you mean?"

"Faith and Raelynn are rich. Both of them. They grew up running together. Their fathers are best friends, and they're kind of like sisters."

"Are you saying they'll do something to hurt me?"

"No. I'm not saying they'll physically hurt you, but I wouldn't put it past them to figure out a way to get you off the team. Just watch your back."

I nodded. "I will. Thanks for the heads-up."

She nodded. Her shoulders lifted in a deep breath, and she started grinning again. "I can't believe it. Our team's always fun, but today was a whole other kind of practice. I'm kind of excited to see what happens."

I glanced over. Grace and Nettie were still chatting up Taylor, who was watching me.

For so many reasons, I was happy Logan had caught her. It felt nice to have someone behind me. I'd been missing Heather since I started at Cain. There'd been random friends, but no one had stuck.

Taylor headed my way. "Ready to go? Logan's blowing my phone up. He wants to meet for breakfast."

Grace and Nettie followed. "Where are you going?" Nettie asked.

"Uh . . ." Taylor opened her mouth.

Courtney cut in, adding, "Because maybe we'll check the place out too. You know, another morning or something."

"No, I was ask—"

Courtney shot her a meaningful look, interrupting again. "We have plans this morning. We'll go another time."

"Oh." Nettie closed her mouth.

Grace frowned.

Taylor tucked some loose strands of hair behind her ear and glanced around, looking anywhere but at the girls.

This had just turned awkward.

Logan wouldn't want new people at breakfast. Taylor didn't have the words to express his exclusivity sometimes, but Courtney knew. Or it seemed like she did. Logan did have a reputation. He liked people, but he was selective. He didn't do breakfast with just anyone.

I cleared my throat. "We have some family things to talk about, but we should do breakfast tomorrow?" I gazed around the group.

Logan wouldn't come. That was the unspoken part of the deal.

Nettie smiled. "That sounds like fun."

Courtney cleared her throat. "And on that note, my stomach is growling. Let's go, chicas. I still have to stop in at my job for a few hours."

After they left, Taylor expelled a breath. "Logan would've been a lot ruder about that."

I chuckled as we started for the cars. "He would've been blunt, not giving a shit if he hurt their feelings."

She glanced at me from the side. "You were smoother. Thank you."

I shrugged, coming to my car. "I'm a little more experienced, that's all. I've been with them since high school."

"Yeah." She looked over at her car for a moment. "I was doing my own thing when Logan and I started dating. Then second semester was just about him—and Jason. My other friend faded. She started doing her own thing." She looked back at me. "I've been so intimidated by you."

"Well, there's no need for that. Whatever changed, I'm happy. I'm glad you're on the team with me."

"Me too." She smiled. "See you back at the house?"

I smelled my shirt and wrinkled my nose. "Yes. I need to shower. Logan can drive."

"See you soon."

⸻

We ended up eating at a restaurant a few miles from the university, and when we walked inside, we weren't the only students there. I recognized a table of football cheerleaders. They weren't in uniform, but their hair was done in pigtail braids, and their faces sparkled with glitter. Some girls I remembered from my freshman dorm were there too, in a back corner booth. We passed several tables of guys as the host led us to our seats. I didn't think anything of them until Logan stopped. A cheer went up, and he pounded fists with a few of them.

Taylor leaned back toward me. "You know who they are?"

I shook my head. "No clue." They weren't football players, but they were tall with long, lean legs. "Some basketball players, maybe?"

A moment later, when we were seated in our booth, Logan confirmed my guess.

"It's a team day here. I wasn't sure if it was today or later this week."

"What do you mean?" I asked

"All the teams are showing here. Mason's coming too. Whoever's around is coming today for a big meal." He nodded to me. "You guys are on the cross-country team." He smirked. "I got in because I'm just awesome. I'm my own team."

Taylor met my gaze. "We weren't told anything about this."

"Really?" He pointed across the restaurant. "That girl has a cross-country jacket. That's your team, right?"

Courtney, Grace, and Nettie hadn't said a word. They'd made me believe we were the ones ditching them, but when I looked over, he was right. They sat at a large table, along with the rest of the team, and at a separate booth with the coach and a woman I didn't recognize were Faith and Raelynn. They both wore smug looks, like they hadn't a worry in the world.

They purposely hadn't told us.

Logan narrowed his eyes. "You guys didn't know?"

"They didn't say a word." I clenched my jaw.

Taylor jerked back in her seat, glaring. "This isn't going to slide."

I shook my head. "Fuck, no."

"Are you guys serious? You were cut out?" Logan whistled under his breath. "And you guys think it's me who's going to get Mason in trouble." He laughed. "What are you going to do?" He glanced at Taylor, but she was watching me.

It was my decision.

I tried to formulate the best plan of action.

Then I saw Faith and Raelynn say something and start laughing. The woman and Coach Langdon seemed oblivious, absorbed in their conversation, but the rest of the team looked over. Faith leaned toward them, saying something, and soon that table was laughing too. The only one who seemed uncomfortable was Courtney. Grace and Nettie laughed, but not as much as the others. The three of them shared a look.

They were talking about us.

My brain shut off. I stood. I wasn't going to be someone's joke. Not now, and not ever. Experiencing flashbacks to my junior year at Fallen Crest Academy, with Jessica and Lydia laughing at me—leading the rest of the students in one big fucking laugh at my expense—some of that old Sam rose up.

I wove through the tables. There must've been some look on my face, because as I went past them, people quieted. I was drawing attention. I didn't care about that either. I was climbing the stairs to the section where the team sat when they saw me.

A collective hush fell over the table and booth. The only two who still had no clue were the coach and the woman. I stopped between them and looked at Faith and Raelynn.

"Whose idea was it to leave us out?"

Courtney looked down at her plate. Grace bit her lip, and Nettie pressed her lips together in a flat line. I looked right at Faith and Raelynn. "Was it you guys?"

Faith flipped her dark braid back over her shoulder and stuck her chin out. "Calm down. This is for the teams from last year. It's an early celebration. It's not anything official."

"Is that true?" I turned to Coach Langdon. "This wasn't official?"

He frowned, a big line marring his forehead. "Faith, Rae, you didn't tell the new girls?"

Faith flushed. "They just joined a few hours ago."

"Doesn't matter. It's for teams. There was nothing said about last year versus this year, and even if there had been, I wouldn't have respected that. A team's a team." He pointed at me, still speaking to Faith and Raelynn. "If you want to go to nationals, you're going to want her on this team." He looked to the woman. "Come on, Ruth. I want to introduce you to some people." He gave the rest of the girls and myself a cursory look. "Let's leave the team to get things right."

Faith's mouth snapped shut, and she glared at me as she swirled her fork through her hash browns.

"Who was that?" I asked her once they were gone.

Faith forced a tight smile and turned to talk to Raelynn, shutting me out.

This bitch—I started for her, but a hand caught my arm and tugged me back. I thought it was Taylor at first, then it registered that the hand was stronger than hers.

"Far be it from me to get involved in a chick fight," Logan began, as Faith and Raelynn both looked up. "I've seen Sam in action. A fair warning: she's not one to piss off."

Faith narrowed her eyes. "That's sweet. Your stepbrother is standing up for you."

So she did know who Logan was.

She leaned forward, propping her elbow on the table and almost posing for us. "Word to the wise. You'll never see a man fighting my battles. I'm woman enough to take care of myself."

"So, I won't see your rich daddy?" I shot back.

Her fake smile dropped, and she went back to glaring. "Like you're one to talk. I know Park Sebastian. I'm well aware of who *your* daddy is, and you're not hurting any more than I am."

This bitch knew who I was. Knew who Logan was. I assumed she knew who Mason was, and she even knew Park Sebastian, the asshole who once tried to recruit Mason into his fraternity and hadn't taken rejection well. At all.

She'd done her homework.

"So this is how it's going to go? Full-out war between us?" I asked. "Why?"

Sighing, Faith grabbed her bag and stood up. Raelynn was behind her. Faith raised her chin, like she was too dignified to breathe our same air.

"If you're expecting a team welcome hug, it's not going to happen. This is my team. Those winning times are mine, not yours. And today was just a small sample of how I can make your time on the team a living hell. Stick around. I'll turn destroying you into a hobby."

She started to leave, but I grasped her arm. When she tried to pull away, my fingers tightened. She gasped, her shocked eyes finding mine.

I didn't take threats lightly.

She was only a few inches from me and I said, in a low, soft, and somewhat lethal tone, "You're going to find out what I can do now. And I *almost* feel sorry for you."

Her eyes widened.

I let go, and she was gone in an instant. She started to shove past Mason at the door, but thought better of it and went around him with Raelynn hot on her heels.

Logan started laughing. "Ice-Cold Strattan is back. This'll be good. But remember, none of this can blow back on Mason."

I frowned. It wouldn't. I wouldn't let that happen.

CHAPTER NINE

I went back and sat with Logan and Taylor for breakfast. Nate arrived not long after, and Mason joined us when the football team was told they could do their own thing. The rest of the girls from my team left the restaurant as Mason settled in. I caught their looks. Several glanced over, and I recognized the wistfulness and jealousy. Grace and Nettie didn't look. Courtney did, but she seemed somber. She lifted a hand in an awkward wave as she followed the rest of the team out.

"You have another run today?" Logan asked.

I nodded, slipping my hand in Mason's. "At three."

"We're there."

"No." I shook my head. This was my fight. I had to be the only one involved. Which led me to Taylor. "You shouldn't come today."

Her eyebrows shot up. "Are you kidding? I joined because I wanted to, and because I wanted to do something with you. You need me there for backup."

"They can hurt you to get to me."

She shook her head. "You're jumping to conclusions. You have no idea what they're going to do."

"If I run with them, I can beat them. They won't be able to catch me." I let the rest hang between us. Taylor wasn't as fast. They could get to her. "I don't want them to hurt you," I added, flattening my hand on the table between us.

"This is stupid." She swore. "*Nothing* could happen. Have you thought of that?"

Nothing wasn't in my history. "I've learned to take threats seriously. I got jumped in a bathroom one time."

Mason's hand tightened around mine. "This is ridiculous. You didn't join the team to deal with this bullshit."

"Oh, you mean it's more ridiculous than the bullshit we normally get involved in?" Logan retorted.

I looked between the two. "Don't get involved. If you guys get involved with girl drama, all bets are off. That could bounce back on you and make you guys look really bad."

"We know," Mason said softly. "I just don't handle it well when my girlfriend is getting jerked around and I can't do anything about it."

"You and me both, brother," Logan added.

"Wait." Nate leaned forward, resting his elbows on the table. "What are those girls' names?"

I tried to remember what Courtney had said. "Faith . . ."

"Shaw," Taylor supplied. "And Raelynn Quang."

"Shaw. She's a junior?"

"I think so." I nodded.

"She has an older sister," Nate said. "I think I slept with her when I was with the fraternity. Yeah . . . Hope Shaw. She told me her mom named all of her sisters like that. Hope. Faith. I think Charity is the youngest."

"What was the sister like?"

He smirked.

Logan chuckled. "She's not asking about the sex."

"Oh." The smirk vanished. He lifted a shoulder. "Hope was cool. I remember she talked about her spoiled little sister, said she was one of those types who has her own coach and everything. She must've been talking about this one."

"You think we could talk to her? Just try to see how far her sister might go with this whole thing about pushing me off the team?"

He nodded. "Yeah. I'll message her, see if she's around."

And we had a plan.

Taylor didn't want to miss the three o'clock run, but I made her. I'd been through too much not to tackle this drama right away, and I planned to say the same thing in Coach Langdon's office that afternoon.

Mason drove me. He was going to go work out and lift weights until I was done with my practice, but I know he wanted to be close in case something happened. I had no doubt Logan, Taylor, and Nate would all be camped out along the running trail. Matteo had probably been recruited too.

After I regaled Coach Langdon with some of my history with threats, he wore a serious expression.

"You think my girls would conspire to hurt you?"

"From what I've heard, I know they would."

"Because they didn't tell you about the breakfast today?"

"Because Faith's exact words were that she'd *destroy me.*"

He pushed his clipboard to the side of his desk. "I don't know what you want me to do, Strattan. They haven't done anything, and I have a girl who's already skipping a practice. She hasn't even been on a full day."

"Coach."

"I'll have to kick her off the team."

He wasn't taking this seriously. He was taking their side. A spark of anger lit in me, but I kept it simmering.

"If I were to take my concerns higher, would others make the same decision as yours? To disregard a bullying concern and instead kick that runner off the team?"

He started to laugh, reaching for his whistle.

"You do remember her last name, right?"

He paused and looked back at me. "Are you doing what I think you're doing?"

"Depends on what you think I'm doing."

"Are you using Taylor's father as a threat? You think my decision will change because her daddy is one of the football coaches?"

"No. I'm reminding you that if I take my concerns to your supervisor, he might weigh the decision differently because of who her father is."

He stared at me.

I stared at him.

We were at a stare-off.

He had to know I was right. The university adopted a strict no-bullying policy last year after some incidents in the dorms and with the tennis team.

I softened my voice. "If I were to look into the history of this team, I'd find other incidents of girls joining and then dropping out shortly afterwards. Wouldn't I?"

I saw the guilt in his eyes. He looked away.

"I'm right."

"That doesn't mean they were bullied," he said.

"It doesn't mean they weren't."

"Goddamn, Strattan. What do you want me to do? Kick my two best runners off this team? They could qualify for the Olympics."

"So could I."

And as I said those words, I felt them ricocheting inside of me. The Olympics. I'd never thought about that. Running was in my blood. I had to run to be happy. It hadn't been something I'd trained or worked hard for. I just did it. But as I heard myself saying those words, I knew they were true.

I could go to the Olympics.

Holy fucking shit.

"Let's not get ahead of ourselves. I saw you run this morning; that was it."

"I held back."

"Why'd you hold back?"

"I was following your instructions. I didn't know the route."

"And the second time?"

I met his eyes. "I didn't want them to hate me even more."

His eyes narrowed, and he leaned back in his chair. "You're saying you can go faster?"

"You know I can. Coach Carillo gave you my times."

"For track, for the mile run."

"Let me know the routes, and don't hold me back."

"And then what? I'm supposed to let your friend join the team and protect her against the other girls? I can't promise they won't do something to her behind my back. I can't watch her at all times. What about the locker room?"

"Who was that other lady today?"

"Ruth. She's going to be your warm-up coach."

"Then she can be in there."

"Strattan." He sighed, pushing the brim of his baseball cap up so it perched on his forehead. "I can't promise you anything, except that if your friend still wants to run with the girls, I'll have Ruth follow in the golf cart. She'll keep an eye out for anything shady. How about that?"

I nodded. I'd been clenching my jaw, and it relaxed now, but throbbed a little. "That's all I want. And for you to keep an open mind."

He leaned forward, opening one of the drawers. Shifting through a few folders, he pulled out a piece of paper and offered it to me. "Here."

I took it. "What is this?" It was a map of campus. I could see the paths highlighted on it.

"Those are running paths." He stood and used a pen to point to the route labeled C. "That's the route you girls are running today. They know all the routes, so you're right about that. I should've given this to you earlier." His pen followed the trail until it connected to another route labeled D. "If you really want to knock my socks off, follow C until it leads here. Then follow D all the way back. You'll have gone twice as far as the other girls today. Faith and Rae do that sometimes. They branch off on their own. I'm offering the same privilege to you."

I memorized the two trails, then folded the paper and put it in my pocket. I'd have to pull it out again later to review. "I'll do it. Thank you."

He held a hand toward the door, grabbing his clipboard, stopwatch, and whistle. "It's almost three. Taylor is excused for the day, and I'll keep an open mind, but my hands are tied beyond those two things. I can't kick off two of my best runners because they said mean things to you. It's not enough to go on. Not yet."

That was the most I'd been hoping for. "Thank you, Coach."

"Now, go get warmed up. I want to see how fast you can really go."

I headed for the door. I was itching to do just that.

Since I was already dressed, I stopped to fill my water bottle before heading out to where the team had congregated. They paused when I pushed through the door, and I made a point of going to a different section of grass to stretch. It didn't surprise me to see Faith and Raelynn stretching on their own too, nor was I shocked by the way everyone looked to them like they were waiting for orders on how to handle me.

Faith narrowed her eyes, but didn't move toward me. She resumed her stretching, and the rest of the team followed suit.

"Samantha." Courtney called my name.

I shook my head. "Save it."

She sat next to me and reached for her toes. Nettie and Grace watched, but they didn't come over with her.

"I can't," she said. "I'm sorry for this morning."

I released my leg and reached for my toes, mirroring her. "You made me feel bad about excluding you."

"I know."

"I felt like an idiot when I saw you there."

"I know."

"Why are you here?"

She looked around, her forehead wrinkling a little. "Where's Taylor?"

"She's skipping today because I was worried something might happen to her."

"Are you kidding me?" Her eyebrows shot up. "You think we'd do something to hurt her?"

"Yeah."

"Faith and Rae might be a lot of things, but actually harming someone isn't something they'd do."

I stopped stretching. "Are you here on behalf of them, or are you here because you feel bad about your part?"

"I . . ." She hesitated, her head dipping down for a moment. She took a breath and looked back up. "I feel bad for my part. I knew they were going to do that, and that's why we asked to join you guys."

"So, we wouldn't know right away that we were outcasts?" My old anger was surfacing. I felt it simmering. "We'd find out later, when something actually happened to hurt me or Taylor?"

Shame flooded her features. She looked back down at her legs. "Look." She twisted her hands together. "I feel bad for my part. And you should know that not all of us follow those two. I think you'll be amazing for our team, and I'm glad you joined."

I looked at her friends. Nettie huffed, looking away. Grace gave me a timid smile back.

"And your friends? Are they on the same page?" I asked.

"Grace is."

"Not Nettie?" Not the drunk girl who'd made out with a guy for everyone to see?

She hesitated again, chewing on the inside of her cheek. "If Nettie has to choose between you and them, it's them." She lowered her voice. "I'm not even sure she'd choose Grace and me over them. Not that it helps."

I nodded. Coach Langdon came out and went over to the two divas. He had a word with them, and both whirled around to look at me. A couple seconds later, he moved on to talk to Ruth. Faith and Raelynn stormed over.

"You narc'd on us? Are you kidding me?!" Faith hissed. She turned to Courtney. "What are you doing over here?"

Courtney straightened, raising her chin. "I was apologizing."

Faith snorted. "You're weak, Courtney. If you want to be on the losing side, so be it. We'll target you too."

"So you're declaring it then?" I stepped in front of Courtney, facing Faith. "You're openly saying you're going to go after me?"

"I already did."

Smart-ass bitch. I only smiled, though. "Okay. Just so we're clear. And you bet your ass I went to the coach. When I think you're going to try to hurt a friend of mine to get to me, I'll do whatever I need to cover her back."

Coach Langdon blew the whistle. The rest of the girls began to gather in front of him. I started forward, but Faith called, "What makes you think I'd go after her first?"

I stopped and looked back. I had a nice fuck-off smile. "If you want to come after me, you need to catch me."

She rolled her eyes. "Like that's going to be a problem."

I kept going, content just to smile to myself. She had no idea.

The run was a joke.

These girls weren't used to my speed. I started strong, and I never let up. Faith and Raelynn stayed right behind me for three miles. Then Raelynn fell behind, and we came to the D route. I went that way, and Faith continued with me. We were too far ahead to see whether the other girls chose to stay on C or come our way. For a while, it was just the two of us, but after another half-mile, I couldn't see Faith either.

I stopped once to check the map.

Then I put my head down, concentrated on my breathing, and kept my arms relaxed. I just kept going.

This was the closest thing to flying for me. I felt it as I soared around the curves and over the hills. This wasn't normal. What I could do wasn't something others could—at least no one here. I kept going, finishing the last few miles strong, and the others were just arriving after their shorter route when I cleared the line.

Coach Langdon looked at me, looked at his watch, and muttered, "Holy shit."

I wanted to do more.

I *could* do more.

I'd run this morning, held myself back, and refueled. I felt like I was just whetting my appetite. My legs should be jelly, but they weren't.

"You can do that every day?" he asked.

I nodded. My music was still blaring in my ear, but I heard enough over it. "You want a runner for the Olympics. I'll do it."

This was it. That was what I wanted to do, whether I succeeded or not. It clicked as I was running today. I wanted to try. I *had* to try.

He sighed, taking his cap off and raking his arm over his forehead. "Okay. Let's do it."

"Coach?" Raelynn pushed forward. Her braid had unraveled, and her hair was plastered to her face with sweat. She must've chosen to stay on the C route. Her hands found her slim hips. I hadn't heard her speak before, but her voice was just as pretentious as I'd thought it would be.

"You can't keep up with her, Rae. Even you have to admit that."

He sounded like he was apologizing, but that was all he said as he walked back inside. The rest of the girls began to stretch.

Raelynn glared at me, her nostrils flaring, before she half-snarled. "Don't get comfortable."

I stepped toward her. "Is that a threat?"

She jumped back, but muffled a scream before plopping down to stretch.

I picked my old spot, away from everyone, and was half done with my stretches when Courtney came over. She leaned down when I laid back and pulled my leg to my chest. She helped push it against my chest and spoke around her counting, "1—lines were drawn today. You know that, right?—4—I'm with you, if you're wondering. Grace and me." She pushed my leg a little farther. "Resist. 1. 2. 3. 4. Relax."

I followed her instructions, and she repeated another two counts until we switched legs. I waited until she released my leg before replying.

"Besides my mother, I haven't had a fight directed just at me for a while." I grinned a little. "It felt kind of good."

Courtney pressed down. "Resist. 5. 4. 3. 2. Relax." She waited a beat. "Resist again. You're used to fights or something?"

I snorted, pushing back as much as I could. "You don't really know my boyfriend and stepbrother, if you have to ask me that."

She laughed. "Relax." She patted my leg, standing back up. "And you're right. I've heard stories, but I never fully listened."

I grunted. "Maybe that's a good thing."

"Yeah. Maybe."

I finished my stretching and sat up to realize the other girls hadn't gone. I'd assumed they would. But instead they had showered, and were standing in a line. I frowned.

"They're waiting for Faith."

"Say what?" I hadn't heard that right. There was no way.

Courtney groaned softly, giving me an apologetic look. "This is what they do. If she's not back, they don't leave. She's the star." She shrugged. "Or she was."

"This is insanity." I felt like I was watching a cult. They were all brainwashed, and I looked over their faces as I moved toward the parking lot. They were blank, except for excitement brimming in a few. Raelynn glowered, and she stood at the end of the line with a hand resting on her hip.

I spotted Mason waiting for me in his Escalade. I ran over and got inside, but when he reached for his keys, I said, "Wait."

He paused. "Something wrong?"

"I just want to watch."

He leaned back in his seat, watching with me.

We waited, and twenty minutes later, Faith ran past us toward the team. They began clapping. Raelynn's glower diminished. As Faith ran to them, they came over and patted her on the back.

"That's strange."

"Why?"

Mason's question threw me. "They support her like a parent would cheer for a kid. That's weird." I looked at him. "Isn't that weird?"

He started the engine. "They're supporting their star runner."

She wasn't the star anymore. It would've been cocky to say that out loud, but I couldn't help thinking it.

"You just started today," Mason said as we left the parking lot. "You turned everything upside down. It takes a while for people to adjust.

They're supporting another teammate. In the future, they'll support you too."

"That'll be weird too."

"She's not going to give up that spot without a fight."

I frowned at him. "I know that."

"No, I mean, she's going to push herself harder. She has someone to catch now. They'll all push harder now."

"So, I'm kinda helping them in a way?" That pissed me off.

He laughed. "Kinda, but you don't stroll through the door and take the spot at the top without a battle. She'll give you a battle. I think she'll do it in a dirty way, but it'll be there no matter what. You just gotta fight for your spot at the top."

"It wasn't like this in high school."

"You were already at the top."

I glanced at him again. "What do you mean?"

"You came in, and you fought Kate. What do you think she was doing? She wasn't just fighting you for me. It was more than that."

"I wasn't at the top in high school."

He reached over. His hand covered mine. "You were with us. We *were* the top."

I turned my hand over and laced our fingers together. "Did you have to deal with this in football?"

"I wasn't the top my freshman year. I'm up there now. Me and another guy."

"It wasn't like this with track."

"Because everyone did different events, but I bet you're considered at the top there."

Maybe, but he was right; it was more individual there. I let out a sigh. I was starting to come down from the adrenaline wave. I could feel myself crashing a bit.

I leaned my head back against the headrest and murmured, "I haven't been this angry in a long time. I mean, I don't know. It's different. It's—"

"How it was when you were at the Academy?"

"Yeah."

"Like I said, it's because you're doing your own fight. And I can't help you with this one." He pulled up to a stoplight and looked over as we waited. "I wish I could."

I squeezed his hand. "I know. I feel the same when you've had your battles."

The light turned green, and after that, we were silent.

I was already thinking about the next day's practice.

CHAPTER TEN

MASON

"Yo."

I was crossing the parking lot to the sports center when I looked over to see Logan behind me in his yellow Escalade. He had the window rolled down and an arm propped on it. He waved me over.

I shifted my gym bag to my other shoulder. It was early in the morning—not Sam-early, but early for me. She was probably already off on her third run with the team, and my day was about to start in thirty minutes. And I'd be busy all day—running drills, watching game tapes, and lifting weights. We'd be here until three or four this afternoon. Yesterday's breakfast had been a one-time deal.

"What's up?" I frowned. "You slept at the house last night."

"I know. I brought Taylor and Sam in for practice this morning. What are we going to do about those two girls?"

"Sam says it's her fight."

Logan dropped the smirk and gave me a knowing look. "Right. Because that's our role. We stand back and let the chicks duke it out."

I stifled a grin. "Sam thinks this is her fight, and she wants us to respect that."

"You're saying you're actually going to *not* do shit here?"

Now I was the one to smirk. "Logan." I shook my head as if to say, *Come on.*

He chuckled, bobbing his head up and down in approval. "That's what I thought. So what's the plan?"

"I'm thinking we should know as much as we can about the whole family. I don't like when people threaten *mine*."

Logan's top lip curled. "I figured your whole passive boyfriend act wasn't real. Call Dad? Have him find out information on this girl's family?"

I hesitated. Things were still tense between our father and us. The speeches we'd made at his wedding hadn't been respectful or loving. "I don't know if we want to push our luck with Dad, not just yet." A horrible idea took seed in my head. Maybe it wasn't so bad, but . . .

Logan's eyes narrowed. He saw it forming too. "What are you thinking?"

If we didn't go to our dad ourselves, who else could go to him? Who else had a vested interest in Sam? Who had said she'd do whatever Sam wanted, and wouldn't attach strings to any favor?

I couldn't. No way. I loathed this person. But she'd proven she could be somewhat sane when it came to her daughter. Lately.

"Mason?" Logan prompted.

"Analise."

His eyes widened. "What? Fuck, no. Have you lost your mind?"

"Think about it. Her psycho button is going to get hit eventually, but not yet. She's still trying to do whatever Sam wants."

"Which is to be left alone."

"She can help us help Sam. That's enough. She won't go to Sam with expectations of being thanked or anything."

Logan groaned. "Team up with Anabitch? Are you sure about this?"

It wasn't ideal, but . . . "I can get Dad's guy to look into this girl and her family, but Dad might have information we wouldn't get any other way. It's worth the try."

"What makes you sure Dad even knows this guy?"

I wasn't. "We have to see. If this chick is wealthy, and it sounds like she is, chances are good that Dad knows something about her family."

"Okay." He nodded. "And when we break the news to Sam that we went behind her back?"

"Remind her she'd do the same for us."

His eyebrows lifted, but he didn't comment.

"Mase!"

Matteo waited by the door. I held up a hand, then turned back to my brother. "Nate's birthday is this weekend. We can pretend to take him to Vegas."

"But by Vegas you mean Fallen Crest?"

I nodded.

Logan laughed. "Nate will be so disappointed."

"Yeah, well, maybe we can use Dad's favor and fly to Vegas afterward?"

"Mason!" Another yell from behind me.

"Score." Logan held out his fist. "Your boyfriend is getting impatient. Pound it. I'll see you later."

I met his fist with mine, then headed for the doors. Logan sped past us out of the parking lot, giving the middle finger as he did.

"Did your brother give you a ride or something?" Matteo asked.

I shook my head. "Just had to talk about something. That's all."

He narrowed his eyes. "The draft is this year for us. Don't do anything to fuck that up."

I understood his concern, and as I nodded, he seemed to relax.

But I had started to wonder if it was worth it.

Did playing professional football outweigh doing the shit I'd always done to protect those I loved? Being good and saint-like versus what Logan and I had always been?

I was beginning to think it wasn't.

CHAPTER ELEVEN

SAMANTHA

A hand on my hip woke me in the night, and I rolled to my back, already knowing who it was. Mason was poised above me, and his hand inched upwards, pushing aside my thin shirt until he cupped my breast.

"Hey," I murmured, touching his chest and sliding my hands around his neck. I raked my fingers up into his hair and grabbed a fistful. There was just enough. "What are you doing?"

He grinned in the moonlight as shadows covered him in a mysterious and alluring way. It didn't matter that he was already above me; I would've been aching for him anyway. I opened my legs a little. He looked down, running his hand along my leg until his fingers rested right there, lightly grazing over me.

"I'm being a selfish ass, and I'm waking you up," he said softly as he kissed my throat, sending tingles through my body. His head lifted; he didn't move to my lips. His hand pressed a little harder, but it still wasn't enough. He was going to tease me. I could feel it in the way he held himself, giving me just a taste.

I grinned, tugging his head back down to mine. "I don't like it when you play like this with me."

"Really?"

"No." I fused my mouth to his.

This touch from him? It'd never get old. Ever.

I felt him still holding himself above me, and I tugged on his shoulders. I wanted to feel the full weight of him. Mouth to mouth. Chest to chest. When he finally rested on top of me, his hand moved between my legs.

"Christ." He pulled away, nipping my lips before moving down to my throat.

He sank a finger inside of me.

The ache was building. I moved against him, letting go of his hair and dragging my nails down his back.

He pushed a second finger in.

I strained against him, lifting up. I wanted his fingers farther inside, but instead he chuckled as he pulled them out. I opened my mouth, ready to protest, and they plunged back in.

"Mason!"

I clamped down on his shoulders, enjoying the feel of his muscles shifting as he ran a thumb over my nipple.

Sensations shot through me as his fingers pulled out and thrust in once again. A third finger joined the other two. He kept going—in and out, in and out. I searched for his lips, needing a taste of him too.

He found me, and his tongue slid next to mine, caressing. As he brought me to a climax, I could only hold on, letting the waves crash through me, one after another. By the time they were done, a new ache had started.

I wanted Mason inside of me, in that primal and most intimate way. It wasn't long until he obliged. I wrapped my legs around his waist. I had already been stretched out, so I didn't need to adjust to the feel of him, but he waited.

I raised a hand to the side of his face. "What is it?"

"I love you."

I grinned faintly, scooting down a little to pull him in deeper. "I love you too."

His lips touched mine in a soft and tender kiss. I felt like he was saying something else with that touch.

"Mason?" I pulled back to look at him again.

He didn't answer. His eyes closed, and he ducked down, kissing the side of my neck as he began to move. I gasped, feeling him push in farther. Then he almost slipped out, but he stopped and thrust back inside. He kept going.

I savored this.

No matter what was going on in our lives, these moments, *this* moment, always connected me to him.

An hour later, I was curled into his side and almost asleep.

"Sam?" His hand came to my hip again.

"Already?" But I was grinning. I knew that wasn't what he wanted. I opened my eyes, but his weren't teasing like mine. They were dark, like they were when we had sex. A shiver went through me, and a part of me wanted him all over again. It just felt right. I shifted, sitting up against my pillows. "What is it?"

His hand traced down my shoulder, cupping my breast and rubbing his thumb over the nipple. "It's Nate's birthday this weekend."

I widened my eyes. "You're going to touch my boob while you talk about Nate?"

He grinned. His hand tightened a little. "I want to touch your boob any time I see you and talk to you. It doesn't matter the topic of conversation."

I chuckled, but sat up farther. His hand fell away, and I rested against the headboard.

"What's going on?" I pulled the sheet up, tucking it across my chest and under my arms. The girls were nicely put away now.

It wasn't that I didn't want him to touch them; I didn't want to associate anyone else with Mason touching them. They were selfish like that.

"We're going to take Nate to Vegas."

I cocked my head to the side. What he was saying made sense, but there was something else going on. I frowned. "Are you lying to me?"

"What? No."

Too quick.

I poked him in the chest. "What's really going on? I can tell when you're lying." I wagged my finger at him. "I've caught on since we first started dating."

The lines around his grin softened, and he leaned down to kiss me. "There was a time when I had the upper hand."

I used the wagging finger to playfully shove him away. "Since when haven't you had the upper hand?" I was joking. Kind of.

"Really?" He loomed up to hold himself above me again. "You think I always have?"

I laughed and twisted away from his kiss, but I didn't go far. He caught me and rolled me back under him. He tried to kiss me, but I kept turning my head.

Part of me believed what I'd said. Mason did have the upper hand. Not in a bad way, like he lorded it over me, but he was the leader. He was the leader of all of us, and in that dynamic, it wasn't just him and me. It was him, Logan, and me. And really, that had expanded to include Nate and Taylor too. We were a fivesome fearsome, with an extended sixth member: Matteo. It was a matter of time before he was all the way in.

Mason's lips landed on my collarbone and he whispered there, "You think it's an unfair dynamic between us?"

Did I?

I was almost panting, loving the touch of him, but I knew the answer. I turned to look at him squarely. "Yes."

He sat back on his heels between my legs. "You think that? For real?"

I nodded. The light, sexual banter was gone. Something more serious took its place.

"Am I wrong to think that?"

He shook his head. His eyes were troubled. "No." His hands rested on my legs. "But I don't like that you think we're not equal. We are."

I sat up, resting my hands over his, and tilted my head to look up at him. "I don't mean it in a bad way. We love each other equally. We protect each other equally, but I've been content to let you run the show. I blame me, Mason."

His eyes narrowed. "What do you mean?"

"It's part of this whole epiphany I had the other week. I have to work on me. I've let my voice go away. It's not that I wasn't heard. It's that I didn't think to say anything. You and Logan make decisions for us, and I know you're just protecting us, but I can help make decisions too. It's you and him. You guys sequester yourselves at times and don't include me. I know Taylor's not included."

He frowned. "Taylor?"

The relationship between Mason and Logan's girlfriend just wasn't there. Taylor was the first girlfriend of Logan's Mason approved of, but I knew he was a long way from including her in the serious talks. She and Logan had been together almost a year, but it'd be longer before Mason trusted her fully, if that ever happened.

I wasn't sure Mason would ever really trust anyone except Logan and me. That's just how he was.

He cupped the back of my neck. "Then I have to come clean about something."

I pulled back. His hand still held me, but I wanted some space. "What?"

He cringed.

"What is it?" I was right. Something else was going on. "Are you not going to Vegas? What are you *really* doing?"

"We're going to Fallen Crest."

"Why?"

"Because I want to ask your mom to ask James for a favor."

My blood turned cold. "What?"

"I want information on that girl from your team. I want to know if my dad knows anything."

"You're going to use my mom?" My voice rose.

This wasn't cool. It wasn't cool at all. I pulled out of his hold, scurrying back against the headboard. I hugged my knees against me and wrapped my arms around them. "You were going to lie to me about that?"

"I . . ."

He was. He was going to completely lie to me, and I wouldn't have had any clue. My entire body felt chilled. "Mason, I—"

"Sam."

I climbed off the bed. I didn't like this. It was after midnight. We'd just had amazing sex, and then he was going to lie through his teeth? And about my mom? This wasn't Mason. This wasn't the guy I fell in love with. I shook my head and started dressing.

"What are you doing?"

I had no idea what to say. My mind was scrambling, and I wanted to run. "I can't believe you were going to lie to me."

"I'm sorry. I am."

I grabbed my pants, pulled them on, and switched my pajama shirt with a tank top. Reaching for an oversized sweatshirt, I whirled around. I slammed the sweatshirt down on the floor, still holding it by the sleeve. "You do this, you know."

"What are you talking about?" He moved to the edge of the bed. He was naked, but he was so confident—if I'd been him, I would've pulled the sheet to hide myself. Not him. He had a gorgeous, mouth-watering body, but it was more. It was his authority. His confidence. He didn't question himself. He didn't doubt himself. I didn't think he'd ever been self-conscious in his life. He probably had no idea how.

I was jealous of him.

Pulling my sweatshirt on, I just kept shaking my head. "When we first started dating, you went after Adam. I had no say. I would've rather not had you guys deal with the Academy Elite at all, but I understood it. You were doing it to protect me, but in some ways, it made things harder for me. And then Logan outed me when he hugged me at that football game. He didn't even think that maybe I wasn't ready for everyone to know I knew you guys. Or even with Kate. You guys had a whole plan for how to deal with her, with video and everything. I wasn't included. Then the frat house. If you had asked, I never would've been okay with you guys burning it down. I mean, my God, you burned a house down! That's insane. But you guys did it, and everyone in the know was supposed to be okay with it."

More and more started bubbling up, but this wasn't Mason. I wasn't mad at him.

I was mad at me.

He opened his mouth. I saw the regret in his eyes, and I knew he was going to apologize.

I held my hand up. "This isn't you." I softened my voice. "This is me. I'm angry with myself because I never spoke up. I've been—"

What the hell had I been doing? Holding on to them? Hoping they'd never leave me? Being beyond scared they'd abandon me like everyone else had? I forced out a breath.

These were the guys who didn't leave. They hadn't left. They never would leave.

Mason always said it. He was the forever guy.

I hadn't been letting myself believe that. I hadn't pushed my way in so they could hear me, though I knew they would.

They weren't the problem.

He wasn't the problem.

I was.

"I'm sorry. I have to go." I slipped on my shoes and headed out into the hallway.

He followed me. "Where are you going?"

I grabbed my purse and keys. "I have no idea, but I have to go somewhere."

"Sam!"

I was out the door and heading for my car.

He paused in the opened doorway. "Sam!"

I turned and waved as I got in the car. "I'll be fine. I just need to think. That's it."

My blood rushed through me, my thoughts bouncing all around my head. I felt panicked, but what I'd said was right. I was the problem. I still had to fix me.

I left, and I had no clue where I was going.

CHAPTER TWELVE

It was the middle of the night, and I was being stupid.

I ended up going to a 24-hour diner, and after my phone blew up with calls from Mason, then Logan, and finally Taylor, I texted Taylor to tell her where I was.

I'm coming. She texted back. **Don't leave.**

After that, my phone stopped ringing, so I assumed she'd told Mason and Logan where I was too.

Fifteen minutes, two cups of coffee, and a glass of water later, she came my way down the aisle between tables. She wore black leggings, an oversized hoodie sweatshirt, and a baseball cap pulled low over her face.

I half-snorted/half-laughed. "You could be in a magazine with that outfit." Her hair was gorgeous. It had grown longer over the year, and some of it was pulled over her shoulder. The rest fell down her back.

I wasn't a girl who got jealous, but I felt the same feeling stirring now that I'd had toward Mason an hour earlier. Taylor always knew who she was. She never questioned herself. I knew that was a quality that had drawn Logan to her.

She frowned, giving me an incredulous look. "Are you joking? You're drop-dead gorgeous, Sam."

So I'd been told, but I never felt it.

I shrugged, filling my coffee cup again from the carafe the waiter had brought over. "Well, I'm being a dramatic girl right now."

Taylor shrugged too. "It happens to the best of us. I think every girl deserves five meltdown moments. It's good for the soul. Cleansing."

I laughed. "Thank you for that."

She grinned. "I should be the one thanking you. I've earned major friendship points here. You texted me, not Logan or Mason. Logan didn't say anything, but I could tell." She pretended to brush dust off her shoulder. "He was impressed."

I laughed a little more this time. "And thank you for that." I felt my insides settling a little. "I don't feel *as* ridiculous as before."

"You shouldn't feel ridiculous at all, but can I ask why you're here and not snuggling up with that man of yours?"

"Because Mason started to lie to me, and I flipped out." I held my coffee mug in both hands. I didn't pick it up, but was content just feeling the warmth from the hot liquid seeping into my hands.

"What was he going to lie about?"

"I asked them to leave the Faith thing alone. They're not going to."

"Oh, yeah." She nodded. "Logan tried to sell me the same bullshit. I saw through it. Vegas, my ass." She snorted.

"He tried lying to you too?"

"He can't lie to me." She chuckled to herself. "He's tried. He sucks at it."

Logan was an incredible liar. That was a testament to Taylor and their relationship.

I let out a deep breath. "I'm not really mad at Mason. I'm mad at myself."

"Why? You're one of the nicest people I know. As Logan would say, you're a big deal." She winked.

I laughed shortly, then waited as the waiter came over to ask Taylor if she wanted anything. She ordered a coffee and some toast. I was content with my water, but did ask for a refill of my carafe. I never claimed my addiction to coffee was healthy.

Taylor groaned as the waiter left. "Our eight o'clock run is going to suck ass."

That was right. And I had to win. I had to beat Faith and Raelynn every time. I shook my head. I would. I had no worries about their running times.

"We'll be running even earlier once classes start."

"Why did I think joining the team would be fun?" She rolled her eyes, talking to herself. "Because I thought it'd be good for me. Good for me to join a team, to be social, to do something with you. I like to run. How hard could it be? I just do a few more miles than I normally do." Her sarcasm was thick, but she was half-smiling. "You might have to remind me in a few hours all of those things. I've got a feeling I'm going to be questioning my sanity at mile three."

"I'll remind you."

"You and me, we're not big social creatures, are we?"

I shook my head. "I've been burned by too many people."

"Yeah." She quieted, staring at the table. "Me too. Is there something wrong with us? And Mason and Logan love us. Is there something wrong with them?" She was laughing, but I sensed a twinge of sincerity in her questions.

The waiter brought over the coffee and refilled both our glasses of water. I picked at a stain on my mug.

"Is it possible to have an early-life crisis? Maybe that's what I'm doing."

"No." Taylor was firm. "You're changing. You're developing; that's it. I firmly believe that."

"Yeah?" I looked up, feeling new hope.

She nodded decisively. "Completely. I thought I was losing my mind when I started to heal from my mom's shooting. And then it just happened one day. The day before, the same shitstorm; things were all in upheaval. And then the next day it settled. I felt okay. I felt I was going to be okay. I don't know if it's the same for everyone, but that's how it was for me." She poured her coffee, eyeing me once she put the carafe back on the table. "You're going through something. Don't stress. Just let it ride, and you'll be fine once you get to the other side of it."

I felt a little more relief at her words. "Does Logan know how smart you are?"

"Are you kidding me? I'm 'majorly awesome.' That's how he puts it. He's awesome, but I'm in the major leagues."

I could imagine them laughing over that.

I felt another twinge of jealousy. And I hated it. This wasn't who I was, but I couldn't hide from it. It's what I was feeling. I had to face it.

"You and Logan have a good relationship."

Her eyebrows shot up. "And is the subtext that you don't?!"

We weren't equal. Mason had been my protector. I protected him too, but it wasn't the same.

"You guys are best friends."

"Again." Her mouth dropped open. She put a hand under her chin and manually closed it. Then she pointed. "That was me almost falling to the floor. Are you insane? You and Mason are beyond tight. Logan and I are good. We're best friends, but you guys . . ." She shook her head, a stunned expression on her face. "You're family. You're tight in a way it takes years for married couples to get to, and that's if they don't divorce. Not that you and Mason are going to divorce. Ever." She frowned to herself. "I have to stop talking. I'm making it worse, aren't I?"

"You're not."

But I still felt the whirlwind of not knowing in me.

And the worst part, I didn't even know what I didn't know. Something was missing. It wasn't Mason. It wasn't Logan. It was me. I was missing a part of me, and I'd just realized it. I still didn't know what it was.

"Can we sit here a bit longer?" I asked.

She nodded. "Yeah. Anything you want."

"Thank you, Taylor."

"That's what friends do."

I looked up, holding her gaze. We *were* friends. It had started slowly when she began dating Logan. It had built a little over the year, then the summer jump-started it, and now—after the team and tonight—Taylor was a ride-or-die friend.

And she was *my* friend.

She stared at the coffee. "We should've ordered decaf."

Mason was in the living room when I let myself in an hour later. Taylor had gone back to her house since that was where she and Logan were staying that night. I glanced around, but as Mason stood from the couch, there was no one else around.

"Nate's still sleeping?" I put my purse on the table by the door.

Mason nodded, rubbing his hands together. "I woke Logan and Taylor, but I didn't think I needed to wake everyone up."

"Taylor came and talked to me. Thank you for doing that."

He nodded again, seeming hesitant to cross the room. "Yeah. Anything."

This wasn't normal us.

We barely fought.

We were never unsure around the other.

I felt horrible that this was us now. Mason was always in control. He was the mastermind, the one who fought for us, and he was always three steps ahead of his enemies. The fear in his eyes now tore my insides apart.

"I'm sorry," I whispered.

He shook his head, taking two steps toward me now. He was still hesitant, and he stopped just on the other side of a chair. He could've taken two more steps and I would've been in his arms. He didn't. He stayed, running his hands down his pants.

He looked so uncertain. "I'm the one who should be apologizing, Sam. I never thought about it from your side, and you're right. Logan and I were just doing things. We were making decisions without consulting you, and I can see how infuriating that would be. It's my fault."

"No." I shook my head. "I came to you broken. You and Logan put me back together, and that was the start of us. But that's how it remained. You protected me. You fought for me, and I let you." I closed my hand into a fist and pressed it against my chest. "Every girl wants that. They want the guy to come in and save them. You gave me that fairytale, but I let it go on too long. I'm supposed to find my own footing and walk next to you. I never did that." I felt the tears falling. I didn't care. "I have to find that in me now, and it's not your fault. Ever. I don't want you to think you're to blame for this."

"But you're in pain."

Another step. He still didn't reach out.

"It's not your fault," I said.

"I don't know how to help you."

A second step. He was within touching now. I ached to reach for him.

My voice was so hoarse. "I know. And I'd feel the same torment if it were the other way around."

He held his hand out now. I took it, clasping tightly.

He looked down at our joined hands. "I really am sor—"

I squeezed his hand. "Never apologize for protecting me. Ever." I inched toward him, feeling his arm pressed against my side. Another inch and I would be touching the rest of him. I held back. I was content to let my mouth water.

"If I can help you, tell me. Please."

I nodded. "I will. Taylor said I'm changing, and that's what's going on with me."

He grinned faintly. "What else did she say?"

"That one day it'll be better."

"Does she know when that day will be?"

I shook my head. "I don't think anyone knows."

He let out a sigh, running his free hand through his hair. "This is going to suck, isn't it?"

"Yeah." I said that so softly, so quietly, I wasn't even sure I said it. Then my eyes closed, and I leaned forward that last inch. My forehead rested against Mason's chest, and his hand held the back of my neck. His thumb moved back and forth, comforting me.

"I love you, Sam."

I felt the words through his chest.

"I know."

That wasn't the problem.

CHAPTER THIRTEEN

As Taylor predicted, the morning's run sucked, but I won.

Logan had given Taylor and me a ride in, and he picked us up after practice. We all went back to the house, and I assumed they napped. I went to my room and slept until the afternoon. Logan gave us another ride back in at two, and the second run was a lot better. I won again.

Mason came home in the evening after practice, and the whole house just chilled. Even Nate. He'd been going out with some of his other friends, but he stayed in tonight. Logan and Taylor were here, and Matteo and a couple other football guys came over.

Someone started a movie in the media room downstairs, and Logan declared it was time that Chef Logan came out again. Forty minutes later, we were treated to another buffet of grilled meat: Steak. Hamburger. Chicken. Brats. I think he even grilled some tofu for Taylor, but while she kissed him on the cheek for his thoughtfulness, she reached for a chicken breast.

Mason and I made love that night, and there was a tenderness to it that had me melting.

The rest of the week passed much the same way: Logan drove Taylor and me to both runs. We napped in between. Mason came home at night, and everyone hung out at the house. Matteo was joined by another couple of guys every night. By Friday, it was just an unspoken agreement that the party was in our basement.

When I asked about the guys' "secret" plans to see my mom in Fallen Crest, Mason said they wouldn't do anything without my opinion asked for and given. I was relieved to hear that, and now the Friday night party morphed into Nate's birthday celebration.

The guys called more people over.

Logan grilled so much meat that it wasn't a third Meat Rushmore anymore. It was now Meat Everest. The guys brought more booze, more kegs, and then the girls started trickling in. They set up a DJ booth, and by eleven that night, the party was in full swing.

I was nestled on Mason's lap, sitting on the veranda with Nate, Logan, Taylor, Matteo, and a bunch of others when Faith and Raelynn moved past us in the yard. Both had drinks in their hands, and their hair was loose and shiny. Raelynn wore tight jeans and a white halter top. I wanted it to make her look cheap and trailer trashy, but it did the opposite. She looked like some wealthy tourist. Faith had a similar top, though hers rested just above her waist and showed half an inch of her stomach. She had on a long and flowing skirt. As she stepped forward, I saw her flat sandals and decided she just needed henna tattoos on her arms to complete the bohemian look.

"Are you lost?" I called as I sat up from Mason's chest.

His arms remained around me, but they moved to my legs. He looked over to see who I was addressing. Everyone did, and Logan was the first to snort.

"They gotta be lost," he added, and with one lithe jump, he was over the veranda's fence and landing right in front of them.

Their eyes rounded, but Faith's jaw firmed. "We're not lost." Her hand tightened around her drink.

"This is a private party." Logan folded his arms over his chest. "Next time we'll leave signs up to alert everyone that you're not welcome, but if you want to save time, just know there's always a disclaimer to our parties." He placed his hand to the side of his mouth and pretended to whisper, "You're not invited." He shot Raelynn a look. "You either."

"You don't have to be rude."

"On the contrary, what are you doing here? I think that makes you the rude ones."

Faith started laughing. She turned to find me. "I've heard stories about your guard dogs. Is this it? I get a vague and sarcastic threat?" She looked Logan up and down, wrinkling her nose. "I gotta say, you're underperforming."

I almost laughed. Almost. I held it in and got comfortable against Mason's chest once again. The whole veranda seemed to share my thoughts. Taylor was shaking her head, grinning. Nate too. The other guys just watched. Logan wasn't one to ignore when a gauntlet was thrown down.

"Say what?" He pretended to wind his arm up, his hand ending cupped behind his ear. Pretending to clean his ear out with a knuckle, he shook his head. "What was that I just heard? Did you say I 'underperformed'?" He twisted back to us. "Mase."

"Yeah?" Mason sat up again, but he held me in place so I wouldn't fall.

Faith and Raelynn looked as well. Faith's eyes caught mine and lingered. I saw a quick flash of emotion, something dark, but it was gone as soon as it appeared.

"All the chicks I've been with, have any of them said I 'underperformed'?" Logan asked.

"Watch where you're going with this," Taylor warned, but she hadn't moved from her relaxed position on the bench. Her eyes were alert.

Logan pointed at her without looking. "See? Right there. That's one satisfied girlfriend. I've never underperformed." He looked Faith up and down again, exaggerating this time. "Though I can't say the same for you. Word through the cross-country grapevine is you've been underperforming quite a bit this week." His eyes narrowed. "You thought you could keep up . . ." His eyes glanced to me, then back to her.

I sat up slowly.

Mason's arms loosened around me again.

Faith stiffened. "It was a learning curve. I know better now."

"You're right. You know how much ass Sam can kick, and she kicked yours." Logan whistled under his breath. "She kicked it all up and down an entire second route."

"Like I said," Faith hissed. "I know better now."

I frowned and called, "What does that mean?"

Faith found me again. That same dark emotion appeared before it vanished. "What?" Her tone was frozen.

"You 'know better now.' What does that mean?"

"It means I know how much I have to train." Her smile turned icy. "Because I'm going to beat you. I should thank you."

That was a bait.

I wasn't going to get hooked.

"I've never been challenged before," she said, her eyes bored.

Raelynn snapped around to look at her friend.

"It's about time it happened." Faith either didn't notice her friend's reaction, or she ignored it. She moved closer, so I was almost staring down at her. "You're going to make me a better runner, but don't get confused. I will beat you. I win. That's what I do."

"You really think like that?" That wasn't what bothered me. I moved to stand by the stairs, and crossed my arms over my chest. "What happens when you don't get your way? What do you do if you can't fulfill what *must* happen in your mind?"

She rolled her eyes. "What are you talking about?"

"I'm going to beat you." I already had. "I will continue to beat you. No matter how hard you train, how fast you can go, I will always be faster. What are you going to do when you're forced to accept the fact that I'm better than you?"

She wasn't laughing anymore. There were no scoffs or cocky attitude. She glared right at me, and that dark emotion showed again. This time, it stuck. I identified it now.

Jealousy.

That was when I knew. She knew I was better. She knew she couldn't beat me.

"Are you going to physically hurt me?" I asked.

I waited to see surprise at the idea of it. There was nothing. That told me one thing: she'd already been thinking about it.

"No." I shook my head. "You're not going to take running away from me." My tone was curt, and I felt shivers down my spine. They weren't there because of her, or what she might do. They were there because of me.

I wasn't sure I *wanted* to know how far I would go to keep the one thing that had saved me.

Running saved my life.

She scoffed now, but saw my darkness too. And she blinked. I heard a twinge of caution in her voice. "Stop trying to claim I'm going to hurt you. You did it earlier, saying I was going to hurt your friend—"

Taylor surged to her feet, coming to stand beside me. She folded her arms.

Faith wavered; her voice hitched as she finished. "I had no plans of doing that, and I have no plans to hurt you either."

"Here's the rule."

Faith looked at me, waiting.

"You hurt us. We hurt you. What you dish out comes back at you."

Her lips pressed together, and her thin shoulders lifted up in a breath. She didn't reply, but I thought I saw a slight edge of fear spark in her eyes.

Raelynn broke the brief silence with a mocking laugh. "Why do you think—"

"Shut up, Rae." Faith grabbed her arm. "Let's go." She glared at Taylor and me, then swept her eyes to Logan. She spoke through gritted teeth. "We're not welcome here."

They left, and Logan waited two seconds before bursting out, "I either wet my pants, or I had the quickest release ever." He waved his hands in a flourish, indicating us. "Well done, and you two together are fucking hot." His hands fell to the front of his pants. "I'm still hard. Honey?" He winked at Taylor. "Quickie?"

She groaned, but her face was already flushing. "You're the most romantic boyfriend ever. How have you stayed single all this time?"

Logan hopped up the steps and grabbed her hand. "With tenacity and battering rams. Those bitches try to break down my barriers, but fuck no. I got SWAT covering me. No bitch could shatter my protest line."

She laughed as he swept her inside. The door shut before we heard her retort.

"Sam." Matteo raised his beer to me. "I got new respect for you."

He wandered down to the bonfire, followed by the rest of the guys who had been on the veranda with us. They nodded to me as well, and I felt an arm encircle my waist. I closed my eyes, feeling Mason's hard body pressed up against me.

"Hmmm." I moaned, feeling his lips settle on my neck. "Is this your version of asking for a quickie?"

His other arm slid around me, anchoring me in place. His lips moved up my throat and landed at the corner of my mouth.

"It'd be longer than a quickie, and I have to give my brother props. That was hot."

"That's my goal in life. To embody my inner she-devil for your viewing pleasure."

He pressed up against me. "Consider this my thank you ahead of time."

I laughed and turned to wind my arms around his neck. I looked up into his eyes. There was a lot of shit going on with me, but him and me? We'd never be on shaky ground.

"Maybe I can ask for a quickie?" I said. I pressed back against him, my ache deepening.

He breathed out, "I thought you'd never ask."

He grabbed my ass and hoisted me up. My legs went around his waist, and he carried me back through the party to our bedroom. We remained there for the rest of the night.

———

The house was empty when I woke around four in the morning. That had been my normal time to get up for a run, and my body hadn't adjusted to cross-country season yet. I didn't want to wake Mason, so I slipped out into the hallway to use the bathroom there. Hearing talking from the kitchen when I finished, I grabbed a robe from under the counter and tiptoed the rest of the way. It wasn't that I was hoping to be sneaky, I was just tired.

"Are you sure?" I heard Taylor ask as I came around the doorway.

Logan leaned against the counter in sweats. His arms were crossed over his chest, and Taylor rested against his side.

"Do they know what happened?" she said into the phone.

I mouthed to Logan, "Who is that?"

He mouthed back, "Her dad."

I sat down on a chair that was already pulled out from the table and slid my hands under my legs to keep them warm. Then I waited.

Taylor nodded as she listened. After a few minutes, she sighed into the phone. "Okay. Thanks for letting me know. Yeah. I love you, Dad."

She hung up and didn't say anything at first. Her shoulders slumped forward as she continued to hold the phone in her hand.

She sighed again. "That was my dad."

Logan frowned.

I frowned. My heart beat faster, and I wet my lips. This wasn't going to be good.

She still didn't look at either of us. "He wanted me to know there had been a car accident. Someone from campus called him."

I expected her to say her friend Jason's name, or one of her other friends. Maybe even one of her relatives.

Then she looked at me. "Raelynn's in the hospital. A drunk driver hit her car."

CHAPTER FOURTEEN

Faith wasn't at Monday's practice.

Courtney told me the girls from the team had gone to visit Raelynn on Saturday. Taylor and I hadn't been invited, but I didn't know what we would've done if we had been. Taylor still had PTSD every time she visited hospitals, since she saw her mom gunned down in one. I completely understood that, but I still felt I needed to show up. So instead of Taylor, Logan went with me on Monday afternoon. Mason was at football. I wouldn't see him till that evening anyways.

"Is this wrong?" Logan was almost bouncing next to me as we walked down the hallway. Our shoes scraped against the floor, and the stench of bleach and chemicals was thick in the air. "I'm a little excited to see if she's really hurt or if she's just faking. My bet's on faking. This whole thing is a scam. They want to pin it on you somehow."

I stopped and stared at him. "Are you joking? Please tell me you're joking. You think this is a huge ploy?"

He frowned. "Uh, yeah. That bitch is crazy. I wouldn't put it past her to ask her friend to sit in her car, then pay a drunk homeless guy to ram a truck into her. I bet she didn't tell the homeless guy her friend was in there either."

"That's horrible."

"Have we not met before?" He held out his hand, much like he had when we were going to the career counselor. "I'm Logan. I'm a jaded son of a bitch. I can't technically call my mom a bitch, but I know Helen is one." He wiggled his fingers. "And you are?"

I knocked his hand aside. "This isn't funny, and stop introducing yourself to me. That joke's getting old."

He twisted around, looking up and down the hallway. "Who's laughing? Not me." He stared down at me, long and hard. "People have done worse shit to us. Fuck. If she *did* orchestrate this, at least it wasn't your car. Remember Nate?"

Budd Broudou had once cut Nate's brake lines, thinking they were Mason's. Nate pulled out of the school parking lot and was T-boned by an oncoming truck. His recovery took weeks.

I didn't know if Faith or Raelynn had orchestrated this, but I didn't want to walk into Raelynn's hospital room with that suspicion in mind. Too late, though. Logan said it, and now it was in my head. I pushed it to the back. I had a feeling she wasn't going to be ecstatic to see me anyway, but I still wanted her to know I felt badly. I was just being a decent human being.

"You've got to be kidding?"

The contorted, half-gasped statement came from behind us. We turned to see Faith in the middle of the hallway. She had a Styrofoam cup in her hand, and the blood drained from her face. She had bags under her eyes and looked like she hadn't slept in days.

"Get out." A mangled growl erupted from the back of her throat. Her eyes blazed, and she moved toward us. "Out! Now!"

I frowned. "Why are you reacting like this?"

She took another step toward us. The liquid in her cup spilled out over her hand, but she didn't seem to notice. She could only glare at me.

"Because for all I know, you paid someone to hit her. Did you have someone follow us home and then get her as she pulled out of my driveway? Was that how it went down?"

This was ridiculous. I held my hands up, shaking my head. "Has it occurred to you that maybe someone hit her by accident? That it really was a horrible, horrible accident?"

"All I know is you joined the team and ever since then, my life has genuinely sucked."

Logan snorted. "That sounds more like a case of bad karma than Sam's agenda. I'm sure she saw you on the team one day, and thought to herself, 'Hmmm. That girl looks evil. I should join the team after a chance meeting with my track coach where he insists I join, and yes, by golly, I'll take that girl down.'" He rolled his eyes. "Hell yes. Samantha Strattan, my stepsister mastermind extraordinaire. That's her, all right."

Faith sucked in her breath. "You don't have to make fun of me. The damage is done. My best friend is in the hospital, and the doctors say she may never run again."

"Bullshit."

"Excuse me?!" She glowered at Logan, perhaps wishing *he'*d never run again.

"Yeah." Logan's head inclined toward her. "I call bullshit. I've been in enough situations to know the chances of having an epic verbal smackdown at a party with someone and hours later, one of the people gets hit and is 'never going to run again' is highly unlikely. It seems to me like you're the one with the agenda. I'm calling your bluff."

She gritted her teeth and spoke through them. "What are you saying?"

"Call the cops. Tell them you think Sam was behind it. That is what you're implying, right?"

Her neck grew red. The color crept up to her cheeks. "Are you—"

"I'm not joking." His tone was dead serious. His eyes were calm. "Make the claim. Make it official. Don't think you can play in our league just by saying you're in our league. Actually do it, then sit back and see how we handle you."

"Is that a threat?" It came out as a whisper.

"Not a threat. A fact. Do it."

"You're insane."

I was tired of this. She was going to sputter and hiss like a broken record. Logan was going to continue to call her bluff. I had come to do one thing, and I turned around to do it.

"Where are you going?" Logan called after me.

"I'm going to see how Raelynn is," I threw over my shoulder.

I hoped Logan would keep Faith distracted. I tensed, waiting for her to hurry after me with more threats, but I didn't hear any yells or footsteps. I got to Raelynn's door and looked back. Logan seemed to be still talking to Faith. I wasn't sure if it was a good idea to leave them alone, but he knew what he was doing. He wouldn't give her any ammunition.

I knocked softly and looked into the room.

Raelynn was curled up in the bed, turned away from me. A sheet completely covered her shoulder, but I saw some bruising on her neck. I moved around the bed, seeing the steady rise and fall of deep breathing, and guessed she was sleeping. When I got to the other side and could see her face, I almost gasped out loud. My mouth fell open, but I covered it and stifled the sound.

Her entire face was black and blue. Her right eye had a bandage over it, and her mouth looked cut up.

This accident hadn't been staged. It was the real deal.

Then her left eye opened, and she saw me.

I shot my hands out. "Please don't get mad at me. I just wanted to see how you were."

Her eye narrowed, and she rolled to her back. Grimacing, she sat up and pointed to a pillow on the chair next to me. I handed it over, and she placed it behind her.

She leaned back gingerly, still cringing. "Are you here to gloat?"

I sat down, my hand covering my mouth. I felt tears threatening. She was clearly in a massive amount of pain. "Faith thinks I had something to do with this. I did not." I gestured to her. "I'm so sorry."

Her mouth was stiff, and her words came out slowly. "The other driver was some drunk guy. He was going home from the bar. The cops arrested him already. It's his third car accident. He'll be in county jail for a while, and he's supposed to get his license taken away. Unless you had someone proposition him, I doubt you'd know Jim DeLuca."

"That's his name?"

"He calls himself Jimbo."

"I'm sorry."

"Don't be. I know you didn't do this. You're not like that."

"Faith said the doctors don't think you can run again?"

She groaned. "Faith is such a liar. That's not true. I can't run *this* year. I'll be running next year just fine."

"That's a relief then."

She looked away. "Not that it matters. Only two people from our team make it to nationals. It'll be you and Faith now. I'd be out anyway. And Faith is going to milk my accident so she gets all the attention. Good luck with her. She'll have everyone convinced you slept with Jimbo to try to kill me, and the cops were paid off by your rich daddy to keep quiet about the whole thing."

"Are you serious?" I tensed.

"'Fraid so. It'll be something like that. She's going to turn everyone against you. She's done it before. I've seen her do it since elementary school. She won't stop either, not until you're so bullied by the others— even other runners in our races—that you're either in the room next to me or you quit out of self-preservation." Raelynn looked toward the open door. "I should stop talking. She could come back soon." She cast me a worried look. "You might want to leave. She'll probably start yelling and get you banned from the hospital."

I gestured toward the hall. "We already ran into her."

"We?"

I nodded. "Logan came with me. He's distracting her so we can talk."

Her eyes darted to the doorway, but it was empty. She looked back to me. "Look, it's over for me this year. I can't run, and that means, I can't be Faith's backup. She and Nettie will become best friends now. Just watch. She's here, but once she starts running again, I probably won't see her until she finds out I'm coming back next year. She'll reach out to me next May, I'm betting. She'll want to run together over the summer. But I'm telling you this because you have to watch out for her. Okay? Watch your back."

I nodded.

She moved her head ever so slightly up and down. The pillow crinkled from the motion. "Can I tell you something? Something no one knows?"

"Yeah."

"I'm in love with her. I have been since elementary school. She knows, but it's not something we talk about. She's not gay. I know what I'm dealing with, but I still love her. I'm an idiot."

I started to reach for her hand, saw how smashed up it looked, and changed my mind. "Why are you telling me this?"

"I'm not evil. She isn't either. She's just spoiled, and she's never not gotten her way. I was going to try to watch her for you. I didn't want her to do something that would jeopardize her future, you know? But I can't anymore. I figured warning you is the best I can do." Her voice grew shaky. "Thank you for coming to see me."

"Yeah. Of course." I was still taken aback by everything.

"I might try to sleep again." She moved her hand until she could press the call button, turning back to her side. "The nurse will come in and give me something to sleep. Come back and visit, will ya? Faith will be around for another week, but she'll drop me like a bad habit after that."

"Of course." I touched the edge of her bed and patted it. "I'll see you in a week then."

"Thanks, Sam. Run fast, okay?"

I nodded, returning to the hallway.

Logan was alone, lounging against the wall with his arms crossed over his chest. He looked over as I approached.

"Your number-one fan went to find the administration here. She's hoping to get us banned. You know, just for standing in the hallway." He whistled under his breath. "That girl is a special one. She's all sorts of delusional, a spoiled princess, and off-her-rocker kind of crazy. You need to watch this one."

"So I've been hearing."

I looked over my shoulder at Raelynn's room as we started back to the car. An uneasiness took root in me. It had been there since the party night and my confrontation with Faith, but it was shooting up at a record speed now. Should I believe Raelynn, or was what she told me complete bullshit as well? If it was some form of concocted manipulation plan, to what end? I didn't know.

Either way, everyone needed to know.

"We need to have a family meeting," I told Logan.

CHAPTER FIFTEEN

"This girl has just never not gotten her way?"

Nate had been asking the same question for the last hour. Logan had called everyone to the house this evening—Matteo too. And after I relayed what had happened, including Faith's reaction to us and Raelynn's warnings, everyone had fallen quiet.

Until Nate started with his questions. He hadn't gotten ahold of the sister. "She's spoiled? That's why she's doing this?"

I nodded again to him. "Yes. From what Raelynn said, yes."

He shook his head, raking a hand over his face. "That's insane." He looked at Mason. "How do we fight a chick?"

Logan grunted, leaning back on the couch. His arm rested on the back of it, behind where Taylor sat next to him. He put his foot up on the table. "I'm thinking it's time we take the JV spot." He clapped Taylor's shoulder and turned to look at me. "Girls, you're up. You're on the front lines with this one."

I'd been standing as I explained everything, but I sat now. Mason shifted his legs so I could perch on a footstool cushion with him behind me.

"You never got ahold of the sister you dated?" Mason asked Nate.

"No." Nate raised a finger and pointed it at me. "I think I must've pissed her off more than I thought. Pretty sure that's a dead end for us."

"Well, that sucks." Logan glanced to Matteo and pursed his lips together. "Feeling up for infiltrating the enemy's bed again?"

Nate grunted. "This time on purpose?"

Matteo grew wary, lifting his hands up in a helpless gesture. "Come on, guys. I felt horrible. And no, I'm not doing that. Not even on purpose this time. Feels too dirty to me."

Logan shrugged. "All this brainstorming got me thirsty. I think we should plan this girl's demise over drinks."

Nate turned to Mason. "Maybe we could do more best friend bonding?"

Mason nodded. His hand slipped under my shirt to rub my back. "Yeah. That sounds fun."

Matteo held his hand up again. "Best friend bonding? I want in."

"Pub crawl. We haven't done that in a long time." Mason kept rubbing his hand up and down my back.

"I think it's high time we get it done." Nate pretended to crack his knuckles. "If we're really nice, we could invite some hangers-on." His grin deepened as he nodded his head to the side, indicating Logan.

"Wait." Logan jerked upright on the couch. "Am I the hanger-on? I had the idea, asshole! If it's anyone, you're the hanger-on."

"Oh. Okay. That's how it is." Nate stood slowly. "I'm the one hanging around you? I remember when you were the scrawny little kid who'd steal Mason's bag just to get attention from him."

"Things changed." Logan stood too. They grinned at each other, but there was a cockiness in the air. It started to feel heavy. Logan tilted his head, challenging Nate. "I grew up and became awesome." He flicked his eyes up and down. "What happened to you?"

Mason's hand paused on my back. "This is the stupidest mock-fight I've heard from you guys. You're funnier when you pretend to be gay husbands."

The tension that had started to fill the air eased. Nate and Logan went back to laughing, and then Logan put Nate in a headlock.

He tightened his arm. "Who's the awesome one, huh? Who's got the hashtags?"

"Shut up." Nate got one of his arms between Logan's arm and his neck, and he reversed the hold. But instead of pulling Logan in for a headlock, he shoved him back a few inches. He was laughing, breathing deep. "No one would ever assume you and Mason have one of those hated-sibling relationships."

"My sister has one of those hated-sibling relationships," Matteo suddenly said.

Everyone stopped and looked at him, sitting on one of the far couches. He wasn't really looking at anyone. He seemed lost in his own thoughts.

When he noticed the looks, he blinked a few times. "Oh. I mean, her cats. One's called Chloe, and the brother is Dingbat. Chloe hates Dingbat. Every time he runs through the house, she takes off after him. The girl cat kept beating him up, so my sister has to keep them separated, but Dingbat always gets loose. Every time he runs past her, she just says, 'There goes Dingbat.' It's pretty funny. But yeah, those cats hate each other."

The silence from everyone held for another beat before Logan snorted. "Speaking of dingbats . . ." He placed a hand on Nate's shoulder. "I think I found your new nickname."

Nate shoved his hand off. "You're such a dick." But he was laughing.

So was Logan, and he lunged for Nate again. As the two started to wrestle, I leaned back to rest against Mason's chest. His arms curved around me, and he kissed the top of my shoulder.

"Did you want us to keep pushing the sister?" he murmured.

"No." It was a dead-end. Nate said so. I watched Taylor as she moved out of Logan and Nate's way. "Maybe instead of you guys asking my mom for that favor, I ask her."

He tensed.

Logan and Nate stopped wrestling, and Logan looked over. "What'd you just say?"

"I said, maybe I should go ask my mom to ask James for that information." Or . . . "I could also just ask James. He won't try to hold anything against me. He wouldn't dare."

Logan snorted. "That's why we didn't go last weekend." He gestured to me as he turned to Mason. "You told her our plan."

"Yeah, and she didn't like it."

"That was the fight you had?"

"You didn't tell him?" I asked Taylor.

She lifted a shoulder. "He doesn't have to know everything."

Logan twisted around to her. "Thanks for that."

I felt Mason's silent laughter behind me, a teasing caress. I felt his breath on my shoulder, and I was torn between paying attention to the conversation and pulling him into the bedroom and feeling his breath all over me instead.

His arms tightened, and he rested his chin on my shoulder. "Leave your girlfriend alone. That was between Sam and me, and she was respecting Sam's privacy."

Logan shot him a glare. "Sam's my stepsister. There's no privacy there."

I grimaced. "Did you really just say that?"

He stopped, thought about it, and shook his head. "You all know what I mean."

"I don't." Nate frowned at everyone. "I have no fucking clue what you guys are talking about, and I don't like it."

"Right there with you, man," Matteo echoed.

"Yeah." Nate looked at him, then back at us. "What happened? You guys had a fight or something? Where was I?"

"Sleeping, and it's none of your business," Mason said. "It's none of yours either, Logan, but no, we're not going to ask my dad for any information about Faith's family."

"Wait." Nate held a hand up. "We weren't actually going to Vegas, were we?"

"I thought you had to be smart to get your MBA." Logan paused for a beat. "Oh wait. That's after you get a bachelor's. That's right, you have to get the one degree first."

"You're such a dick."

Everyone tensed. This had become something between Logan and Nate. I looked at Taylor and saw her frowning right along with me. I wondered if she knew the cause for this friction.

Then Nate just said it. "Don't get pissed at me because I'm the one here, and you're not. I'm not the one who chose to get a girlfr—"

"Shut up, Nate." Logan growled.

He didn't. "A girlfriend who continues to choose to sleep at her place, and not here. If you're missing being around Mason and Sam, that's on you. Not me. I'm getting real sick of you putting your shit on me. I've never done anything to you, Logan."

"Shut *up*!"

Nate added, unperturbed, "Unlike you."

Logan stood completely still, the unnatural and dangerous way. A shiver went down my spine, and I swallowed over a lump. Nate had just gone dirty in a way that wasn't dirty at all.

"Are you serious?" Logan's eyes were narrowed to slits, everything about him tensed. This was Logan right before a full attack. Whether it was words or fists, it was coming. And he was going to do some damage.

Mason suddenly lifted me to the side and stood up. "Stop. Both of you guys."

"No." Nate shook his head, still glaring at Logan. "I'm sick of it. Any time Logan starts feeling pissy about something, he takes it out on me."

Mason moved to stand between them.

Nate leaned forward, looking at Logan around Mason. "Guess what? I've done nothing to you. I left when I was a kid because my parents moved away. They didn't want me to be around Mason. When I came back, you'd replaced me. It wasn't the other way around. You pushed me out, Logan. And I did nothing. I let it happen." A cutting laugh came from him. "And that wasn't even the biggest change. Sam was in our lives. I went from being number two to being number four, if that spot was even included in shit. How do you think that made me feel? And I put up with it," he spat, his eyes blazing. "I thought we were good too."

"STOP!" Mason shoved him, then turned to make sure Logan was still holding back. Satisfied that he was, Mason sighed. "This is all bullshit. We're all family by this point." He looked at Matteo. "You too, even though we don't show it all the time."

Matteo perked up. "Thanks. I appreciate that." His tone was cheerful.

I laughed softly to myself. No one except Nate and Logan seemed too upset about their fight. Matteo must've gotten used to us by now. Fights flared up, but they always blew over. We all loved each other. That's how we were. That, in itself, was comforting.

Then I looked over. "Where's Taylor?" Her spot on the couch was empty.

Logan cursed.

She was gone.

CHAPTER SIXTEEN

Logan took off to find her, then backtracked for Mason's Escalade. Taylor had taken his.

Fighting back a smirk, Mason dug for his keys.

Logan's head hung low. "Don't start." He held out his hand.

Mason didn't drop the keys, prompting Logan to look up at him.

"Just tell her the truth. She'll understand," he said.

"Yeah." Logan nodded and took the keys. "I'm hoping I get the chance."

"You'll be fine. She loves you. You love her." Mason patted him on the shoulder, but he was looking at me. "Check the ego, be vulnerable, and anything's possible."

Warmth spread inside of me. I knew he was talking about us—about my fear of marriage and his need to protect me without me even knowing. He was right, though. Everything would be fine. I believed that.

"Thanks." Logan glanced back at me. "Don't know what's going on with you two, but take it easy on him. Whatever it is, Mase is trying. He's a lot less bossy than normal."

Mason laughed. "Okay. Leave now. Go fix your own relationship."

Logan nodded and was out the door in the next instant. Nate and Matteo declared that they didn't have girlfriends, and that was reason enough to go drinking, so the two took off. Since Matteo and Mason had practice the next day, I was surprised they weren't back when we went to bed around eleven that night. They'd left in one vehicle.

"Nah. Matteo will take a cab home if he's had too much," Mason said when I shared my concern. He'd been changing in the walk-in closet and came back out in lounge pants. They were deliciously low on his hips, showing off all those lovely stomach muscles and the V that cut down into his pants. I pulled the covers back as my mouth began watering.

Four years and I still had this reaction to him. I felt the flutters in my stomach, and as I climbed onto the bed, I hugged my knees to my chest and hoped this feeling would never leave me.

"What?" He noticed my reaction.

I just grinned at him. "I am completely head over heels for you. That's all."

A soft grin lingered on his face, then slid away as his eyes sharpened. "Are you worried about this Faith girl?"

I shrugged. "I don't know." I hugged my knees tighter to me. "We've dealt with worse. I don't know why Faith Shaw would top that list. I think we'll be fine."

"Then why aren't you looking at me?"

The lump I'd felt when Logan and Nate were fighting came back. "It's nothing." I didn't know why I couldn't meet his eyes.

"Sam."

The bed dipped under his weight as he sat next to me, resting a hand on my knee. "What's going on?"

I shook my head. I felt so stupid. It was the night I'd left the house all over again. "Really, Mason." My voice grew hoarse. The lump pressed on the bottom of my throat. "I'm fine."

"Hey."

That word was so soft, so tender. It was my undoing, and I felt the tears start. Making a frustrated sound, I used my palms to clear my face. "This is so annoying."

He leaned closer, and his hand replaced both of mine. He began wiping the tears away. "Do you know why you're crying?"

"No!" I cried, looking at him through a haze of tears. I pointed at them. "I hate this. I have no idea what's going on with me. Taylor says I'm going through something, but this is what crazy girls do. They cry at the drop of a hat. I don't do that. I have issues, and sometimes they come up and make me cry, but I don't even feel sad. I'm just crying, and I have no fucking idea why."

He laughed softly, sitting closer on the bed. Tugging on my arm, he pulled me over to sit on his lap. His arms came around me, like they always did, and I curled into him.

I sighed.

This feeling, being like this with him as he sheltered me was one of the most wonderful things about Mason Kade. No other girl could understand this feeling, no matter how many wished they could. It was me, all me. I tipped my head back, my eyes closed as his hand brushed down my hair and back.

"You really are wonderful," I murmured, feeling my tears start to subside.

"Hey." He tapped gently under my eye. "Can you look at me?"

I did. The tears were there, but I could see him.

He looked down at me, so adoringly. "I don't care what's going on with you. Whether you think it's ridiculous or not, I'll always want to know. It'll always matter to me. You'll always matter to me."

I cupped the side of his face. "Why did you choose to love me? Because I was there? I was the girl who moved into your house? That could've been anyone."

The corner of his lip tugged up. "Are you serious?

I nodded.

I hadn't been wracked with doubt, but as I asked now, I realized it'd always been with me. It had been in the back of my mind.

"I was a nobody."

He started to protest, but I kept going, shaking my head.

"No. I know you're going to say I wasn't, but I was. I wasn't even popular at my own school. I had two best friends, a boyfriend, a mom, and a dad. That's it. Then I lost everyone in the same week. You and Logan didn't have to do anything for me. You didn't even need to be nice to me, but you were. You were kind and supportive, and you guys made me one of yours."

"We weren't that nice. You're giving us more credit than we deserve. I stayed back from a party so I could grill you about you and your mom. That wasn't me being nice. That was me being an asshole."

"That was you looking out for yourself and your brother. My mom and I invaded your house. I expected you to hate me in the beginning." But I'd never felt that from them. Never hate. "Why didn't you hate me?"

"Why would I?" He leaned back, resting on his hands.

I was still curled up on his lap, but I sat further upright to hold myself steady.

He shrugged. "I hated my dad. I didn't particularly like your mom, but I never hated you. You didn't do anything. You were just collateral damage like Logan and me. Now, if you had started to do things, then maybe I might've started to dislike you." He tucked a strand of my hair behind my ear, and his hand lingered on my cheek. "I don't even hate your mom. After all the shit she did to you, I seriously dislike her, but I don't hate her. I can't. She brought me you, and a part of me is thankful to her for that."

I pressed a fist to his chest, just holding it there. "Any other guy, and that would sound like the cheesiest line ever. But you." I gently tapped him with that fist. "You, and I'm almost swooning."

"Yeah?" His grin deepened, his eyes warm and loving. They darkened into something more, and he sat back up. His arms came to circle me, but he kept them loose. His thumb rubbed back and forth on my thigh. "Look." He sounded so serious. "I don't know what's going on with you, but as long as you're not going to leave me, I'm not too worried about it. I think Taylor was right. I just think you're processing something, and you'll come out the other end better. Stronger. And things are kinda weird right now, since we're engaged, but kinda not engaged at the same time. Almost everything's come full circle, you know? You got both your dads. You got Malinda as a mom. Heather is a good best friend—and that's saying a lot from me—and Taylor seems cool. Plus, Logan's finally your official stepbrother now. And you got

107

Mark. You got everything you lost, and then some. You and me, I figure we're the icing on the cake." His eyes sparkled. "Right?"

"When you put it like that . . ." I teased. The lump was dissipating. "I think you're right. Everything will be fine."

He nodded. "Damn straight, Strattan."

"Strattan?" I arched my eyebrows. "We've moved to last names now?"

"Fuck yeah." His hands tightened, and he pulled me closer. He leaned toward me, and I knew those lips were going to rest on mine in seconds.

"When I'm deep inside you tonight, I want to hear you scream my name," he murmured, his breath caressing me. "We're that kind of last names to each other."

I laughed because that didn't make sense, but I don't think he cared. I didn't either, and then his lips were on mine and the laughter turned into a moan.

So many sensations flooded me, and soon he was inside of me, and I *was* screaming his name. I hoped this, like everything else, would never ever go away.

CHAPTER SEVENTEEN

Glass shattered.

Thump!

Then complete silence.

I jerked upright in bed. Mason sat up with me, and I looked at the clock to see it was around four in the morning. He slid out of bed without a sound and reached for his phone. He handed it over, and as he did, we heard another sound. It was like someone shuffling, then another thump.

"Fuck."

My eyes found Mason's. That word was whispered, but we both heard it, and it hadn't come from either of us. Someone else was in the house.

He mouthed, "Nine-one-one."

I nodded, lifted the phone with trembling hands, and expelled a silent breath. I had to close my eyes for a second, just to steady myself. When I opened them, Mason was at the door. I reached out for him. My heart was pounding. I didn't want him to go, but I couldn't stop him, not unless I made sounds. And I couldn't—then the intruder would know we'd heard him.

As Mason slipped out the door, tiptoeing down the hallway, I moved to the edge of the bed and stepped into the closet. I shut the door and dialed the numbers.

My heart was almost deafening, and I barely heard the operator answer my call.

"What is your emergency?"

I whispered, "Someone broke into our house."

"Where are you?"

I gave her the address, my name, and Mason's name. I told her everything I knew. I didn't know if Nate was home. I didn't know if Logan and Taylor were here. She told me to stay on the phone and stay in the closet.

That was when I hung up.

I wasn't leaving Mason alone. I silenced the phone and put it in my pocket. Mason had held something in his hand when he left. I didn't know if it was a weapon, but I suddenly wished I'd agreed to take gun safety class when Logan suggested it. I didn't like guns.

My thoughts were changing.

My hands shook. I was sweating, but so cold at the same time. Fear choked me, but the thought of never seeing Mason again was worse. It propelled me forward until I saw him poised by the front closet. It was close to the stairs, and as I heard a third thump from upstairs, I realized it was the closest place he could stand without being seen.

I edged out into the living room, but Mason saw me. He motioned for me to go back.

Part of me stopped thinking now. Part of me slipped away, no longer standing in that room with him. I was back in the closet, the phone in my hands, the door locked shut. I was safe, and the cops were coming to take the bad guy away.

That wasn't what was really going on, though.

I watched myself as Mason continued to try to get me to go back.

I kept shaking my head. I wouldn't go.

A fourth thump above us. Footsteps.

Someone left a room, moving into another.

"Shit."

A second whisper from someone I didn't know.

My knees began to shake, but they weren't making noise. Thank goodness. I couldn't get them to stop. The girl they helped support was frozen in place.

She couldn't do anything.

Her eyes moved upwards.

The person upstairs was moving again. Whoever it was wasn't being as quiet anymore.

Drawers opened.

Things dropped to the floor.

A door clicked shut, and a different one opened.

A light was flicked on now, then off right away.

Someone was in the bathroom.

They moved back into the hallway.

I could see the thoughts whirling in the girl's head as I watched myself. Her forehead wrinkled, and she bit her lip. She was biting too hard, she drew blood. She never noticed.

I watched all this, but I couldn't tell her (*myself*) to stop.

She'd stopped listening to herself long ago.

The person moved in one bedroom, then the other. Only Logan and Nate had rooms up there. The person walked by the bathroom. The only other door was a closet.

The footsteps continued.

They didn't stop at the closet.

They were coming down the stairs.

They were coming to where we were—Mason and the frozen girl.

The alert blared inside me, but I couldn't say anything. I couldn't do anything. Then Mason lifted his hands, and the moonlight glinted off something metal.

A handgun.

He held it, poised with two straight arms and his feet braced. The footsteps stopped at the top of the stairs. Suddenly red and blue lit up the room. It was small at first, then brighter and brighter.

Someone above cursed again and started down the stairs.

Everything in me paused. My heart. My breathing. My thoughts. The girl's eyes were so wide, so frightened, but she couldn't say anything. Her voice was paralyzed.

Mason's finger moved as he took off the safety.

Sirens broke through the girl's fear. She could hear the cops coming closer and closer. It was no longer just a colorful landscape. They'd parked. They were on the other side of the door. She heard another type of running. The kind that was coming to help. Those feet sounded different than the intruder's. The footsteps were fast, but sturdy. The others had been accidental, then less tentative, and finally filled with the assuredness that they were alone in this house.

But that was wrong.

It all happened in one second. Mason was braced against the closet door. The cops would burst into the house, and the front door would hit him. The intruder was coming down the stairs and would be right there, right in the spotlight as the cops barged in.

If Mason shot, it might be self-defense.

If the cops shot—well, they might not need to.

Sam had to do something. *I had to do something.*

Summoning all the strength inside of me, I burst out of my paralysis. I stopped my knees from shaking, my hands from trembling. I was suddenly right here. I felt the chill in the room; I rode the upper crest of the feeling that something wrong was about to happen, something that would change lives.

"Mason, don't!" My voice finally ripped from its prison.

The intruder froze on the stairs, whirling to me, then looking for Mason.

He cursed.

The cops banged on the door. "POLICE!"

Mason thumbed the safety back on. He locked eyes with the intruder, and both sprang into action.

Mason tossed the gun to me, launching himself forward.

The intruder tried to jump over the bannister, so he would land right where I stood.

I caught the gun as the two crashed into each other.

The door burst open.

Guns, lights, and yells filled the room as four cops rushed forward. Two grabbed Mason and hauled him backward.

"He lives here!" I yelled.

The other two cops grabbed the intruder and slammed him against the wall.

"Sam!" Mason bucked against the cop's hold.

I looked down and realized I had the gun. I slipped it inside my pocket. The weight sagged my pajama pants, so I scrambled and tightened the drawstring, tying it so it couldn't budge.

"I'm fine," I called out, my voice cracking.

I'm fine.

I'm fine.

I kept repeating that in my head.

I wasn't fine.

"Let me go. She's scared."

One police officer nodded, and the other released Mason. He rushed over to me. I was caught up in his arms, and we both turned to watch.

The cops turned the light on, and one pulled off the intruder's ski mask.

"Adam?!"

CHAPTER EIGHTEEN

This is insane.

I kept shaking my head, thinking that. It was insane. Adam Quinn broke into our house, and not even our house in Fallen Crest. He drove to Cain, found out where we lived, and then broke into this house. Why? That was the big question. He told the cops it was a good-natured prank.

Mason and I had changed into our clothes now, and the police were still questioning Adam in our living room. He was able to look over at Mason and say, "Right, Mason? We're in a big prank war. That's all it was."

The asshole wanted us to cover for him.

I was about to say *hell no*, but Mason took my hand to stop me.

"Yeah. Just a really stupid prank. That's it."

The cop lowered his notepad. "You don't want to press charges?"

Mason shook his head, just slightly. "No." He stared right at Adam, his eyes almost calm, but there was a dangerous aura coming from him. I felt shivers down my spine. Mason had something planned for Adam, but he wasn't going through legal channels to do it.

"Hey!"

We heard a commotion and raised voices from the front door.

"Mason!" Logan was there, waving. The police stationed in front of the house were holding him back. "I live here. Tell 'em so I can come in."

"So we can come in." Nate popped his head out from behind Logan. "I'm here too."

"Yeah." Mason turned to the cop holding the notepad. "That's my brother and my best friend. They live here too."

The cop narrowed his eyes, then gestured upstairs with his pad. "Their rooms are the ones upstairs?"

"Yeah."

The cop looked at Adam as he said, "The rooms this guy was searching in." He let out a sigh, putting his notepad back in his pocket. "What do you wager those two guys don't have any idea about this 'prank war' you're in? You went through their stuff. I wonder if they'll want to press charges?"

Adam just closed his eyes and folded his head down. He was dressed for the part, in a black long-sleeve shirt and black pants. He'd had a flashlight with him too, but the cops confiscated it, along with his ski mask.

The cop waved for Logan and Nate to come in. Taylor came with them, holding Logan's hand. Logan went right to Adam, his jaw clenched.

"What the fuck, Quinn?! I could've been here. Taylor could've been here."

Adam opened his eyes and held his hands up in surrender. He shot Mason a look. "It was a prank. That's it."

Logan snorted. "Right. Because we're in one big fucking prank war, huh? My ass, a prank war." But he looked at Mason. "Were you aware of this prank war?"

Mason half-grinned. "I was. Not telling you was part of it."

Logan shook his head. "That was the best part, right?" He was laughing, but his eyes were dark with anger and his tone was biting. He sent Adam another glare as he tugged Taylor away.

The cops said they had a few questions for Logan and Nate, but they had them both look through their rooms first. Taylor went too, since she half-lived here. When they were done, and hadn't noticed anything missing, they convened in the kitchen to talk to the police, and Mason went over next to Adam on the couch. I moved with him, but kept a little farther away. Mason's arms were crossed over his chest and he spoke low, so the cop left in the living room couldn't hear him.

"What the fuck were you doing?"

Adam eyed the police warily. "Can we wait till they leave? I'll tell you everything then."

"You'll answer now."

Adam let out another breath, raking a hand over his face. "Fine. You know about my dad's case." He spoke quietly too. "It's because of you guys he was arrested."

Mason knew. He'd been the one to find the evidence against him. He didn't need to be reminded.

"My dad wanted to send a bunch of guys to see if you had anything else on him. He's worried more evidence might come to light. You were at the cabin, and the security feed shows that you went into the garage. There was something in there that his men can't find now."

Mason frowned, glancing over at me. He'd kept relatively quiet about going to that house. I knew Mason had made a copy of the files on the computer, but that's all he said he'd found. He glanced over at Nate and Logan from where he sat with the same impenetrable mask, but I knew. He didn't have anything else. If someone went into that garage, it wasn't Mason.

But all he said to Adam was, "He was going to send 'guys'?"

Adam nodded, casting a worried look toward the kitchen. "I offered to come instead. I worried if they came in, they'd hurt someone." Adam glanced to me. "I didn't want anyone to get hurt."

Mason caught the look. His eyes narrowed.

I had to blink a few times before I caught the significance. Adam was worried about me?

I narrowed my eyes too. "Please. Don't pretend you care about me. You know it's because of Becky's loyalty to me that she gave us the full footage of Mason." I moved closer. "Why are you really here? Were you hoping to hurt me? Because Becky dumped you and you blame me?"

"Contrary to your low opinion of me, I never stopped caring about you."

I searched his face. Nothing. No reaction. He didn't look away. His eyes didn't widen. There were no twitches or anything.

I shook my head, moving away. "I don't believe you. I don't believe anything you say. You've already proven how deceitful and manipulative you can be."

"Like you guys aren't?" he shot back. He was still sitting on the couch, but he strained to sit as tall as he could. "Like you guys don't lie to protect your own? That's all I was doing. I sent that footage in to discredit Mason for my father's case. That's all. There wasn't any other intention to hurt you guys."

"That could've ended my football career."

"Boo fucking hoo." Adam glared at him. "So, you'll make your millions through your father's company instead? Am I really doing you such a disservice? You have to toe the line and act like a good little saint so you don't get kicked out of your football career? Newsflash, Mason." Adam's eyes sparked in anger again. His hands balled into fists, pressing against his legs. "You're not a saint. I bet it's killing you to act like the model citizen. You want to beat the shit out of me just as much as your brother does over there, but you can't because if it's caught on tape or if someone witnesses it who shouldn't—there goes your football future." He sneered. "Get over yourself. You're no longer going to play in the NFL, and you know it. You just can't admit it."

"Is there a problem over here?" The notepad cop came back from the kitchen.

Logan, Taylor, and Nate trailed behind.

"No problem." Mason kept his gaze locked on Adam. "We're just fine, sir."

"Well." The cop looked around everyone. "You all insist this was some stupid prank. If you discover anything missing, give me or the station a call. We'll arrest the guy then." He handed his card to each of us. "Would you like a ride somewhere?" he asked Adam.

Adam gazed around the room and cleared his throat. "No. I'm fine. I have my car. Thank you."

"All right." The cop waved his hand. "We can clear out." He reached for his radio, and we heard him speaking into it as he left the house.

A moment later, all the squad cars were gone, and it was just as quiet as it had been before we woke to glass breaking.

Logan looked to Mason.

Nate looked to Mason.

Everyone was waiting for our leader, but Mason turned to me. "You wanted to be included—"

I felt sick to my stomach, but I knew what they needed to do. Mason couldn't let this go. He'd let the video go, but not this.

I stepped toward Adam. "Is there anything else you haven't told us?"

"No." He frowned, rubbing at his forehead. "Why?"

"You're really here to search for something for your dad?"

His hand fell back to his side. "I told you, Sam. I came so my dad wouldn't send those guys instead. If he had, they were on order to remove anyone or anything that got in their way. They would've hurt you guys."

"They would've tried."

Adam turned to Mason. "What?" He looked around the room, and saw the intensity on Logan and Nate's faces. A different awareness settled over him, like a veil lifted and he was seeing them for the first time. "What are you guys going to do?"

Logan shook his head. "Adam, who the fuck do you think we are? You think we'd take you breaking into our home and let you go with a pat on the back? You can't be that stupid."

Fear finally appeared in his eyes. Adam looked at me. "Sam, don't—"

Mason blocked me from him. "You got a pass. Not anymore."

"Are you guys serious?" Adam started to rise from the couch.

Nate stepped up and shoved him back down. He kept a hand on his shoulder.

Mason turned back to me. "Sam?"

He was asking for permission. I nodded. "He's all yours," I said, quietly.

Then I took Taylor's hand and left the house.

As we walked away, Adam began to cry out, "What are you guys doing? Wha—you *guys*! Please!"

Taylor stopped once, looking back over her shoulder. She frowned. "What are they going to do?"

"Do you have your keys?"

She nodded, faintly. She touched her purse. "Yeah."

"Let's go to that diner. They need to do this."

Taylor's frown remained as we got into her car and drove away. This was new to her, but if you hurt one of us, we hurt you back. That was our motto. That was what I'd promised Faith, and that was what was happening right now.

That was how we were.

CHAPTER NINETEEN

MASON

I spoke two words. "Grab him."

That was the cue. Adam knew to run, and he tried. It was futile. Logan and Nate were on him in a second. They pushed him against the wall, and Nate and I switched places. I stood right in front of Adam as Nate went around the room. He locked all the doors and windows and drew the curtains. No one would see what we were about to do.

Adam's eyes grew frantic as he watched Nate's progress. He tried kicking back against Logan, but as he surged forward, Logan and I slammed him back in place. "Wha-what are you guys going to do?"

Logan kept quiet. So did Nate.

It was my turn to talk.

"What do you think, Quinn?"

Logan snorted.

Nate shut all the lights off except one lamp in the far corner. Then he came over and took my spot. I stepped back, my arms crossed over my chest.

Adam wasn't fighting anymore. He'd grown completely still. He just looked between us, waiting.

"There's no weakness in us," I told him. "Is that what you're looking for? A way out? You think my brother or my best friend is going to turn against me?"

Adam swallowed. Beads of sweat formed on his forehead. "Let me go, Mason. I won't say anything. I swear."

Logan laughed again, but he didn't speak.

It was still my turn. "And what are you going to say? You broke in here. The cops asked if you wanted to go. You stayed on your own. It's on record. And that's just tonight. That's not counting when you sent the FCPD a video trying to get me arrested, and your own fiancée—"

"Ex," Logan supplied. "She dumped him."

"Ex-fiancée cleared me. Any way you slice it, it will look like you're trying to set me up again. You already tried once, didn't you? Not to mention that Caldron went on record that your father was paying him to go after Samantha, that same girl you keep declaring you care about. If you're rolling the dice, it always lands on our side. Always."

"So what?" Adam was sweating profusely now. "You're going to beat the shit out of me?"

I flexed my hand. My knuckles were already bruised from football. "Maybe." I stepped forward, and without speaking, Logan and Nate backed away. I held Adam in place now. "Why are you really here?"

"I told you."

"You told me lies." We walked through the garage, but we didn't search it. It was the one spot we hadn't looked through.

He pretended to frown. "What? My dad told me you did."

I waved to Nate. "Go see if you find anything he planted." He nodded and went upstairs.

"I wouldn't do that!"

Logan ignored Adam. "You think that's why he's here?"

I was sure of it. "Go check your computer, if he could even get on it."

"You sure?" Logan eyed Adam.

If the prick made a move, I'd have the perfect excuse to hit him.

I nodded. "I'm sure."

When he left, Adam began shaking his head. "I didn't plant anything. I swear, Mason."

"Then why are you here?"

"Because my dad—"

"No, he wouldn't." I raised my voice. "Your dad would never hire goons to come in here and rough us up if we got in their way. If he did that, it'd be war between my dad and yours. It'd hurt his case, and if you're actually here because of his case, you know that too. All roads lead back somewhere. Trust me. My dad would hire the best to find that trail, and he'd use that information against your father. That's what I'd do."

Adam started to protest, saw I wasn't going to budge, and started laughing instead.

This one had a ring of truth to it. My shoulders relaxed. Finally we were going to get somewhere.

"Fine," Adam bit out, rolling his eyes. "I fucking hate you guys. Yeah, I came here to plant something, but I didn't want to plant it on Nate or Logan. I was looking for your room. I assumed it would be upstairs."

"What was it?"

"A virus. I was going to load it on *your* computer."

"Is it on you?"

He nodded. "My right pocket."

"The cops searched you. They didn't take it?"

"They did. But they put it back. Why wouldn't they? It's not drugs or a weapon."

I didn't move.

He arched an eyebrow. "Aren't you going to grab it?"

"I'll get to it." I had more questions. "What does the virus do?"

"It's just a bug. It gives me access to everything you have and you'd never know. Your emails. Your school account. Papers even. Your social media. Anything you opened on your computer, I'd have a back door into it."

"What were you going to do with that information?"

"Anything I wanted. I wanted to make your life hell."

Logan was coming back down the stairs, and Adam looked up.

"I believe your threat, that you're going to law school to torture me." He focused on me again. "You've already made my life hell. You did it in high school, and you'll continue to do it as we get older. We're going to be competitors. No matter where you look, it's always you against me. I wanted to start early and get as much dirt on you as possible."

Logan narrowed his eyes, but he didn't say anything. This was still my show.

Nate came down the stairs too. "I couldn't find anything," he said.

I motioned to Adam. "Strip him. I want to know what he might have on him."

Adam looked at Logan and Nate, his hands up. "Come on, guys—"

They grabbed him, and he was soon standing mostly naked in our living room, holding a pillow in front of him. Logan went through his pants, pulling the pockets inside out. Nate searched the shirt. They dropped keys, the flash drive, and change on one of the tables.

Logan held up a condom. "Really? Were you planning on raping someone?" He tossed it on the table. "And please say yes. I want any excuse to beat the shit out of you."

Adam shivered from the cold. He clutched the pillow closer. "No. That's just, you never know. I was going to drive to see Becky after this."

"Ah. That's so sweet. You were going to rape your ex-fiancée instead?"

"No! Shut up," he barked at Logan. "I wasn't going to—no rape. Nothing like that. She loves me, and I thought I could get her to take me back. That's all. I swear."

Nate tossed the shirt on the floor. "I can't find anything."

I gestured to Adam's socks and shoes. "Take 'em off."

"What? Are you joking?"

"Please." Still holding Adam's pants, Logan put his hands together in a prayer. "Pretty please, refuse us. Give us that excuse."

"I'm buck naked." Adam looked at his underwear lying on the floor, and his shirt on top of it. "My socks and shoes are all I have."

"Give them now."

Adam scowled, but Logan and Nate started to advance, and he backed against the wall. "Okay. Okay! I'll do it. Hold on." He held one hand up to stop their advance and began to toe off his shoes. One by one, he kicked them toward his pile of clothes, followed by his socks. He kept the pillow in front of him the whole time. When he was done, he said, "There. Happy?"

"Dude," Logan grunted. "If you think we're doing this because we find enjoyment in your nudity, you might be batting for the wrong team.

You know, my girlfriend has a friend. I can introduce you? Though I think Delray could do better."

Adam glowered. "Fuck you."

Logan finished searching the pants. He tossed Adam's wallet on the table, then let the pants fall on the rest of the pile.

"That's the point, Quinn," he retorted. "Delray *could* fuck you, but I still think he could do better. He runs with crime bosses, not with the guy who would be *that* guy's bitch in prison." He winked at Adam. "If you know what I mean."

Adam didn't comment.

I knew Logan was waiting for the go-ahead from me. There were a few things my brother liked to do more than others, and burning shit was on that list.

I nodded, and he exclaimed, "Yes!" He grabbed the clothes and took them out.

"Wait. Where's he going?"

Adam went to follow him, and I slammed him back in place. "You stay."

"But—" He pointed beyond me. "My clothes."

"What made you think you'd be allowed to wear them out of here?"

"Bu—" Understanding dawned, and his hand fell back to his side. He gulped. "You're joking."

Nate laughed behind me. "It was funny at first, but now it's insulting. Of all the shit we've done, and all the people we've gone against, you still think we'd let you leave unscathed? It's like you don't know us anymore. Has nothing bad happened to you since high school?"

"But—"

"Shut up with the buts." Nate shook his head. "It's becoming annoying."

A fireball erupted in the backyard. That'd be Logan, who probably doused the clothes in gasoline and threw a match on the pile.

"There go your clothes," I murmured a moment later as Logan came back in.

"They're doused real good," Logan said as he came to stand next to me. "I put 'em in the bonfire pit. Don't worry. They'll be ash real soon." He glanced to me. "Now what?"

I wanted to hit Adam. I wanted it so badly, but if he didn't move against me, I had no real excuse. Burning his clothes was one thing, but actually assaulting him was something else. I couldn't justify it in my head, not this time, so I glanced at my brother and shrugged.

"Now it's time for him to go."

Logan groaned. "I wanted more fun." He *tsk*ed at Adam, shaking his head. "Thanks for being a pussy and not fighting back. You saved yourself some bruises. Too bad." He grabbed the flash drive and tossed it to me.

"Hey!"

I gave Adam a look, catching the flash drive and pocketing it. "Stop insulting us. You're just being stupid."

"Come on, you guys . . ."

Adam started for the table as Logan tossed his keys to Nate, then grabbed his wallet. He pulled out the cash and went through the rest.

"Nothing in here except credit cards and some other ID," he said to me.

"Leave the credit cards and money. Burn the rest."

"What?!" Adam surged forward.

I shoved him back against the wall, harder than necessary. "Unless you'd like to fight me for them?"

He fell back, still holding that pillow in front of him. "You guys are assholes."

Nate laughed, going to the front door. He took one key off the ring. "And yet you're the one who broke into our house."

"What are you going to do?" Adam watched him, warily.

"What do you think?" Nate stepped outside, hauled his arm back, and threw Adam's keys as far as he could. "We live next to some woods. Those fuckers are gone." He came back inside and slapped Adam on the back. "Have fun walking into town."

There was nothing left except the wallet. Logan threw it back to him with the credit cards and cash inside. Adam caught it against his chest, dropping the pillow as he did.

And as he bent to grab it, I kicked it out of reach. Then I pointed to the door. "Get lost."

"We're really letting him go without a beatdown?" Logan asked.

Adam wavered, as if waiting for the answer.

"Go!" I clipped out. "Before I change my mind."

"Oh, hey." Nate stepped next to me. He produced that one key and waved it at Adam. "We'll leave your car at some gas station. So don't bother coming back here for it."

Adam went to the door, stark naked, and reached for the handle. "I really hate you guys."

"Trust me," I said. "Not as much as we hate you. Come back here, and we won't be as nice next time."

Adam left, and as soon as the door shut behind him, Logan asked, "Why the fuck didn't we pound him?"

I gave him a look as I reached for my phone. "Because *that* doesn't look suspicious. He was at our house and then he gets beat up? They could charge us for that."

"And stripping him naked and sending him on his way isn't something we could get charged for?"

I shrugged. I was willing to bet they'd let that slide.

"Who are you calling?" Nate asked.

I grinned. "A cop who's friendly with Sam's dad. Garrett summers here. He gave me a few names of people we could call if we ever needed anything. I figure this guy might want to know about a naked dude walking away from our house, and that it's the same guy who broke *into* our house earlier tonight."

Logan laughed. "Okay, that's good." He turned to go burn the rest of the stuff Adam had in his wallet.

"Logan," I called. "We'll get him another time," I added when he looked back.

"We better. The punk needs to be dealt with."

He did. And we would.

I was sure of that.

CHAPTER TWENTY

SAMANTHA

Call me a vindictive bitch; I don't care.

But when Mason told me what they did and what they'd found out from Adam, I went the extra mile. I called Becky, told her Adam had showed up at our place with a plan to see her afterwards to "make up." I told her about the condom, because every girl enjoys knowing she's an assumed sure thing. Then I followed that by letting her know he hadn't just "dropped by" our place. He'd broken in because he wanted to plant a spying malware program on Mason's computer. I ended the call with a warning not to let him anywhere near her computer.

And thinking about that call now—how Becky had been beyond pissed—gave me an extra boost of speed on my run.

It'd been two weeks since Raelynn's accident, and a week since our latest run-in with Adam. Everything Raelynn predicted had come true. Faith milked her accident like a cat licks every last droplet of milk. By the end of the first time Faith rejoined the team at practice, everyone was acting like it'd been her in that car. And when I dropped by to see Raelynn yesterday afternoon, she told me Faith had already stopped visiting her.

I was keeping a healthy skepticism, but it looked more and more like Raelynn was telling me the truth. Her words hadn't been part of an elaborate plan of manipulation.

As I ran, I continued to stay hyper-aware of my surroundings. I usually liked to tune everything out and just go, but I couldn't do that with Faith behind me. It wasn't that she was breathing down my neck. She was a good half-mile or more away, but I still couldn't relax. The moment I did, I worried she might pounce—or have someone pounce for her. Coach Langdon was happy with my times, but I knew staying watchful had cost me some of my speed. Once I could tune the world out again, he'd be even happier.

And I soared over the finish line once again.

Coach Langdon clocked it and called out, "Another fast time."

I felt more in me. Today was an "easy day," and Coach wanted us to lift weights too. Instead of pushing for another go-around like I wanted to, I slowed to a walk and waited until Taylor crossed the finish line. Courtney came next, then Grace, followed by another prediction of Raelynn's that had come true. As Courtney and Grace headed my way, their third friend went to Faith's side. Nettie had replaced Raelynn as Faith's go-to, right-hand girl.

Nettie crossed paths with Courtney and Grace, and she didn't spare them a look. It was as if they were complete strangers.

Taylor shook her head. "That's sad."

"Yeah." I agreed.

Courtney's jaw seemed clenched, and Grace looked over her shoulder at Nettie, who talked excitedly to Faith. Her hands were all over in the air, yet Faith seemed to be mostly ignoring her, only glancing up every now and then

"Raelynn's coming back next summer," Grace said. "What does Nettie think is going to happen then?"

We stopped walking and found a spot on the grass to stretch. Grace pulled one leg over the other and leaned toward it

"I have a hard time imagining Faith won't want her best buddy back," she added.

"Unless she's not as fast as Nettie," Courtney said.

Taylor started laughing. "Sorry. I was remembering the first night we met you guys."

Courtney grinned. "True. Nettie's fast in that way too."

"Hit the weights this afternoon, ladies," Coach Langdon barked before he headed back to his office.

We wouldn't see him again until tomorrow morning when we had an easier run scheduled, then our first meet of the year this weekend.

I'd run races in high school, but I knew college was more. The mileage was double what it had been in high school, and everyone was more intense. I didn't know what to expect, but I thought I'd be okay. I just had to beat Faith. That was my main goal.

"The football team is in there today," Courtney mumbled.

"What?" I looked over at her as she frowned off into the distance.

As if everyone heard her, the rest of the team looked over in time to see the football team walking down the sidewalk toward the doors that led to the weight room. Coach said we might run with them, but it looked like we'd be lifting weights instead.

Some of the girls wore eager grins, some groaned.

"Great," Courtney grumbled. She reached to grab the bottom of her feet. "Now we either have to use the shitty weight room, or we have to wait in line for the machines. Coach should reserve the weight room for us."

"You'd think, right? That'd be the smart thing to do." Grace switched into a different stretch, and for the next few moments everyone was quiet until we finished. Then we began walking across the lawn toward those doors. Courtney and Grace fell in step behind Taylor and me. This was the first time we were going, and as we went inside, I heard all the noise from the weight room and wondered if it might be worth it to get a gym membership somewhere else.

I stopped just outside the door.

Massively built guys were everywhere.

I recognized a few, but this was different territory. We used the room too, but there was something primal about the way these guys were claiming the weights as theirs.

"This can't be as terrifying for you guys as it is for us," Courtney said from behind me.

I looked back at her. "Yeah, you'd think, right?"

Taylor clapped her hands together, beaming. "Follow me, ladies. I'll show you how to throw your weight around." She started forward. Courtney and Grace followed, and I brought up the rear.

My plan was to find Mason. I knew he'd be nice, regardless of how the rest of these guys were. As I was looking, Taylor stopped at one of the leg machines.

"Do you know who my dad is?" she asked.

The guy grumbled, but he got up and walked away.

Taylor laughed as she climbed on.

And that was how we lifted weights. Taylor would approach and ask her question. By the third machine, the guys saw her coming. They always got off, and the rest of us would use it after she did. We were half done with our regimen when an arm snaked around my waist.

Mason nuzzled my ear. "What are you doing?"

Gasping from the instant tingles, I laughed and pointed at Taylor. The only problem was the guy using the machine we wanted this time was Matteo.

"It's entertaining to watch all the guys want to refuse Taylor, then realize who she is and slink away with their tail between their legs," I told Mason.

His hand slid down to grasp my hip. He kept me anchored in front of him. "Nah. The tail between the legs is because they want to hit on her, then remember she's Broozer's daughter and Logan's girlfriend." He looked down at me. "I didn't know you'd be in here at this time. I was going over some new plays with Coach. If I'd known, I could've done that later."

I tipped my head up, resting against his chest. "I didn't know myself until we finished an hour ago."

His eyes were warm as he looked down at me. "If you do weights during your season, we could do them together."

"Matteo!" Taylor yelled. "Let us use the machine."

He snorted, adjusting the weight and sitting back down. "You don't scare me, Bruce. I know all the same people you do, and you and your line of ducklings can wait for me to finish my rep. That's the right way to work these machines. You get in line and wait your turn." He leaned down and began pumping his legs.

Taylor's hands found her hips, and she glared down at him. "You take twice as long as we do with this machine. We're runners. We don't have to bulk up. We're just toning."

"Not my problem. I refuse to give in to favoritism." He motioned behind him with his head. "Get in line, Broozer Jr."

I started laughing as Mason tugged me to a different machine. "Have you used this one already?"

I hadn't, and after that, I followed Mason around for the rest of my weights.

Taylor came over at one point, her eyes blazing in frustration. "I'm going to do something to Matteo. I don't know what, but I am."

"Can you really blame him?" I asked. "We *were* cutting in line."

She wrinkled her nose, crossing her arms over her chest as Courtney and Grace came over. They all watched Mason finish his last rep before it was my turn. Though their eyes widened like they normally did around him, Taylor barely paid him attention.

She turned to me. "I know, but now all the others took notes from him. Only a few will get off the machines for us. He ruined our fast time in this room. Plus, he's in here with his team. He doesn't understand. Girls don't like doing weights with all this testosterone. The smell alone is uncomfortable enough."

Mason finished his last pump, then stood and adjusted the weight for me. "Why don't you have Logan lift weights with you?" he said as I climbed on.

"You think that'd work?" She gazed around the room. "You have to admit, there's a lot more of you guys than us. I think half the girls are too scared to come in here."

"Just call Logan. He does weights, though he talks shit more than he lifts, but he'd do it. And he'd love to give Matteo crap too."

"We're almost done today, but I'll be doing that next time. I didn't realize Logan lifted weights that much."

Mason grinned, moving to another machine as I was finishing up. "I think it'd be more about talking shit." He nodded to Taylor. "And showing off to his girl too."

She laughed. "Maybe I should give him a call today after all?"

As I got off my machine, Taylor moved for it. Matteo showed up, appearing from around a different machine, but he jumped back as Taylor got on it first.

She held up her middle finger. "Aha! You were totally trying to cut there."

"Oh, come on." He reached for her finger, but she pulled it away. He grinned, casting a sideways glance to Courtney and Grace. "Can't hurt a guy to try, right?" He asked the last question with his focus on Grace, whose eyes suddenly looked like they were going to bulge out.

"Wha—what?" she stammered out.

"You can't blame me for trying. Right? Now I gotta wait for all three of you ladies." His head perked up, and his grin deepened. "Though, now that I think about it, maybe I've been doing this wrong all along."

Taylor finished and got off.

Courtney and Grace waited, but Matteo waved them on. "After you, ladies. I just realized the benefits of being a gentlemen." He winked at Grace, who waited as Courtney got on the machine. "I get to spend more time with you."

Grace's cheeks pinked, and she yanked her eyes toward Courtney. The back of her neck was reddening too.

Matteo grinned over at us. "Thanks for bringing your friends, Sam."

Mason laughed, moving out again and adjusting the machine for me. "Yeah." He rested a hand on the frame as I sat down. "That's what my girlfriend is: your personal pimp."

"Works for me."

I did my rep and then stood, standing close to Mason for a second. "Girlfriend?" I cocked my head to the side in a teasing manner.

His eyes darkened. He knew what I meant. I wasn't just his girlfriend. I was more now.

His hand grazed mine. "You know what I mean."

We hadn't talked much about the engagement in weeks. There'd been other issues on our radar. He was still supposed to ask again with the ring, and in the meantime I was becoming more and more okay with the idea of getting married.

I was not Analise.

He was not James.

We were a completely different couple.

As we moved to another machine, I watched Taylor continue to fight with Matteo. By now, it was mostly in jest. She'd caught on that he was more interested in hanging out with Grace than fighting to get to the machine.

After one more machine, she admitted defeat. Taylor held her hands in the air and told Grace, "Go with Matteo. I think he'll help you better than me."

Grace's entire face was beet red, but we could hear her giggling the rest of the time we were there.

Courtney and Taylor stayed with Mason and me. Courtney seemed a little quiet around Mason. She watched him as he moved around, and I thought I caught a twinge of jealousy in her eyes, but it was always gone by the time she looked over at me. I wasn't insecure. It was the opposite with Mason, but I was more on edge because of the way girls reacted to me because of him. I didn't want another Kate situation, but that wasn't Courtney. If that were going to be anyone, it would be Faith.

A little while later, when we were done and walking back out to the parking lot, I saw Faith getting into a Yukon.

Speak of the devil.

Taylor stopped next to me. "I really hate that girl."

I grinned. "Is there another weight room on campus?"

Courtney was on my other side. "There's a VIP room that only some of the star players get to use." She frowned at me. "You should have access to that, actually. You and your boyfriend."

Mason came up behind us, and I turned toward him. "Do you have access to a VIP weight room?"

He paused. "Yeah."

"Could you have taken me to the other room?"

"You, yeah." He glanced to the others, and I got his drift. The others couldn't have gone, and he didn't bring it up because he knew I wouldn't have left them.

I frowned. "That's not fair."

"It's for the players who need more attention," Taylor said. "If someone is rehabbing, they get to use it too. But yes, it's generally for the star athletes—the ones who bring in boosters and more money. It's exclusive, but it kind of does make sense."

"You knew about it too?"

She gave me a look like I'd grown two heads. "My dad is Broozer. Yeah, I knew."

"Oh."

Mason unlocked his Escalade and stored his bag inside. He shut the door, waiting for me. I glanced to Taylor. "What are you doing now?"

"I've got this guy I'm dating. I haven't seen him all day, and I thought maybe I'd check in with him. Maybe give him a smooch or two." She grinned at me.

I arched an eyebrow. "Logan's sarcasm is infectious. Who knew?"

She laughed. "He's at your place. I was hoping to hitch a ride since he brought me this morning." We glanced over to Courtney. Grace and Matteo were coming out of the building and heading our way.

"What about you two?" Taylor called over. "I bet I can get Chef Logan to make an appearance. He can cook for all of us."

"I'm down." Matteo gave her a nod, his eyes skirting to Grace beside him.

Taylor touched Courtney's arm. "You and Grace want to come over?"

"Uh." Courtney turned around to look at me. I'd migrated over to Mason by his Escalade. "Is that okay with you?"

I shrugged. "Why wouldn't it be? But to be honest, I think if Logan found out we didn't invite you at this point, he'd be chewing my ass within seconds." I grinned, sinking into Mason's side. I noted how Grace was touching her hair and grimacing. "If you guys want to go shower and change, just head over when you're done. You know where we live."

"Okay. Sounds like a plan."

Mason's arm came down around my shoulders. "Matteo, are you coming over right now?"

"Yes. If that's okay?"

Grace and Courtney took off for their vehicles, their heads bent together. It was obvious the topic of conversation. Grace kept looking back at Matteo, and he seemed receptive.

He turned toward Taylor once the two girls got into a car.

"Can I give you a ride to your man?" he asked. "I have questions to ask. You have answers to give."

"Really? Do I?" Her eyes rounded. "I'm just kidding. I'll take the ride, but I'm not divulging any secrets Grace might've confided in me." She looked over to me. "See you guys there?"

I nodded, but once Mason and I were in his Escalade, he said, "No, she won't."

"What do you mean?"

He started the Escalade and pulled out of the parking lot. "I'm going to be selfish. I want alone time with you. Being in our bedroom when the house is full doesn't cut it for me sometimes."

I leaned back in my seat, grinning at him.

That sounded more than all right to me.

CHAPTER TWENTY-ONE

I wondered where Mason was going to take me. I assumed a hotel. We'd get a suite, have some hot and rough sex . . . when he pulled up to a construction site and hopped out to open a gate, it was the last place I expected to be.

Well, to be honest, I wasn't sure where we were.

He got back in and pulled the Escalade inside before parking and closing the gate behind us again.

I started to get out, but he waved me back. "I gotta drive a little bit still."

There were buildings and walls all over the place, along with construction trucks and machines.

"What is this place?" I asked, as he went down a small trail.

"You remember hearing about that old amusement park Logan took Taylor to last year?"

I nodded. "This is it?"

"This is it while it's being torn down and turned into a big resort kind of thing. James bought it, and I came across some of the plans they have for it this summer. I did a little more digging and found out some of what's already done." He grinned. "I swiped the access code, and I know they're not building tonight or tomorrow. They have those days off for some reason, so it's ours."

"Oh." I laid my hand on his arm. "You're so sweet. A construction site. It's where every girl dreams of being ravished."

His grin only deepened. "Joke will be on you when you see where I'm taking you."

I laughed, leaning my head against the headrest again. "I was teasing, but I do mean it. I appreciate the gesture for some time alone."

"I'm going to miss Logan when he goes to law school, and I know Nate will be moving out eventually, but we do have a full house."

I agreed. It seemed to be getting fuller every year.

"We're here," he announced.

Mason parked outside of a large building. As I got out and he took my hand, I tried to guess what we were stepping into, but nothing could've prepared me.

"Mason!"

It wasn't just a pool; it was one of those you find at water parks. There were slides and a kiddie pool. There was a large butterfly statue in the middle of one section, off to the side, and it looked like a real oasis. The wings were made of material that shimmered all different colors. Just watching it a moment, it was blue, green, orange, and a stunning teal color. The whole place looked almost like a fairytale.

Palm trees overshadowed the edges of the pool. Foliage hung from the tops.

It all looked so real.

A bar was at the far end, with stools to sit on in the water.

"It's useable too." I could smell the chlorine in the air, feel the humidity from the room, and a second later Mason switched the lights on.

He came up behind me and kissed my cheek. "They've been using it for office pool parties and some other events. I think they've rented it out a couple times. This is the next big deal in Cain. I thought my dad was going to sell it again, but he got approached by some guys, and changed his mind. It's smart, if you think about all the sports the university has. That's a lot of cash flow. James is going to capitalize on that."

I turned back to him, feeling one of his hands fall to my hip. "And does James know *we're* using it?"

Mason shrugged. "I know it's empty tonight. That's all that matters." Then his grin darkened, and before I could register what was going on, I was in the air. I shrieked, and the sounds echoed off the walls. Then I was in the water.

It felt warm and refreshing all at once, and just like that, my inner kid surged out. I kicked off the bottom and broke the surface just in time to see Mason pull his shirt off. His sweatpants were on the floor too, along with his shoes and socks. Then he launched himself over me, sinking into a cannonball so I was splashed all over again.

I waited, my heart picking up pace, but he didn't come back up. Instead, two hands grabbed my waist and pulled me down.

"Ah!" I yelled when I popped back up, but by then he was at the far end of the pool.

His eyes danced. "Come and get me, Strattan."

The challenge was on.

I climbed up, pulled off soaking clothes until I was in my bra and underwear, then dove in and was at his side within moments. He dropped below the surface, watching me under the water. I tried to grab him, but he caught my hands and found my waist. He lifted me in the air again, tossing me once more.

I got in a few good dunks when I surprised him, but Mason was strong and quick. I was dunked more often than he was until we'd been swimming for an hour, and our touches started to linger. The grins and laughter turned more serious, more lust-filled, and it wasn't long before I was pressed against the edge of the pool.

Mason trapped me, his arms on either side and his legs underneath me. I wasn't even going to attempt to get away. This was exactly where I wanted to be, and I sat down, straddling him instead. I had my hands on the pool's edge behind me, but I pushed myself forward so my breasts touched him.

He groaned, his eyes almost black with desire. "You're killing me, Sam." He nuzzled my neck, just under my jaw and murmured, "They could have cameras."

"Then turn the lights off," I whispered, searching for his mouth.

I found it. His lips claimed mine, and a tingle went through me.

I was beginning to ache for him, feeling throbbing between my legs, and I just wanted to feel him. Only him. The rational side of me was turning off quickly. I let go of the edge and wound my arms around him.

"Mason." I kissed him, feeling his tongue sweep inside.

He groaned, pulling back. "You sure?"

"God, yes."

He pulled himself up and went over to the panel. A second later, the pool was plunged into darkness, and not long after that I felt his hands on me again. He pulled me into a darker corner of the pool, underneath the butterfly statue, and then his lips found mine.

I raked my hands through his hair, still kissing. I couldn't get enough of him.

"Sam," he breathed.

His hand slid down my back, caught my leg, and pulled me tighter against him.

I moaned. The ache was building, and I moved against him, needing to feel more friction. God, he was right there. A quick shift of his boxer briefs, he could tug my underwear to the side, and he'd be in. But he waited. I waited. I was breathing hard, grinding on him.

He kissed down my throat.

His other hand rested at my waist, and he turned me so I was against the edge of the butterfly. I was almost immobile as he continued kissing. Then he tugged my bra, unclipping the back and pulling it completely off. His mouth found my breast, sucking on my nipple.

I gasped, then arched into him.

I clamped my legs more tightly around him.

He kept kissing. He kept caressing. His hand swept between us, and his finger slid inside.

A guttural groan left me. I just wanted him. Like always.

"Mason." I was damn near begging. I panted.

He kissed me again. Home. That's how he tasted. My arms went around his neck, and I moved my hips in rhythm with his finger. He slid two more inside, and I was soon riding him.

"I love you." His words were a teasing caress against my lips, and then he sunk his fingers inside me again.

I kept going, kept feeling him thrust inside of me until I was damn near falling apart in his arms.

"Mason!"

He continued, holding off on his own pleasure until I had mine. I held on. I loved this Mason. His will was iron strong. He always made sure I came first, and when I was a puddle and my bones weren't firm anymore, he'd slide inside and take me on a whole other ride.

That seemed to be his plan this evening too.

I cried out, feeling my climax rip through me, and then Mason removed the rest of our clothing and sheathed himself inside of me. He pushed in, holding me as his muscles trembled and rippled. He waited, but he didn't have to wait long. He gave me time to adjust to him. But I didn't need any of that. I grabbed his ass and began.

I was moving before he was ready.

"Sam!" My name ripped from him.

"Let's go." I pushed my hips at him, starting the ride.

"Fuck, yes." Then he was going with me.

He thrust out, and I went with him. He went deep inside.

Anywhere he went, I was there too. How fast, how slow, it didn't matter. My heart was a fucking stampede inside of me. Pleasure, desire, lust—it all swirled in me, building into a frenzy until all I could do was beg, plead, and answer any command he made of my body.

I felt he was near, but he held off. He kept thrusting in and out. He was giving me time to match him, to be right with him as he came.

A primal need clambered inside of me. I grabbed his shoulders and urged him to go harder. I wanted it rougher.

"Sam."

"I want it." I gritted my teeth, needing something deeper, darker in me.

And then he gave it. He began pounding into me. He grabbed my shoulder. Half of his hand was on my throat, and he held me in place as he pounded into me.

I came undone in his arms and nearly wept as a second climax ripped through me. I felt like I was torn in half, and then Mason came. His body surged one last time, almost crushing me, before he pressed a tender kiss to my shoulder and swept his hand down my arm and side lovingly.

"You okay?"

I nodded. I was more than okay. I touched the side of his face. "I love you."

His eyes were clouded. I knew he didn't like to think he hurt me, and this had been rough, but I wanted it. His eyebrows dipped together.

I kissed his lips. "I wanted that."

He frowned, slightly. "I might've hurt you."

I shook my head. I felt alive. So much alive. I kissed him again and wrapped my entire body around his. He slipped out of me and held me for a moment. We stayed like that, our heartbeats next to each other, until I began shivering. He moved through the pool, carrying me the whole way, and set me on the edge.

"Stay here."

I wasn't sure what he was doing. I heard some splashing before he pulled himself up and out behind me. He padded somewhere, then a small light was turned on. It was in the corner of the room, enough for us to see, but not to be seen. I could make him out as he came over, handing me my clothes and some towels.

"I'll start the Escalade and make sure the heat is on."

I left my clothes off. They were still wet anyway. Instead I wrapped myself in two large towels. Mason came back in, barefoot in his sweatpants and shirt. He took one look at me and whipped off his shirt. He handed it over.

"Here. It's something."

I grinned, pulling it over me. I was more than okay with him driving home shirtless. "You're going to attract attention from other drivers."

He shrugged, then bent and threw me over his shoulder.

"Mason!"

He smacked me on the ass. "I'm being all gentlemanly. Let me carry you outside."

I stopped struggling and pointed for him to grab my shoes. He must've taken his to the Escalade already. He locked the door behind him, double-checked it, and then deposited me in the passenger side of his vehicle.

I was pulling my seatbelt on when he paused. "Shit."

"What?"

"Hold on."

He went back in and returned ten minutes later.

"What'd you do?" I asked when he climbed inside again.

"I moved us to a place you couldn't see on camera, but I still wanted to make sure." He put his seatbelt on and pulled away from the building. "I just deleted the whole thing."

"Are you going to get in trouble for being in there?"

"Nah. No way." He got out to the open the gate, and then again to close it behind us. After that he found my hand. "I'm sure Logan's blowing up our phones, but I needed that."

I squeezed his hand. "Me too."

We shared a look before he turned back to the road.

When we pulled up at the house, there were too many cars for him to pull into the driveway. He still opened the garage, and we went in that way. As soon as we opened the door to the house, loud music and laughter greeted us. Mason hit the garage button, then went on ahead of me. I huddled behind him, thankful for his bigger build.

"Hey!"

I heard Logan, but darted for the bedroom. I was inside and heading for the bathroom when I heard Mason saying, "We went swimming."

"You couldn't have told me? Dude."

"Give us a minute to shower and chan—"

The door shut on Mason's words, but as I turned on the shower and stepped under the water, I knew he'd be joining me here as well. A few minutes later, he did, but this time I didn't turn around and find his mouth with mine. I leaned against him as we soaped our bodies and washed our hair. I could've turned around, pressed into him, and asked for round two, but my restraint was ironclad. That and I was exhausted. I smiled up at him, watching as he watched me, until we were both clean and there was no reason for us to remain.

I groaned. "How many were out there?"

"More than just Matteo and your two friends," he said.

Another party.

I nodded, stepping outside as Mason turned off the water. "Chef Logan must've called some people."

I handed him a towel, drying off with mine.

"I think some are Nate's friends, and I'm pretty sure Matteo called a few guys from the team."

"Nate has friends?" I was joking. Kind of. I knew he did, but they rarely came over.

Mason finished drying and grabbed new clothes from his closet. I could hear him as I found my own.

"He's bartending at that place where Taylor worked last year. I think she put in a good word for him."

"Really?"

I pulled on underwear, considered a sports bra, but tossed it for a regular one, and pulled on sweatpants. Mason's had looked comfortable at the pool—I wanted to feel that too. I also grabbed one of his football shirts. I wanted to feel like this, like his, for the rest of the night.

His eyes darkened when he saw me wearing his shirt. He grabbed the sleeve, feeling the cloth. "I like when you wear my stuff."

"Me too."

He would've pulled me to him, but I slipped on some flip-flops and ducked out of his reach. He groaned.

Heading for the door, I promised, "Tonight."

"Hell, yes."

Then he reached for the door over my head and opened it for me. When we went out to greet everyone, we went together.

CHAPTER TWENTY-TWO

Two days later, my first cross-country meet had arrived. I had my leg pulled up behind me to stretch when Logan pointed a finger in my face.

"May you be the strongest. May you run the hardest. And may your ass beat some bitches and be the fastest."

"Hey!"

He moved his finger to Taylor beside me. "Hold on a second." He turned to face her, his finger in her face. "May you be the strongest. May you run the hardest. And may your cute and fine ass that I really loved impaling last night be the fas—"

She finished stretching and grabbed his finger. "You couldn't have used a different word? Impaling? Really?" She rolled her eyes, letting go of his finger. "We got it. Thank you." She gave him two thumbs-up. "Best cheerleading boyfriend ever."

He straightened and saluted her, then me. "I'm doing my duty as boyfriend and brother. I hope you both kick ass, but Taylor, let's be real." She'd started to lift her other leg for a stretch, but he yanked her to the side and thumped her on the back. "We all know Sam's going to be legend today. Legend, Samantha. L-e-g-e-n-d." He said it slowly again, one last time, drawing it out.

I clipped my head in a nod. "Thank you."

I wasn't sure if he was helping or hurting. To say I was nervous would've been an understatement. Every inch of me was sweating, and my pulse was racing. I could feel it through my forehead.

This was it. This was the day I proved I could live up to the hype—and I knew there was some about me. I'd caught the looks the other teams were giving me. Or this was the day everyone learned I was a choker and a failure.

I tried to calm myself. I'd been annihilating Faith at every practice run, and I wasn't even trying. According to records, she and a runner from another school had taken the top two spots last year at this meet. When I'd visited Raelynn earlier in the week, she'd filled me in. She said she was sure Faith had probably looked in on this runner's times, and instead of focusing on beating me the last couple of weeks of practice, she might've been more centered on her previous rival.

When we lined up for our starting spots, it wasn't hard to recognize the runner in question. She had the same diva aura Raelynn and Faith had had the first day I ran with them. She walked like a ballerina, with razor-straight posture and her almost-white hair up in a high braid. Girls didn't worry about a lot of makeup for runs, but everyone did a light bit because of pictures. This girl had a smattering of glitter over her cheeks, but then again—I scanned the rest of her team—they all did. It must've been a team-bonding event.

"That's Emily Kostwich," Faith announced as she took her spot next to me. Our coach had put us in spots up front and in the middle. "She and I are your competition today," she added, shaking her hands out.

"Does she know that?"

Emily lifted her chin and turned a haughty look our way. Her eyes were cold, and they seemed even chillier once she made eye contact with Faith.

"Oh, no." Faith laughed under her breath. "I guarantee she thinks the hype about you is all made up. Nope."

Emily wrinkled her nose and looked back to the front line.

Faith groaned. "I hate her. I'm not one of your fans, but if you beat anyone today, make sure it's her. She needs to be brought down a couple notches."

I made sure there was a deadpan expression on my face. "Funny. That's what everyone says about you." And fuck Coach. I moved over a couple girls, instructions be damned. I was going to run beside someone I trusted, and starting a packed race, Faith Shaw was not in that category.

"Strattan!"

I ignored his yell and bent slightly. The start would be any moment.

I knew the route. There would be no surprises. We were on a golf course, and I'd walked it the night before with Mason, Logan, and Taylor. I wanted some familiarity, and today the entire way would be lined with flags and signs, and someone would be at every mile.

Some runners waited the first half, then pushed the second. Others were the opposite. I never had any strategy—I just ran, and with the crowd today, I had a feeling I wouldn't be needing any extra adrenaline.

I breathed out, feeling my clammy hands. I needed to calm down. I could do that.

Stay steady. Stay strong. Stay true.

That was my phrase, and I started repeating it in my head. None of this mattered.

I began to strip it all down.

The other runners.

The whispers.

The rumors.

The hype.

Faith.

Even that Emily girl.

None of them mattered.

It was me. It was the course. It was the run.

It was my old friend. This was just another night I needed to run. Maybe I was pissed at my mom. Maybe I was pissed about Kate and her group that had jumped me. Maybe I was fuming about Cass, Mark's girlfriend who'd hated me since high school. Or maybe I was thinking about Becky and Adam, about how he tried to set Mason up. Or maybe it was Budd Broudou in the back of my mind, when he was looking for Mason's girlfriend because he wanted to rip her up with his dick.

All of those enemies flashed through my head.

There'd been so many, but the one that stood above the rest was Analise. And she was no longer my enemy.

They were all gone. I was done with them.

No. This was just me today. Me and my friend, the run.

Then the gun went off, and we started.

———

Everyone came off the line fast. I heard people from the sidelines yelling for us to slow down. We weren't supposed to start this quick, but it didn't matter. No one slowed. Faith surged ahead of me. That Emily girl was right behind her. I held back, just a little. There were a few runners between us.

The first mile passed.

The lead group pulled ahead of the others. This was my competition. I positioned myself at the back of that group.

Mile two passed.

We had fourteen more to go.

The lead group strengthened its advantage. The middle group was back by half a mile, at least. I still waited, content to sit behind the others, but once we passed mile six, then seven, then eight, I began feeling the itch.

I needed to go faster.

Faith and Emily were out in front. Emily had taken the lead a mile back, but Faith was on her heels. She was almost breathing down her neck.

Come on.

I heard the voice in my head. I didn't know if it was mine, or Mason's, or even someone else. It sounded like my mom, but no. It was me. My voice.

It's time to go.

Tears streamed down my face. My stomach was still clenched in knots, but the voice was right. I could go faster and harder. We had eight more miles to go, a little less than that by now.

It's time.

I moved to the side, and I picked up my pace. In thirty yards, I was ahead of the last ones in the group. Another thirty yards, and I was past the two behind Faith and Emily. They were farther out. It took me another half-mile to be right behind Faith.

She felt me. I knew she did. She glanced back once, but she didn't react. She'd been waiting. I dug my heels in even more, and I was beside her. We matched our strides. Our arms swung in sync. Our legs tuned in to the other's, feeling a teammate near. We moved together, and she gave me the slightest of nods. We forged ahead.

We reached Emily together.

She looked back and saw Faith. Her eyes were flat. They were full of pain, and she was exhausted, but she showed no other emotion. Then her eyes moved to mine and rounded a little bigger. But she couldn't focus too much on me. She returned to facing forward. She couldn't lose even that tiny bit of time, though it didn't matter. She just didn't know that.

Faith and I pulled ahead, then moved over to run right in front of Emily.

We went a half-second faster and began to put distance between us and her.

Tears streamed down Faith's face as she looked at me and said, "Go."

It was all I needed.

I ran.

I stopped thinking.

I tuned the people out.

I tuned the runners out.

It was me.

It was the course.

And I had my friend—the run.

Just her and me. Just doing what we always did.

In the beginning, I heard Coach Langdon yelling for me to slow down. He was worried I would burn out. I wouldn't. I didn't look behind me, but I was alone. I knew it was only me in the lead, and when I passed each mile marker, people were surprised. Either they were surprised it was me, or they were surprised I was there sooner than they'd expected.

I didn't care.

I ran the rest of the race with no one behind me, and when I crossed the finish line, the crowd was quiet for a moment. When I stopped, my chest heaving, the tears were still falling. Something had happened. I didn't know what, but I knew I had run one of my best times ever.

Then Logan was there. He let out a cry and picked me up, swinging me around. Nate came with him. He hugged me too. I knew it was just those two. Mason couldn't come. He had a football event today because they were getting prepped for their game tomorrow, but I knew Logan had been on the phone with him. He had it in his hand, and I reached for it. I wanted to talk to Mason.

My whole body was buzzing, so when Logan tapped me on the shoulder and said something, I didn't hear it right away.

His mouth was moving before I heard the words. "You beat the record, Sam!" His hands held my shoulders. "The record."

"No." Coach Langdon was next to him now, a shocked expression on his face as he looked from me to his watch. "According to this time, you would've qualified for the Olympics."

It was all a rush afterward.

I took first, and even Faith was happy. She hugged me as soon as she crossed the line.

"That was my best time ever," she gasped into my ear. "You helped me do that." She pulled back, and then hugged me once more. "Thank you. Thank you. Thank you." She kept crying and saying the same thing. A bunch of people came over to hug her. They were congratulating her, then me.

Everyone congratulated me.

Taylor was crying. She came in fourteenth out of seventy runners.

Coach Langdon had a frazzled look in his eyes, even after the medals were handed out. Our team took first, and wondering if I could get some favoritism, I asked if Taylor and I could ride back with Logan and Nate. He said no. We needed a team-bonding ride back, but that was fine.

We stopped for food on the way, and so did many of the runners' family and friends who'd traveled to our meet. We took over an entire restaurant, and the whole time, I just wanted to talk to Mason.

I'd only gotten a few words in with him over the phone before, and it hadn't been enough. People kept coming over to me, and I couldn't hear. Then he had to go.

After eating and going to the bathroom, I slipped outside for some privacy and called him again. I didn't know if I would catch him. It was around six, so he'd either be in the weight room, or already heading home to rest before his game tomorrow.

"Hey."

I sagged in relief. "You picked up."

He chuckled. "I'd pick you up any day of the year."

I smiled. "You sound like Logan."

"I have a sense of humor. Sometimes." Then he grew serious. "I hear some major congratulations are in order."

He'd already said it, but I loved hearing it again. My throat swelled up. "Thank you."

"Even the guys heard about it here."

I clutched the phone tighter in my hand. "Really?"

"It's a big deal if we might have an Olympian at our school." He was somber. "Your life's not going to be the same, Sam."

He was warning me.

I nodded. "I know," I whispered. I'd watched him go through it. "I can't believe it, but it might not happen. This was just the first race. It might've been a fluke."

"Stop."

"What?" But I knew what he meant.

"You know it wasn't a fluke. You know the rest will be the same. The only difference now is that everyone else knows how good you are."

Those damn tears. I felt them again. They were threatening to spill. "I heard your voice in my head."

"Yeah?"

I laughed. "It was telling me to go." It had also been my voice, and my mom's too, but I kept that to myself. I didn't know what it meant, and I didn't want to give her any credit. She didn't deserve it.

"I hear your voice in my head sometimes too."

"You do?" I sat down on a bench. Some people had started to leave the restaurant, heading for their vehicles.

"I do. When I'm holding back, and I have to make a good play or something. You're always yelling at me—why am I holding back? Why aren't I going for it?"

"Are you messing with me?"

He laughed softly. "Kind of. I never hold back when I need to make a great play, but I do hear your voice. You're always urging me on. You make me stronger. It means a lot to hear that I do the same for you."

I fell silent. I just held the phone and listened to him on the other end.

"I love you," he said.

"I know. You tell me often."

"I feel it often. I mean it every time."

"I love you too."

The door opened, and I heard Logan's voice.

"I should go. I think Logan's looking for me."

"Tell him I'll be at the parking lot to pick you up. I want that privilege."

"You're still there?"

"I am. I'm waiting."

He wasn't alone. When the bus pulled up to the building, the entire football team was waiting. The family and friends who had gone ahead of the bus joined them, and they all started clapping as we got off.

I started crying. I couldn't stop. I stepped forward and just stood there. I was dressed in the warm-ups the university had given us, and I held my bag in one hand. I covered my face with the other. I hated crying, but I hated crying in front of others even more.

Mason broke from the crowd and came forward. He lifted me up, and I wound my legs and arms around him.

Then I let everything go.

CHAPTER TWENTY-THREE

"Honey, your father and I are coming today for Mason's big game. I only wish we'd known about your first run, or that you were even on the team. We had no idea. And that's so exciting, hearing about how fast you ran. I'm not surprised at all."

Malinda was gushing in my ear as I tried to dress and talk at the same time. I'd slept late since Mason didn't wake me when he got up to go in earlier.

My stepmother kept going. "And don't you worry about making room for us at the house or even cooking. We'll get a hotel room. I already have it reserved, and we'll be treating you to dinner. All of you."

I paused. "Dinner?"

"Of course. We have to celebrate your run and Mason's first game."

I was scrambling, trying to remember if we had any set plans. Last night had been a blur. Coach Langdon and my track coach both mentioned celebrating with the team. I couldn't remember when they'd said it was happening, but then again, I hadn't known Malinda and David were coming to town until she called this morning.

Mason's game was at two. I had to find Logan, Taylor, and Nate, and we all had to head to the stadium to get seats.

No—I jerked upright from reaching for my shoes on the floor.

That was it.

Coach Carillo had mentioned us joining him in a private box for the game. How did Coach Carillo have a private box? I frowned, trying to remember what I'd said in return.

Actually Mason had stepped in, saying, "She'll probably be sitting with my brother and a few others. Can she get back to you tomorrow?"

Coach Carillo had bobbed his head up and down. "Sure thing. That's understandable."

And then we'd gone home. There'd been more celebrating, but Mason had to go to sleep right away. And since Mason had to sleep, Logan suggested going out for some drinks. But I declined. I wanted to be with Mason.

Now tonight was supposed to be the main celebration night. And Malinda and David were joining the festivities.

This should be fun.

After hanging up with Malinda, I finished getting dressed and reached for my phone. I needed to call Logan, but instead saw a bunch of text messages from my biological father, Garrett.

Hey! Sharon and I are coming to Mason's game. It's last minute, but my firm has a private box. Did you and the others want to join us? Seb stayed back in Boston with the grandparents.

Shit.

I texted back, **Do you have room for me, Logan, Taylor, Nate, Malinda, and David? They're in town too.**

He replied almost right away. **There's a few seats, but there's standing room. As long as they're okay standing? We'll have food and drinks too.**

I typed back, **Sold.**

Maybe I should've chosen my track and cross-country coaches, but it didn't feel right sitting with them over family. The jaded part of me wondered if they would've asked if I hadn't run so fast yesterday. I was guessing not.

Heading out to the kitchen and living room, I stopped to see if I heard anyone. Nothing. There was complete silence.

"Logan? Nate? Taylor?" I called.

Still no answer.

I started upstairs and knocked on Nate's room first. "Nate?"

I heard a crash from inside, followed by a curse and a grumbling, "Yeah?"

"We have Mason's game soon. Are you up?"

I was lying, but everything would take longer. This was a major D1 game. Traffic would be backed up, and getting into the stadium would take forever. Since Taylor and I were on an athletic team now, we'd gotten special parking permits for spaces closer to the stadium. I hoped we could park there today and cut back on some of the walking. I also wondered how many other athletes might be thinking the same thing.

I went to Logan's door, but it opened before I could knock.

He peered out at me. He kept the rest of himself hidden, and he said, "I love you, Sam. You're my sister, but if you yell for me in the next half hour or knock on this door, we're going to have problems."

I didn't need to guess. "You're having sex?"

"Yes. Go away."

The door slammed in my face.

I turned around, and a girl was slipping out of Nate's room. Her hair hung loose, and she was holding her shoes. Her dress had twisted up, only covering half of her body. I listened and could hear Nate's shower running. This girl was trying to sneak out.

"Hey."

She screamed, jumping around to see me. Her eyes were wide, and her face drained of blood.

"Oh." She cursed, raking a hand through her hair. "Fuck. Hi. I'm Valerie." She started to hold her hand out, saw it was still full of her shoes, and cursed a third time. She switched her shoes to her other hand and held it out again.

I waved. "You don't have to worry about being formal. Do you need me to call a cab?"

"Could you?" Her voice was hopeful. "Oh, that'd be wonderful."

She kept sneaking glances back to Nate's door. After the third time, and after her eyebrows pulled together in apparent confusion, I asked, "Do you remember last night?"

She bit her lip, following me down the stairs and into the living room. "I remember going to a club with some friends. I remember shots. Lots of shots. Then we went to another bar. It was a little pub type of bar, but it was so packed. And I remember a hot guy . . ." She kept biting her lip and cringing. "Yeah. The rest of the night is a long blur, but I remember having really hot sex." She groaned to herself. "Really hot sex. Oh boy."

I checked outside to make sure somehow her car hadn't gotten to the house, though if it had, I didn't want to know how. I was relieved to see the front was empty except for Logan's Escalade and Taylor's car. Nate's and mine were parked inside.

I started dialing the car company. "They'll be here shortly, I'm sure."

"Oh good." She looked around the house again, bending her knees. "Uh, is there a bathroom around here? That I . . . could . . . use . . . ?" Her soft voice trailed off.

I pointed down the hallway. "First door on the left."

"Oh, thank you." She took off, rushing around the corner.

I was just hanging up with the cab company when Nate hurried downstairs. He took the phone away from me. "No, don't call a cab."

"Wha—" I pointed to the phone. "They're coming."

He cursed, then yanked it to his ear. "Hello?" He waited a few seconds, then said, "Yes. I want to cancel that cab. She didn't know she didn't have to call it." He frowned. "Of course she's safe. Here." He thrust my phone back to me. "They want to make sure you're okay."

I took the phone. "I'm fine. I was calling for him, but it's not needed. Thank you." I hung up and frowned at Nate. "What are you doing? She wanted a cab."

"Where is she?"

The toilet flushed down the hallway.

He looked that way. "Oh." Then he leaned closer to me. "I'm not doing anything shady, but I'll take her home. I don't know who she is. I want to find out a little more about her before sending her on her way."

"Why?"

"The bar was filled with reporters last night."

I touched my chest. "Because of me?"

"What?" He frowned, shaking his head. "No. Not you. That's not news yet. For the game. I don't remember a lot about last night, so I want to make sure this chick isn't a reporter."

The door opened then, and Valerie came out. Her hair had been smoothed; it was even glossy somehow. It had looked mostly blond before, but I saw some reddish tints to it now. Her dress was back in place and covering all it was supposed to be covering, and her shoes were on. She had a clutch in her hand that I hadn't seen before. She started toward me, but saw Nate and jerked backward.

"Oh." She caught herself on the doorframe to keep from falling. "Oh, hey."

He waved to me. "I hope it's okay, I had her cancel the cab. I'll give you a ride home."

I hit his arm. "The game."

"Yeah." He pushed my hand away distractedly. "We'll be fine. I'll be back." He gestured to her. "Is that okay? Can I give you a ride home?"

"Sure." She came forward a few steps, walking stiffly. She held onto her clutch with both hands in front of her. "But I don't go to Cain U. I don't live here. I'm in town with some friends for the game."

"You are?"

His relief was evident. I hit him, just because.

Nate shot me a look. "What?"

Her eyebrows drew together again, and she lowered her head slightly.

I gestured to her.

Understanding dawned. "Oh! No. I thought you were a reporter. If you're with friends for the game, I'm hoping you're not a reporter."

"Why would you worry I was a reporter?"

"Because there were a lot at the bar last night."

She shook her head slowly, like she was trying to remember. "I think that's why my friend wanted to go to that bar. She has a thing for one of the ESPN commentators."

"But you're not a reporter, right?"

She shook her head. "No. I go to Gammit."

That was the team we were playing today.

I forced a smile, grabbing onto Nate's arm. "Do you mind if we have a moment?"

She stood there.

So did we. And then her eyes got wide again. "Oh!" She pointed to the door. "You want me to—okay." She power-walked to the door. "I'll be right out here. Don't forget about me."

As soon as the door closed behind her, I let go of Nate's arm. "You like her, don't you?"

He lowered his voice, sneaking a look at her on the other side of the door. "The sex was really good last night."

"Good enough that you want to threaten Mason by telling her who you are?"

"How would that threaten Mason?"

This girl was a stranger. He might want to stay in her pants a while longer, but there was a reason we were a tight-knit group. Not just anyone got in. And this wasn't normal for Nate. I felt an underlying alarm to press this point to him.

"Nate."

Then he held his hands up. "Okay. Okay." He backed up, and his tone was serious. "I got it. I know what you're saying. She won't know anything about Mason."

"Do you?"

"Yes." He lowered his hands, letting out a sigh. "I won't tell her my last name. I'll give her a ride back to the hotel, and I'll distract her the whole time. It's obvious she's not like us. She's not guarded, so I can ask her questions without telling her anything. I'll keep her talking, and I'll get her number without her having any clue who I am."

And that meant who he was in relation to Mason.

"Okay." Good. It might not be anything. She could be an ally, but why risk it? This girl could be a one-night stand. Or a two-night stand. He didn't have to make it anything else.

"Okay." Nate nodded again, collecting his keys and wallet. "I'll call when I drop her off. Let me know the plans from there. Traffic is going to be a bitch today."

"Garrett said we could all watch with him in his firm's private box."

"Your bio dad?"

I nodded and pointed upstairs. "I'm waiting for the Sex Machine to finish before telling them too."

He grinned. "Sounds like a plan. I'll call you guys."

"Hey." I stopped him as he went to the door. "I can tell you like her. I'm not saying not to like her or pursue anything. I'm just saying—"

"I know. Be cautious. Be smart."

"Yeah."

He opened the door. "I'll call you in a bit."

"Okay." I waved at Valerie, who turned toward us as we opened the door. "Nice to meet you."

"Nice to meet you too!" She waved back, then asked Nate, "What's her name?"

"Just a roommat—" The door shut, and I couldn't hear any more.

"Yo!" Logan came down the stairs.

I turned and grinned. "That was quick."

He braked on the last step. "Ah. Not funny, Sam. Not funny."

"I thought I was funny."

He glanced around. "What's going on? You don't usually knock on my door."

I filled him in on everything, and he agreed it was a good idea to head out as soon as we could. He went to get dressed for the game, saying he'd let Taylor know the plan too, and I went back to my bedroom to change. I'd pulled some things on in a rush, thinking I was way behind schedule. Now that I had a moment, I grabbed different pants that were still comfortable but a little more fashionable.

I knew my biological father and his wife. They ran in elite circles, and that meant they were always dressed so they looked wealthy without trying to look wealthy. It was a skill. Sharon was nice, but she was one of those socialite types. She looked beautiful and put together every time I saw her. And now that I thought about it, Malinda was too. I always forgot about that. Malinda was just Malinda to me. Loving, warm, and sassy, but she could play in those top circles too. She had more bite than Sharon, but this was Garrett and Sharon's alma mater. I had no doubt they'd be seeing old friends.

All in all, I wasn't sure what to expect from the day.

Forty minutes later, Logan, Taylor, and I were heading to the game with instructions to pick up Nate at the hotel where he'd dropped Valerie off. We figured it was easier to go in one car because we were already going to be meeting both sets of my parents there.

I talked to Malinda. She and David would meet us at the stadium. And since we were going to Garrett's box, I assumed we'd meet him and Sharon there too.

After picking up Nate, it took another half hour to get to the stadium.

Swarms of people were already descending on the stadium, and by game time, it'd be filled to the max.

"Hey." Taylor pointed to a group going in through the same entrance as we were. "Look."

Faith and Nettie were there, along with a bunch of other girls from the team.

"I don't see Courtney and Grace," she added.

I frowned. "Were we supposed to invite them with us?"

She shrugged. "I'll text them and mention that we saw Nettie and the other girls at the game, see if they're coming too."

We hadn't talked much about it last night. Everything had mostly been about the meet, but as we followed the group inside, and then proceeded to continue following them, I realized they were in the box next to us.

I stopped Taylor. "Did you already text them?"

"Yeah."

A cold feeling spread in my stomach, and I peeked into the next box. Faith was there, along with the rest of the team. The only ones not there were Taylor, me, Courtney, and Grace.

"Do you need something?" Faith came to the door, a drink in one hand and a haughty expression on her face.

"What happened to 'Thank you for helping me go faster'?"

She shrugged, sipping her drink. "That was on the course. This is off the course."

"You're cold."

She laughed. "I've never pretended to be otherwise." She angled her head to look at the door to our box. "Unlike you. I'm betting whoever you're sharing that with, you didn't invite your two other buds from the team."

"Are you sharing with Coach Langdon?"

"No. This is my dad's private box. Coach usually sits with the other coaches. They all share one box."

I didn't tell her I'd been invited to that one. "Well, have fun watching the game."

"I will."

"I'll have fun watching *your boyfriend*," she added.

I wasn't sure what she meant by that, but I turned to Taylor as we entered the box. "Text Courtney. Invite her and Grace up here."

They couldn't be the only ones left out. I wouldn't do that to them.

I looked over and saw Garrett and David waiting for me.

I took a breath, then approached both of my dads.

CHAPTER TWENTY-FOUR

Garrett and David had settled in together, sitting side by side.

Sharon and Malinda also sat together.

They were all happy to see me, as well as my friends. And they were happy about my race time. Garrett and Sharon hadn't known about my first meet, and Malinda loved telling them. She followed that up with insisting that my biological father and his wife join us for dinner too.

Actually, she invited everyone, including Matteo, Courtney, and Grace. When they agreed, Malinda called ahead to alert the restaurant, and when we arrived after the game, we were led to a private room in the back.

"Honey, you must be so happy today." Malinda linked her elbow with mine. She pulled me to the side as everyone headed in and took their seats.

There it was, that word. *Happy.* Everyone seemed happy. I just wasn't used to the emotion being genuine around me. But I'd done well in my race, and Mason had scored two touchdowns to help Cain U win their first game of the season. I was surrounded by friends and family . . .

"I am." And I was. I really was. I nudged her with my elbow. "I'm glad you and my dad came up today."

"Yes, me too." She craned her neck to look into the room. "Everyone's sitting down. I should head in there, but I wanted to check in with you real quick. How are you? I was shocked when you told me you'd joined the cross-country team. I know you haven't the last two years."

"I know, but I wanted to do . . ." How could I explain this without feeling selfish?

"Something for yourself?" she supplied for me.

Some of the tension left my shoulders. "Yeah. It's been fine so far, but we start classes next week."

"Well, that'll be more of a challenge, but you and Mason will be fine. You've already been through so much, and you're going to have moments like these. Especially if you guys get married, or stay together for life. Some husbands join the military and are gone for years. I think you and Mason are very lucky to have what you have, and I know you two are committed to the relationship."

David came to the door and waved for Malinda to join the rest of them. She laughed softly under her breath. "Trust me. When you have a good one, you hold onto him. You might not get another." She shook her head, clearing away whatever else she'd been thinking, and gave my arm one more squeeze. "Maybe not you, though. You're amazing. Any guy would be lucky to have you. I gotta go in there. You're waiting for Mason?"

I nodded. Mason and Matteo needed to shower and change after the game, not to mention all the people they needed to talk with before they could leave.

She kissed my cheek before going to the room. I could hear her saying, laughing as she did, "I'm here. The party has to start now, right, Logan?"

"Damn straight, Mama Malinda."

I wandered back to the front of the restaurant and was content to wait outside until Mason and Matteo arrived. There was a warm breeze, and after all the attention I'd gotten in the box and since yesterday, I was grateful for some moments alone. I drew in a deep breath, watching people come and go. This was one of the nicer restaurants in Cain, so maybe I shouldn't have been surprised when I saw Faith walking up from the parking lot toward the entrance.

She never goes away.

She wasn't dressed in the jeans and light sweatshirt she'd worn to the game. Instead, she now wore a black dress and heels with her hair on the top of her head. A white shawl draped around her back and arms. If I hadn't known Faith from the team, I would've assumed she was a celebrity or something. She had that air about her.

She was with Nettie, who was also dressed up in a white dress. No white shawl for her, though. She held a black shawl instead, and her hair was curled and hanging loose down her back.

I couldn't stop myself. I snorted.

The sound drew Faith's attention, and her eyes widened before narrowing. She stepped onto the curb where I was sitting. "Are you stalking me, Strattan?"

"My memory tells me I got to the football game before you."

She rolled her eyes. "Slightly. You were at the entrance first. You followed us inside. That's what my memory says."

I kept going as if she hadn't spoken. "And again, I'm here before you." I narrowed my eyes at her. "Are you stalking me? Is that what's really going on here? I know you're in love with me on the course now, apparently, but maybe it's time you admit how you feel about me off the course too."

"That's easy." She gave me a fake smile. "Loathing. Deep, dark, loathing. That's what I feel for you, and don't get confused. I am grateful to you on the course because of one thing: competition. Until you came, I was never motivated to really push myself, and yesterday I beat Emily Kostwich. I can beat anyone now."

"Except me."

She tsked me, waving her finger in the air. "Don't get cocky, Samantha. You never know. Someday, you might not be able to run." She paused. "Like Raelynn." She tilted her head to the side. "I hear you're great friends with her now."

"I hear you dropped her like a bad habit."

She frowned. "I can't stay by her side all day long. I still have to train and have a life."

"I would think that's completely understandable, except for the first time I visited her. She predicted you'd drop her like an anchor. She's coming back to running, you know. She's just out this year."

"Is that what she said? That's funny. That's not what the doctors said. But hey, you were in the room when they were, right? Oh wait."

She dropped the pretend smile and politeness. "You weren't. I was. Rae's been my best friend since elementary school. I'm not dropping her as a friend, but I do have to live my life and continue to train." She pulled her shawl tighter and raised her chin. "We're meeting my father inside and some family friends. Excuse us, would you?"

She started forward.

"Rae's not your friend," I called after her.

She stopped, her back stiffened, and she slowly turned to me.

Her eyes were full of caution. She knew what I was going to say, but I had such pleasure saying it anyway. I made sure my voice was cold, like her.

"She's in love with you, but you already know that."

She sucked in her breath. "Do you know what you just did?"

Yes. Because when I'd visited Rae, she asked me to call Faith out on it. I nodded. "Trust me, I was given permission to say this to you. If you really do care about her, go talk to her. Her feelings matter."

"I'm not some lesbian."

"Right." I nodded. "Because that's the best reaction you can have when you find out your best friend since elementary school is in love with you. Say you're not a lesbian." I was struggling not to say too much, but I did add, "The loathing is mutual, you know. And mine just went up a whole other level. I love having you on *my* team."

"It's my team!" she snarled. "It's not yours. It'll never be yours."

I saw Mason and Matteo approaching from the parking lot, but I couldn't stop. I didn't just loathe Faith. I was beginning to truly hate her.

"If you don't start beating me, I can only assume you mean to keep the team a different way. Tell me, Faith," I chided, softly. I wanted to know. I wanted to see a crack in her mask. "If you were to take me down, how would you do it? A shove? Would you hope my ankle broke? Or a different way? How would you do it?"

Her ice-cold exterior remained intact. "I want to beat you in the truest way there is: I'm going to be faster than you. It's just a matter of time before you feel me right behind you. Like I said before, I've never really had competition."

This was the second time Faith referenced not having any competition. I'd sensed a reaction from Nettie the first time, but I ignored it. I looked this time, and she wasn't glaring at me like a good sidekick. She was frowning at Faith, her arms hanging loose by her side. The shawl was slipping. She didn't notice.

I jerked my head toward Nettie. "Look at that. Seems like at least one of your friends might not agree with you."

"Sam," Mason called.

He and Matteo stood at the door in jeans and Cain University shirts. They weren't dressed up, but they didn't need to be. Mason held his own, no matter what he wore. A commanding presence, and a slight shiver of danger clung to him. Nettie and Faith both reacted to his presence, and I wasn't the only female to take all of him in. Nettie touched her stomach and flipped one of her curls over her shoulder.

"You okay?" he asked me.

I nodded. "Yeah." I moved around the two girls.

Mason touched the small of my back, letting me precede him and Matteo back inside. I walked past the front desk, then stopped abruptly.

Valerie, Nate's one-night stand, was waiting with a group to be seated. She was dressed the way Faith and Nettie were, in a shimmering dress. A bunch of others were with her, but Valerie was one of the only girls not standing next to a guy.

She turned and saw me. "Oh. Whoa—" She started to fall backward.

"Val!" A guy twisted around and caught her. He helped to right her. "Come on."

She waved a hand, mumbling a thank you to him, but her eyes were stuck on me. She started to smooth out her dress, not noticing she'd caught the jacket of the guy who helped her. His suit jacket had opened, and she was raking it down her dress repeatedly.

"Val!"

"What?" She snapped to attention, looking down and realizing what she'd done. "Oh. Sorry." She handed the jacket back to him and looked away, trying to appear casual. She fluffed her hair, and I walked past her.

"Do I want to know?" Mason asked.

"Ask Nate." I patted him on the arm.

We wove through the last of the tables before coming to the private room, but Mason took my hand and pulled me to the side. "You okay? Things seemed heated back there."

"Yeah." But I felt a headache forming, and I pressed a hand above one of my eyebrows. It hurt the most there. "She's just . . . She's not a good person. I'll leave it at that."

"Let me ask my dad about her family."

"Mason," I started.

"Let me help you. I'll talk to my dad."

Suddenly, and so completely, I was just thankful Mason was with me. I slid my arms around his waist and tipped my head back. I didn't have to say anything. He knew, and his lips were right there, meeting mine.

CHAPTER TWENTY-FIVE

MASON

"Mason."

Garrett, Sam's biological father, held his hand out as Sam and I stepped into the private room. Sam paused, looking up at me. She was silently asking if I wanted her to stay and be a buffer between us, but I shook my head. It meant a lot that she was even offering.

I shook his hand. "Mr. Brickshire. How are you? Thank you again for helping with that incident earlier this summer."

"Garrett. We've been through too much for you to call me by my last name, but I admit, it's a lot nicer reception than I used to get from you guys."

And since he went there, I replied, "Yeah, but that was when you were a dick to your daughter. You haven't been for a while, and you helped me out."

Logan was sitting close by, and he snorted, looking back to watch us.

Garrett let out a soft sigh. "I guess I asked for that. I did disappear for a while."

It was for two years, but who was counting?

I just smiled back. "Thanks for coming to the game."

"Of course." He seemed relieved to move on. "And it was a great one, especially for your first of the season. Two touchdowns. They were raving about you on ESPN earlier."

I nodded. "Yeah, well, everyone at the university is raving about Sam's race time yesterday." I turned toward her. She had taken a seat at the end of the table and was conversing with some of her running friends, but she looked back to me. A warm glow emanated from her.

The buzz about her was small, so far. That wouldn't last. I knew the other runners were talking about her race, and that would only spread. People would watch to see if she could continue that time. I was sure some thought it was a fluke, but I knew better. Sam had been running like that since I'd known her.

Thinking about it now, I hadn't pushed her to join cross-country. I'd asked her once if she wanted to, but she'd said she was fine with just doing track. I was ashamed now that I hadn't pushed her harder. I knew I was part of the reason she'd chosen only the spring sport. I should've done everything I could to make sure she wouldn't regret not joining cross-country.

At least she was there now.

Sam didn't like attention, and I knew a part of her was happy, but a part of her was freaked out. My job was to be there for her, and I would be, but as I gave her bio dad a look, I hoped he read between the lines. I wanted everyone to be there, including him.

It was her time to shine.

He coughed, narrowing his eyes. "Yes, that's what I've heard. I was ecstatic when I found out."

"She's running pre-Olympic times. Did you hear that?"

He stilled, and his eyebrows stretched apart.

He hadn't.

"It's going to get crazy for her."

"Yeah," he murmured, his eyes falling thoughtfully to his daughter. "Yeah, I'm sure it will be." He paused, then looked back to me. "Pre-Olympics?"

"Yeah."

Was he getting it now? Did he understand?

"You know, I couldn't have done what I've done without support," I said. "Support. That's really important. Support. From family and friends." Did I have to say it again?

He shot me a look.

He got the message.

"Mason." Malinda stood at the other end of the table, a glass of wine in hand. "Stop interrogating Garrett and sit down. Both of you sit down."

She waved to the table, and I slipped into my seat next to Sam. Garrett returned to his at the other end next to his wife and David.

Malinda raised her glass. "A toast to Mason for his exceptional game today." She beamed with pride. "And to Samantha, for making Cain U history yesterday and continuing to do so. And to everyone here." She indicated the whole table. "If you're here, that means you love and care for one of our kids, and that means the world to me. Thank you from the bottom of my heart. To everyone!"

We saluted, then sipped.

Malinda had already ordered appetizers, which were now placed down the middle of the table. Once they were done, the servers came around for our individual orders.

Matteo leaned across the table from his seat next to Grace, with Courtney by her. "Hey, what was up with you and Bio Dad?"

Sam put her water down with a little extra force, like it slipped and she caught it in time. "Do you have to call him that too?"

"What's his name?"

"Garrett. Call him Garrett."

Matteo thought about it, then shrugged. "Bio Dad seems more appropriate, but okay." He turned back to me. "So? You and—" He glanced at Sam. "—Garrett. What's up with that?"

"Nothing. Just small talk."

Matteo snorted. "Right, because that's what you Kades are known for. Small talk."

Nate leaned over the table and asked in a mock whisper, "What's going on?"

My eyes met Sam's. I knew we were thinking the same thing. Then I looked at Logan and saw the suspicion there. He knew something was going on too, so I shrugged.

"We ran into a friend of yours out there," I told Nate.

He had been reaching for a roll, but he dropped it. "What?" He cursed under his breath, grabbing the roll before it hit his water.

"Someone recent. Like, last night and this morning recent."

Logan started laughing. He was keeping it quiet, but he was still laughing. "Is he talking about a chick or a dude? If it's a dude, I'm all for that, but give me a heads-up. I am your husband, remember?" He winked at Nate.

Nate scowled. "Shut it." He cursed again under his breath. "You ran into her?" He shot Sam a look. "And thanks for telling."

She shrugged. "Sorry." She didn't sound it.

I hid a grin, rubbing a hand over her back. "Back off her. I would've figured it out anyway. The girl wasn't real smooth."

"I liked her."

Logan frowned at Sam, then me. "Who is she? I want to meet her now."

A third curse from Nate. "This isn't funny, you guys. We're at a family meal. It's not the place to talk about my sexual escapades."

"Mmmm?" That perked Malinda's ears. She straightened in her chair. "What's going on? Nate has sexual escapades?"

Logan smothered more laughter.

I started to open my mouth, but Nate shot me a dark look. "Mason."

I heard the warning and held a hand up. "We're just joking. We didn't even talk to her. Sam just said you knew her, that's all." I pointed to Logan. "He told me about the one-nighter."

Nate stiffened, turning to Logan. "Are you kidding? That happened just last night."

Logan frowned. "Why are you getting all uppity about some chick? Unless—"

Nate's eyes flashed.

Logan dipped his head in a small nod and cleared his throat. He looked my way. "So, Matteo."

"Oh no." Matteo stopped eating a fancy-looking pizza roll. "Don't start, you guys. Please." He gestured to his plate full of appetizers. "I just want to eat. That's all."

Logan ignored him. "Have you asked Grace out yet?"

Grace squeaked at the mention of her name, and her face reddened. She looked around, saw she was the center of attention, and squeaked again. "Oooh boy," she breathed.

Matteo shook his head and pointed at Logan. "No. You're not going to do this. You're deflecting. I won't let you do that. Deflect elsewhere, buddy."

Logan's eyes darkened. He and Matteo were friends, but he didn't like getting orders from anyone except Sam or me.

He narrowed his eyes. "I was? Really? I think I'm more curious now than ever. I think you're the one deflecting. Hey, Grace."

She stiffened, but looked at him with caution.

"Logan, don't." Matteo's warning was low.

An evil gleam started in my brother's eyes, and his lips curved. "Has he asked you out yet? Or maybe you guys already went out? Did he underperfor—"

"Watch it, Logan."

I couldn't see Sam's eyes, but her tone was a warning too.

"Don't be disrespectful to my friends."

Logan stopped, seemed to realize what he'd been about to do, and closed his mouth. He leaned back. "Maybe we should adopt a new policy where we dine with enemies? I'm in the mood for a target right now."

Sam pointed over her shoulder toward the rest of the restaurant. "Faith Shaw is out there. Have at it."

Logan didn't stand up, but I could tell he was considering it. His eyes met mine. Sam had stopped us from proceeding before against Shaw, and if he went after her now just to release some of his anger, it could backfire.

"Chill," I said, quietly.

Logan groaned, but did as I said, and the silence that followed was thick and awkward.

"Okay." Malinda stood again, a second glass of wine in hand. She raised it up like last time. "I want to do another toast, but this one might make me a little teary." Her eyes shone, and she pressed a hand to the corner of her right eye.

She sniffled, clearing her throat. "Okay. Here it is." She raised her glass higher. "I'm not trying to purposely leave anyone out, but I have to focus on these three children of mine." A tear slipped past her hand, making its way down her cheek. She used the back of her hand to wipe it away. "Nate, Matteo, I don't know you guys as well, but I already love you, and I know both of you love these three too."

She smiled at Sam's runner friends. "And you both seem very lovely." She turned to Taylor, sitting across from Logan and next to Courtney. "I've only recently gotten to know you, and you seem perfect for Logan. I can tell he's very happy with you, but you three." Her eyes warmed, and her lips started to tremble. She looked at Logan, Sam, and me. "You three have rocked my world. I am beyond happy to have met David, but then his daughter came along, and, Samantha, you took my breath away." She pressed a hand to her chest. More tears slid down. "And you got along with my Marcus. Oh, my boy. He'll always be my baby, but he got a sister in you, and everyone now knows that Samantha is a package deal. Mason and Logan come with her, no matter what."

She chuckled hoarsely and glanced to David. "I have to admit that we agonized over what to do with you, Mason. You had more claim on this new precious baby girl than I did." Her hand fell to David's shoulder. "More than David too. You were protecting her from us. That stopped me in my tracks. I couldn't get over it, but then I heard more, and I started to understand. You and Logan, you're her guard dogs, and I hope that never ends. Ever. You protect her against the world, and Samantha is one of the luckiest people I know."

She paused, clearing her throat. "Samantha, what you have with Mason and Logan, I am beyond envious. And I'm an adult, but the three of you continue to humble me. The loyalty and love you have for each other, I can only strive to create the same bond with David and my boy. And I am so very grateful to have met all of you, and to you three

. . ." She raised her glass once again. "To the love you have. May we all be lucky enough to experience that once in our lifetimes."

She stopped and turned to each adult, touching their glass with hers. Garrett's wife looked like she was fighting back tears, and they all sipped from their drinks, joining the salute.

Sam looked between Logan and me. She had a stunned look in her eyes, and her throat was working. She reached for her drink and raised it toward Malinda.

"Thank you, Malinda," she whispered.

Everyone sipped their drinks, and another bout of silence filled the room.

Logan frowned, swinging his gaze to me. I raised my eyebrows. If he thought I was going to follow that toast with one of my own, he was a moron. I gave him a look back, letting him know what I thought.

He snorted, grinning slightly. "Fine." He took his glass and stood up. "I love you, Mama Malinda, and my speeches aren't usually so nice, but—"

"Not another wedding speech," Malinda interjected. She was firm on that. "Nothing like that. We were at James and Analise's wedding too."

Logan laughed. "No, but technically, my speech was fine that day. *I* had to be nice. Mason's was the mean one."

"Truth." I coughed. "I just spoke the truth."

Logan swung his glass in my direction. "And on the same theme of being true—"

Nate slumped back in his chair. "Oh no." He tossed his cloth napkin on his plate.

"Logan." Malinda gave him a small warning.

"Can you all relax? I'm going to be honest, but not in the way you think." He paused, waiting for their permission.

"Logan, just talk," I told him.

He nodded. "I will. Thank you, brother." He cleared his throat and hit his chest. "There once was a little boy."

"What?" Nate frowned, shooting forward to look at me.

I lifted a shoulder. "Just let him talk. This is Logan. We never know what we're going to get."

"Thank you, brother."

Nate groaned, leaning back again. "That's what I'm worried about."

"Ahem." Logan shot him a look. "Like I was saying, there once was a little boy who grew up in a palace, and there was a sad and lonely mother, who liked to drink her misery away with wine and diet pills, and there was also an older brother. And this older brother was looked upon by the little brother. He worshiped him. He idolized him, and when the older brother would get angry, get drunk, or get into fights, the little boy wanted to be just like him."

I sighed. I'd asked for it.

Logan kept going, laughing, "And one day, when the wicked king of the palace came home, riding on one of his many *w-horses—*" He coughed. "I mean mares. The older brother had enough. He yelled and swore at his father, and he turned his back on the king that day. That was the day everything in the kingdom changed. The queen, who was still lonely and sad, moved to a different kingdom and found her love of traveling. She was never heard from again, but the two brothers banded together. They kicked the evil king out of the kingdom, along with his new prized mare."

His lip twitched. "The one he had fallen deeply in love with, who was as evil as he. But you see, the story didn't end there. No. The king and his new evil mare, who turned into a human and became his new queen, brought a daughter with her. And this daughter needed to be saved from the evil king and queen, and the two brothers knew they couldn't just live happily ever after in their own kingdom with all their own mares." Another lip twitch. "They knew they had to save this new daughter, and so they rode out on their mares, and laid waste to their father's new kingdom to save their new queen."

"Logan." I leveled him with a look. "Wrap up this fairytale."

"You were all about transparency at the wedding. And excuse me, but this is a fairytale. Everyone knows I'd never insult a horse by calling it a whore."

"Let him finish." Nate gestured to Logan. "I'm enthralled."

"Thank you, and you didn't want me to do a speech."

"I stand corrected. Please go on. I enjoy hearing about the *mares*."

"Oh, yes." Logan smirked. "There were lots and lots of mares in this story, but when the two brothers brought back the new evil queen's daughter, she cast a spell over their kingdom and both brothers. But it wasn't one of evil or one she meant to do. It was magic. One became destined to be the new reigning king at her side, and the other was destined to always protect and cherish her as a brother should."

His gaze lingered on Sam before he kept going, forcing a lighter note in his voice. "And there you go. The new kingdom was created, and the new and loving queen replaced both the evil queen, and also the sad and lonely queen, who was never heard from again." He held his glass out. "And let's all drink to that odd and kind of twisted fairytale."

Logan was about to sit down as everyone sipped from their drinks, when a new voice spoke from the room's doorway. "Is that what you think of me?"

Helen stood there, a hurt look in her eyes. "You think I'm sad and lonely, and that you've never heard from me again? You think I abandoned you?"

Logan didn't reply.

I knew my brother. He did think that, but he wasn't going to say anything because he still felt some loyalty toward her.

I did not. "If the shoe fits, *Mom*."

CHAPTER TWENTY-SIX

SAMANTHA

"That's hilarious." Helen gave Mason a scathing look, folding her arms over her chest. She was dressed in a pencil skirt with a white silk top. With her pointed heels, she looked like an older model who'd stepped out of a business magazine. Her blond hair was pulled up into a fancy twisted bun, but every time I saw Helen, that was how her hair was done.

Garrett stood. "Helen, to what do we owe the pleasure?"

A gargled sound came from Taylor's throat, and when everyone turned her way, she held up an apologetic hand. "Sorry. She texted and said she couldn't get ahold of Logan. I told her we were at dinner and he'd probably call when we were done. I had no idea she was in town."

"Or that your phone pinpointed the actual restaurant you were at?" Helen didn't sound amused. "Yes, well." She swept a cold gaze over everyone. "I'm afraid I have to interrupt. As happy as my sons seem to be with my arrival, I need to pull them away."

She turned to Mason. "A journalist friend of mine gave me the heads-up about an article coming out on Monday. I may be sad and lonely, and I may have abandoned you, but with this bit of news, I could not stay away. Can we talk in private, please?"

Mason narrowed his eyes, but a half hour later, we were in Malinda and David's hotel suite. Malinda had insisted, and Helen took a minute to scan the room again. Mason had insisted the parents be present, along with Nate, Logan, and myself. The only adult who'd excused herself was Sharon, Garrett's wife. I wasn't sure if that was because of Garrett and Helen's brief dating history or because she just didn't feel her presence was necessary. Either way, I couldn't blame her. Helen hadn't seemed happy to see her, and Sharon only managed a brief smile as everyone left the restaurant.

"Is everyone necessary?" Helen asked Mason again.

He shrugged, standing behind where I sat on a couch. Logan stood next to him, and both had their arms folded over their chests.

"They'd all find out anyway. Besides—" He gestured to Garrett. "Meet my new lawyer. If memory's right, you two know each other, in a biblical way?"

My biological father grimaced, rubbing a hand over his face.

Helen bristled. "Is this what's to come? Have you and Logan switched roles? You're the sarcastic one now?"

"No." Logan leaned back against the wall, giving his mother a dark look. "He's just a bit meaner to you than I am. You took me to Paris. And you're actually nice to my girlfriend. Mason doesn't have those reasons to be kind. You like to be a dick to *his* girlfriend. Remember?" His voice indicated that he wasn't all right with that, but he bared his teeth in a forced smile. "Trust me, mother. I'm walking a fine line here between being pissed at you too about Sam and being somewhat grateful to you about Taylor. Keep being a dick, though, and I'm certain Taylor won't care to have anything to do with you either."

"Noted."

She glowered at me before letting out a loud sigh, pulling out a magazine, and tossing it on the hotel's table. "This is running on Monday. It's an article saying my son was given special privileges because of his 'promising' future. He was arrested for assault and battery, but was released and received no consequences from the Cain University administration."

Mason let out a savage curse.

Helen kept going, as if her son hadn't reacted, "It was supposed to run later in the month. They wanted to wait for a bowl game, but it was pushed up because Samantha ran an impressive race yesterday afternoon. A second article is coming out on Tuesday where they'll talk, at length, about my son's history, along with his Olympic-hopeful girlfriend and my other son. Now," she said, looking around. "Was I wrong in interrupting such a cozy family meal?"

"Come on, Mom." Mason moved forward to pick up the article. "Don't be snide because you weren't invited. If you were ever around, I'm sure we would've *thought* about inviting you."

Logan snorted.

Helen sighed. "I'm having déjà vu. Aren't we missing a few people?" She glanced to Nate and added, "And we've picked up a few new ones too." Her eyes fell on Malinda. "Were you at the first meeting? When we learned how sexually active Mason and Samantha had become?"

Logan's head tipped back. "I can't. I can't keep quiet." He shook his head, letting out a dreamy sigh. "Fond memories. We all bonded together over our hatred for Analise." He glared at Helen and drawled, "Sorry, Mother, but apparently hell's frozen and you're now taking the Anabitch's place." His tone cooled. "Stop being a *bitch*."

"Okay, okay." Garrett held his hands up and moved into the middle of the room. "There are issues that need to be addressed, I agree, but—" He pointed to the article in Mason's hands. "Can we brainstorm on how to get that pulled? It'll be very bad if that article comes out."

"You can't." Helen shook her head. "I got an early copy out of consideration because my friend works with the magazine."

Mason finished reading and handed it to me. His jaw clenched, but that was his only reaction. "Who's your friend?" he asked.

Helen paused.

"Answer the question, Mom." Logan growled.

She flicked an annoyed look his way. "You're nicer when you're not around these two."

"I'm nicer when you're not a bitch."

She sucked in an angry breath. "My God, can you be more disrespectful?"

Logan started laughing again, and I read enough to feel my heart sink. Everything was there. Everything that had happened this summer.

I stood, fed up with the mudslinging. "*Stop!*" I couldn't read it. I'd vomit if I did, and threw the article on the floor. "Your friend told you about the article. You're in the best position to fix this. Why are you here?"

"What?" Her eyes narrowed.

I stepped toward her, folding my arms over my chest too. I lowered my voice to the same cruel level as hers.

"This is something you could've fixed. If you have the pull to get an early copy, you could've flown to your friend instead of here. You knew about this days ago. You would've had to get the story, book a flight from Europe, and have the foresight to text Taylor and not your actual sons. Did you even text Logan, like you told Taylor you did?"

"No," Logan answered. "I checked. There were no messages from her."

"Am I blocked?"

"No, Mom," he shot back. "Why the fuck would I block you? You just took my girlfriend and me to Paris. We were on good terms until this."

"Why are you blaming me?" Her question was directed to Logan and me. "I'm the one bringing this problem to you."

Logan was about to say something, but I spoke first. "Because you're the parent. No matter James' faults, he would've handled this before even bringing it to Mason's attention. My mother too."

The last was meant as a jab, and Helen closed her eyes. She shuddered briefly as it made contact. When she looked at me again, the loathing had gone up a notch. "I hate that my son is infatuated with you. It's because of you that all this is happeni—"

"SHUT UP!" Mason burst out.

He lunged forward, and everyone jumped at his quickness, but he only took my arm with a gentle touch and pulled me behind him. Logan moved forward so both were shielding me.

"You hate Samantha because she's Analise's daughter. That's the only reason. Get over it." His words were calm, but there was rage in them. They sent shivers down my spine, making him seem almost deadly, even though I knew he'd never touch his mother. "I'm going to spell it out once and for all. If you don't get right with Sam, you and I are done."

"Me too, Helen," Logan added.

I couldn't see her, but I heard her sharp intake of breath.

"I don't give a shit if you like Taylor," Logan continued. "You better love my sister, or we're done. And don't think you can go around my back to have a relationship with Taylor. She's loyal to Sam."

Garrett cleared his throat. "Look around, Helen." There was a firmness in his voice too. "Everyone in this room is loyal to Samantha, who is *my* daughter."

"She's my daughter too." Malinda stood, sounding like she was fighting back tears.

Nate was next. "Sam is family to me. I know you don't care about my opinion, but I wanted to offer it."

Then David cleared his throat.

I held my breath. That man raised me. He put up with Analise's cheating. He knew I wasn't his by blood, but he stayed anyway. He didn't want to risk losing me. He didn't speak a lot, but when he did, his words meant something. I was already trembling, and I leaned forward, resting my head against Mason's back. His hand swept back to touch mine. Our fingers intertwined together, and then I heard my father speak.

"I've held some sympathy for you in my heart because even though Analise didn't directly affect your marriage, I know she had a part. I also know she's the woman who has kept your ex-husband faithful when you couldn't."

Helen expelled a shuddering breath.

"I know I don't talk often, and I can't have any voice on your relationship with your sons, but I stand with everyone in this room," David continued. "It's time you stop tearing into my daughter. She was not the one who tore apart your family, and she's not the one who continues to keep it apart. That's you. You're the adult, and you have to take the first step toward mending your relationships with your sons. Even if Samantha were like Analise, which she is not, the responsibility would still fall on your shoulders. You're the mother. Not her. You're the top of the family hierarchy, you and James. When you continue to put your sons above you on that line and expect them to model unconditional love and support, that never works. You're cheating your sons out of being your sons. Malinda has been remarkable in modeling the kind of unconditional love and support a parent should. I think you would love my daughter very much, if you would allow yourself to be humbled. You can learn from a child, but it always starts with the parent. Be a mother. Stop being the scorned wife."

I couldn't stop shaking.

Mason felt me. I was pushed up completely against him. As if sensing that I didn't want anyone to see me like this, Logan shifted to further block me from view. Nate came to Mason's other side, acting as a third shield.

I drew in mouthfuls of air, and I tried to think calming thoughts. None of it worked. I was falling apart inside, and I didn't know why.

Mason glanced back at me. "Can we have the room for a moment? Just Nate, Logan, Sam, and me?"

"What?" Helen started.

"Please. Give us a moment."

"We have to still talk about the arti—"

"Mom!" Mason spoke over her. "Give us the goddamn room. For a minute."

Nate and Logan didn't say a word. They didn't move a muscle either. As soon as the last adult was gone and the door shut, Mason turned swiftly and held me in his arms. "What's wrong?"

I couldn't speak. I shook my head and lifted my arms and legs around him. I just wanted him to hold me. I just wanted him to soothe me.

He cradled me in his arms like a child as he sat on the couch. He kept rubbing a hand down my hair, arm, and back, then he'd circle up and repeat.

We stayed like that for a long while. After ten minutes, as Logan and Nate both sat waiting in silence, Logan said, "She's used to only being supported by you and me. Even Nate wasn't supportive in the beginning, and now everyone stood for her, not against her."

God.

The trembling started again.

I was being such a baby.

"Sam?" Mason pulled back to see me. The entire front of his shirt was wet from my tears. "Is that what it is?"

I shook my head. "I have no idea." I could barely talk. "I've been feeling like this since the beginning of summer. I've just felt something wrong with me. It got better when we came back and I started running, but your mom being here, and hearing my dad talk—" My voice trembled. "I don't know why I'm reacting like this. I wish I did."

Mason nodded, bringing me back to his chest. "It's okay. Whatever it is, we'll be fine." I felt his words floating over my head to Logan and Nate as he repeated, "We'll all be fine."

"Sam, can we talk about the article?" Logan asked. "Is that okay?"

I nodded against Mason's chest. I wanted to participate, and I was trying to get there. The shaking had almost completely subsided. I still needed some time, just a little. Mason's hand kept caressing my side.

I needed a bit more of that too.

I turned my head so I could see Logan when he pointed to the article. "What do we do about that? We all know Helen's not going to do shit."

"Everything is in there from this summer." Mason's chest rumbled under my head as he spoke. "It was the Quinns. I'm sure of it. I bet if we ask Garrett, he'll say Adam's dad's trial is starting. They did this to throw blame my way instead of his."

"You look like a wealthy, privileged boy getting off when you shouldn't," Nate added, nodding.

"Pretty much."

"This will end your football career."

Mason let out a silent breath. I felt his chest lift and fall under my head. He agreed with Logan. "Probably, especially with our history in school."

Nate held up a hand. "Can we spin it? My parents are always saying stuff like that with scenes in movies. Maybe we can do that here. You go out before this gets out. You tell everyone about your past, and about this summer, and you show the correct footage from that day at the carnival. We have shit on Quinn Jr. I say use it."

Logan leaned forward with his elbows on his knees. "It's risky. That's what it is."

Then a thought occurred to me, but it was one I didn't like. I didn't like attention. When it came, I'd been taught that it was usually negative, and this—this would be the spotlight of all spotlights.

But . . .

I pushed down the fear. It was a big, fat lump that formed in the bottom of my throat. It was always there. It was always waiting for bad stuff to happen. Even though I'd gotten some good things lately, a part of me was always tense, waiting for the other shoe to drop.

This time, I decided.

I sat up from Mason's arms. "Use me."

"What?"

"Use my story. I wasn't always wealthy and privileged. I came from a family that barely held its head above water. My dad was the only breadwinner, on a high school teacher and coach's salary. My mom suffered mental illness all her life. She went to a treatment facility for two years, and you guys gave me back a family. Use me. I'm the underdog." I cracked a grin. "Who doesn't root for an underdog?"

Logan's grin had been spreading as I spoke, and it stretched from ear to ear as I finished.

He snapped his fingers. "And an underdog who's going to the fucking Olympics one day."

"Exactly."

I ignored my ice-cold panic.

CHAPTER TWENTY-SEVEN
MASON

It wasn't right to use Samantha.

She'd already made the decision to sacrifice herself. The hope was to champion her as the underdog, and people would like me for 'saving' her. Maybe it would work. Or maybe it wouldn't, and it would backfire completely. But I knew it didn't feel right. I didn't want to use the woman I loved. People would either like me or they wouldn't, it didn't matter to me.

And the truth wasn't that I saved Sam.

Still, we made the decision to come out with our story before the article, and we all went home. Logan, Taylor, and Nate came to the house with Sam and me. We stayed up till early morning, just drinking and sharing stories. I don't know why. It seemed like we were kind of memorializing my life or something. If this didn't work, I'd still live, but a part of my dream would be dead. Our lives would definitely change. I didn't know how. No one did, but we all felt it.

I held Sam on my lap, drank whiskey with my brother, and laughed with my best friend. This was my family, and as they talked about how this was going to be Sam's official ascent into the public eye, I was doing what I always did.

I planned ahead.

I thought ahead.

I calculated, and I tried—I really did—to imagine using my girlfriend as a crutch to explain why I'd done all the shitty things in my life. But every time I went down that path, the same decision came to me.

There was no fucking way.

I loved this woman.

Sam was livid with the world when I first saw her. She had a stone-cold exterior, but I saw the fire inside, and I was drawn to her even that first night at the gas station. She looked at me, dead in the eyes, and I felt her message. A solid *fuck you*. I'd wanted her then. I wanted to take her, bend her over, and stick myself so far in she'd never feel another guy. The primal part of me had just wanted to claim her as mine, and I usually never gave two shits about that stuff.

I liked sex. It was what it was. It was a pastime for me, but I answered to no girl.

That changed the second I saw Sam's *fuck you* attitude, when she looked at me and never looked away. She challenged me without knowing it. I knew then that Logan would want her, but no way. This one was mine. I felt her inside of me. I didn't like that part of it. No one got in there, only Logan. But she'd gotten in, and she continued to get in deeper over the next weeks. I couldn't get her out.

I tried.

God, did I try.

I tried to ignore her.

I tried to intimidate her.

I tried to fuck her out of my mind.

I tried everything except bullying her—I couldn't do that.

I was an asshole, still am one. Bullying was not beneath me. If someone came at me, or came at someone I loved, I did what I had to do. I fought people. I fucked other girls. I didn't give a damned thought or care about who someone was. I hated adults. That was why Nate's parents took him away. They didn't want me rubbing off on him, and I'd begun to.

I was not a good guy, nor am I one now.

I am the bad guy. I'm the asshole.

Sam is the one who saved me.

The only part of me that was good was her. She curbed my anger. She taught me how to love. She made me want to be a better version of me, but I only went so far. Even now, I wanted to fuck people up. I wanted to hunt down Adam Quinn, and I wanted to beat the shit out of him until he was in the hospital. I didn't give a shit how much damage I inflicted. I wanted it. I almost needed it sometimes.

And my brother, I'd condemned him. I'd made him what he was today. Like at dinner when he needed someone to take his anger out on? I did that. I put that hatred and darkness in him. Logan lived for the fight. I used it to extract my demons, but not him. I raised him in that world of hatred, loathing, and violence. He's addicted to it. I could walk away. He can't. That'll always be a problem in his life, and it's my fault.

I couldn't let anything else be my fault.

As they talked about my speech for the press conference, I already knew. I wasn't going to let anything fall on them. Not even Nate, who wanted me to talk about how he'd joined the fraternity and how Sebastian became our enemy for two years.

This was me, all me. And this was probably the last time I'd make a decision for the group without consulting them. I was their leader, at least for one more day. I might not be after this, but it didn't matter.

My life.

My history.

My faults.

My problem to fix.

———⌐——

"Are you ready?" Coach Broozer clasped a hand on my shoulder.

The next afternoon we stood outside the room where we did interviews for the team sometimes, and it was filled with press. I realized it was probably my last interview in there too. I could hear the telltale sounds like I always did after a game, but this time the reporters didn't know the reason for the conference. They didn't have questions prepared for me. I was the one to prepare them.

"Okay." Coach opened the door and eased back out. Lights and voices filled the hallway before he shut the door again. "They're all here." He looked at me. "Are you sure you want to do this?"

I nodded. I had no other choice.

Coach took a deep breath. The nerves were getting to him. He kept squinting—that's what he did when he was agitated about something.

"I'm going to do everything possible to keep you on the team," he said. "You might have to do some suspensions, but I'm still going to try."

It wouldn't matter. If that happened, no NFL team would touch me. This was the only card I had to play, if I even wanted to attempt to stay in the game. I knew the odds. They weren't good. I was just hoping for hope right now. That was all.

"I'm ready."

"Okay."

Coach reached for the door, but I heard a slight hitch in his voice. That wasn't normal. He never showed emotion, and hearing that now, I hung my head.

"Mason." Broozer touched my shoulder, holding me back. "Are you sur—"

"I'm sure, Coach."

"No, I meant, are you sure you don't want Logan or your girlfriend here? I understand that you're trying to spare them in some way, but if Taylor were going through something like this, I'd want to be there for her."

"That's your daughter. You're being a good dad."

"She's family. They're your family."

Maybe. Maybe I should've told them when it was happening. They were at home, expecting me to come back after talking everything out with the coaches, and then we'd call a press conference later tonight. But when I left the house, I knew it wasn't going down that way. I told the coaches and asked them right then and there to call the media. I wanted it done before Logan and Sam had any idea.

Coach was still waiting, ready to open the door, and I said again, "I'm ready."

We stepped out, and the room grew quiet. The flashing lights remained constant. The press room was usually hot and stuffy, but not this time. A cool breeze swept through the room like someone had propped the door open, or maybe it was just me. Maybe this time I wasn't hot and sweaty from a game.

It didn't matter. None of that did.

I'd expected to be alone when I walked out here. I wasn't. Both coaches sat beside me. They didn't say anything. This was all me, but it meant something that they were there. It meant a lot, and I was man enough to wish that either of these guys had been my father. Maybe then I wouldn't have been in this position. But that wasn't right. Maybe I wouldn't have had Sam if that was the case, and if there were a choice between her and anything else, I would always choose Sam.

She was the only direction that made sense to me.

"What's this about, Coach?"

It was go time.

The reporters jostled to get their mics closer.

Coach pointed to me. "Mason asked you guys to be here. This is his show, and no matter what you hear, I ask you to remain respectful." He glanced to me.

That was my cue.

I looked at the room, but I didn't speak right away. This was the end of one part of my life. Emotions surged up in me, and I stomped them down. My problem. My mess to clean up.

"Mason?" It was the same reporter who asked the first question. He had a friendship with Coach, and as he'd softened his tone a bit, I had a hunch he already knew what this was about.

This reporter, he was being cautious right now, but he'd called me by my first name. He acted like we were friends. I didn't even know the guy, and I looked over the rest of them. They were all the same. They'd been like this since I came to Cain U. They called me by my first name. They gave me friendly smiles, joked like we were all pals. Then they'd go back and write whatever kind of article suited their magazine. Some were scathing, some were reluctantly respectful, and yeah, sometimes they were nice articles.

Okay. Fine. They wanted to act like we were friends, then I was going to make them my friends right now. Or I was going to try.

I cleared my throat and leaned toward the mic on the table.

"Tomorrow, a magazine is going to print a story that says I was given special privileges because of my athletic ability and because of my father's wealth."

An interested buzz started to filter through the room. Any dull or glazed eyes sharpened now. Almost as one, everyone moved a little closer.

"I wanted to come out before the article appears and tell you what part of it isn't true." I paused. The one reporter's frown deepened. "And I wanted to tell you what parts of it are true."

Both my coaches turned to me.

Broozer hissed under his breath, "Mason!"

The mic caught it, and the room shifted once again. An underlying seriousness filled the air. This was a real story, and as I watched, one by one, they drew out their notepads.

"Mason." That first reporter again. "What exactly will be in that article?"

"My father is James Kade," I told him. "He owns and runs a multimillion dollar company, and he has a lot of off-shoot companies. I interned for him this summer. I was placed on a joint project with a guy named Adam Quinn, Steven Quinn's son. My father wanted me to get close to Adam to see if I could find out anything illegal his father was doing."

I was about to confess to corporate espionage. This was one charge I'd be found guilty of, but I had no choice.

"I didn't find anything, at first. And I didn't get close to Adam. I don't like the guy, never have, but I did go to his family's cabin, and I found files on a computer there."

"Were you invited in?"

"What?" I frowned at a different reporter. He had his pen ready and poised against his notepad.

He asked again, "Did you break in?"

"No. It was unlocked."

"Did anyone mention the cabin to you?"

I wasn't following his line of questioning. "Yeah." I overheard it, but I did remember a time Adam brought it up in conversation with me.

"Did they maybe suggest spending time there at one point?"

Did they?

"Did they?" Broozer asked, giving me a meaningful look.

"Uh . . ." I rubbed my throat. "Yeah, I think Becky and Adam both suggested it at one point." I couldn't remember.

"So maybe you got confused? Maybe you went there and just wanted to check your email or something?"

He was giving me an alternate storyline. I could only sit there, dumbfounded. I didn't even know this guy, and he was throwing me a line.

"Uh . . ." I dipped my head back to the microphone. "Maybe. I'd have to ask my lawyers about that."

A smattering of laughter rippled through the room.

I kept going. I had to. "I found emails that showed he illegally paid off officials for permits. Steven Quinn was also paying one of my father's employees to harass and threaten my girlfriend at the time. When this was taken to the police, Adam retaliated against me by showing a video to the police where I protected my girlfriend. The video was edited to make it look like I was assaulting a guy. I was picked up by the cops, but I wasn't officially charged. They held me over the weekend, and during that time, Adam Quinn's fiancée gave the full video to my girlfriend. It showed that the guy was about to hit her. She took it to the police, and I was released. No charges were brought against me."

"That's it? That's what that article is going to say?"

My throat started to burn. "No. The magazine is going to say that the coaching staff was notified of this incident, and they should've done an investigation. They did not do that."

"You were never charged."

"What?" We all turned to the first reporter.

He lowered his notepad. "They can't do an investigation if you were wrongfully picked up by your local police. It seems to me they did the right thing."

I frowned. What? But . . .

The reporter asked, "Who do you think leaked the information for the article to this magazine?"

"The Quinns."

"Why?"

"Because they blame me for Steven Quinn's arrest, and my guess is they're trying to distract attention from his own case."

"What facts do you have for this claim against them?"

"Adam Quinn always wanted my girlfriend in high school. I told him to fu—screw off on more than a few occasions."

A few reporters cracked grins.

"Anything else?" The same reporter looked like he was getting at something, like he already knew.

"The guy the Quinns paid to harass my girlfriend attacked my best friend, my brother, and me with fifteen guys."

The buzz started to grow. People began getting out phones and texting.

"Any other run-ins?"

"He and ten of his friends attacked me and my girlfriend at an event in Roussou, California." I paused. This guy *did* know. He was leading me there. I leaned down again into the microphone. "And Adam Quinn broke into my house here in Cain."

All the heads snapped back up.

"Can you say that again?"

"Adam Quinn broke into my home two weeks ago. My girlfriend and I were the only ones home. The police came and caught him."

"Did they arrest him?"

"No. I didn't press charges."

"Why not?"

"Because I knew he wouldn't be honest about why he was really there if I did. After they left, he confessed that he wasn't there to steal anything. He was looking for my computer because he wanted to load a virus onto it so he could monitor my email, and everything else I had on there."

"Why did he want to do this?"

"He said he wanted to make my life hell." I waited a beat. "His fiancée broke up with him after he tried to get me arrested for assault and battery. He blames me for his dad, and he blames me for his broken engagement."

"You said there was bad blood between you two in high school? That was over your girlfriend?"

"Yes. He wanted her. She chose me."

The second reporter, the one who'd led me toward a different storyline about how I got on the Quinns' computer raised his hand. "Is there anything else you want to tell us today, Mason?"

I didn't even have to ask myself. I said without hesitation, "I'm not a nice guy. I have a history of fighting and protecting people I love. I called you guys because I wanted to come clean about that, and I wanted to share my side before you read all about how I'm privileged and wealthy and another prick who got off easy. That's not my life. That's not who I am—"

"Your father is a multimillionaire, correct?" It was the first reporter again.

I nodded.

"Yet you and your brother chose to attend *public* high school when you could've chosen a private academy in your town?"

"Yes."

"Your best friend's brake lines were severed because of a high school rivalry, correct?"

"He was in a car crash because of that."

"Your girlfriend was hospitalized because she was jumped in your high school's bathroom. That's right?"

I nodded. Where was he going with this?

"Did you do anything against anyone in high school or since you've attended Cain University?"

"Yes."

His eyes widened.

"But only to protect people I love."

"Did you set out to hurt this Adam Quinn?"

"No."

The first reporter glanced around the room. They all seemed to be following his lead. He shrugged. "I guess I only have one other question. You stated before that your girlfriend was your 'girlfriend at the time.' Why is that? Did you two break up?"

Oh. Fuck. *Forgive me, Sam.*

But I couldn't lie, not about this, not about something I was proud of.

"No. She's my fiancée now."

CHAPTER TWENTY-EIGHT

SAMANTHA

An hour earlier.

"Sam."

I was lacing up my sneakers. Mason had gone to tell his coaches what was going on. We'd slept super late, and half the day was gone already. I wanted to get a run in before he called to let us know their plan. I looked up from the back patio when Logan said my name, opening the back door. My heart sank at the look on his face.

"What is it?" My hands were suddenly clammy. I rubbed them down my running pants and stood.

He gestured behind him. "Just come in. You need to see this. It's on the university's cable channel."

I think I knew even before I stepped inside.

Mason had been calm when he left, too calm. He'd been like that all night too, and the way he'd made love to me last night—I suppressed a shiver, one of the good kinds. He'd been tender, loving, giving. He'd worshiped my body, and then he'd taken us both on an almost-frenzied ride. It had been exhilarating, but now I knew why.

I heard his voice from the television in the living room. " . . . My father is James Kade. He owns and runs a multimillion—"

Logan growled behind me, his arms crossed over his chest and his jaw clenching. "This is fucked up. He went alone."

"Did you expect anything different?"

Nate came down the stairs. He wasn't shocked like me, or furious like Logan. He was resigned, and a hint of fondness played over his features. He ran a hand over his face, then held it out toward the television. "This is what he does, Logan. You know that."

"This was all of our decision."

"No." Nate shook his head. His voice was so calm, so understanding. "This is his career, his life. It was his decision. It was never really ours."

"Nate—" Logan whirled to him, his eyes blazing. He took a step like he was going to hit him. He stopped, and his jaw clenched again. "Shut up."

"No." Nate was firm. He stepped in front of the television. He raised a finger in the air. "You need to give him this space."

"This affects all of us."

"It affects him the most," Nate shot back. His eyes blazed right back at Logan, just not as much. He wasn't as angry. "He won't name us. He won't put any of us in danger, and you know it. He's taking the whole blame. I don't even need to hear it to know I'm right."

Mason's voice filled the silence in the room. " . . . I found statements on the computer there that showed a discrepancy, and it also showed—"

"You see that?" Nate turned and looked at the television. "I. He's saying *I*. He's not saying *we* or my name, your name. If you're going to be angry, at least be angry for the real reason."

Logan had grown silent, but flicked his eyes to Nate.

"You're mad because he shut you out," Nate murmured, almost too quietly for us to hear. He rubbed the back of his neck, grimacing. "But that's his way of protecting you, and you know it."

Logan remained silent, his chest rising and falling as he breathed.

I sank down on one of the couches, placing my hands in front of my mouth. I couldn't listen, but I couldn't leave. He was doing this all on his own. My stomach twisted. He must've been so scared, but Nate was right. He was protecting us in his way.

I focused for a moment and finally realized the two reporters were helping him. They were flipping his story into something else, something where he was the victim, where Adam and his father were the bad guys.

Good! A part of me growled.

"You were never charged," a reporter said to Mason.

Mason frowned at him. "What?"

The reporter's voice sounded from behind the camera, "They can't do an investigation if you were wrongfully picked up by your local police. It seems to me they did the right thing."

Logan swore, sitting in the chair closest to the television. "They're helping him."

"That's my fault."

I closed my eyes. I knew Taylor's voice, and it all started to make sense. She was wringing her hands together when I looked at her.

She flashed an apologetic smile. "I couldn't not say anything."

She turned to Logan, but I knew what she was going to say.

"You disappeared last night after we got here," I said. "You called your dad, didn't you?"

She jerked her head in an unsteady nod. "I had to."

Logan was quiet again. She kept skirting her gaze to him, then back to me.

"This isn't the first time an athlete has been in trouble," she said. "My dad knows guys. They can pull some strings and get favors. I had to let him know ahead of time. He needed a chance to see if he could help. Mason deserved that."

Logan pointed to the screen. "It's working."

She nodded, sitting down across from him. She was on the edge of her seat, her hands pressed together on her knees. "Are you mad at me?"

His eyes softened. "No, baby. Never."

She sighed, her shoulders relaxing.

One of the reporters was speaking again. "Did they arrest him?"

Taylor nodded toward the television. "That reporter and the other one you guys heard talking, those are heavy-hitter sports reporters. They've always tried to help my dad, if they can. Sometimes they can, sometimes they can't, but they're going over and above in this press conference. My guess is that they don't like Steven Quinn for some reason." She lifted a shoulder. "Or they just really like Mason."

We all looked at each other.

"Nah." That came from Nate.

Logan shook his head. "No way. Who likes Mason?"

I only laughed, content to hear the jokes from them. My stomach had stopped twisting, and the press conference seemed to be coming to an end. I stood. I needed to be there for Mason now, and I moved to grab a sweatshirt and my purse when I heard, ". . . You stated before that your girlfriend was your 'girlfriend at the time.' Why is that? Did you two break up?"

No.

I froze, my hand in mid-air, and then I heard Mason answer, almost too quickly.

"—she's my fiancée now."

I gulped.

He hadn't.

He had.

I turned swiftly. Everyone in the room stared at me with varying expressions of surprise. Nate's eyes were wide, Taylor had the beginning of a smile, and Logan—he was the one I was most afraid to look at—his eyes were hooded, his face unreadable.

I started for him. "Logan."

He held up a hand, stopping me in my tracks. He didn't say a word, just stood and walked outside.

Taylor stood too. Her eyebrows pulled together. "Sam, I—"

"Go after him." I stepped back.

She rushed past me, but squeezed my arm on the way and whispered, "Congratulations!" Then she was gone, slamming the door behind her.

It was just Nate and me.

His hand moved from his neck to the side of his face. He held it there a second before letting it fall. Then he lifted his arms. "Congratulations, Sam. Come here."

I stepped into his hug, but I was tense. He was tense. Logan was pissed, and I needed to get to Mason's side.

I hugged him, though. "Thank you, Nate."

He squeezed me once more before letting me go. "Logan's just hurt. You know that."

I nodded. "Doesn't make it hurt less."

I started for the door, but Nate said my name again, and I looked over.

"You know we're going to have an epic party now, don't you?" He gave me a half-grin.

I felt myself smile, but my stomach twisted back up. "First things first."

"Right." He pointed to the door. "Go be with your man. Oh, hey—"

I paused once more.

"He doesn't lie about you," Nate said. "You're something in his life that he is beyond proud of. He never wants to make you feel that he isn't. That's why he said it."

My smile grew sad, but I still felt a flutter in my chest.

"I know." Then I left.

———⌐

Mason was shaking hands with two men when I got there.

His coaches were next to them, and I overheard one of the men saying, "There are a lot of ways we could've spun your story, but we're not idiots. All of us, or most of us, have covered Steven Quinn. The guy's a prick. Finding out he hired someone to attack and harass you? Not shocking to us. Trust me. I think you'll be shocked at the reception you'll get after our articles come out. I wouldn't be surprised if the article retracts and issues an apology."

The guy who'd been speaking clasped a hand on Mason's head coach's arm. "It's been real, Hank. Thanks for the heads-up."

He and the second guy took off.

Mason said to his coach, "You knew?"

"Taylor called me as soon as Logan told her. You're going to be family one day, Mason. And the truth was on your side this time. You and your brother might do asinine things, but this time you didn't. You really were just protecting your loved ones."

Broozer glanced over, saw me, and nodded in my direction. "And I hear congratulations are in order. Congratulations, Samantha. I know Taylor's really grown fond of you."

He held his hand out, and I shook it, feeling dazed.

He patted Mason on the shoulder. "I can't say anything official to you, but if you still want a career in the NFL, I'm pretty sure it'll be there waiting."

Mason let out a breath. "Thank you." He looked to his other coach. "Thank you both."

"This is part of our job. We don't like to let our kids hang out to dry. We'll protect you as much as we can, every goddamn time."

They left, and Mason turned to me. His eyes were haunted, and he seemed to brace himself. "I couldn't lie. Not about you. I can never lie about you."

But I knew a time he had lied about me. He'd sent another girl to take the assault that should've been for me. He was protecting me then, like he was protecting me now.

I nodded. "I know. We can talk about it later."

I rested a hand on the side of his face, and he leaned into it, his eyes closing for a moment.

My throat grew thick. "How are you?"

He pulled me in for a hug and held me so tightly. He buried his face in my neck. "Better. I'm so much better."

I hugged him back, just as tight, and we stayed like that for a long time.

CHAPTER TWENTY-NINE

"So, how pissed is Logan?" Mason asked.

We'd gone back to our spot, and we were once again submerged in the pool underneath the butterfly statue. Mason treaded water in front of me while I sat on the edge, dipping my legs.

"He was hurt that you did the press conference without us, but Nate took up for you, and Logan got over it." I looked away, feeling a knot in my chest. "Then you announced our engagement. He left after that."

He cursed under his breath and narrowed his eyes at me. "Why aren't you mad?"

"Nate reminded me that you said it because you're proud of me, and that you probably couldn't lie about me." I wasn't mad, but I was hurt. That was what I was.

"Oh." He was moving his arms under the water in small circles, and he looked down at them now. "But you're hurt, aren't you?"

My shoulders sagged. Why did I even try to keep something from him? He looked back up to me, and I let him see the truth.

"Yeah."

"I'm sorry."

I lifted a shoulder, holding it pressed against my cheek. "It is what it is. We can't go backwards now."

"Meaning?" He swam closer to me, his hands resting on my legs.

"I am hurt."

His hands dropped from my legs, and he flinched, but he kept looking at me. He didn't drop his gaze.

"That was our news to announce together, and you said you were going to ask again." He had to know the truth.

His voice grew hoarse. "That's what you want? You still want me to ask again?"

I nodded. "With the ring, and I want it to be romantic again."

He watched me, studying, and I saw a lingering question lurking in his depths.

"You'll be ready this time?"

Was I ready? I had to look down. My insides trembled.

"I'm scared."

He looked back down to the water.

I saw how his shoulders went rigid, and just like that, I knew my fears were garbage. That's all they were. Just excess trash I needed to expunge. I slid into the water, and Mason's head lifted in surprise as I wrapped my legs around his waist. He was going to give me space. I knew it instinctively, and I didn't want it right now. So I went to him before he could move away. I could feel him right between my legs, where he always belonged, and I wrapped my arm around his shoulder. He caught me, holding me in place, and I drew my fingers through his hair. Our faces were inches apart.

"You can't lie about me? I can't lie to you." I brushed my lips over his. "I don't know how it might happen, but I'm scared. I couldn't handle losing you."

"Sam," Mason whispered, raising one of his hands to cup the side of my face. His thumb rubbed over my cheek. "You might've seen your mother at her worst, but you also watched David. He stayed. He held on because he loved you. She left him, but he never left her."

"But he did. One time."

Mason cursed again, his lips falling to my shoulder. He lightly nipped me there, tightening his hold around my back. "I'm sorry. I forgot the time she . . ."

Killed her babies.

He couldn't say it. Neither could I.

I rested my head on his shoulder and hugged him. I didn't know what the future would hold. I was sure there'd be challenges, but I was sure there'd be good times as well. There was a layer of strength and belief in us, but underneath it, I couldn't deny there was a layer of fear.

I felt tears forming, and before they shed, I whispered, "Let's get married now."

"What?" He pulled back to gaze down at me.

Those tears fell. "Let's do it now. Before—"

Before it was too late. Before we built walls around our hearts, because that was what my mother taught me to do.

I finally figured it out, and the realization spread through me at breakneck speed. I guarded myself. At first it was against her, but it'd be against Mason eventually. It was part of my DNA, a part of me. I wouldn't know I was doing it until it was too late.

That couldn't happen. I couldn't safeguard myself against him.

My fingers gripped his skin. "Let's go now. Let's do it before we fuck up and something horrible happens."

"Sam."

He was going to say no. He was going to say everything would be all right. He was going to say all the right things, that we'd be fine, that we loved each other, that we'd never do what our parents did. Maybe he was right, but I still felt there would be a time when neither of us would realize what was happening. Something would put us on opposite sides of each other, and that would be the end.

"Please, Mason."

He began threading his fingers through my hair, tucking my strands behind my ear. "Do you trust me?"

I nodded. I didn't trust myself.

"If you trust me, believe me when I say that we're going to be fine. I've never done anything to hurt you. You've never hurt me. We will be fine. I promise."

My hand wrapped around his wrist where he cupped the side of my face. I clung to him, wanting to accept what he was saying, but my gut was saying otherwise. Something was going to happen. Something neither of us would foresee, and whatever it was—it was going to rip us apart.

I closed my eyes and rested my forehead to his shoulder.

"Sam." He smoothed my hair down my back. "Everything will be all right. I promise."

I trusted *him*. I was the problem.

All I murmured was, "Okay."

"Okay?" He was smiling, searching my face, and his eyes darkened. His lips found mine, resting there softly. "It'll be fine. I won't let anything happen to you or me. I promise."

Again, that word.

I was starting to hate that word, just like when Analise would promise me. She made all sorts of commitments. She failed on all of them.

But I nodded and breathed out. "Okay."

"Okay?"

I nodded again, closing my eyes. I felt his lips on mine again, and this time they didn't pull away. They held there and applied pressure. They took me away on a different journey, and when Mason slid inside of me, I moved with him, but I couldn't shake what my gut was saying.

We were on borrowed time.

CHAPTER THIRTY

MASON

Sam fell asleep on the short drive home.

I didn't have the heart to wake her, so I was carrying her inside when Logan stepped into the hallway. I held a hand up before he could start and gestured to her. I held up a finger. One minute. That's all I was asking for, and his eyes fell to Sam before he nodded. He stepped back into the living room while I slipped into the bedroom.

Sam and I had rinsed off before leaving the pool, and I'd done my thing, going back and making sure the cameras were wiped during our time slot there. When I got back, she'd had the Escalade running, the heat turned up, and was curled into a ball in the back. I knew she was asleep even before hearing her deep breathing.

And as I placed her under the covers now, she didn't even stir.

I grabbed new clothes and moved into the hallway bathroom to change before going to find Logan. I didn't want to wake her.

He'd poured himself a drink while waiting for me. I smelled the aroma of bourbon, and he waved toward the liquor cabinet with his glass. "Have at it. I'm in the mood to get ripped tonight."

Even if Sam hadn't told me, I would've known instantly. Logan was furious, more hurt than anything else.

I poured myself a glass, then turned around. "I'm sorry."

"For what, big brother?" His face showed no emotion. But his eyes were raging. "For going to self-sacrifice without me? Or asking Sam to marry you and not telling me the news?" He flung a hand toward the television. "I heard about it on the fucking TV! Like everyone else!"

"I'm sorry."

205

He grunted, sipping from his glass. "You better damn well be. You cut me out. I'm not everyone else. I'm the one who's never left your side."

"I know."

"Do you?!" he spat. "I'd tell you before I asked Taylor to marry me. Fuck. You'd be in on the planning. And if you weren't, you'd be my first phone call after she said yes." He laughed, and the sound was bitter. "You'd be my first phone call if she said no too." His eyes grew wary. "How long ago?"

"When I asked her?"

He nodded. "How long have you been engaged and you haven't told me?"

"A month."

His head tipped back. "Are you serious? A whole month."

I sat down at the table. Logan kept the lights off, which I was grateful for, and he followed me. He brought the bourbon with him, placing it on the table between us.

"She didn't say yes."

He went still, and his eyes lifted to mine. "You shitting me?"

I shook my head, finishing my glass and refilling it. I had practice in the afternoon tomorrow—or I hoped I still did—but I didn't care now. Logan was right. I should've told him right away, and admitting Sam's reluctance was like a weight off my shoulders.

I leaned back in my chair. "She's scared, and she wasn't prepared. I wasn't even prepared. I just decided that day, and I did it. I lit a bunch of those fake-candle things girls like, and I put them all around on this path Sam likes to run."

"Ah . . ." Logan mocked me, grinning. "How romantic of you."

"Shut up. You'll do something twice as romantic for Taylor, and you know it."

"Yeah," he conceded, reaching for the bourbon again. "You're right. I'll blow your proposal out of the water."

I cringed, hearing that word. I remembered holding Sam in the pool, moving inside of her. She was with me. She had felt all the sensations

I did, but she wasn't quite there. I could feel her doubt. It clung to her like a blanket sometimes, and marrying me—she was nervous. I felt a knife inside every time I admitted that to myself.

I was ready.

I could wait, but I was ready. There was no doubt for me. No fear.

I'd do anything for her, but the woman I placed on a pedestal above me wasn't sure about marrying me. She said she was, she whispered the words, but I knew she wasn't. Even though I said on television we were engaged, a part of her wasn't my fiancée at all. A part of her wanted to run from me.

I downed my glass and filled it for a third time.

"You okay?"

I looked over, hearing Logan's concern. "You still pissed at me?"

"Shit, no. Not after hearing she said no."

I nodded. It sucked. It more than sucked. It burned me raw. "Yeah."

"You want to go do something stupid? Like we did in high school?"

I glanced over. "Like what?"

But I was going. Whatever he suggested, I needed to slip back into that skin where it was him and me against the world. Everything made more sense then.

"Let's go find Adam Quinn." He grinned crookedly at me. "Let's go light his car on fire."

I grinned back at him. "Like we did with the Broudous."

This was wrong.

This was stupid.

This was something we'd do in high school.

I finished my third glass. "I'm in." I pointed the glass at him. "But just the car. Nothing else. We can't be that stupid."

He nodded. "Of course. We're never dumb."

We both cracked grins, and I said, "We need a driver."

As one person, we looked up at the ceiling. We were waking Nate within thirty seconds.

"Hey!" I shoved at his shoulder.

Logan didn't waste time. He yanked off Nate's blanket and both of us turned away, in case there was nudity.

"HEY!" Nate reared up. "I'm naked."

There was nudity.

"Yeah." I made a hurry-up motion with my hand. "We need you to drive us somewhere. Get dressed."

Logan was heading back to the hallway. He slapped a hand on Nate's wall. "Get your ass in gear, Monson. We've got a mission to fuck some shit up."

Nate growled, but we heard him moving around as we left. Logan went to change, but I was ready to go. This wasn't a smart decision, but I didn't care. I filled my glass again as I waited.

Logan's grin was wicked when he saw my fourth glass. "This is what I love." He filled his fourth too, and we went to the kitchen until Nate showed moments later. He stopped in the entryway, dressed in jeans and a black sweatshirt.

He eyed us. "Do I even want to ask?"

Logan pointed to me. "He and Sam are kind of engaged, but kind of not. She said no at first."

Nate's eyes rounded in surprise. "Really?"

I didn't want to talk about it, and I downed the rest of my drink. "Let's go."

"Where are we going?"

Logan finished his too, leaving the glass on the table. He grabbed Nate's car keys from the wall where they were hanging and hurled them to him. "You're driving. We're doing a road trip to Adam Quinn's place."

"Are you serious?"

Logan nodded, pulling his phone out. We were heading out to Nate's vehicle when someone answered his call.

"Tate!" he said. "Hey, you owe me one." He paused. "I don't give a shit what time of night it is. Where's your cousin's ex-douchebag staying these days? Call it a hunch, but I've a feeling she'll know." He waited again, then said, "Okay. Got it. Thanks, and hey." His voice turned ominous. "Don't think ahead of yourself and give someone a heads-up. Got it?"

As we got into Nate's truck, he said, "Adam's staying at the cabin to get away from the news media. Apparently, they haven't located the cabin yet."

Nate started the engine.

I looked back. "His parents?" I was sure his dad was out on bail.

Logan's grin looked a little dangerous. "Daddy dearest is in town so he can meet with his lawyers more easily. His mom is in Fallen Crest too. Adam's alone."

I'd once whispered to Adam that if he fucked with my life, with Sam, with anyone I loved, I was going to end him. I didn't know how, or when, but one day he would look around and realize no one was there to help him.

That day had come.

SAMANTHA

Something wasn't right.

I felt it even before I woke up, and when I did, I knew Mason wasn't next to me. I had no reason to know something was going on, but I did, and I acted on that instinct. I dressed, pulled my hair up into a ponytail, and went to wake Taylor. I wasn't surprised to see that Mason, Logan, and Nate were gone. I checked the kitchen, living room, outside, and Nate's room as I went up to Logan's room.

Taylor was curled over on her side, her body rising and falling in deep breaths.

"Hey." I tapped her on the shoulder. "Taylor."

She woke with a gasp, whirling over to stare at me. She clutched the blanket. "Who—Sam?" Recognition eased away her panic. She ran a hand through her hair, blinking and squinting at me. "What are you doing here?"

"Something's wrong." I couldn't explain it. "The guys are gone. I think they're going to do something bad."

"Like what?"

She hadn't been around for all those fights. She'd seen them defend her, save her from her friend's enemies, but that was it. Logan had shielded her from the dirty stuff. I wouldn't do the same. She needed to know, but for now I just shook my head.

"I don't know. It's just a feeling I have. We need to find them."

"Okay." She rose and reached for a robe, then paused as she took in my getup: jeans and a sweatshirt, all black. She let out a wary breath. "Why do I feel like I'm not going to be getting back to sleep anytime soon?"

I turned and headed for the door. "Because you're not."

I went downstairs to wait for her and pulled up a tracking app I'd put on Mason's phone. He knew about it. He wanted one on mine, so I insisted on one for his phone too. I'd also put it on Logan's phone. He just didn't know about it, or I doubted he did. He had so many apps on there.

"Where are we going?" Taylor asked as she appeared.

I held my phone up. "You drive. I'll tell you where to go."

We got into her car, and she pulled out a moment later.

I looked down at the dot on the screen that was Mason and said, "Head out of town. We're going back to Fallen Crest."

CHAPTER THIRTY-ONE
MASON

"Do we have a plan?"

Nate asked the question after we'd been on the road for three hours. First we had to go toward Fallen Crest, and then we'd been taking a county road north for the last half hour. We were getting close.

Logan leaned forward. "Besides picking a fight?"

Nate frowned. "I thought we were just going to throw some fireworks in his car or something."

Logan snorted, falling back to his seat. "Right. Because we're traveling three hours just to pop some sparklers in his car. You're kidding, right? Are you not with the program?"

"Well, you two *are* drunk."

Logan hid a grin. We'd brought the bourbon with us, though the drive was starting to sober me up. Logan rolled his eyes in the rearview mirror before shaking his head.

"What?" Nate looked at me, then Logan in the mirror. "We're not really going to do anything. We can't. Mason, you just went on television and pointed the finger at him."

"He's at the cabin," Logan said. "He's hiding."

Nate looked back to Logan in the mirror again. "And that means what?"

"You really think we're going to not do anything? He tried to frame Mason. He could've fucked his entire football career. He broke into the house. He was in your room, dude. *Your* room. He didn't actually get to Mason's, because he went to both of our rooms first. What if he planted that virus on your computer?"

Nate straightened in his seat, like he hadn't thought of it that way. His hands gripped the steering wheel. "What are you saying? You think he put that shit on my computer?"

"I was with you when you checked your room. Your computer was on. It's not password-protected. He could've."

A vein popped out of the side of Nate's neck. "Are you messing with me, Logan?"

"That's the point." Logan's tone cooled. "Quinn's not some fucking innocent, and you have to stop treating him like he is." Logan's eyes skirted to mine as he said to Nate, "And you know it."

Nate quieted for a minute, then looked to me. "Are you going to hurt him?"

I wanted to end him.

"We'll see what happens," I said.

"Which means Mason's going to wait and see what we can do without getting into trouble."

I grinned back at my brother. "It's like you know me."

He shot back an answering grin. "Only since the day I was born."

The cabin came into view, and Nate cut the lights, turning down the long driveway. He parked, still close to the highway.

"Just don't do anything that could get you arrested," he said. "Shit's different now that we have to be mature."

Logan got out and shut his door. "Mature? What's that?"

I got out next to him. "I think it's some type of STD."

Logan barked out a laugh, then tried to quiet himself. "I suppose I'd be the one to know what it is then."

Nate caught the end of the conversation as we met at the back end of his car. He skimmed Logan up and down. "You have an STD?"

"Only if it's called maturity, and I'm pretty sure I have an ointment for it."

We both started laughing.

Nate shook his head. "Mason, you need to sober up. I can't handle it when you drink like this. You're just like Logan, only quieter."

"Hey." Logan kept laughing, his shoulders shaking. "Oh, fuck. I just lost what I was going to say."

"Thank you." Nate's eyes flickered upward, then back to us. He was smiling, though. "All right, guys. I asked before, but you didn't answer. What's the plan?"

They turned to me. The jokes were done, and slowly, everything started to come back to me. I remembered Adam. I remembered all the shit he'd done to us over the years, but I especially remembered that one time at Nate's cabin. He'd been talking to Sam in a hallway, and I could see how he was moving in. He was grinning and flirting with her, and I remember how my blood went cold. Sam was mine, and I didn't want to remind him of it. I wanted to show him.

I'd set him straight, going in for the kill. *"What do you want here?"*

I asked him that, and he had pretended to be surprised. Maybe he had been. Or maybe he was surprised that I was calling him out. If he wanted Sam, he had to man up and show me he was even a worthy opponent.

He hadn't been. *"What are you talking about?"*

That had only made me more pissed. *"What do you think, dickhead? What do you want? Her?"*

I wanted it all out on the table. I wanted Sam to know who she was dealing with.

"What do you want? Yes, I want her. I want her, okay?"

I grinned now, remembering it like it happened yesterday. That's what I wanted. I had wanted him out and exposed, where he couldn't hide anymore. *"How long have you wanted her?"* I asked him then.

"Since seventh grade . . ."

I remembered Sam had started to become uncomfortable. She'd felt pity for him, but I wouldn't allow it. No. I moved so she was behind me, and I did it slowly, smoothly, almost so Adam didn't notice at first.

He tried to come back at me, saying I wanted Sam too.

Hell yes, you fucker.

Then I'd felt Sam behind me. She'd pressed her body against mine, and I felt her trembling. Her heart was beating so fast, but I knew it wasn't because she was scared. I wasn't going to let her claim that. She was trembling because of me, because I was staking my claim, because as I told Quinn she was going to be mine, I was letting her know too. And she was almost wet because of it.

Then Adam had started to squirm. I saw the hesitancy on his face. He was going to take it back.

"I'm not denying it," I had told him. *"But I'm not going to screw another girl wishing she were Sam. I'm not going to do that. You know why?"*

I went in for the kill then and turned to Sam. I had been doing this for her too. She couldn't deny me either. She couldn't hide.

I had pressed into her. My knee wedged between her legs, and I felt her throbbing. She closed her eyes, feeling what I could give her. And I had moved closer, nuzzling against her cheek. She sagged into me so I was holding her up, and then . . .

Her hands had slid up my arms, over my shoulders, and began to knead the back of my neck. Even now, my heart picked up as I remembered. I felt it all over again. I could feel her in my arms as I pressed her against the wall back then.

I had cupped her ass, and she wrapped those long, toned legs around me. She pressed against me.

She was mine, then and now.

Quinn had been there, but that moment was all mine. I lifted her from the wall. I had wanted to feel all of her weight against me.

A tremor wracked through her, and I kissed her ear, her cheek, her neck. I was whispering to her about something else, but everything had been about her.

"Mason," she had breathed out.

There. Right there, she had succumbed to me.

I turned to Quinn. *"This is why I'll never do what you have to do. I have her. I won't have to dream about her."*

And it hadn't stopped there. He'd still wanted Sam. He'd tried to be her friend, and he'd held her when she cried on his shoulder. That was the worst, when I heard how he'd been there for her, and I hadn't. That one burned deep.

"He was our first, you know," Logan said, pulling me out of my memories.

I looked over to him now. I knew what he meant.

Nate didn't. He frowned. "Huh?"

"We had our fights and rivalries, but Adam was the first one we fought for Sam. He wanted her, and he kept trying to take her from us."

From us.

From me.

We'd called a truce, but that had ended this past summer. We weren't fighting Adam for Sam anymore—but I couldn't help but wonder if we were. Did he still want her, in some deep part of himself? Had our dad's beef been an excuse for him to make one more go at her?

I started forward. "Let's go."

There was no plan, but it was time to deal with Adam.

Falling silent, Nate and Logan followed me, and we found Adam outside on the patio. He lounged on a bench with a cigar in his hand. The smoke trailed up into the air as he exhaled. He was raising the cigar to his mouth again when he saw us.

He jerked up, and his eyes became panicked as he looked out into the darkness. I could see the whites rounding, and then he scrambled to his feet.

"What are you doing here?"

There was a quiver of fear in his voice.

I moved forward. "If you were to take a guess?"

His eyes narrowed, and he began to ease toward the door. "I'm not alone, you know."

"You got some chick in there?" Logan craned his neck to see. "Because our intel says you're here all alone."

Nate added, "You're hiding."

"Yeah." Adam growled at me. "Thanks for that press conference, by the way. It really helped my dad's case."

"You're the fuckhead who broke into our house."

I was seconds from grabbing him. I tried to remember why I shouldn't. There was a voice in my head—was it Sam's? She wouldn't want me to hurt him, but he wouldn't go away. We did the right thing at our house. We let him off. We didn't hurt him, nothing. There might've been some humiliation, but he walked away from the house on two legs. And he would keep coming back.

"What am I going to do with you, Quinn?" I gave him a hard look as I stepped up on the patio.

"What are you doing?" He jumped in front of the door, still holding his cigar. He looked down at the cigar, then back to me, and put it down, laying it on the bench he'd been sitting on.

"Get out of my way."

"Mas—"

Nate and Logan jerked into action. They grabbed him, but instead of pushing him behind us, Nate opened the door, and Logan pushed him inside. I stepped through last, circling the living room. Rap music played throughout the house, but it was low, and the smell of bourbon mixed with the cigar.

"Well, looky here." Logan shoved Adam back one more time before going over to the liquor cabinet and reaching for the glass. An ugly smirk showed on his face as he picked up Adam's glass. "You celebrating something, Quinn?" He lifted the glass to his nose, took a whiff, and tossed the liquid to the floor.

"Hey!" Adam started forward, but Nate moved in front of him now, shoving him back. Adam took a breath, staring at Nate for a second before looking past him to Logan. He turned to me. "What are you going to do?"

"I made you a promise a long time ago."

Did he remember?

"I promised that if you fucked with me, Sam, or anyone I loved, I'd end you. I'd take away everything you hold close." I gestured around the room. "I'd take your home. I'd take your girl. I'd take your money. And I'd take your reputation. Then I'd leave you alone, but not before I ruined you. We've decided it's time to follow through."

Adam started to laugh. "What? What can you do to me now?"

"You're going to watch." I nodded to Logan. He knew what to do, and he took off.

"Wha—" Adam pressed against Nate. "Is he looking for something?"

"What do you think? I just told you what we're going to do. Think, Adam! Guess what we're doing." And as he frowned and pulled back from Nate, I looked to my best friend. "Mind taking one for the team? For a while anyway?"

Nate cocked his head to the side, then groaned. "Are you serious?"

He knew.

I nodded. "Sam said you liked Becky."

He groaned again, letting his head fall back. "Seriously, Mason? I don't want to date Becky Sallaway."

"What?" Adam's eyes locked on us. "What did you say?!"

He surged toward us, but Nate and I both lifted a lazy hand. We pushed him back, and he fell to a couch behind him.

I dropped my voice. "Just for a little bit. You want to date that other chick right now, anyway? This could get messy."

"Sam's going to know."

"Sam doesn't have to find out right away. And yes, Becky will know, but she's not going to care."

We turned as one toward Adam, who was shaking his head, his hands in his hair.

"I have a feeling she'll take you up on a date," I told Nate. "Maybe more than a couple times even."

"Okay." Nate pulled out his phone and dialed. "It's late, but maybe she's awake. I think Sam called her from my phone once. Let's see if she still wants to talk to us."

"Be—" Adam surged to his feet, yelling for Becky.

I rounded on him, my hand cocked, and hit him in the face. He fell back to the couch almost in the same motion as standing, like he was jerked back by the couch itself. I knocked him out.

Nate turned and grinned at me, his eyes on Adam. He ended the call. "What he doesn't know, right?"

I grunted, heading into the bedroom Adam used. Logan found me a few minutes later. I was sitting on the edge of Adam's bed.

"All the security footage is destroyed. We're covered." He nodded to the camera I had in my hand. "What's that?"

I handed it over to him. "Push *Play*."

He did, and a girl's moans came from the machine.

Logan's eyes widened. "Holy shit. Is this . . . ?" He pressed *Pause*. I stood as he zoomed in on the naked girl on Adam's bed. She was spread-eagle, her tits and everything showing as he bent over, kissing between her legs. She had a blindfold on, and her arms were handcuffed to the bedposts. "Yeah, that's Sullivan."

He didn't mean Adam's ex-girlfriend either.

"I know," I told him.

"Fuck." He went to the next video. It was Tate again, and another. He kept going. There was a new girl in the tenth video. "Isn't that—is that Miranda? No wait, it's the other chick that was in the Fallen Crest Elite group. Amelia or something?"

I took the camera back from him. "Sam told me Becky was worried about some other girls, but she couldn't find anything that showed Quinn was cheating on her."

"But her gut said otherwise?"

Always trust your gut.

"Shit." Logan shook his head. "House, rep, money, and girl. That's what you take from someone if you want to cripple him."

I scowled. I didn't want to cripple Quinn. I wanted to destroy him. "You think I'm going too far?"

He laughed. "When you say *you*, you mean *us*, right? You're not doing this alone."

"I'll take the blame."

"For what? We're not going to get blamed for this."

"Sam's going to be furious with me." Sam wanted me to stop making decisions for her. She wanted to be included on these things.

He grew somber. "We're not excluding her. We're shielding her from the bad shit we do sometimes."

He was right, but she'd still be mad. I rose, heading back into the living room after grabbing Adam's laptop. I hadn't found anything else in his room, just the camera, his computer, and some dirty magazines. I'd show Sam the camera. She could decide then.

Nate looked up from his phone. "It's been fun, but . . ." He let his sentence hang in the air, and I got his drift.

We'd come in half-drunk, but we were real sober now. Seeing Adam on his porch, stepping inside and finding the camera in his bedroom, I knew I was changing.

"You know, there was a time when I would've burned this place down," I murmured.

"We still can," Logan said.

I shook my head. "No." We were better than that. I gestured to the camera. "We have enough to destroy him. If he does anything, we release those videos. It'll destroy anything Quinn tries to build over the years."

"What videos?"

I tossed the camera over, and Nate caught it. He began looking through the videos and swore under his breath.

After a minute he handed it back over. "If you release those videos, you have to crop out the girls. Their identities have to be protected."

I nodded. They would be. "I will. I gotta show this to Sam too."

They both nodded.

A moment of silence passed as the three of us looked at each other. This was it. Nate would take the girl—or so Adam thought. I would take his reputation. The money would be worked out later. But there was one thing left.

Logan looked around the room. "So, just to be perfectly sure about this, we're not torching the house. Right? Because we could. I'd be up for that."

I laughed. "We can't."

I wanted to. The old Mason would've, and he was still inside of me, but I *had* changed. I was becoming better. Slightly.

I held up the camera. "This is enough."

"You're sure?"

I gave my brother a look. I heard the hopeful tone in his voice. I shook my head. "Apparently I have that STD called maturity too."

Logan cursed. "That's the worst of them. Such a shame." He smiled, though.

Nate laughed. "Let's get going in case Quinn tripped some alarm. You never know with him."

Adam was still unconscious, and we left him where he was. We were in the vehicle and leaving the driveway when Nate hit the brakes.

"Wha—" I looked up to see why he'd stopped.

Sam and Taylor stared back at us.

CHAPTER THIRTY-TWO

SAMANTHA

Logan leaped from Nate's car and hurried over to ours.

He flung my door open. "Let's switch. I'll go back with Taylor."

I was slow to release my seatbelt. "What did you guys do?" I asked as I stood.

"Nothing really." He cast a worried glance over my shoulder, to the road. "But we gotta go in case any alarms were tripped. It's not good if we're seen here."

He took my seat, and I jumped in next to Mason, who moved over behind Nate. Taylor reversed her car, and we pulled out after them.

I waited a few minutes before asking, "Do I want to know what happened?"

Nate's eyes flicked up and met Mason's in the rearview mirror. Mason's jaw clenched, but he handed over a camera from on the floor by his seat. "You can see for yourself."

The first video disgusted me.

The second had my stomach churning, but the third actually made me retch. I grabbed for the door handle, but Mason was there. He caught my hands and pulled me back to his chest.

"Hey, hey," he soothed. "It's okay."

The vomit was still coming. I shook my head. I couldn't say anything to alert him.

He stuck a bag in front of me, and I let loose.

I saw enough to know there were more girls on the camera, but it was the video of Becky that sent me over the edge.

As I threw up more, Mason ran a comforting hand down my back. He'd picked up the camera and was clicking through the ones I'd looked at when I heard him say, "Oh, man."

"What?" Nate asked.

I looked up, feeling all sorts of disgusting.

Mason looked at me first, his eyes clouded. "I didn't know. I didn't see that one."

I closed my eyes and leaned back against him. His hand curved around me as he spoke over my shoulder. "I didn't look through all of the videos. There was one . . ." I felt him turn to me, though I still didn't look. "It was Becky."

"Oh." Nate quieted. "Shit."

"I'm sorry, Sam," Mason added.

I shook my head, but my stomach was better. It was empty now, and I tied the ends of the bag together. "We should drop this off somewhere."

Nate nodded, and he pulled into a gas station not long after that. I went inside to clean up a little, buying some toothpaste and a toothbrush. Taylor came in as I was finishing in the bathroom.

She ran a hand through her hair, looking harried. "Are you okay?"

I didn't want to tell her about Becky.

I didn't even want to tell her about the videos.

She knew Becky and Adam from the summer, though not like I did. Maybe it was ridiculous, but I wanted to protect her a little bit.

I just nodded, rasping out, "I got carsick."

"You get carsick a lot?"

"No. Hopefully it was just a one-time deal." I tried to smile, but I knew it didn't meet my eyes, and Taylor didn't look convinced.

She bit her lip and followed me back outside. Logan was jumping around Nate, while Mason lounged against Nate's vehicle. All turned toward us as we crossed the gas station to them.

Logan stopped jumping, a shadow coming to his face. "You okay, Sam?" He glanced to Mason, the unspoken question there of what happened.

Mason nodded.

Logan's whole demeanor shifted to pity. "Ah. I'm sorry, Sam."

I pressed a hand to my stomach. "Me too. Getting carsick sucks." I held his gaze, wondering if he'd get my unspoken message.

"Yeah." He nodded. "Carsickness sucks ass."

Mason smiled. "Let's get back. I think I went right from being sober to being hung over. I need to sleep a little."

It was nearing six in the morning when we staggered inside. No one spoke as we ventured to our own rooms, but the sleep would be short-lived. Tomorrow / this morning was our first day of classes. Worst timing ever.

Once we were in our bedroom, I gazed up, my hands resting against Mason's chest. "I'm tired."

"I know." His hand cupped the side of my face, and he leaned down. "Are you mad at me?"

I knew what he was asking. My hand covered his. "I was mad that you left. I was mad when I realized where you were going, but I'm *not* mad at you in a way too. I'm furious with Adam. I'm livid at what he did to Becky, and I didn't ask what you guys did to him, because I don't know if I'm going to be mad about that or not. And I know none of that makes sense." My hand slid around his shoulders and my other arm wrapped around his neck. I pulled his mouth down to mine. "But I also don't want to talk about Adam right now because I really, *really* just want you."

He groaned softly before his lips descended to mine, and all the same flutters started. I sighed into him, letting my body dissolve. It was a gentle nip at first, then another, then he stopped and opened his mouth, commanding the same from me. I just held on and did as he wanted. My body heated up, and pleasure swept through me.

"Sam." He breathed my name, bending down to pick me up.

I moved with him, lifting my legs to wrap around his waist.

I felt him hold me, all of me, and his shoulder muscles contracted. He didn't lay me on the bed right away. He kept holding me, kissing me, and I knew this wasn't going to be anything quick. Even his kisses—he slowly dragged his lips over mine, like he was stealing a touch from me and relishing it.

Then he moved one step toward the bed and lowered me down. My back rested on top of the covers, but he still didn't do anything else.

He bent over me, my legs and arms wrapped tight around him, and he just kept commanding my mouth.

I felt like he was trying to feel inside of me, all the way to my soul.

"Samantha," he whispered again, lifting me and scooting me farther up on the bed. Then he sank down, letting me feel all of his body weight. He pushed himself against me, our jeans rubbing over each other, and held himself still, poised right there. I felt his back muscles trembling from the strength it took.

It just made the ache rise.

A small whimper left me. I couldn't stop it, and I moved my hips. He was there, and if there hadn't been clothes, he would've pushed inside already. I was wet. I was ready, but I heard a soft chuckle, and he lifted his head to peer down at me.

"No, no. I'm taking my time tonight." He bent and pressed a kiss to my jawline, then my neck, next my shoulder. "I remembered tonight when he tried to take you from me." A kiss. "And I felt it all over again. How you're mine." A second kiss. "How you'll never be someone else's." A third kiss. "How I'm yours."

He lifted heated eyes to mine. I saw the lust swimming in his depths. Shifting so he was resting on an elbow on the bed, he laced his free hand with mine and pressed it next to my head, pinning one of my arms in place.

"I wanted to claim you all over again," he said. "I wanted him to remember."

My throat was swollen. Loving, wanting, needing—that was all I was feeling.

"I think Adam got the memo a long time ago."

Mason shook his head. "Maybe. But I can't help but feel everything else was an excuse to come after you again."

I lifted my head, trying to concentrate. His thumb rubbed over my finger, and that caress alone was driving me crazy.

"If it was, I'm sure you reminded him again tonight."

Mason's eyes were so dark. The green was almost gone, and he pressed into me.

I sucked in my breath, my free hand falling to his hip. I licked my lips. His eyes fell there, and he groaned, dipping his head back down, and I felt him take another kiss. I'd give him any kisses he wanted, but there was something else I wanted. I undid his jeans and slipped my hand inside.

I felt his warmth first, then moved farther and caught him. I held him in my hand, but he was already hard.

He closed his eyes, resting his head on my shoulder as I began to stroke him.

"You felt the need to claim me, didn't you?" I whispered.

"Mmmm-hmmm." He could hardly answer. "It's not the first time, you know."

I paused, looking up. "What?"

He opened his eyes, watching me as I held him in my hand. "The first time I needed to claim you. There was another time." His grin grew lustful, and his eyes were almost simmering. "The shower."

My hand tightened, just a slight bit. My heart skipped a beat. "The shower?"

"Before we turned evil on your mom." He gave me a knowing look. "You remember."

I did.

The memory came back to me.

I was in the doorway and Mason was just turning on his shower. He was naked, and he didn't care who saw.

All the same confidence he had now was just so much more pronounced back then. He knew I was there, and he didn't care.

I grinned up at him now. "You asked me to join you."

He laughed, his voice ending on a moan as my hand moved down his length. "Uh yeah. I did."

But there'd been more.

I wanted to go to him. I had. I took a step inside, then the cockiness left him and his eyes had been smoldering, like he was waiting for me, like he'd been waiting the whole time for me.

"I kissed . . ." My voice trailed away. We hadn't. We stood close to each other, close enough to touch. It'd been before we were together, when Mason's presence was enough to implode my senses, and that was what he did then. His hand touched my hip, just a small caress there. It was enough. A need for him began to throb between my legs, and I sighed now.

"You scared me."

"I did?"

Mason was still watching me, intent.

Feeling a euphoric sense of power, I ran my thumb over his tip, and he shuddered. I laughed huskily, remembering the rest. "You kissed me on the forehead. That's what scared me. I wanted you so much, but it was like I knew if you took me then, everything would change. I wasn't ready for it to all change, not yet." I paused and glanced up again. "You said something to me in that shower, but I couldn't hear you. I never told you that." I cocked my head to the side. "What did you say to me?"

"Oh." He laughed, his grin turning wolfish. "You're holding my dick in your hands and you want to know what I said back then when I was still in high school? I was a young punk."

My hand tightened again, and he bit out a moan. "God, Sam!"

"What'd you say? I want to know now."

He groaned. "I told you that I'd fuck you until your legs couldn't work."

"You did?" My body reacted, suddenly feverish and aching. I was beyond wet.

He nodded, watching me warily. "I thought I was being a gentleman by offering to make you explode."

I laughed, breathless at the same time. "Goddamn." My own grin turned wolfish now. "Maybe I should return the favor right now?"

"Wh—Sa—" He bit off his words with another groan as I began running my hand the full length of him.

"You wanted to claim me, and I feel the same." I tightened my legs around him, bringing him even closer against me with my hand between our bodies. As I talked, I stroked—slowly, making him groan. "I know other girls want you, but they can't have you." Stroke. "You're mine." Another stroke. "You'll never be someone else's."

My hand moved a little faster, and I could hear him breathe.

"And I'm going to make you explode tonight." I drew it out, knowing just how to touch him. When to stop, when to go soft, when to go faster, when to wait, when not to wait. I knew him like the back of my hand and I was showing him right now. I whispered, lifting to kiss his throat. "Maybe your legs won't work tonight."

"Fuck." A guttural growl burst from him, and he adjusted his position, bringing himself back on top of me. My hand was knocked away with the movement, and his mouth found mine as his hand went inside my pants. He must have unbuckled them earlier—I hadn't noticed. I did now. I gasped as his finger slid in, stretching me. He paused once, then went deeper.

I felt him grin against my lips, and he asked, "You like that?"

God, yes.

I clamped his shoulders tighter, raking my hand down his back.

He arched over me and pushed a second finger inside, stroking in and out. When he brought them out, my hips went with them. I was moving for him, like we were attached and couldn't come undone. Then he pushed his fingers back in, all the way. He started a rhythm.

I could only lie there, gasping, as I felt the tremors swirl through my body. They kept spreading, building as he worshipped me. He bent and pushed my shirt up, and his lips went to my breast. His tongue swept around it, then sucked, tasted, and his teeth found my nipple.

I cried out, the sensations almost carnal inside of me. I was intoxicated.

Goddamn, I loved this man.

"Mason," I whimpered. I needed him inside of me. I wanted the feel of his entire body over me. He was mine. No one else's, and he never would be.

He laughed again, lifting his mouth to grin at me before he went back to teasing my nipple. His fingers were still thrusting.

"Please." I groaned. I was almost mewling with wanton need.

"No." He kept plunging his fingers in and out, in and out. His eyes smoldered, gazing back into mine. "I'm going to make you come, Samantha."

My name, the way he said it, sent tingles through my body.

"And then I'm going to take my time and make sure I explore every part of you." He whispered those words as he tasted my nipple, then my chest, then my throat. He moved back up to find my lips again, and his tongue slid inside, meeting and tangling with mine.

The only way I could be closer was if it were him moving inside, not just his fingers. I wanted to feel his surrender, and a frustrated growl came from me. He was holding himself back, ravishing me first. I wanted him to lose control. I didn't want it to be just me.

"Mason." I moved my hand back between us and caught him, wrapping my fingers around him.

He paused, tensing and catching his breath.

"If you don't get this inside of me, I'm going to torture you right here and now."

He had a wolfish look on his face. "What are you going to do—"

I ran my thumb over his tip, and he sucked in his breath again.

"That." I offered so much promise and warning in that one word. And I closed my hand back around him, holding still.

His fingers kept moving, almost ramming into me, and I felt the climax building. It was rising, increasing. I was just on the cusp of coming, and he knew it. He smirked down at me as I tried to hold him hostage. It wasn't working.

I opened my mouth, only able to lie there, pant, and stare up at him.

I was right there. And then he slid a third finger into me, pumping it deep, and it was enough.

I groaned as I felt the sensations flood me. I rode over the waves as he watched. He looked smug, and I cursed, feeling my body tremble, but it was payback time.

I managed to keep my hold on him, and then I began rubbing. Up and down. No, that wasn't enough. I wanted to taste him and I began to shift so I could lower my head.

He was already rock hard. He'd be delicious, but Mason swore he had other plans.

With my body still shaking, he dislodged my hand and pulled his fingers out. He undressed himself and me within seconds, then he was back. I hadn't even had time to register his absence. His hands went to my thighs, and he spread them wide.

He impaled me in the next second, and he went deep, all the way deep. I felt him in my stomach. He lay on top of me, then with a soft kiss dropped to my shoulder, he began moving, and soon I was writhing all over again.

A little while later I whispered, "What are you going to do about the videos? About those girls?"

"Nothing." He shifted, tightening his arm around me as he held me from behind. He kissed the back of my neck. "But if Quinn fucks with us again, I'll do to him what he did to me. I'll edit that video so those girls' identities are protected, and then I'll release it." He slid his leg up between mine. "Oh." He gently nipped at my shoulder. "He also thinks Nate is going after Becky, but don't worry. He's not. It's just a bluff."

I twisted around to him. "What?"

CHAPTER THIRTY-THREE

Everyone stared.

Everyone talked.

Everyone knew.

The first day of classes sucked. The second we stepped on campus, all attention was on us. Logan saw Mason and me coming—he'd come earlier with Taylor for some reason—and he came over to throw both his arms around our shoulders.

He hugged us to him with an extra squeeze. "Look, we're celebrities. Dreams *do* come true."

Mason shot him a look. "Thanks for the sarcasm."

"I charge extra for the attitude. You get the family discount." His arms dropped, but he bumped me with his hip before falling in line on the other side of me. "You too, Sam. *Sista*." He winked.

"Lovely," I remarked, rubbing at my forehead. A headache had already started. "Let me guess. We're the Soul Sista Connection?"

"SSC." He beamed back at me, puffing up his chest. "I had to ask Matteo if we could branch out, but he okayed it."

Yep. The headache was definitely there. It kept growing the more cheerful Logan became.

"Why doesn't the attention bother you?" I asked.

He shrugged, dropping some of his extra bounce. "Used to it since high school." He jerked his head toward Mason. "My brother kinda set the bar, you know?" He swung his hands as we made our way to the coffee cart. Every now and then, people would call out a greeting. He pointed at each person as he responded. Most of the greetings were for Mason, congratulating him or coming over to bump fists with him in a show of support, but it didn't matter to Logan. His head was up. His shoulders were back, and he was embracing everything with his usual Logan cockiness.

He talked as we walked. "So Taylor talked to her dad, and he told her everything is good. No investigation is going to happen since the original charges were dropped, and you 'came clean.'" His fingers did air quotes. "That did a lot of damage control. You should be in the clear. We don't have to worry if that other chick says anything either, about our party."

He was talking about Nettie. I, for one, was relieved by that too. Even if she did twist things around, Mason's press conference was already out there. People would be more inclined to believe him than her now.

I glanced up when Mason didn't say anything. His eyes were on me. I reached for his hand, and his finger began rubbing over where my ring was supposed to go. We hadn't fully discussed the engagement announcement yet. Images of us together, our limbs tangled up with each other, and him watching me as he slid inside—it all flashed in my head, and my body jolted at the sensation.

God. I wanted to groan. Just the small reminder and I was aching for him again. I tightened my hand with his. I was definitely and completely addicted to him. I didn't even know if I could function without him.

"Whoa." Logan slowed to a stop, his gaze fixed to the right of us.

I looked, then gritted my teeth.

Faith Shaw was coming our way, with Nettie glued to her side. A few other runners were with her, but no Courtney or Grace.

"Samantha."

That one word was my greeting.

My tone matched hers, cool as ice. "Shaw."

"What?" A faint smirk teased at her face as she raised an eyebrow. "We're not on a first-name basis now?"

"New policy. Only friends are called by their first names."

"Since when?"

"Since whenever the fuck I talk to you."

Her face fell flat. "You're such a bitch."

"Uh." Logan stepped forward, half in front of me with his finger in the air. "You came to us. Us." He pointed from himself, to me, to Mason, and he looked back to her. "We're not really nice people. Do you think it's a good idea for you to approach Sam and start by insulting her? We might not able to physically do anything to you, but if we see a window where we can make your life suck, trust me." He leaned forward, whispering. "We'll take it, with pleasure."

Her eyes narrowed. "You can't do anything to me."

His grin turned evil. "You haven't slept with a guy named Adam Quinn, have you?"

"Okay." I reached for him at the same time Mason clapped a hand on his shoulder.

He yanked him back, saying, "Enough."

Logan was undisturbed. He merely leaned to the side so he could see Faith again. "If you haven't, let me know. I can hook you up."

I'd had enough. If he stayed, he was going to get more and more mean.

"Take him with you?" I asked Mason.

He nodded. "We have psych together, right?"

"Save me a seat." I nodded. "I'll be there in a bit."

"Okay." He reached for Logan's neck. "Come on, little brother, before we get in even more trouble."

Logan allowed himself to be pulled backward, his eyes narrowed and locked on Faith. He finally turned around. Mason's hand dropped from his neck then, and the two were quickly swallowed up by an entire crowd of guys. I recognized some football players, but there were others I didn't know. I spotted Matteo heading toward them, his bag slung over his shoulder. Nate was next to him. I didn't know where Taylor was, but I assumed she'd be busy all day in her nursing classes. We no longer had morning practices, at least for a few weeks.

Faith cleared her throat.

I sighed, looking back to her. "I hoped you would've vanished."

"Like a genie?"

"Like a fart." I wrinkled my nose. "It's just as bad smelling."

"Har har." She rolled her eyes. "You and those two guys. You're all so mature."

"Yeah." An image of exploding cars, burning fraternity houses, and Mason tossing a bat to me before he evaded a punch flashed in my mind. "That's one word to describe us." I shook my head. "What do you want?"

It was her turn to send her crew away. She did so with a dismissive bob of the head, and once they'd all hugged and waved, making promises to see each other later for lunch, she faced me again. Her hands folded in front of her.

I frowned. "Let me guess. You're here to offer congratulations?"

"What?"

"Nothing." Apparently not.

"No." She shook her head. "I wanted to talk to you before practice today. We have another meet on Thursday, and Coach is going to talk to both of us. I thought I should give you a heads-up, maybe discuss the developments before he does. You and I can be on the same page then."

That was it? I almost smiled. "No." I turned to follow where Mason and Logan had gone. That was the easiest decision ever.

"What? Wait!" She ran to catch up.

"Stop chasing me. I can beat you, if I want to."

She groaned. "There's that maturity again."

Oh, fuck this. I stopped and whipped back to her. She almost ran into me, but I didn't wait for her to regain her balance.

I put a finger up in her face. "Back off of me. There's no way I'm going to believe anything you say."

So much had happened over the weekend, but I remembered how she hugged me after the race. Then I remembered how cold she'd been at the restaurant the next night.

"You're a cold, deceitful bitch. I will never trust you. Go away." I flicked my fingers like I was shooing a fly.

A barely contained scream erupted from her throat, but she kept her mouth shut and only stomped once. I suppose I should give her a little credit there? Only one stomp, not two. She was like a five year old throwing a tantrum.

"What?" I asked. "Can't control me? Can't manipulate me? I'm not falling in line like all your other girls? Please." I was the one to roll my eyes now. "Get outta here."

"Stop!"

I had started to go again, but swung back. "Make it quick, Shaw. I have no patience for you today."

"My God! What is wrong with you? Your attitude is tenfold what it normally is."

I had a whole list I could've recited for her:

My boyfriend/fiancé's mother was in town, who hated me.

Our engagement was out on a national scale, and I didn't know how I felt about it yet.

That same boyfriend/fiancé went and found a camera where another old friend of mine had been videotaped having sex.

Oh, and I had some incredibly hot sex, which had left only thirty minutes for sleeping this morning.

"Talk while I'm still standing here."

"Coach is going to make us run together."

"No." I started for class again.

She began walking with me. "I hate you on a personal level, but I admire you on a runner's level, and I'm sure you feel the same—"

"Not even a little bit. I don't give two shits about you: personal, professional, runner's, any way."

The group of guys that had been standing around Mason and Logan was still there. I spotted both of them, but didn't feel like fighting to get to their side. I moved past them into the building and headed for the classroom. We'd all synced our schedules to have this class together—except for Taylor because she'd already taken it. So they'd be coming my way eventually.

I reached for the door, and Faith grabbed it as I went through. She was right with me.

"Okay, I get it," she said. "Insults, insults, insults. I got it. I was more than a bitch to you in the beginning, and deserve this. I do. I'll take it, but I mean it when I say that Coach is going to have us run together. He wants us to push each other even more, and if it's just you and me, he thinks that'll happen. If we run with the others, there's more distraction."

"For you." I turned right down the hallway.

She was still hot on my heels. "You too. You get distracted because of your friend Taylor. You're distracted when you worry about her."

"Courtney and Grace can run with her."

"You know what I mean."

I kept going. The door was just in front of me.

"Hey!" She stopped behind me, her voice getting the attention of other students as they came and went from the classroom.

I braked. "What?" I looked back to her. "What do you want me to say?"

"That you'll run with me."

"And why should I do that?" I started toward her, one step at a time. I knew when she clued in that maybe she should be wary of me. Her head straightened. Her eyes grew alert, and she began to edge backward.

"Why not? We're running mates."

"We're on the same team. Unfortunately." I advanced one more step.

She began to look around, but for what or who, I didn't know. She stopped backing up and tucked her hands behind her back this time. Her head lowered a little too, but not much. She chewed on the inside of her lip.

"What are you saying, Samantha? That you won't run with me? You don't have a choice. We're on the same team."

"You're right. I don't have a choice about that, but I do have a choice if I'm going to run with *only* you. I don't trust you. What part of that sentence don't you understand? I know why Coach wants us to run together, but it has nothing to do with my distraction. I'm a pro at shutting things out. If I want to go, I will go. No, he wants me to help you. He wants to hone in on your competitiveness, and if the two of us run together and only together, only one person is going to be helped by that arrangement. You. You'll get better."

She swallowed, her throat moving up and down. She seemed timid, then suddenly it was all gone. Her eyes closed to slits, and she almost hissed back at me. "Because of your race time on Friday, this university now has an Olympic hopeful. Do you know what that's going to do for this school? For money? They can blast that all over their promotions. It's huge. And because of my increased race time, it's proven that I can get even better than I have been. You're helping me, yes. You will continue to help me, yes. You're going to do that just by being on the team, but if you think you have a say about running with me, think again. This isn't Coach's idea. This is coming down from his boss's boss. You will run with me, or you won't run at all. I'm here to save some time because we both know that when Coach brings this to us later today, you'll have the same fight we just did. But you're new to college sports. You don't know the politics that go on behind closed doors, and trust me when I say that you'll find it's easier to accept that you're going to be running with me alone than fighting it in the long run. And you're wrong. I *will* help you too, because the better I get, the more you're going to hate it, and the more you're going to push to destroy me."

Matteo and Nate rounded the corner and faltered to a stop.

There were other guys with them, but they went around them. I waited. Logan and Mason came next. They stopped just behind where Faith stood, all four of them wearing varying frowns. Matteo seemed mostly curious. Nate was wary, casting furtive looks to Logan and Mason beside him, and the last two: the same dark frowns they wore when they dealt with Adam were on their faces again. This time, their target was Shaw.

She had no clue. She was almost brazen, finishing what she'd been saying and placing her hands on tiny hips. "Got it?"

Now it was my turn.

"You don't think I know what politics are?" Did she not know who Mason was? He was almost as high up on that totem pole as an athlete could go. "If you think I don't know how to play ball, you're stupid. No matter what anyone says, I'm not helping you. And no one's going to make me. Got *that*?"

A silence had fallen in the hallway. I knew where it came from. The sight of Mason, Logan, Nate, and Matteo drew attention and slowly, everyone else stopped to watch whatever they were witnessing. Half the attention was on Faith and me, the other half on the guys.

Faith frowned, realizing the attention we had drawn, and she turned around.

"Oh." Her mouth fell open a little.

A part of me was smug. If this attention unnerved her, she really was an idiot declaring I was the inexperienced one. Politics was politics. I met Mason's gaze and knew that if orders came down that I didn't want to follow, I'd find leverage to get my own way. Eventually. *That* was manipulation 101.

Mason's eyes shifted to Faith, and she gulped, feeling the full force of his stare. She never had before, and I remembered what that felt like. He could stare at a person, making them feel like they were stripped bare so he could see into their soul and thoughts. Faith tried looking for an escape. She scooted over two steps, but the crowd didn't budge. She was locked in place now. We were completely surrounded.

"Are you here to threaten, order, or intimidate Sam?" he murmured, his voice almost a weapon in itself.

She didn't answer. I wasn't sure if she'd registered that he asked a question. She only blinked a few times.

"Which one?" he asked again.

She jumped, and one of her hands rose to pat her hair absentmindedly. "Wha—huh? What did you say?"

Logan snorted. "Yep. You're a real threat. Sam should be quaking in her boots." He shook his head. "Don't bother, brother. She'd piss her pants if she played in our league for even a day. The girl's a sheltered, ignorant princess."

"Thank you."

He snorted again. "That wasn't a compliment." He stepped forward as if he were going to pass her to head into the classroom, but he paused next to her and raked her up and down. He shifted his bag to his other shoulder. "Mason and I could've grown up sheltered, just like you. We chose not to be because we don't respect people who put their heads in the ground. In fact, we loathe those kind of people." His disdain was clear. Then he brushed past and winked at me. The crowd parted, and he walked into the room.

All heads, or it seemed like all heads, swiveled in Mason's direction.

"If you give Sam one more threat, one more order, one more time trying to intimidate her, you'll learn how inept you are," he said. "We've held back because she asked us to. We won't anymore. You hurt one of us, we hurt you back." Then he went past her too, but unlike Logan, he took my hand and pulled me with him.

The crowd remained parted, and as easily as Logan had gone, Mason and I went through too. Logan was in the back row where a few other guys had sat down, but when we walked up the stairs, those guys stood up and moved down. They sat in front of us, and our entire group took the last row.

I moved past Mason and Logan to sit at the end. Everyone was openly staring, or trying to hide their staring. I had a feeling this was how it was going to be for the rest of this semester.

Then the professor came in and announced, "Welcome to Sports Psychology."

CHAPTER THIRTY-FOUR

"Hey."

I was heading to the library after lunch when Logan came up and fell in step next with me. "Did you eat?"

"Not really."

I went into the food court. I tried to eat. I really did, but left after staring at my food for thirty minutes. The whole confrontation with Faith was weighing on me. I'd felt a momentary break after Mason's press conference. I didn't have to worry about what might happen to him anymore. I wasn't worried about Faith trying to use Nettie against us, but the whole fight with her didn't have to happen in the first place. I regretted allowing myself to be baited, but then again, I was also sick of people trying to push us around.

Logan stopped me with a hand to my arm. "What's going on?"

"Nothing." I shook my head. "I just felt like a run." And I winced. I ran at irregular times when something was wrong with me. Logan knew that, and I cursed softly.

"Yeah." His tone was soft. "What's really going on?"

"I went after her today."

"Who?" A line marred his forehead, and he rubbed a hand over his jaw. "Shaw? She's like an Anabitch Jr."

"She's come after me before, and I never backed down, but it was different today. She came to me and gave me the heads-up that our coach is going to want us to run together. She was still a bitch about it, but it was a truce. She was bringing a truce to me, and I spit on her. I told her to try and come at me."

"No." Logan started to shake his head.

"No offense, but I'm a little worried what you guys will do this time. I thought you were going to do something horrible to Adam last night," I told him. "This is my fault. My problem. I'll fix it."

"You're just like Mason."

I'd started off again, but he grabbed the back of my jeans and hauled me closer. "Stop trying to storm off. Don't do anything about Anabitch Jr. We'll deal with her together."

I gave him a look.

He grinned ruefully. "This chick is different than Quinn. We'll handle it differently, but we *will* handle it, and everything *will* be fine. Okay?" His hand came back to my arm and he squeezed it gently. "Okay?"

"Okay." My neck was stiff, but I tried to nod.

"What's going on?" Nate had found us. "What's up?"

Logan looked to me. It was for me to say.

I shook my head. "Nothing. It's nothing. I just felt like a run."

Nate's eyebrows shot straight up. "Oh no. Now I'm really worried."

Logan started laughing. "You need a new lie, Sam. We know you too well."

I wanted to roll my eyes, but refrained. I was irritated, but not with them. "I realized I might've poked a sleeping bear, that's all."

"Sounds ominous." Nate looked to Logan. "Decode."

Logan pointed to the food court. "Shaw. Sam's worried about her."

Nate shrugged. His response was automatic. "It'll be fine. We'll deal with her if we have to."

"See?" Logan beamed at me, clapping Nate on the shoulder. "There's the confidence you need to have in us, Sam. Anabitch Jr. will be fine. She was stuttering before. I doubt she's going to be much of a problem." He pulled me in for a hug. "You know everything will be fine. We'll shut her up, somehow. Maybe we can get some dirt on her and do the whole blackmail thing." He asked Nate, "Did you ever get in touch with her sister?"

"No. I pissed her off more than I thought."

Logan clapped a hand to his shoulder. "I may be out to pasture, but if you ever need lessons—"

Nate laughed, but shoved Logan's hand from his shoulder. "Stick to your la—"

Logan's phone started ringing, interrupting Nate.

Logan pulled it out, then paused when he saw who was calling. He swore under his breath, and a second later we heard why.

"Hey, Mom."

Nate and I shared a look. Helen calling was never good.

"Dinner? Are you sure?" Logan didn't sound enthused. "Cut the bullshit. What are you planning?" Another second. "I'll tell Sam and Mason, but if you're going to fuck with Sam, this dinner will end badly. For you." He started to hang up, then put the phone back to his ear. She wasn't done talking. "Okay! I told you. I'll tell Mason and Sam. Mason will let you know, and no. Taylor isn't coming."

He hung up, not saying anything right away. He expelled a deep breath. "Fuck." He looked at me. "She wants to have a family dinner tonight."

"What?"

"Who's that include?" Nate asked.

"Mason, me, and Sam. No one else."

"She invited Taylor too?" I frowned.

"Helen was nice to Taylor, and she kind of likes my mom, but tonight . . ." He faltered, shaking his head. "If she goes after you, all bets are off. Taylor's not some innocent, but I still want to shield her from some of the worst moments of my family."

"Your family?" Taylor's voice piped in, joining us. She had her bag over her shoulder.

Logan instantly transformed. He went from scowling to smirking, and he pulled her against his side, his arm around her shoulders this time. "It's nothing. How are you?"

She gave him a look. "Logan."

His arm dropped. "I'll tell you later, but I don't want to talk about it right now. How was your first day of nursing classes?"

She sighed. "Fine, but it's going to be a hard year. I have a lot of labs." She said to me, "I might have to quit the team. I don't think I'll be able to do both. I'm so sorry."

Faith's words came back to me. " . . . *Your friend Taylor. You're distracted when you worry about her.*"

"No. I'm okay with that," I said quickly.

"Are you sure?" She looked to Logan for clarification, but he didn't react. Her mouth turned down.

"Yeah. I'm fine with it. You have to focus on your studies."

"Yeah, but you won't have the extra backup."

"I have Courtney and Grace. Besides, I might ask Coach if I can do some runs alone this week."

"Oh." She perked back up, her frown disappearing. "Are you sure? That'd be good if he let you do that."

I nodded. I was going to make him, if I had to. I glanced at Logan, but spoke to Taylor, "Yeah. I'm sure I can figure some way to twist his arm."

Logan nodded, just the slightest of movements so Taylor didn't catch it, but my message was clear. If we were finding leverage to use against Shaw, we could find some to use against Coach Langdon too. I knew there was no way I could kiss Faith's ass or run with her, so we had to find something.

"Okay," Nate spoke up. "I have business economics next. I think I might actually go and prep for it." He started off, walking backward. "See you guys tonight. Or wait . . ." His eyes lingered on Taylor. "Maybe not. Never mind." He held his hand up, rotating around to walk forward.

"Okay. What's going on?" Taylor asked. She leveled Logan with a warning look. "And don't try to placate me and say nothing. I can tell. I know you guys."

I cut him off. "Nothing. It's nothing."

"Sam?"

I winced at the hurt in her voice. "You're right. It is something, but trust me. I'll tell you later. I promise."

It wasn't that I wanted to keep her out of the loop, of us finding leverage against Faith or even Coach Langdon, but Taylor was like Courtney. She had some bad shit happen to her, but she was still good.

I didn't want to take the 'good' part out of her. She'd already been too involved over the summer. Logan's eyes met mine, and I knew he understood where I was coming from. He looked relieved.

"It's not to exclude you, Taylor," I added, softening my voice. "It's to protect you."

"Isn't that what you were pissed at your boyfriend for doing before?"

She was right.

I didn't care.

Call me hypocritical.

"I'll explain it, but not yet," I said. "Not until something actually happens."

She'd just said she was going to quit the team. If she were brought into the fold, she'd refuse. She'd keep running, and Faith was right. I would be distracted, worrying about her. She was out of the line of fire this way. Everything would work out.

She set her jaw in a determined line.

"Please?" It worked. I saw her softening when I used that word. "I'll explain later. I promise."

"You promise?"

I nodded, feeling some of my unease lessening.

"Okay." She sighed, raking a hand through her hair. She leaned back against Logan. "I suppose it's for the best anyway. I wasn't lying when I said this year is going to be hard. I'm even worried about finding time with you."

Logan's arm curled around her. "You can study at the house. We'll stop partying there as much." His eyes flicked to mine. "Classes and all."

She groaned. "Yeah, maybe, but I'll be at home tonight. I want to try to get a head start on things. See?" She pointed to herself. "Me getting ahead of my studies, totally believable." She waved in the direction Nate had gone. "Him, not so much." She pulled away from Logan and glanced at her phone. "I have lab in twenty minutes. I should grab something to eat, then jet over there." She pecked Logan's cheek before walking toward the food court. "I'll see you guys later, and I gotta talk to Coach about quitting, so maybe I'll see you at practice. Bye!"

We watched as she turned around and picked up her pace.

Logan said quietly, even though it was just the two of us, "If this spreads to Taylor, and Shaw hurts her." He looked at me. His eyes darkened in a dangerous glint. He didn't say anything more, but his threat hung in the air.

"Nothing will happen. We'll find something." We had to. "I promise."

"Don't make promises you can't keep."

He'd been the one reassuring me not long ago. But I did what we did for our family.

"Nothing will happen." I touched his arm. "I promise, Logan."

CHAPTER THIRTY-FIVE

Coach Langdon never got around to that meeting with Faith and me. Taylor was in his office by the time I got there, and he was distracted afterward. I didn't know if it was because of her or something else, but it didn't matter. Everyone finished stretching, and he lifted his whistle to his mouth.

He blew it and hollered, "Get running. Friday was a good race, but don't start slacking now. Strattan, no holding back. You go as far as you want and as fast as you want."

I looked to Faith, who was already scowling in my direction, and gave her a smug grin. *Game on.*

As soon as we started, I felt her breathing down my neck. I knew she'd gotten the memo. It wasn't long till I pulled away, and after another half-mile, I never saw her again.

I did as Coach said.

I ran for two hours, and I ran hard. I felt my phone buzzing at one point. It was a text from Coach, asking where I was. I told him I was still running, and his only reply was that I needed to log my miles and time when I finished. Everyone else was done and had gone home.

I'd gotten a ride with Mason that morning, and he texted too, asking if I wanted a lift home with him. My reply was the same to him as Coach, but I added that I was just going to run home. I felt it in me. I hadn't run all weekend, and it showed.

I did just under twenty miles in two hours, ten minutes, and twenty-three seconds.

I had already showered and was sitting at the kitchen table to study when Mason came home. He walked over, kissing my forehead. "How was your day?"

"Good." I'd tell him later about Faith and my concerns. "How was your day?"

He looked tired, with bags under his eyes, but he was freshly showered. He had changed from the clothes he wore this morning into a Cain University black blazer. I pulled my attention away from the way it fit over his shoulders. My mouth watered, but I needed to eat, not engage in even more physical activity.

He grabbed a sports drink from the fridge and an apple, then sat next to me. "It was fine. I had to officially meet with all of the coaching administration, and they just gave me a warning not to pull something like that again."

"Like the press conference?"

He nodded. "And admitting that they knew about my charges this summer and didn't do anything about it. Telling the press that wasn't my decision to make."

"I thought your head coach and Taylor's dad were okay with the press conference."

"They were, but they didn't know I was going to admit to that part."

"Oh." I snagged some of his sports drink.

He frowned at me. "How far did you run tonight?"

"Farther than normal. I didn't run this weekend. I had energy to burn." I shrugged.

His eyes narrowed, darkening with suspicion. "What's going on?"

"Nothing."

"You're lying to me. Stop."

I pressed my lips together.

"Sam." That one word was a warning from him. "I know you. I know you inside and out. I know you bare naked, and I know you to your soul. You're lying through your teeth right now. What happened?"

I leaned back in my chair and told him my concerns.

He agreed with Logan, saying, "We'll find something. Don't worry about her or your coach. She got put on the back burner, but I can still call my dad if you want."

"Yeah." Maybe that was the best course of action finally. Forget my mother, just for them to go to James? But there was a nagging feeling in the pit of my stomach. I didn't know what it was about, why it was there. It just wouldn't go away since this morning.

I reached for his sports drink again, and he just pushed it in front of me instead. He got up and got a new one for himself. "My mom called earlier."

"About dinner?"

"You knew?"

I explained that part too. "I was with Logan."

"And he doesn't want Taylor involved?"

I nodded.

"That's smart of him, but she wants to meet tonight."

"Not tonight." Thirty minutes of sleep, an adrenaline-packed day, and twenty miles later, the exhaustion was going to hit me any moment. I was just waiting for it.

He ran a hand down my back. "We could handle this without you. Are your parents still in town?"

I shook my head. Malinda had texted Sunday morning to say they were heading home, and Garrett told me at the game they were leaving last night. I knew both were gone. "Just your mom."

"You don't have to deal with her, you know. Logan and I can go."

"I want to." I needed to. Everyone else was done and dealt with. There was no one else to handle in the family. I even had closure with Analise. Helen was the last one.

"Okay." He ran a hand down my back again before standing up again. "Have you eaten yet?"

I gave him a rueful look. He already knew the answer to that.

"I'm taking that as a no." He grinned at me and grabbed his phone. "Let me call Helen and move dinner to tomorrow night, then I'll make some food."

Helen argued, but accepted the dinner date delay. We were supposed to go to her hotel suite, and she was having it catered in. As soon as I heard that, my stomach dropped. If Helen was pursuing a private venue like that, it meant she wanted to talk about real business. I wasn't looking forward to it.

After that, Mason opened the fridge and found it was almost empty. There was nothing to cook. My stomach was growling and so was his, so he suggested going to get food instead. I went with him, and fifteen minutes later, he pulled into the bar where Taylor used to work.

"They do pick-up here?"

"Nate texted when we were leaving. He said to stop in. He's picking up a late shift."

"I'm going to get sleepy soon."

He took my hand in his. "I'll carry you home."

I gazed at him a moment.

He was dangerous at times. He was loving *all* the time. And he was all mine.

He was literally my other half.

"I love you," I breathed.

His eyes grew warm, and the faintest grin back was my reward. "I love you, too."

When we got out, he took my hand in his and we walked into the little pub. It wasn't long before people realized Mason Kade was in their presence. More and more attention came our way. I leaned into him as he waved to Nate behind the bar.

"Hey, guys." Nate came to our booth in the corner a moment later and slid in next to me. He leaned his elbows on the table. "Change of plans. I told you the sister wouldn't respond to me. Well, she's here."

"Here?" Alarm sliced through me. I turned to look around, but only saw half the pub watching us back. "Is she in the back?"

"She's with Matteo in the back." He glanced to Mason. "I have that girl I'm interested in, so he took point. He's going to flirt with her, see if she tells him anything."

"He slept with Grace." And as soon as the words were out of my mouth, I was wondering why I cared. Sleeping with multiple girls wasn't rare for these guys, at least until they committed like Mason and Logan had. "Never mind. I don't know why I said that."

Nate laughed, standing up. "I don't think he's going to sleep with her. He's just hanging out to see if the liquor loosens her tongue."

He seemed to think about that for a moment. "And not in the usual way we'd use that term. Okay. I gotta go back to work. You guys need anything?"

"Some food?"

Nate nodded to Mason. "You want a beer?"

"Just water."

"I'll get you the nice stuff, the stuff that doesn't come out of the tap. Don't tell the other customers." Nate winked, grinning, before he headed back behind the bar.

Mason got out and came around to my side of the booth.

"I like that Nate works here," I said.

"Yeah?" He sat next to me, resting his legs on the seat he'd just vacated.

We could see everyone else in the room and at the bar too, but if we pressed back into the booth, only a few tables could see us. It gave us a modicum of privacy, and I had no doubt that someone would end up joining us. I'd be curled in the corner sleeping soon.

I nodded. "Yeah. It's like we have our own hangout—that's not our living room."

He ran a hand down my back. "You okay?"

"Just the stuff about Faith."

"You sure?" He grasped my hand, our fingers sliding together.

I nodded.

He shifted back so we were sitting side by side again. I laid my head on his shoulder.

Nate brought our food over a few minutes later, and by the time we were done, a couple football players had come over. I sat with Mason, holding his hand under the table as he talked and laughed with his teammates. I saw the envious looks from some girls, and a few even came over to flirt with the other guys, but if a girl tried with Mason, he ignored her. He didn't shoot her down in an embarrassing way, but the girls stopped trying after he ignored them on their second or third attempt.

I started to fall asleep around midnight, my head still resting against Mason's shoulder. His arm was around me now, holding me in place, his hand heavy and warm on my leg. It was an anchor I savored.

At one point I woke to see a group of girls leaving the bar. Matteo had his arm around one as he walked out with them, but he came back in and pulled up a chair next to Mason. I registered his laughter, hearing that it was a little more carefree than normal. Either he was buzzed or he just got laid.

I struggled to remember why that mattered to me, but then my eyelids shut once again.

———

I woke sometime later, hearing laughter.

Nate was saying, "Last call. Do you guys want anything?"

I was curled in a ball next to Mason. His hand was on my hip, holding me in place. Something soft was under my head.

I was out again.

———

I lifted my head from Mason's shoulder; he was carrying me. The back door of the car opened, and he laid me down.

"Mason?" I caught his hand as he started to back away. "What's going on?"

"Go back to sleep. We're going home."

Then the door shut, and I heard Matteo climb into the front passenger seat.

Mason asked him, "What'd you find out from the sister?"

"That she thinks her little sister is a spoiled bitch."

Mason sighed. "She didn't go into specifics?"

"No, but she was wasted. And I got the feeling the two aren't close. You want me to keep pushing her?"

"No. I think I'll just ask James to find something. If we owe him, then . . ."

I started to fall asleep again, but not before I heard Matteo ask, his voice sounding clearer like he'd looked back at me, "Maybe we shouldn't have stayed as long as we did?"

"If she wanted to leave, she would've asked. Besides, she sleeps best next to me anyway. It doesn't matter where we are." Mason started the engine.

I felt myself smile. He was right. Wherever he was, I wanted to be.

I fell asleep again.

Mason put me in bed and took my clothes off. He started to put my little sleeping shorts on me, but I sat up and draped my arms around his neck.

"No."

"Sam?"

I ran a hand down his chest and stomach and shook my head again. "No." I pulled him down to me, fastening my mouth to his.

Naptime was over. I wanted something else now.

And a second later, his arm slid under my back and he lifted me farther up on the bed before coming back down to me. I wanted to feel his weight all over again, the way that made me writhe underneath him. Mason did just that.

CHAPTER THIRTY-SIX

"No."

The next day Coach Langdon gave Faith and me his pitch. He wanted us to run together. We were the only three in his office.

I folded my arms over my chest and said again, "No way."

"Why not?"

He sounded aggravated, and he should've been. We were going on minute thirty-five of him trying to change my mind. It wasn't happening.

"Sam." He stood from his desk.

I didn't care. He could stand. He could pace. He could wring his hands together. He could do anything he wanted. None of it was going to work.

"You have to tell me why." He took a deep breath, seeming to calm himself, and sat back down behind his desk.

Faith sat in the corner next to me, her legs crossed and her arms folded over her chest. She'd turned to sit at an angle so she was more comfortable to watch this spectacle. And that's what it must've looked like to her.

Hell, if she'd been eating popcorn, it would've looked like she was at the movies.

"I already did. I don't trust her."

"But—that was in the beginning. I thought things had changed."

"No." I shook my head. "She thought she could keep up with me in the beginning because I held back. Only thing that's changed is that she knows she can't now."

His eyes flicked to hers, like he was worried about Faith's reaction.

I spoke for her, almost sounding bored. "She knows it. She's just learned running against me makes her a better runner. Why would I want to help her with that?"

"Because she's your teammate!" He threw his arms out wide before they rested on his head.

"She didn't choose that. I did. I joined the team. She tried to kick me off." I wanted to sneer at her, but it was obnoxious and rude. I refrained. With effort. "It didn't work."

Faith snorted in laughter, but didn't say anything.

"This makes no sense to me." He shook his head. "No sense at all. I've never had a teammate who didn't want to do everything she could to help another teammate."

"Bullshit."

"What?" His eyes latched to mine, shocked.

"I call bullshit. Have you met Faith Shaw?" I jerked a hand to my right.

"That was uncalled for."

"No." I thought about it. "It's not. She got the whole team to exclude Taylor and me from a breakfast thing. She threatened us too. She threatened Taylor, saying I couldn't protect her if I was running ahead of everyone else. She's a prime example of someone who didn't want to help another teammate."

"You know what I mean."

I leaned forward, my arms still folded over my chest. "You're right. I do, but you don't realize you're being biased here. You're not putting yourself in my shoes, and if you did, you'd understand why I don't want to run with her. The only kindness she's showed me was after Friday's race when she thanked me for helping her. That was it."

He frowned, seeming to see me for the first time. His eyebrows pinched together, and he looked at Faith. "That can't be right."

"It is."

I turned to look at her. She was being honest now?

Noticing my look, she shrugged. "What? I mean, there are witnesses to everything. Even if I tried lying, I know at least Raelynn would back you up. Or she would've. And you were right. She thought I dropped her friendship."

My lips parted. That didn't sound good. "I take it that's not the case anymore?"

She preened back at me, giving me a close-mouthed smile. "Don't say I'm not a quick learner. You threatened me, and I read between the lines. I circled the wagons, so to speak, and yes, Raelynn is back to being one of my besties. Thanks for that."

Well . . . Fuck.

She grinned. "I should thank you again. You've made me a better runner, and a better friend."

It burned. Deep down. There were all sorts of burning going on down there.

"Look, Coach." Her arms unfolded, and she sat forward. "Samantha has a valid point. I was horrible to her in the beginning, still am actually, so based on our past, you can't force her to run with me. If she fought you and wrote a claim against you, she'd win eventually. Even public opinion would side with her, so you can let it go. I'm not going to force my teammate to do something against her will."

I rolled my eyes. "That's so considerate of you."

"I'm trying, actually."

I studied her; it seemed she *was* genuine.

Then she flashed me another smug grin and ruined it. "You're wrong about one thing, though." She stood.

I waited.

"I am going to beat you. Eventually. It might not be this year, but it'll happen. You're not the only one qualifying for the Olympics."

She seemed so sure of herself. Her head was high, and she held my gaze steadily. She meant what she said.

Well, fuck. Again.

"Let us both run on our own," she said to Coach.

He frowned heavily. "I don't like this."

"Come on," she said. "The other girls distract me too. You want us to do better. This is the way."

"You'll do your sprints and weights too?" He was asking both of us.

I nodded.

"You know I already do," Faith answered.

"I lift with my boyfriend."

He pointed at me. "You do sprints with him too from now on."

I stood next to Faith. "I will."

He waited a minute, staring at us, and then he gestured to the door. "Fine. Go. Our next meet is Friday. Check in with me every day with your progress."

I followed Faith outside and asked, "What are you doing? What was all that about in there?"

She stopped and turned to face me, cocking her head to the side. "Why do you think that was a charade? Maybe I really am grateful to you for making me a better runner and friend. I'm a better person, thanks to you."

"You have an angle. What is it?"

"Right." She snorted, starting to walk backward, away from me. "Because that's a good battle tactic: declare your intent to the enemy." She rolled her eyes. "I thought you were better than that."

I was . . . but no. I wasn't. That was Mason and Logan's job. They fought the fights. I just followed behind and reaped the benefits.

"You're right."

"What?" She stopped, her forehead wrinkling as she frowned at me.

"You're right. I've never been good at this kind of fighting. Mason and Logan have done everything for me—the plotting, the manipulation, the deceit. I have verbal exchanges. That's my fighting. And the last time I really went against another girl, she and her friends jumped me in a bathroom. They put me in the hospital."

Fuck you, Kate, and your old clique.

But Faith was right. She was a female Mason. She was the mastermind. I wasn't. A sudden, different kind of humility swept through me. I'd judged Mason, getting mad that he didn't include me with his decisions before, but who was I to be upset about that? Everything he did was to protect me. Everything.

Faith was watching me as if I'd grown a second head. "You okay, Strattan? What's going on with you?"

"Nothing." But I was distracted. "Thank you, Faith."

"Me?" Her eyebrows shot up to where her hair met her forehead. "What did I do?"

"You helped me too."

I wanted to see Mason. He had practice, and he wouldn't be done till later in the evening. I promised Coach I'd do sprints and weights with Mason, but that would push us back another hour, and we had our dinner with Helen tonight.

I couldn't do anything now, and for once, I didn't want to do the one thing I always wanted to do.

I did it anyway. I went on a run.

CHAPTER THIRTY-SEVEN

MASON

"You won."

Those were two words I normally would've loved to hear from Adam Quinn, but as I put my gym bag into the Escalade, the sight of him standing at the end of my vehicle didn't give me a good feeling. He was pale, bags under his eyes, and looked like he needed a meal or a good night's sleep.

"When's the last time you slept, Quinn?"

A broken laugh barked from him, and he shoved two fists into his baggy coat pockets. "That's your greeting to me? I just told you that you won."

"I heard. What are you doing here, Quinn?"

He snorted again, still sounding bitter. "At least have the decency to call me by my name. I'm here. I'm conceding defeat. You. Won. You won. You can be happy now. Right? Because that must be why you destroyed my life." His voice rose, and he was almost spitting out his words. "Right?" His nostrils flared. "I mean, you did what you said you'd do. You ruined me. Becky wants nothing to do with me, and that video—you're always going to have that over me, aren't you?"

My phone was in my pocket, not my bag. I shut the Escalade's door and faced him squarely.

He kept going. "The case against my dad is bad. He's going to go away, but it doesn't even matter. His reputation is ruined." Another hard laugh. "And that's what you have against me now. You took my girl. You have my reputation, and I can't even get mad at you. I set myself up. The video I used against you. I broke into your house. It's perfect." He looked down at the ground, shaking his head. "It's just perfect."

A sad echo.

He wanted me to feel pity for him? Fury lit a flame inside me. He'd tried to take my life away. He tried it again, and that was after a few years of peace. I clenched my jaw. I didn't feel pity for this guy. He was a feral animal. Wounded, backed into a corner, but he'd come back fighting. I had no doubt about it.

I eyed him. "Why are you wearing a coat?"

"Huh?"

I nodded at him. "This is California, and it's eighty. Why are you wearing that coat?"

He looked down at it like he hadn't realized he had it on. "I don't know." His voice was strained again, quiet. "I don't remember putting it on."

"Why are you here, Adam?"

His eyes flicked to mine at the mention of his name. I saw something lighten, like he was thankful for that. Then he closed his eyes and took a deep breath.

"I don't know." He was almost murmuring to himself. His head hung low. "I think I came to let you know that. You won." He rolled his eyes up and let his head fall back. "What am I going to do? My dad is furious, but he's going to prison. He'll get convicted. The evidence against him is rock solid. Becky won't talk to me. I have no one anymore."

The parking lot was almost empty. I had taken longer than usual to get ready because the plan was to meet Sam and Logan at the hotel for Helen's dinner. I could feel my phone buzzing in my pocket. It was probably Sam or Logan, or both of them, wondering where I was. I could've reached in and hit one button to let them listen to the conversation, but then they'd know Quinn was here. They'd come.

They couldn't come.

If he was going to do something, he was only going to get me. No one else.

"I was going to go to law school, Mason." His shoulders crumbled before me. He was almost shrinking in size. "I was engaged to a great girl. Becky loved me for me. She was there in the beginning. She was always there for me, and I wouldn't look at her. Not like that. It was Sam for me." He cursed softly. "Man, Sam was so beautiful."

He looked up again, a sheen of tears in his eyes. "I fell for her before Sallaway did. I wanted her first. She was stunning. I tried to talk to her, but she never saw me. Then he swooped in and got her, and she was gone. I started dating Ashley after that, but Sam was the one I wanted."

That flame inside me was building. I wasn't enjoying this walk down Adam's memory lane.

"Then when I heard he was cheating on her, it was only a matter of time," he continued. "She'd find out, and there was no way she'd stay with him. No way. Not a girl like her. She had spine. Morals. Values. And those stupid friends of hers. Both of them. They were horrible. One was screwing the boyfriend, and the other knew about it. I ended things with Ashley. First excuse I got, I jumped on it. Everything was lined up. It was a matter of time. I was willing to wait, then move in when Sam dumped him, and she would fall in love with me."

He looked at me again, his jaw hardening. "Then you came along, and I didn't even know it. That was the thing. I had no clue."

I lifted an eyebrow. "You would've moved faster?"

"Yeah. I would've asked her out right away. I wouldn't have tried becoming friends first."

"You had since first grade to become friends with her. Don't put that on me."

A vein popped out in his neck. "Shut up."

My eyebrow went up. "Excuse me?"

"You heard what I said." A growl started in the back of his throat. His hands were in fists again, pressing against his side. He looked like he wanted to lunge, but restrained himself. "You and your fucking brother. I had no idea how much I would hate you guys."

I frowned. "And if you had? What?"

"I would've handled it before now."

What the fuck was this guy saying?

"You want to elaborate on that?"

A car's lights swept over the parking lot as it turned in, but it parked far away. I tried to see who it was, but couldn't. The air was thick with tension. If I moved, I didn't know what Quinn would do.

I was still wondering about that damn coat. Why wear a coat? He didn't grab it by accident. There was a reason.

"I don't need to." He started shaking, but he didn't seem to realize it. Fury shone in his eyes. "You took everything, Kade. Everything."

Voices sounded from the gym's door. It was two football players, but they didn't come our way. They headed to the section where the other car had parked. Who had that been?

"And Becky," he started, his head hanging back down.

We were on a loop. I didn't know why he came here, but he was going to repeat everything he just said.

Then someone appeared behind him.

He wasn't looking at me, and I opened my mouth to tell them to leave, but the words died in my throat.

Sam looked at me. She saw me, then Adam, and I watched the blood drain from her face. Horror filled her eyes.

No.

No.

Icy dread formed in my gut, but I could only shake my head and motion for her to go.

She started to come forward.

I mouthed, "NO!" I put my hand up in a stopping motion.

She skidded to a stop again, her eyes on Adam. I could see a question in there, but she closed them for a moment.

I breathed a little easier. She was going to stay silent.

I motioned for her to leave.

She shook her head.

I did it again, an abrupt and almost savage motion.

She shook her head again, crossing her arms over her chest.

This woman—

Adam lifted haunted eyes back to me. "Why'd you have to take Becky from me?"

Sam's frown deepened. Her forehead wrinkled.

"Kade!" he barked at me.

Fuck. He'd been expecting a response. "What?" I rubbed a hand over my face.

This could go from bad to worse. Sam had to get out of there. How the hell could I make her leave without letting him know she was there?

"Monson called her. What did he say?"

My alarms were blasting. This was why he'd come. Not Sam. Becky, because Nate called her. I stilled. Nate never actually talked to Becky. It was a bluff, one that he bought.

"How do you know he wasn't honest with her?"

His nostrils flared again. "You told your best friend to take her from me. Logan slept with Ashley. You took Sam from me. Now it's Nate's turn, right? He's going to make Becky fall in love with him, isn't he?"

What?

I was distracted.

Sam was here.

He was talking.

Nate.

Becky.

"Kade!" he yelled, a vein pulsing in his neck.

"What do you want? You tried to set me up, you fucker." *Take the offense. Make him go defensive.* I started for him. "That video could've put me away for years. My future would've been ripped from me."

He stepped back.

It worked.

"It wouldn't have," he said. "You always get off. You and Logan. You get the girl. You get the life I wanted. You get the future."

"I don't want to be a lawyer."

"Logan does."

"Because of you. Because you and your dad kept fucking with us. He sent Caldron after Sam. He sent him to hurt her, and you were there." That flame was a full fire in me now. Fuck what I did to his life. He tried to take mine. "You were there, you fucker. You did nothing. You stood there and *did nothing*!"

"I didn't know. I didn't. I didn't see them, and when Becky told me, I couldn't stop him. He was there with his friends. All of them against me. It wouldn't have worked." Some of his rage left. He sounded sorry. "I never wanted to hurt Sam. That was one concession I made with my dad. I insisted she'd never get hurt. Caldron went rogue that day."

"Or the first time he attacked me and her? Are you not remembering that time either?"

"That was at your friend's fight?"

I nodded.

"He wasn't supposed to touch her. Just you."

"Him and ten of his friends."

Adam shrugged. "Whatever it took."

To hurt me. That was what he meant. Whatever it took to hurt me.

I wanted to hurt him. All over again. I could feel it rise up in me, and I had to remind myself that I *had* hurt him. That was why he was there, but he wouldn't go away. This asshole was never going to go away.

"But why Becky? Why her?"

"Because you loved her, and you lost her. You. Not me. And she doesn't even know about the video." I grinned, knowing it was a hard smile. "Imagine what she'd say if she knew what you'd done there."

He paled, but he didn't respond. He couldn't. Those were all his fuck-ups, and he knew it. He couldn't spin it around to blame someone else, and my patience was growing thin. If he was here to do something, he needed to get on with it—and before he realized Sam was here. I didn't trust him. He claimed he didn't want to hurt Sam, but I felt no guarantee.

"You lost her," I ground out. My hands moved into fists. "You did that. Maybe I was pissed after you tried to set me up. Maybe I was even madder after you broke into our house. Who the fuck cares? Or maybe Nate knew she was single. She told Sam she broke it off with you. Maybe he wanted to see how she was doing, and he called once to do that, and that morphed into something else."

"You're lying." His voice was shaking. "Stop lying!"

I moved toward him again. One more step. *Come on, fucker. Do what you came to do.*

I kept my voice level, steady. "Have you asked yourself why she answered the call? If it was something about you, Sam would've called. Or maybe she didn't answer? Maybe he called, and she waited for him to leave a message?" I waited one second. I wanted his mind following along. I wanted him to imagine her perspective, to understand what I was saying. I was lying through my teeth here, but I didn't care. I wanted him to act now, not later, not when he knew Sam was here. "That means she would've called him back. She would've dialed him up."

His shaking was worse. I didn't think he could get any paler than he was, but he did. He was almost as white as a piece of paper, with fury in his eyes. They were near black. "Stop it."

No. Fucking. Way.

"Whatever the reason she's going with him, she decided to do it. Her. Not me. Not him. Her." I looked him over. "She already left you, but that's insult to injury. She's going to hook up with your enemy's best friend."

The coat remained in the back of my mind.

Why the coat?

I risked a look over his shoulder. Sam covered her mouth with her hand, and she was visibly trembling.

I wanted her to go. My eyes caught and held hers. I tried pleading with her.

She shook her head, lowering her hand and crossing her arms over her chest.

"Go," I mouthed once more.

Another head shake.

Quinn was watching me. I had to look back at him or he'd notice. I couldn't let him do that. If he did, if he turned—I'd take him down.

The coat. I started eyeing it again, forcing myself to look away from Sam.

She didn't like when I toyed with Adam. That was what she thought I was doing. I was the better guy, tormenting the lesser guy. She didn't see him for who he was. He was toxic. He kept coming back. He kept trying to take *mine* away.

I didn't know what else to do.

But Sam was good. I was not.

I wouldn't let him hurt her. Ever.

"Why are you doing this?" he asked.

I jerked my gaze back to him. He'd reached into his coat pockets again.

"I came to you," he said. "I should be attacking you, but you're attacking me. Maybe that's my fault. That's what you do, isn't it? When you're backed in a corner, you go on the offensive."

Like an animal—the way I thought of him.

My lips parted at the irony. "Maybe I'm just impatient?"

"No." He shook his head, his eyes falling again. "That's not it. You're patient. That's a quality you use for your success. I know. I know you. Logan's the impatient one. Not you. You . . . if you attack, you're doing it for a reason." He looked back to me, and I was chilled.

He was dead inside. I saw into him.

I wanted to edge back, but I stopped myself. No matter what was coming, I was here. I'd take him down before anything could happen.

His hands were still in his pockets, and a sick thought came to me. I saw his hands moving in his pockets. No. Only his right hand. Like something was in there.

Like he was grabbing at it, getting ready to pull it out.

I didn't want to give *it* a name, but I looked over his shoulder to Sam. She had to go. She had to run.

Tears streamed down her face. I didn't think she was even aware of them. She had both her hands pressed over her mouth, and seeing what I wanted, she shook her head. She wasn't going to go.

She had to.

I pushed back the ice that lined my organs. I shoved away the rage that was just underneath it. I only wanted her to see love and warmth right now from me. I saw the dawning recognition in her eyes. It was slow and still horror-filled, and she began shaking her head even harder.

She was going to say something, or choke back a sob. She was going to make a noise, and he'd know she was there.

He couldn't—I tore my eyes from her and tossed out, "What the fuck do you want, Quinn? You want me to call Nate off Becky?"

I picked those words on purpose, and he grimaced like I'd hit him.

I advanced, softening my tone. "Because that's what's going to happen. And you know it. Whether she goes out just to talk, it doesn't matter. You know how charming Nate can be. Girls like him. They unzip their jeans for him, raise their skirts for him. They pull their panties off and give them to him, if he asks. They finger themselves, if he asks. I know they do because he's told me. How does Becky like it? Does she like your fingers in her first? Is she going to pull his fingers into her? Buck her hips on them, like she's riding a horse? Is that what she does?"

He couldn't talk. His hate for me was right on the surface, and my gut was right. He was here to kill me.

A chill went through me. I ignored it.

"You want to know the worst thing about this? Even if he was honest and told her he called her because I asked him to do it, she *still* decided to go with it. *She* did. She's choosing him. How's that feel? To know you're going to lose a second woman you love because of me?"

It was enough.

A primal roar erupted from him, and he started to pull his hand out. I rushed him.

Sam screamed.

I grabbed his arm and pushed him back, hitting it hard against my vehicle.

He screamed too, but I kept hitting his arm against my Escalade. He had to let go of the gun. He still wouldn't. His hand was still in there.

Adam grunted. I held him against my truck, and he grinned at me. Sweat poured off him.

"I could never hurt you, Mason. I've tried, but it doesn't work. That's why I came. I wanted to give you this—" He started to pull his hand out.

I released him, stepped back, and rounded with my fist.

One punch across his face, and he slumped to the ground.

Sam was still screaming in the background, but I had to get the gun. He was unconscious, and his hand fell out . . .

There was a letter crumpled in his hand, and it fell onto the parking lot's cement.

A letter.

I couldn't—a goddamn letter.

My heart raced. I reached for it, turned it over.

It was addressed to Becky.

CHAPTER THIRTY-EIGHT
SAMANTHA

"Sam?" Gentle hands touched my shoulder. Mason. I didn't know why he was being gentle with me, but I launched myself at him. I held him tight, burrowing into him. I wanted him to take me away. I didn't want to be here. I didn't want to be a part of this. Any of this.

He crushed me to him, his hand running down my hair and back.

I drew in a ragged breath. I tried to speak. I couldn't.

He just held me.

Then someone pulled up by us. Car doors opened and shut.

A muffled, "Oh, no."

Mason spoke over my shoulder, "Check him. I thought he was going for a gun."

"Sam?"

A soft female voice. I looked. Taylor stood next to me, tears cascading down her face. She touched my arm. I didn't release Mason, but unwound one arm and pulled her in. I couldn't think about what was happening behind us.

"Shit."

That wasn't Mason.

I looked. Logan had fallen back so he was sitting on the cement. His eyes were wide and his mouth hung open. He looked at Adam like he'd just realized he was an alien. The letter was still on the ground, but . . .

. . . Next to it was a gun.

Red and blue lights flashed in the night.

Someone had called campus police.

267

We sat on the back end of an ambulance. Two of them were here, one for Adam and a second for us. We were fine. Adam was the only one who got carted off. Mason had broken one of his ribs from when he shoved him against the Escalade.

The campus cops told us Adam would be charged for bringing a weapon on campus.

They asked Mason what happened, and he told them. He thought Adam had a gun.

They talked to me. I just wanted to talk to Mason; that's why I'd come to find him.

I wanted to thank him for always protecting me.

They talked to Logan and Taylor. Logan explained that we weren't at the dinner, so he wanted to come see if something was up. Mason wasn't answering his calls, and that wasn't like him.

What happened when they got there?

There was a pause at that question.

I didn't look up, but I felt Mason tense next to me. He shifted, looking over. I assumed he and Logan shared a look, and then Logan's tired voice spoke.

"Quinn was on the ground. Mason was consoling Sam, and he told me to look for a gun."

"Who?"

I jerked. The cop was so impassive, so brisk. Like he dealt with this all the time.

A sad laugh bubbled up in my throat. He was campus police, but maybe this was a normal day at the office for him. Which was so sad, in so many ways.

"Uh . . ."

I looked now. Logan had a hand in his hair, his other arm around Taylor, who leaned back against him.

"Mason did," Logan finished.

"This one?" The cop pointed at Mason with his pen. He looked almost bored.

"Yeah. My brother."

The cop stopped, his eyes narrowing. "You guys are brothers?"

Who was this guy?

Mason was still so stiff. "I'm Mason Kade. That's my brother, Logan."

The cop cocked his head to the side, his eyes locked on Mason. "You're that football star, aren't you?"

Mason swallowed. "So?"

The cop pointed the pen back to where Adam had been laying. "Was he an avid fan or something? Why would you think he had a gun on him?"

"Because things have been shit between him and me lately." Mason's jaw clenched. I could feel his anger stirring.

My hand covered his leg, and I spoke, explaining what all happened over the summer, except the last visit to Adam's cabin on the ocean.

The cop didn't say a word once I finished. He kept staring between all of us, but lingering the longest on Mason. A minute passed. I felt Mason growing more and more tense next to me.

Then the cop said, "You have enough history to get a protection order. I don't think you'd have any problem, and it sounds like you need it."

The questioning took on a different feel after that. The cop's supervisor came, along with Mason's head coach. Coach Broozer pulled up in a car after that, and Taylor went running into his arms. The cop noticed that too, frowning.

"My girlfriend," Logan said. "His daughter."

The cop snorted. "Nice to be so connected." He turned back to Mason. "You got some folks waiting for you at the hospital. You all need to go get checked out."

Logan stood from the ambulance. "Shouldn't that have happened before the questioning?"

The cop shrugged, smiling slightly. "You'd think, right?" He held up his notepad. "I got enough. Thank you all and stay safe." He stepped past his supervisor, who came over to shake Mason's hand. The first cop went over to talk to the two coaches, who then called Mason over to join them.

Taylor came to see me, her arms wrapped tightly around herself. She kept glancing over her shoulder to her dad. "We're going to go to the house. Do you mind, Logan?"

He shook his head, pulling her in for a hug. "Not at all. I'm sure this brought up flashbacks."

She shuddered in his arms, closing her eyes as he kissed her forehead.

He promised to go to her house later. Taylor nodded, almost like she was relieved. She gave him one last kiss, hugged me, and started for her dad's car.

Seeing her, Broozer clapped Mason on the shoulder and departed as well. The two drove off together.

I turned to Logan. "You okay?"

That's when I saw the truth.

He blew out a breath, running a tired hand over his face. I saw the worry lines around his eyes and mouth. I saw the fear in his eyes. I saw how he'd been keeping himself together until Taylor left.

"Oh, Logan." I pulled him in for a hug.

He clasped on to me, pressing his forehead down on my shoulder. "Holy fuck, Sam. I couldn't lose you guys." He was shaking, just a slight tremor. "Holy fuck." He tightened his hold.

I looked over his shoulder to Mason. A frown marred his face, but he didn't come over.

This was . . .

I was comforting my stepbrother because he thought his family could've been shot.

That wasn't supposed to be my life. This wasn't supposed to be happening.

If a gun was involved, it was supposed to be a random act of violence. We were supposed to be the victims. We weren't supposed to be part of the reason.

We weren't supposed to *be* the bad guys.

I heard Adam. I knew why he was here.

When Logan saw Adam's gun, he retreated as if it had burned him. The sight of it shook him. It shook all of us, because the truth was Adam *had* brought a gun.

But it wasn't to shoot us.

At least that's what Adam said when he became conscious. The cops questioned him as he was placed on the paramedic's gurney. They kept questioning him until the ambulance doors shut, and then they were told to continue their questions at the hospital.

Only the officers' supervisor was still here. He didn't seem to care about the incident. He was all smiles now, laughing with Mason's head coach. And I knew why Mason remained over there with them.

He had to put on a show.

He had to make the cop happy so he wouldn't investigate further. His head coach was schmoozing him too.

It hit me then. No matter what happened, they did not want to lose Mason as a player.

Mason was going to be fine . . .

As a football player, he was going to be fine.

That's what we'd been worrying about this whole time—his career, his future in the NFL.

We were so stupid.

We never worried about his life, if he would remain breathing, if he'd be buried six feet underground.

I started shaking all over again.

Logan lifted his head. "Sam? You okay?"

God.

His soft voice helped the unraveling.

My tears were falling.

I couldn't stop them. I couldn't stop trembling.

We'd never considered that Mason could die.

I could've died.

If Logan had gotten here five minutes earlier, he could've died too.

Taylor!

She would've endured her second shooting incident.

This was insane.

This was reckless.

This was wrong.

This was us.

I shook my head, and once I started I couldn't stop. I pulled away from Logan.

Mason came walking toward me. "Sam?"

I put my hand out to stop him, but even my hand wasn't steady anymore.

I couldn't do this.

Someone was going to die.

"Stop." I whimpered. I wished it had come out strong, but I didn't have it in me.

I couldn't . . .

"Sam, we're fine. I'm fine."

"Now."

He stilled. "What?"

"You're fine *now*."

What about next time?

There *was* going to be a next time. This wasn't because of Adam. This was because of what we'd done to him. What Mason had done. What Logan had done. What I had done. None of us were innocent. I remembered the cop's words in my head and started laughing. The sound slapped against my ears, an edge of hysteria attached to it, but I kept laughing.

We didn't need a restraining order from Adam. He needed one from us.

"Sam." Mason lowered his voice.

I closed my eyes, pausing. In his soft and tender way, he could say anything, and I felt loved by him. I felt protected by him. It made me believe nothing would ever happen to us.

I was wrong, so goddamn wrong.

Adam had brought a fucking gun to this parking lot, where my fiancé was. Adam told the cops it wasn't his. It was his dad's, and he was supposed to put it in a bank safe. He wasn't going to use it or anything. He came to bring the letter. He figured it was best to ask Mason to give to me, and I would give it to Becky. He didn't want to approach me without going through Mason first. He was trying to be respectful.

That was the ultimate kicker.

Adam brought the letter to Mason because he was trying to put an end to this war. He was doing the right thing.

Right? Was he? Or was that the lie he'd made up in the moment?

Did that even matter?

Regardless, we weren't doing the right thing. We still weren't. They were saying Adam was out to get Mason. But he'd looked broken.

That's the reason he came. The letter was the excuse. He was admitting defeat.

Mason won.

We won.

No one won.

We were the bad guys. And it was never going to stop.

Anyone who went after us, Mason and Logan would retaliate. It was their way. They destroyed their opponents, but this time Mason could've gotten destroyed instead.

He was going to jump in front of the gun for me.

Maybe I should've swooned at that, but this wasn't a random act.

It never should've happened. Mason never should've needed to make that decision—his life for mine.

I couldn't do this anymore. It had to stop.

I had to stop it.

"Sam." Mason was still saying my name. I heard the anguish in his voice, and I jerked back to reality. He was holding on to me. His hands were tight on my arms, like he was scared I was going to slip out of his hold.

I did. I lifted my arms, disengaging and stepping backward.

"Sam?" One word, one name, whispered in agony.

He knew. I saw it in his eyes. He knew what I'd been thinking, because he'd been thinking the same.

I spoke quietly. "We did this."

"No."

"We did."

"I did. I did this," he said as he moved close, his forehead resting on mine. I sensed Logan nearby, but I didn't know if he could hear us or not.

I felt more tears on my face. "This can't happen again."

"It won't. I promise."

He couldn't make that promise. My eyes searched his, and he waited, holding his breath.

"I love you," I whispered.

He knew.

He closed his eyes and whispered, "Please don't."

This wasn't going to stop. Nothing was going to change. So I had to. I had to change. I had to stop it. I had to do something.

I stepped back from him.

"Sam?" He reached for me, but stopped. His hand closed into a fist, still hanging in the air between us.

I needed space, but I couldn't bring myself to say the words. I didn't think I'd ever be able to. I moved back another step, though I couldn't make myself turn and walk away.

Mason saw the torment in me, and he let out a soft breath, bringing his hand back to his side. He nodded.

He made the decision for me.

He let me go.

CHAPTER THIRTY-NINE

Mason had gone to stay with his mom last night, and I'd slept one last night in our bed, but I couldn't stay any longer. Maybe no one would understand, but I had to do this. What it was, I wasn't sure. If Mason and I were completely done, half done, a separation, a momentary break—I didn't know, but we weren't together. And we hadn't talked about it yet, but that would come. I just wasn't ready.

The only thing I did know was that if I stayed, Mason would die. Somehow. Some way. I knew it would happen.

Logan had gone to Taylor's last night and told her what was going on. She made him promise to stay there, but he hadn't. So she came to the house and slept in the bed with me, and I overheard her on the phone later. Logan had gone to his mother's hotel too. Nate never came home. I didn't know where he'd stayed, but I was glad Taylor had stayed with me.

She held me as I cried, and she was the one who suggested Courtney and Grace. They had a large storage room in their apartment. They'd joked one time that it could be turned into a bedroom if they ever had a third roommate. She'd called them and asked, but then she had to go. She had studies, though I knew it had killed her to leave. I appreciated everything she'd done, and gave her an extra tight hug before she left.

I wanted to hug her again and again, like it wasn't her I was saying goodbye to.

I don't know how long I stood there after she was gone. I went back to the room at some point, and I'd been trying to pack all day.

"Why?"

My heart was splitting open, my chest the only thing keeping it inside me. But still, I moved around Logan in my bedroom and continued packing my stuff.

"You know why," I told him.

Mason knew. I'd explained it to Logan, but he wasn't accepting it.

He crossed his arms over his chest and glowered at me. "This is bullshit, Sam. Bullshit."

I stopped and looked at him. My hands were full of shirts, and for a moment, I considered hurling them at him. I didn't. I placed them inside the suitcase and tried again. "If Adam had shot Mason, he would be in the hospital right now."

Or worse.

My voice dropped. "Something has to change."

"You think this is going to do it?" He flung his hand out toward the suitcase. "Fuck, Sam. We were worse before you. You made Mason softer. You know what he's going to be like now?"

I couldn't . . .

God. I couldn't breathe.

Everything was open and bleeding inside of me.

I glanced down. If I'd actually seen blood seeping out on my shirt, I wouldn't have been surprised.

"Stop, Logan."

"Stop? Are you fucking kidding? You're leaving." He grabbed my suitcase.

"Don't."

I tried to say that loud and strong. It wasn't. It came out as a hoarse squeak instead. "Don't, Logan. Please."

He lifted it like he was going to throw it across the room, but just tossed it back on the bed with an extra bounce.

"What the hell are you doing?" he yelled. "You and Mason? He's off drinking with Nate and Matteo right now. You're leaving. You can't leave!"

This was making it worse. I was going to give up, collapse on the bed, and wait for Mason to come back and pick me up. I was two seconds from doing that, but I snapped.

"He could've been shot! SHOT! He could've been killed." Rage gave me power. Rage gave me the strength to say, "Something has to change. It has to. This is the only card I have. If I stay . . ." Nothing would change. "I have to go, Logan. Please understand."

Maybe I was wrong. I didn't want to go. Even thinking about it, I staggered. My knees buckled, and I fell to the edge of the bed.

But I had to. It was the only thing I could do differently. It was all I could do.

"I don't have to accept this, and I don't. You're my stepsister, so you're stuck with me anyway. You and Mason." Logan's disdain was evident. His lip curled up in a sneer. "You both make me sick."

He swept past me.

I should've felt a break in the tension. I should've been able to breathe easier.

The outside door slammed shut a second later, rattling the entire house.

I couldn't. If anything, I felt like I was choking instead.

But I couldn't do this.

That phrase was on repeat in my head. I couldn't stay because eventually a gun was going to come for Mason, eventually someone was going to die. But I couldn't go either. I was leaving half of me here.

"Sam?"

A new voice.

I tensed, wondering who else was here to assault me, but it was Courtney. She pushed some of her strawberry blond hair behind her ear and smiled, coming toward me from the doorway. She took the shirt I had in my hand. Her touch was gentle. Everything about her was gentle.

"I can help," she murmured.

More tears flowed down my face. I was numb, but I wasn't. I was dazed. I was too aware. I could feel everything. I couldn't feel anything.

I was a mess.

I just choked out, "Thank you."

Grace stood behind Courtney, and she stayed in the doorway, a sympathetic smile on her face. "Hey, Sam."

Courtney shared a look with Grace before clearing her throat. "Maybe I could finish packing for you? I'm sure Taylor will bring anything I missed?"

I couldn't answer. That meant I had to actually leave. I had to stand and walk out. For real.

I sat.

"Um . . ."

"*SAM?! SAM!*"

I froze. That voice was Heather's. Someone had called her. She hurried down the hallway, pausing at the sight of Courtney and Grace, but rushed to me. "Oh, Sam."

That's all she said. That was all she had to say.

I'd been crying before, but I sobbed now. "Heather." I could only gut out her name.

"Sam." She grabbed me in a hug, cradling my head to her chest, and she just held me, like a child. I was gone after that. Heather was there. She would take care of everything, and I just cried.

We went to Courtney and Grace's apartment.

I would remember later how Heather took over. She introduced herself, found out who they were, then took one look at me and the room. She announced, "Okay. Let's pack up her things."

And just like that, they did.

Heather told me later that Channing came with her. I couldn't move, so he's the one who carried me out of the house and to Heather's car. He helped carry me into the apartment too, but he left again. I didn't know where he went, and Heather said later that Channing left to join the guys.

She was there for me. He was there for Mason.

The rest of that night, I cried.

Heather held me, and I kept crying.

I didn't know when I would stop.

It was dark. Heather's even breathing beside me told me she was sleeping soundly, but something had woken me up.

A flash!

There it was. I looked over. My phone was flashing. I already knew who it was. I felt him inside of me, and I clicked on the screen.

You okay? I just want to know that much.

Sadness lined every organ in my body. I didn't think it would ever leave. **Crying. But awake. You?**

I didn't wait long.

A minute later, **Drunk.**

It was a dagger to me. I didn't want Mason to hurt. I didn't want to hurt.

Thirty seconds later. **How are we going to do this?**

I took a deep breath. My hand started to tremble. **What do you mean?**

His reply: **We should talk. I know why, but we should still talk.**

He was right. I thumbed back, a hollow ache filled my chest, **Give me a bit. I can't talk and not break down yet.**

Can I text you? Can we still do this?

I let the breath out. I already knew my face was wet again. I didn't think it was going to be dry any time soon. A thousand knives were in my lungs, in my throat. I couldn't breathe without pain. I couldn't swallow without pain. I couldn't move without pain.

Have to. I can't do this without you.

My phone buzzed back his reply. **Love you.**

Love you. Be safe.

You too.

I'm at Courtney and Grace's.

I know. Taylor told Logan. He told me.

Logan's mad.

He doesn't understand.

He doesn't understand. Those words. I stared at them. It felt right to be texting with Mason. It felt like we were back together. I was just at a friend's house, but that wasn't real. I'd walked away—no, that's not even right. He let me go. He walked for me, and then I was carried away.

Those thousand knives suddenly became ten thousand knives.

I wanted Mason back. I wanted to be in his arms. I heard Heather's deep breathing behind me and wanted that to be him. I wanted it with each of the knives pushing inside of me.

I couldn't respond. My hands were suddenly clammy, and the shaking was too much. I wouldn't be able to hold on to the phone in a few seconds.

Then, it buzzed. **I will make things right. I promise.**

One large teardrop fell onto the phone. It blurred his words. I wiped it off with my thumb, but tucked the phone under the pillow next to me. I slept with those words in my head.

The next day passed in a blur, and the following night, Mason texted again as I lay in bed.

Sam?

Mason.

I wanted to smile, but I didn't. I couldn't. I wanted to ignore how I needed to hear from him. I couldn't do that either.

Still okay?

I wouldn't answer that. **Did you go to class?**

Have to. I can't play if I don't.

I didn't care if I ran this weekend, but it was different for him. Thousands cared if he played. One missed race from me wouldn't go noticed by too many, for now. That would change, but for now I was okay.

I texted, **You're loved and adored.**

Fuck. I don't care about that. You know that.

I did. And I felt my tears. They always came. **Are things right yet?**

I didn't know what we could do. I knew I was being irrational to ask that—nothing could have changed that quickly—but I couldn't stop my fingers. I couldn't stop the swell of hope filling my chest, even though I knew what his answer would be. But still, I waited.

Another minute.

Then, **We should have the official talk.**

I could only grip my phone as I stared at his last response. *Talk. Official.*

That's right. We were still unofficially broken up, and ice-cold dread sliced my veins. If we talked, the unofficial part would become official. Call me a coward, but I was okay living in the in-between.

Not yet. I typed.

Can I tell you I love you?

Deep breath. **Always.**

Then I do. Always.

I didn't go to classes that week. Heather remained at my side, and while Courtney and Grace went on with their lives, mine was at a standstill. I didn't go to practice. I was given time off from the team because of the parking lot incident, but it wouldn't have mattered. I wouldn't have gone running anyway. If I started, I wouldn't stop.

Late one night, I woke hearing raised voices in the apartment. Heather wasn't next to me, and as I padded barefoot down the hallway, I heard her say, "Back up, Kade."

My heart jumped.

Mason?

I hurried forward, then heard Logan's angry voice, "She's mine too, Heather."

I stopped, seeing Courtney and Grace in the kitchen. They were in my line of sight and both saw me. Their eyes were wide, filled with an emotion I didn't want to recognize. I pulled my gaze away. Grace sat at the kitchen table, a blanket pulled around her. Courtney stood in front, with one hand on the table and the other resting on her chest. I could understand the fear in their eyes.

Logan was here. Logan was pissed off. I felt their intimidation even before leaving the bedroom, but the other emotion I saw in their gazes—I swallowed hard.

I didn't want their pity.

Why would they pity me?

"You don't think this is hard on her?" Heather snapped. "You're going to make it worse. You can't come here and bully these two girls—"

"She's my family! Stop protecting her from me."

"She's mine too, and you're damn straight I will. Back off, Logan. I mean it."

A deep growl came from him. "Jax, I swear—"

Courtney and Grace jumped. Their eyes grew even wider.

Grace gasped.

Courtney jerked forward, then braked when Heather shot back,

"What? You're going to threaten me? You're forgetting I know you. I'm not like these two girls who are probably scared of you right now. I know you love Sam, and I know you're hurting, and I know all this anger is because you're scared you're losing another family member. You're not. Okay?" She softened her tone. "I don't know what's going on, and I'm guessing you don't either, but they do. You have to trust them."

"He's not doing anything!" Another eruption from the hallway.

Smack!

Something hit the wall.

"You don't know that either."

"He's not here."

Heather sounded tired, but sympathetic. "She's texting at night."

"What?"

"She texts. At night. She thinks I'm sleeping, but I wake up too. I'm assuming it's Mason on the other end."

He was quiet. Then, a few beats later he asked, "How do you know?"

He asked like his life depended on it.

"Because she sleeps better afterward."

"Oh."

She coughed, clearing her throat, and her voice took on an edge of kindness. I knew that was just for Logan. "I'll tell her you came and wanted to hug her. That's all I'll say."

I hadn't heard Heather talk like that to anyone else.

"Thank you."

I closed my eyes, feeling a pang in my chest. I pressed against the wall and tried to stop the waterworks. These fucking tears.

"How do I fix this, Heather? I don't know how to fix it."

He was a broken little boy.

I was Helen. I had just ripped apart his family—again.

I sunk to my knees. Oh, God. I couldn't . . .

"Sam!"

Courtney rushed to my side, her hand touching my back, but then it was brushed aside. Two strong arms lifted me up, and Logan carried me back to the bedroom. He laid me on the bed and stepped back.

He hung his head, his hands pushed into his pockets. "Is that true? Is he texting you?" he asked, his voice so raw and gruff.

I nodded. My throat was scraped clean. It wasn't working anymore.

Logan drew in a breath, and his shoulders grew rigid. "Is he going to fix this?"

I paused.

I hoped.

And I nodded.

Logan's eyes met mine. I saw the unshed tears. "I want to stay. Let me stay."

I was Helen. I was Analise.

My throat still couldn't work. It had swelled shut. Shame and guilt crushed my windpipe.

But Logan was waiting. I saw that little boy in him, the same one Mason told me stories about, the one who would sit outside his door waiting for his big brother to leave so he could follow or steal his bag for attention. He stared at me now, waiting for my answer.

I reached forward and grasped his hand. "Thank you," I choked out. I nodded, in case he couldn't make out my words.

He let out a relieved breath and sat on the floor by the bed.

Courtney and Grace were in the doorway with questions in their eyes. They didn't know what to do, but Heather did. She moved past them and held out a beer to Logan. He took it, and she sat next to him with her own. The two saluted each other, and the three of us just settled in as Courtney and Grace slipped away.

Logan had his back against the bed, right next to where I lay. Heather sat beside him, and I kept my hand touching my phone.

I had done this. Now I had to fix it.

I couldn't be like our mothers.

Is Logan there? He's not answering his phone, but Taylor won't tell me where he is.

Later that night my phone lit up, and I looked over. Logan was curled in the corner. Courtney and Grace didn't have anything for him to sleep on earlier, so he made them drive him to a nearby store since they were sober, and he was not. He bought a cot, a sleeping bag, and a travel utility bag.

He set everything up, and he now slept soundly. He'd refused to move to the living room. Heather asked what his girlfriend would think, and he replied without hesitation.

"She knows what it's like to lose a family member."

The conversation was dropped.

He's here. Refuses to leave. I texted.

You're okay having him there?

Yes. I hit send, then paused with my fingers over the buttons. I typed out, **I think I fucked this up. I did a Helen.**

You didn't. I did a James. I'll fix this.

How?

We need to talk still. We can talk about it then.

Okay.

Love you.

So goddamn much.

So goddamn much.

I put the phone away, and Heather was right. I slept the rest of the night through. When I woke, I knew—I was ready to talk.

CHAPTER FORTY

"Sam?" The next evening Courtney knocked on the open door.

Heather and I looked up from where we were lounging on the bed. Logan was at Taylor's, and Courtney faltered in the doorframe, scratching behind her ear.

"Um, there's a lady here to see you."

"Me?" I gave Heather a look, starting to put my pen and book away. "She didn't say who she was?"

"Helen or something?"

My eyes found Heather's again. *Helen*?

Heather raised her eyebrow and scooted to the edge of the bed. "You want to talk to her?"

I shrugged and stood, hugging myself. "I guess."

Mason and Logan's mother never sought me out. A red alarm blared in my ears, but I went down the hallway to the door. It was closed, so I guessed she was in the hallway.

I opened the door and stuck my head around. "Ms. Malbourne?"

Dressed like she'd been out at a benefit, she wore a cream-colored shirt and wide-legged pants. They looked like a skirt, but I knew they were slacks because she stood with her legs apart. Her hands rested on her hips, one shoulder propped against the neighbor's wall. I also saw a slit that ran underneath her arm, showing some skin. It was a very sexy, but also classy look.

My eyes lingered on her pearl necklace.

I forgot Mason and Logan's wealth. When I was with them, they rarely mentioned it, or dressed to proclaim it. James didn't either. He was authoritative, but he didn't exude his place in society. And, somehow, Helen emanated it so well in just one look.

She did so now, pursing her lips together at the mention of her name. A slight flick of her hair, and she gestured to me. "It's Helen by now. I think it's time we had a talk, yes?"

I moved forward slowly, letting the door close behind me. I kept my hands touching it, crossed behind me, in case I wanted to go back in at a second's notice. Mason and I might not be together, but I knew he'd come in a heartbeat if I called.

But even as I thought that, I knew I wouldn't.

No matter my status with Mason, I had to get along with their mother. If she deemed this the time for a real talk, so be it. I only hoped no one drew blood, and feeling that small amount of bravery, I tipped my head up and gazed steadily at her.

She smiled slightly, like she'd been waiting for me to make that decision. Her hand pressed to her hair, keeping it in place. "Should we go somewhere more private?"

I didn't have to think about it. "Here's fine."

A dry glimmer of humor showed in her eyes before she masked it, her lips pressing together again. "Okay."

Then she stopped.

I waited. She'd come to me, but she didn't say anything. I narrowed my eyes. Was I supposed to start?

"You'll have to give me a minute," she finally said. "Coming here is, well, humbling to say the least."

Her hand rested on her pearls, and I saw the intricate detail of her nails. They were long and shimmering, matching her pearls and outfit. Everything about her had been exquisitely put together.

She mused again, almost to herself, "Logan told me that you and my son have broken up." Her hand fell from her pearls and began to play with the diamond bracelet around her wrist. It was like she didn't know she was doing it. Her eyes lingered on me, narrowing slightly. "I had an epiphany when I heard that."

A soft chuckle came from her, but her lips never moved. It was like a ghost laughing beside us.

"I've always hated you," she said, her eyes downcast. "What your father said was true. I blamed you because you're Analise's daughter, and she took my family from me." She lifted her face now. "But if I'm being honest with myself—and my sons will attest that I hate being honest with myself—it wasn't your mother at all. It was James, and me. He destroyed our family, and I let him, but I have been blaming you in the back of my mind ever since."

This wasn't news to me.

"And I haven't cared one iota what that did to you. I'm not one of those mothers like Malinda. No. James has a type. He likes the cold types, and I'm one of them. It's perhaps why my sons are the way they are. They can be cold bastards at times, can't they?"

My lips thinned. "Did you have a reason to come here?"

She raised her chin, elongating her slender throat, and smiled. Almost. It was gone in a moment. The cold disdain never wavered from her eyes.

"My epiphany was that while I don't care for you, and I never will, my son does. He will never waver from his love, and I am here being the most motherly I'll be in a long while. I don't know what happened between you and Mason, but I would like you to fix it."

I almost laughed. Almost. "You're telling me to fix it?"

She nodded. "Yes. I am."

I couldn't hold the laughter in anymore. "Who do you think you are?"

Helen squared her gaze at me. She didn't bat an eyelash. She didn't flinch or look away. I could see some of Mason and Logan in her, and while I loved those qualities in them, I hated them in her. She replied, so smoothly, "I am the mother of two boys you love infinitely. That's who I am, darling. Who are you?"

I raised my own chin. There was no flinching from me either. "I'm family."

An approving look swept through her eyes, but she checked it, the coldness coming forth again. "Then do as I say. Fix it."

"No."

Her eyes widened, just a fraction. "No?" The beginning of a smile started, but it was just a tease. She kept it in check too.

I would see Mason. It was time to talk to him. I had already decided to, but I would not be ordered to do it. I would not be ordered at all.

"You may have birthed them, but you don't give me orders. That's not your place."

"I'm their mother."

"You're not mine."

She drew in a breath. "I am your elder. Don't you show respect to your elders?"

"Not to you."

She raised an eyebrow.

I gave her a nice fuck-you smile. "You can go now."

We were at an impasse.

She ignored my order, staring at me.

I stared back.

Neither of us looked away. Neither blinked. Neither flinched. Neither fidgeted.

Then she broke, drawing her chin to her chest and gazing at me from under those long eyelashes. "I'm at a loss then. I want to ease my son's pain, but you seem unwilling to do that."

I grunted. "They must get their intelligence from James."

Her eyes sharpened, but she only murmured, "What do you want then? Money?"

She thought she could bribe me.

"No?" Her nostrils flared. "What would you like? I can send you and Mason to Paris too? An all-expense paid trip? Or a cruise for you and your girlfriends? What would you like? What will it take for you to go and make my son not hurt anymore?"

"Not a goddamn thing." *From you.* "You don't scare me, Helen. Have you not met Analise?"

She laughed then. The sound rippled out of her, and she stopped, her hand resting on her throat like she'd surprised herself. Then she dropped it and started laughing again. She shook her head.

"You're right." She kept laughing, finally wiping at the corners of her eyes. "You're right. That's what it is. That's why they love you so much." She shook a finger at me. "And you're right about Analise. I thank you for implying I'm not as scary as her. That will help me rest better at night." She dabbed some more at her eyes, the laughter leaving her. "I suddenly feel like a thirty-year-old, young and refreshed."

I frowned. I wasn't sure what to think anymore about Helen.

"Okay." She seemed to speak to herself, pulling a handkerchief from her purse. Folding it into a small square, she smoothed out the ends. "I came here with the purpose to ask you to get back together with my son, something I never would've thought I'd do. I've only wanted you out of my son's life, both of them actually, and now this. I am indeed humbled." A half-bitter/half-amused laugh came from her. "So, what is the problem? I know it must be world-ending for you and Mason to have gone separate ways, or as separate as the two of you can be."

My mouth hung open an inch.

Was Mason's mother asking me because she cared?

I closed my mouth. I didn't know how to respond. I shifted my foot from side to side against the hallway's carpet. "That's none of your business. If Mason chooses to tell you, that's his decision. You and I have no relationship."

She did that. Not me.

"Okay." She graced me with another soft smile, the disdain lifting a bit from her eyes. "Noted. And I didn't expect you to tell me, but the mother in me had to try." She looked away. "Mason doesn't share much with me, ever."

There was a reason, but I kept quiet.

She added, "Not that I blame him. Logan's the one who shouldn't confide in me, but he does sometimes. I still think of him as my little boy. Mason was . . . older. Angrier. He shielded Logan from a lot of it. Lord knows, he didn't have to, but he stepped into the roles that James and I had ceased playing."

Her eyes grew haunted, and she looked over to me. Her lips pressed together in a tight smile. "I came tonight with a white flag. I'm not the nicest, and I won't be the warmest person after this either, but I do wish to cease being your enemy. It's something my son does not need to worry about." She inclined her head. "I hope you have a good night, Samantha."

She didn't wait for a response. She whisked past me, her silk pants flowing, and I had no doubt there was some fancy driver waiting for her in the apartment's parking lot.

Heather, Courtney, and Grace were all sitting in the kitchen, waiting for me.

They looked up as I came in and Heather asked, "So?"

I shrugged. "It was weirdly okay."

"What was she doing here?" Heather spread her hands in question.

"I think she was trying to help Mason, in her own way."

It felt odd saying these things, but I couldn't lie to them. Helen had only been a cold bitch to me, and she was still cold, but I wondered if she might no longer be a bitch.

I slipped into the empty chair at the table. "Yeah. I think she and I might be . . ." These words felt so alien in my mouth. " . . . Okay after this."

Then again, she didn't really matter.

Mason did.

CHAPTER FORTY-ONE

The next night Mason wanted to meet at the butterfly.

When he said those two words, I knew exactly where he meant. He said the renovations had been completed, and this time he'd gotten permission from his dad for us to be there. They changed the security codes to the entire place, so Mason was forced to ask.

This meant I got the codes too, and I was sitting in a lounge chair next to the pool when he walked inside.

My heart soared.

He came in with a fierceness. His eyes were blazing. As usual, he was gorgeous. Wearing jeans that molded perfectly to his trim waist, showcasing his firm upper legs, and hugging his ass, he twisted around to make sure the door was shut.

I took a breath. I wanted to touch him and cry all at the same time.

He wore a black Cain U football jacket, which molded to him just like his jeans, like perfection. His body was a well-oiled machine.

"Hey." He ran a hand over his black crew cut, and my hand actually jerked.

That was my job. I got to run my hand over his hair. I did it when we were in bed. I had to tuck my hand on my lap to keep from going to him.

"Hey." I flinched at how hoarse my voice was. "Sorry."

Sadness flared in his eyes, replacing the fire. His shoulders slumped, and he pushed his hands into his pockets. He didn't sit next to me, just leaned against the closest pole, which was ten feet away.

He opened his mouth.

I leaned forward to hear, but tensed at the same time.

Then he closed it.

I was right there with him. "It was weird coming here alone," I said.

"Yeah." He looked away.

His hand went back to his hair. I smiled bitterly. Logan did that all the time, but I'd never seen Mason do it until now. Why? Because his hands were usually touching me.

I asked softly, and because I had to know, "What are you feeling right now?"

His eyes met mine, searching.

"Like my soul was yanked out of me," he said.

I could relate. "I'm sorry."

He lifted a shoulder, but looked away again. "I know why you left."

Technically, I hadn't. I made the decision, but there were no words shared. Only looks and years of reading each other's thoughts. I might've made the decision to go, but I was the one who hadn't been able to do it. Mason did, so technically, it was just one more thing he did for me. He was the one who left.

"Yeah." I had no other words.

He shook his head, letting out a deep sigh. "Where do we go from here? Do we share custody of Logan or something?"

So quick. "Is that it?"

"What?" He frowned, looking back at me again. I saw anguish there. His eyes darkened, and he blinked a few times, holding back tears.

"You don't want to talk about it?"

I wanted him to. I needed him to.

He raked a hand over his face and jaw. That chiseled and strong jaw that had faced down so many enemies—some of them for me, some for other loved ones, some for him, and some just because he'd been hurting at the time.

He dropped his hand to his side. "I don't know what you want me to say. I'm ashamed, Sam. I hate that it happened. I know I'm a part of it. And I know why you walked. To be honest, I was glad. A gun—fuck's sake. He said it was for his dad, but who knows if that was true.

What if he'd been more depressed that day? What if I hadn't seen it coming? Depression translates to anger real quick for guys. I thought he was there for another fight, and I kept thinking, *He won't go away*. I wanted him to leave, but not for me. Not even for Logan. For you. No matter what Quinn says, he still has a thing for you. I know he does. I see it in him."

"Adam."

"What?"

"His name is Adam."

Some of the anger in him softened. "Adam. I broke him. I realize that now." Mason's voice broke, and I felt a new wave of my own tears forming.

"We all did that," I whispered.

"No, Sam. It was me. You know it. I set the tone. I set the pace. Logan might be raring to go, but I can let him go or rein him in. It's all on me. You know it is."

"Then why do I feel this?" I pressed my hands to my stomach, feeling guilt and shame there. They weren't moving. I didn't think they'd ever leave me. "I had a hand in it."

"No." He shook his head, coming to sit on the lounger next to me. He reached forward to take my hand, then thought better of it.

I reached out and caught his instead. I wanted that, and he expelled a ragged breath, his head falling down. He squeezed my hand.

We sat there for a moment. Just holding hands again. No words.

"I've been trying to understand where it all went dark, but I can't," he said. "What we do, all of us—it's too much. We went too far with Adam. I've been able to walk the line, but this time we went over it. I can deal with protecting Logan, or myself, or Nate, but you . . . I can't see that line when it comes to you. I get so angry, and I want to beat the shit out of anyone who hurts you. I enjoyed hitting Adam. I enjoyed rushing him and pushing him against my truck. I wished I could've hit him a second time, even after he was unconscious, even when I knew why I was hitting him. I still wanted to do it again. That's too much." He paused a beat. "I could kill someone. That's how far I would go for you."

Were those words supposed to scare me? Maybe.

Should I have been disgusted to hear them? Maybe.

Should I have felt justified by leaving? Maybe.

I felt none of that.

I left because I was scared *for* him.

"I know who you are." I adjusted my hold on his hand, lacing our fingers together. "I fell in love with who you are. Who you are is not what I'm scared of."

He lifted his eyes.

"You're going to break someone one day. And someone's going to die if we keep going as far as we do."

We. Not him. We. Us.

"I remember when you told me you loved me. I remember when we left that bedroom and when I saw that Logan had slept with Miranda Stewart. I know he did it for me, and he was setting her up to protect me. I also know he did it because *you* told him to do it. You did that for me. That's when I signed up for this." I lifted our hands.

"I thought Qui—*Adam* had a gun. I thought he was going to kill you. You were there because of me. He was there because of me. This whole thing was because I didn't pull back when I should've. I don't see that line when it comes to you."

I started to shake my head.

"No, Sam. It killed me when I saw you were leaving. I saw it in your eyes, and I couldn't even fight you because I knew it was right too. It still is right."

My heart clenched. My chest felt like it was going to cave in.

"Something *has* to change," he said. "I don't know what, but something."

Was he . . . I couldn't finish that thought. My stomach dropped to my feet.

"What are you saying?" I asked.

"We should stay like this."

I flinched. "Mason . . ." I started.

I know he didn't mean to do it, and I know this whole train started going because I climbed behind the wheel, but I still felt a knife slice into my chest at his words. This was right, but it hurt. It hurt so damned much.

"Mason," I whispered.

He sighed. "I know." His hand held onto mine so tightly. "I know."

"How can we do this?"

He shook his head. He was pale. His eyes were tortured. "I don't know. Can you stay where you are? Do you need a house or something?"

God—another knife pushed in and made the cut even wider. "I'm okay."

"You sure?"

I nodded. "I have Garrett's inheritance, remember?"

"Oh yeah. I forgot."

I couldn't talk. I couldn't see. I just held onto his hand, not knowing the next time I would have it again.

His eyes darkened. "I'll figure it out. I'll fix something. I just don't know what yet."

This was the part of the conversation where we should have stood up to leave.

We didn't. We stayed.

I just held on to his hand.

CHAPTER FORTY-TWO

"So, what's the plan?"

Heather asked that as soon as I got back to Courtney and Grace's. They both waved from the living room as Heather followed me to my bedroom.

I'd been a bit more with it the last couple days, but I remembered how my roommates had acted when Heather came in, took over, and handled me. They idolized her, and after she stood up to Logan, they idolized her even more. I didn't blame them.

I lay down on the bed.

Heather raised an eyebrow and turned around. She'd been putting on lipstick in the mirror. "What's that look mean?"

I pushed myself up, resting on my hands tucked behind me. "Thank you for coming and staying."

She shrugged, her eyes still narrowed and studying me. "You're my best friend. You haven't told me what happened, so I can only imagine it was bad."

I cocked my head to the side. "Why didn't you push?"

"It's your business." She turned back to the mirror and pulled her lipstick out again. "You'll tell me if you want, but I know you guys. If you don't tell me, I figure it's for a reason."

I nodded. "Still. Thank you." I gestured to Logan's empty cot in the corner. "Thanks for being okay with him being here too."

She finished applying her lipstick. A fresh red coat in place, she came over to sit next to me. She sighed. "He loves you. They all love you."

I glanced to her.

"I love you too," she said.

"I know." I sat up and squeezed one of her hands. "I love you too."

"And Taylor's freaking adorable. Her and Logan. He really loves her."

I nodded. "He does."

"That's good. Taylor completes him. He's found his someone. You're a lot happier now," she added. "Are we moving back to the Kade house?"

I shook my head, running a hand through my hair before sitting forward and leaning my elbows on my knees. "No. We went too far with something, but we're going to fix it."

"Okay." She stood up, patting me on the leg. "I have no idea what that means, but I trust you. And personally, I don't want to know. But I do know that you have two friends out there who really care about you. It's Friday, and technically, you're single tonight."

"I'm not single." I was. *Was I?*

Pain sliced through me. I didn't want to think about it.

She pulled me up, grinning, and headed for the door. "I'm not saying you should hook up with someone. That guy would just wake up in the hospital, and we'd both know who put him there, single or not. But you can do what single girls do." She let go of my hand and led the way to the living room.

Both Courtney and Grace had drinks in front of them. They looked up.

"What's up?" Courtney was grinning, her cheeks red.

Grace tried to stifle a laugh.

"You guys are both single, right?" Heather asked.

At the question, Grace spilled over onto the rest of the couch. She couldn't stifle the laughter anymore, and she buried her head in a pillow.

Courtney said in between her own laughs, "We were just talking about that. Matteo made a cameo here last night. He and Logan ran into each other in the hallway. Neither was expecting to see the other." Her eyes suddenly widened and she sucked in her breath, looking to me. "I was supposed to tell you they slept together. I forgot."

"Logan and Matteo?"

"No."

Grace was laughing again.

Courtney scowled at her. "You should tell her. You're the one who slept with him."

But Grace couldn't. She was still laughing.

Courtney rolled her eyes. "Grace and Matteo slept together."

She waited, watching me.

Heather frowned, turning to me too. Grace finally stopped laughing. I shrugged. "So?"

"So . . ." Courtney and Grace shared a look. "Is that a problem? You know, is that going to cause drama or anything?"

I looked at Heather before raising my shoulders again. "I don't know why it would."

"Oh." Courtney blinked a few times, relief flashing over her face. She nodded to Grace. "She's okay with it."

Grace was nodding. "Matteo said she would be." She turned to me. "Are you feeling better?"

She was asking about Mason. I changed the subject.

"Matteo and Logan ran into each other? We missed this?"

"Yeah." Courtney's cheeks reddened. "Logan was dressed. Matteo was not."

Heather chuckled. "I'm sure that was a fun time. So, are you and Matteo lock, stock, and barrel?"

"Huh?"

"Did Matteo wife up?" I asked, trying to explain.

"No!" Grace's entire face flared up. "No. I mean . . . no."

"All the more reason for tonight." Heather clapped her hands together. "I have a feeling I won't need to be here much longer, so how about we go to a club and pretend we're all single ladies tonight." She held her hands out. "Not as in hooking up with guys, but some fun drinking and dancing. No guys involved. We can do stupid dances, if we want."

"We have a race tomorrow." Courtney looked at me. "Coach asked me earlier if you were going to come."

I wasn't.

I said, "I'll email him."

Coach would understand, and I would start running again tomorrow. It'd been two weeks, and I was feeling the itch to pound pavement. I wouldn't be able to stay away now that I felt sturdier.

I knew I could stop.

"Will one bad race affect you guys that much?" Heather asked.

I had to laugh. Heather wasn't messing around. We were going to drink. We were going to dance. And we were probably going to get fucked up doing it.

Why we were outside the loud nightclub still escaped me, but we were here. Taylor was coming, and Courtney and Grace were in line right next to Heather and me. The music was booming, and the rest of the people in line with us were talking, complaining, smoking, or already dancing. I'd been to the club once before, when Mason was a freshman and I was visiting him from Fallen Crest. Nate's fraternity had a private room that night.

That felt so long ago.

Heather snuffed out her second cigarette and came back over. "This is ridiculous." Her hands found her slim hips as she surveyed the line. "Can't you use Mason's name to get us inside? If he were here, you know we'd get in right away."

"Yeah, but Mason and I broke up."

She waved that off. "Yeah, right. You'll get drunk tonight, call him, and I'll end up sleeping on the couch. I can read the writing on the wall." She rolled her eyes. "Sorry. I'm not the most patient one."

Her phone had buzzed nonstop the first couple days after she came to Cain, but it had stopped after she stepped outside for a heated conversation with Channing. I knew he'd come up with her and spent time with the guys, but I wasn't sure what had happened after that.

"You and Channing have a fight?"

She groaned.

"I'm sorry."

She shook her head, still scanning the line. "It's fine. He partied with the guys for a night, then headed back to Roussou. There are things going on with his sister, and he's got this idea we should chill for a while, for her benefit. It's all bullshit."

She'd mentioned Channing's sister before, but I'd never met her. "I'm sorry I've not been the best friend this week."

She squeezed my arm gently. "Samantha, seriously. You and Mason broke up. Granted, I don't think that's going to last long, but still. That's apocalypse sort of stuff. Like, end of the world stuff—"

"Are you Samantha Strattan?"

A security guard stopped and blinked a few times at me as he passed.

"Yeah?"

Heather nodded. "That's Mason Kade's fiancée. And she's an Olympic hopeful."

"What are you doing in line?" He motioned for us to come with him and gestured to the other security guards at the door. "Just tell those guys who you are. You should never have to wait." He led the way and held the door for us. As we swept in, he winked. "Just use my name if they don't believe you."

"And your name would be?" Heather turned to walk backward behind me. Her tone dropped low.

"Bass."

"Bass?"

I glanced back and saw a slow smile spread on his face, his eyes darkened. "Oh yeah. Bass. That's all you need to find me."

"I might put that to the test one day," Heather said.

Courtney and Grace laughed as they ducked around Heather and me to get inside. Once Bass closed the door, the nightclub was startlingly dark—until red, pink, blue, and green neon lights lit the way and we found a bar. That's when the shots started.

Shot one. Shot two. Three. Four.

It wasn't long until I was fucked up.

I began feeling the music. The lights blurred around me. The edges of my vision closed so I wasn't aware of anyone except my friends, and before long, I was smiling. I was laughing. I was enjoying time with these girls. Mason was still with me—he was always there, always in the back of my mind, but he was sleeping right now. He wasn't active in my mind, not like these friends.

Feeling someone behind me, I turned, a wide smile already on my face.

"Taylor!" I threw my arms around her.

"HEY!" Courtney raised her drink, sliding off her stool, and she hugged Taylor too. "You made it."

"I did." Taylor was laughing but as she took us all in, she shook her head slightly. "When you said you were going out for drinks, I thought one or two." She eyed the half-empty glass in Courtney's hand and the shot I'd just taken. "How many are you guys on?"

I held up my hand, my fingers spread out. "Seven!"

Grace tripped over to us, giggling, and she held up two fingers next to my hand. "Now that's right."

"Oh yeah." I turned, looping my arm around her shoulders. "Thank you for that. I forgot."

Heather handed Taylor a glass. "Here. Drink up. You have a long way to catch up."

Taylor took it, still eyeing us with raised eyebrows. "We're cabbing it home, right?"

I nodded. Even drunk, my cheeks were hurting. "And no calling Logan for a ride."

She would call him, and he'd call Mason, and both of them would come, and then Mason would find me. We'd find a dark corner, and tonight would be for nothing. I held up a finger. "Tonight is about friends. Not boys. Friends."

Taylor watched me, sober.

Courtney's eyes were glazed over as she propped an elbow on the bar to rest her head. She was watching me. So was Grace, weaving, her cheeks flushed, and a hand over her mouth to keep in the infectious giggles that'd been spilling out all night long. And then Heather stood next to Taylor. Her long dirty-sexy blond hair was messed, and her black eye shadow was smudged, but her eyes were still alert.

I took a moment, looking at all of them watching me back.

They were here because of me, for me.

I opened my arms to them. "I love you guys." I couldn't look away from Heather. "How'd I get so lucky? Why do you like me?"

"Oh, Sam." Taylor sighed.

Courtney brushed a hand over her eyes, and Grace's hand fell from her mouth.

Heather reached for me. She held me tight, whispering against my hair. "I've got my dad and brothers, and I've got Channing, but you're family too. You gave me a family too, you know."

I clasped on to her. I meant what I said—why did she like me? Why did anyone like me? Some days I was weak, whiny, and wishy-washy. And those were the only W characteristics I could think of when I was intoxicated.

I was so goddamn lucky.

"You're not any of those."

I pulled back.

Heather shook her head, wearing a wry grin. "You're not weak. You've never whined. And you're damn sure not wishy-washy. You love, and you love hard, and you never complain. I know you stepped away from Mason, and I know it probably killed you to do that. Don't think of yourself that way. Anyone who says that shit about you is the weak one. They're the whiny ones. Don't ever let yourself be defined by someone else's biases. Got it? You're one of the strongest people I know, and that's saying a lot." Her hands caught my shoulders. "Got it, Sam? Tell me you got it."

"Got it."

The words spilled from my tongue. I hadn't realized I'd spoken out loud. But she was right. I *was* strong. My shoulders lifted and straightened. I *did* love hard. I was more than what others might say. *They* were the things they said.

"Thanks, Heather."

Her smile turned gentle.

I groaned. So many tears. I was sick of them. "I think we should do more shots." I lifted my hand to order them, but Heather pulled it down.

"I think you're good with those," she said. "Here." She gave me a different drink, like the one she'd given Taylor. "That's a Long Island Iced Tea. You can sip on that the rest of the night."

"Sip?" I sneered. "You mean chug?" And I proceeded to do just that.

"No!" She laughed, and so did Taylor. Both tried to pull the drink away from me.

"I don't think I've ever seen you like this, Sam."

I rarely was. I'd drink one or two, then stop. I couldn't remember the last time I was really inebriated.

"Me neither," Heather added.

Then Grace announced, "I'm so glad we became friends this year."

"Yes! Friends!" I reached for my glass again. This time it was half-full. I could finish the rest, no problem.

"No!" All of them kept it from me.

"Come on."

"No." Courtney grabbed it and pushed it far behind her on the bar. I couldn't get to it without losing my place by my friends' side. The bar was dramatically busier than when we first arrived. I swayed on my feet, taking it all in.

"Where'd all these people come from?"

Taylor chuckled again beside me, and Heather said, "They've been here since we got in."

"Really?"

Everyone nodded.

"Oh."

I hooked my fingers around the loops on my jeans and tried not to sway. They were staring at me, waiting for something.

"What?"

I felt another wave of gratitude crash over me. Jessica and Lydia were my best friends growing up, but neither was loyal.

Then there was Becky.

Oh, Becky.

I had loved Becky.

She stood at my side when everyone deserted me, and she continued to stand there even during the ridicule and attacks. Even when the guy she always loved showed interest in me. I never should've become friends with Adam. That was on me, but it didn't matter in the end.

She chose Adam over me.

Adam . . .

He was the friend gone wrong. How had that gone *so* wrong?

I was starting to sober.

Could I have done something different? Not been friends with him. At all. But that was before Mason and Logan. Could I have read the writing on the wall? Was there writing on the wall? Could I have known what would happen almost five years later?

If I had, maybe this rivalry with Mason and Logan wouldn't have built itself up. Maybe Adam's ego wouldn't have been bruised. Maybe Mason wouldn't have continued to see Adam as a threat, as someone coming to take me away.

Maybe none of those things would've happened.

But I didn't know.

Could I have known? Had there been signs? Had I been like my mom all over again without realizing?

She strung men along. Had I done the same?

No . . . But . . .

"Hey, hey." Strong feminine hands took my shoulders again. "Look at me," Heather ordered.

I couldn't. I shook my head instead. "Heather, I'm to blame for all of this. I didn't want to be like Analise, but I was. I am. I became her when that was the last thing I wanted to be."

"Look at me!"

I did, through watery eyes. "It's all my fault."

"No. It is not."

"It is. It's all my fault."

She glanced to Taylor. "Okay, what happened? I haven't pushed her to tell me, but I have to know."

"Adam Quinn brought a gun to the parking lot, to see Mason."

Courtney and Grace gasped.

In the back of my mind, I was surprised it wasn't around campus yet.

I heard Heather curse under her breath. "Are you serious?"

Taylor nodded, tears in her eyes.

"Fuck's sake." Heather focused on me again. She lowered her head so her eyes were looking right into mine. "That is not your fault. Adam Quinn is not your fault."

"But I could've not been his friend—"

"Samantha, stop it. You are not your mother. I know what you're thinking, but you did not toy with one guy while screwing another. That's not who you are. I wasn't there in the beginning, but I wasn't too far behind. You were explicitly honest about who you loved and who you were with."

I tried to stop crying. I did.

"You never went there. Ever. You are loyal. You are strong. You are selfless. You are all those good things that your mother was not. She helped you learn who you wanted to be despite her, not who you could've been. Give yourself a break, Sam. You aren't to blame for any of this."

"Neither are the guys."

We both turned to Taylor. She seemed to have spoken without realizing, and her hand touched her mouth. Her forehead wrinkled as she saw us looking at her.

"I mean it. The guys aren't either. They just love you, and they protect you. It's what they do. The whole thing was Adam's fault, not yours, not Mason's. Adam's. He brought the gun. Mason didn't give it to him. Mason didn't tell him to bring it. Adam did. Whether what he said was true or not, why he had it there, it doesn't even matter. He made the decision. Just like he chose to go along with his dad's plan of spying on Mason, just like he chose to find that video and edit it to set Mason up, just like when he chose to break into your house. He made all those decisions. Not the guys."

I didn't say anything. But I clung to everything she said.

"Mason didn't set Quinn up. He didn't break into Adam's house to try to spy on him for the rest of his life. What he did was fight back and try to push him away so he'd actually stay away. He was protecting you."

I frowned. My thinking was becoming a bit more rational. Was she right? Had I been wrong to leave in the first place? Was Mason wrong to believe he couldn't see the line when he was protecting me? Was this all really just an accident? Or Adam's fault in the first place?

Everything was so muddled up.

My head felt heavy. My neck was stiff.

Why had we gone out drinking again?

"Okay." As if reading my mind, Heather reached for my drink that Courtney had pushed away and put it back in my hands. "We're not here to save the world. Heavy thoughts are not welcome now." She included Taylor in the last statement, her eyes sweeping over and back to me. "And now . . ." She clinked her glass to mine. "Let's get fucked up, because to be honest, we all need a break. One night." She picked up her glass and chugged the entire thing.

I wasn't far behind.

The music was already blaring, and Courtney jumped to her feet, grabbing Grace's hands. "Come on. Let's dance. I love this song."

After that, the rest of the night was a different kind of blur.

I danced. I smiled. I laughed.

And I didn't think about anything else because I just couldn't.

CHAPTER FORTY-THREE

MASON

From where I was sitting, I could see Nate coming a long way off.

"This is the last damned place I thought I'd find you." Nate grunted as he sat on the step next to the track. He sat carefully and made sure to lean against a thick and sturdy post. "Shit, Mase." He pulled his knees up, resting his elbows against them. "I thought you were scared of heights."

"Nervous of heights." He was right, though. It was the last place I thought I'd end up too. I intended to go to the pool, but found myself climbing this rollercoaster instead.

"Same thing. Why the fuck are you here?"

I shook my head. "This is Logan's spot. He likes to come and sit here. I think that's why Dad hasn't had it torn down yet." I leaned forward to rest my own elbows on the front of my seat. "Guess it felt right."

I nodded in the direction of town. We were above everything else, and the whole place spread out beneath us, like it was ours for the taking.

"She's out there. I wanted to be somewhere maybe I could see her." Even though I knew it was crazy, I didn't care. I wanted to feel like I could still watch over her.

Nate looked out, then swung his head back to me. I could feel his gaze. "Fuck, man." He let out a quiet sigh. "Talk to me. I know things changed, but I was your number one at one point."

I gave him a rueful grin. "We never really talked back then. Not really."

He looped his hands together, and his Adam's apple bobbed up and down. He was settling in. "I know, but that was how guys talked to each other at that time. We were kids. You were angry and hurting."

I was. I closed my eyes and cursed. "I don't even know why I was so mad sometimes. It's not like I had a family then lost it. They were always like that." I glanced at him. "You never talk about your parents."

Nate grinned. "Because I have good parents. I love my mom and dad. I don't like to rub it in your face."

I grinned back. "Just did."

"You deserve it."

My grin grew. He was right. I did. "I've been a shit friend to you over the years."

"No." He grew serious, shaking his head. "No, that's not true. I left. Things changed. I came back, and I was jealous. You were right to be cautious with me, but you never cut me out. I did some weasel things, and you could've. You never did."

I owed him.

"You let me come to you, to your parents' party, and you let me go upstairs and start a fight," I said. "You knew I was going to do that, and you said okay."

Nate snorted. "I think that was the turning point. My parents knew you were hurting, but when you did that, they were like, 'Okay. Enough's enough.'" His laugh had a sad ring to it. "They didn't want me to become like you. But instead, all they did was hurt me. I lost my place as your best friend when we moved. I never fully got it back."

Logan grew up. Logan became my ride-or-die, and Sam came along.

"I'm sorry for back then." I glanced over to him. "I wasn't an easy person to be friends with."

"No." He shook his head again, his tone thoughtful. "You were the easiest there was. I just had to be loyal; that's all you asked for."

"You were loyal—"

"No, I wasn't." He frowned. "Why are you trying to rewrite history? I wasn't. You said to stop sleeping with the girls. I didn't. I continued to fuck Parker. Then the whole video thing. I didn't tell you about that right away, and I should've. Logan would've. Logan would've gone ballistic if Kate tried to blackmail him into drugging Sam. And freshman year here, I knew Sebastian was using me to get to you. I knew it, and let it happen. I even tried to make you feel guilty for not liking him. I did those things. Not you. Sam never would've. Logan never would've. You never would've. No. Your solid two are right where they're supposed to be, right at your side. I lost my place, and I didn't get it back for a reason. It took me until Sebastian to get my priorities right. You never have to apologize to me, and you never have to feel sorry for anything. You've been my friend. You never turned on me."

I had to grin. "I don't usually have heart-to-hearts with Logan. And even the few we have, it's usually me telling him to shut the fuck up or him telling me the same."

Nate shrugged, leaning his head back. He extended his legs, his heels resting on one of the tracks. "It's overdue, if you ask me."

"You're wrong."

"It's not?"

"No. You did prove your loyalty." I didn't say the words, but our eyes met and he knew. The frat house. "You proved it."

He nodded, then asked, "What are you going to do about those videos? Cops never showed up asking for them, so I'm guessing Quinn never mentioned them."

I snorted. "Would you?"

Nate smiled faintly. "No. I wouldn't. You still have them?"

I nodded. "I'll keep them, in case he comes after us again. Just in case."

But maybe I shouldn't have them. Maybe that was the bad part of me I could help make good? Maybe that was part of why I was even sitting on a fucking abandoned rollercoaster in the first place. "I could delete them."

"Why would you do that?"

"We did that to Quinn. He brought a gun to campus. I mean—" I suppressed the rage that flared every time I thought about it. "Sam was there. I'll never forgive myself for that."

"So don't, but don't let it change you completely."

"What do you mean?"

He leaned forward, looping his hands together, resting them on his legs. "The problem would be ignoring this whole thing. Don't do that. You pushed a guy. We all pushed him, and maybe it was too far, but we could've pushed him further. We could've burned the place down. We've done it before. I could've actually screwed his woman. You could've released those videos. It could've been worse."

"I don't think Sam would agree with you."

"You didn't do anything wrong."

My eyebrows went up at that.

"You know what I mean. You were protecting. That's what you do. Sam knew who you were when she fell in love with you. She signed up for it. She can't claim ignorance now and back out. That's not right. If she's scared, that's another thing, but she can't blame you. You're being you. None of us are saints. That's for sure, but it could've been worse."

I shook my head. "He had a gun, Nate."

"Yeah," he clipped out, jerking forward. His eyes were blazing once again. "And the problem would be to ignore what happened. You're not ignoring it. Neither is Sam. You're both doing what's right, but you don't have to change. You already have."

"What do you mean?"

"Not being scared, that would've been wrong. Acting like it was no big deal. Pretending it was all him, and not you or us. Not realizing how close you and Sam came to your lives being threatened. All of that would've been wrong. You guys aren't doing any of that. You took notice. You're acknowledging it. You don't want it to ever happen again. You're scared it could. That's the right thing you're doing. You've learned that you don't want this to repeat again, and my guess is that it never will. You'll read the signs. You'll know when you're going too far. You'll rely on the rest of us too. I'm here. Logan's here. We're all here. No one's leaving. It's never just you. Ever. You can trust us. If you don't see the line, we will. Trust us. Trust Sam. Trust yourself. You don't have anything more to repent. You already have. You get that, right?"

Goddamn. I felt tears in the corner of my eye.

I scowled at him. "If you make me cry, I'll punch you in the face."

He barked out a laugh. "You do that, you'd have to carry me back down. You'd probably knock me out."

"I'd call Logan. He'd figure out how to get you back on the ground."

"Fuck." He grimaced, some of the blood draining from his face. "He'd probably lower me down with a rope tied around my waist. He'd get me killed."

"But it'd be on me because I punched you in the first place."

He laughed, and I joined in.

I rubbed a hand over my forehead. "You're right. My brother would kill you, somehow."

"Speaking of death," Nate looked over his shoulder and down to the ground. "Can we please leave this thing? Logan's batshit crazy for coming up here whenever he does."

I stifled a small shudder and stood. "Let's go." Once we were heading down, I asked, "Where is Logan?"

Nate was ahead of me and he tossed back over his shoulder, "Said something about picking Taylor up. She went out with some girls and got drunk."

"Girls?" I paused, mid-step.

Sam?

CHAPTER FORTY-FOUR
SAMANTHA

Kapow!

I hopped, threw my hand out in a karate chop, and let out a half-growl/half-gurgle. Then I snapped up my leg.

"Uh . . ." Heather traded looks with Taylor. Both were holding back grins. "Whatcha doing, Sam?"

"I'm karate-chopping your ass." And I leaped in a circle, my hand out in another *chop!* before I raised my knee. I pretended to take someone's head in my hands and rammed them down on my knee. "This is what I'm going to do to Faith Shaw if I see her on a bad night." I swung my arms around in a wide circle, then brought them together as if I were praying. As a snarl formed on my mouth, I shoved my hands out, palms flat. "And I'll break her nose, just like that."

I was panting.

I frowned. That didn't make sense.

I was drunk. With that realization, I lifted one leg, my arms to the side like I was going to do the crane kick move from *The Karate Kid*. "And hi-ya!" I smiled at them. "Did you hear that? I just dislocated her shoulder, all with one move."

"Okay." Heather moved around me out the door. "Bring those fighting moves this way. You're holding up traffic."

Taylor had left the group when we decided to leave. I had to run to the bathroom, and when I came back, Heather said Taylor had called a car for us and was waiting outside. Courtney and Grace were giggling at me, but I didn't care. Each move I made, they erupted in more laughter, their hands trying to hold it in. I didn't know why they tried.

They weren't the only ones watching. I declared after dancing that I needed more zen in my life. I was going to make Mason take yoga with me, but I couldn't practice any positions on the nightclub's floor—because disgusting—so I turned to my own rendition of tai chai. Heather said it was tai chi, but she was wrong. It was chai, just like the tea. I was adamant, and then that turned into my stealth ninja moves.

Each step I took out of the club was a ninja move. I was just through the doors.

We'd started ten minutes ago.

"Sorry." I heard Heather say to someone just behind me.

"No, no. This is entertaining as hell," an amused guy responded. "I think I reached my black belt just watching her."

"Hi-ya!" I leaped again, rounding back on whoever was behind me, and I pretended to ram my elbow into his chest.

Two guys were there, smiling and looking me over approvingly. The first one, who looked a little like Mason, smirked and stepped even closer. If I shifted an inch, my elbow really would've been pressed against his chest.

"What's your fighting name?" he asked.

I paused, frowning. This didn't feel right.

A door slammed behind us, and Heather cursed under her breath.

"Ninja Sam," I said, a death warning on the tip of my tongue. But three things happened then.

First, the guys looked over my shoulder and paled, stepping back. Then my hair stood on end, and finally, a strong and masculine arm wrapped around my waist. It lifted me and threw me over a shoulder. My mind considered struggling, but my body was already melting. It recognized its mate.

"She's mine," Mason growled.

He carried me across the sidewalk and into the opened back door of Logan's Escalade. I glimpsed the yellow, then Logan's smirking face before Mason climbed into the backseat and lifted me onto his lap.

"Hi, Logan." I waved a hand.

His eyes met mine in the mirror, but he only shook his head and waited until the rest of the girls got in. Once the last door was shut, he took off, and I curled into Mason's arms and rested my head against his chest.

I looked up at him. "What are you doing here?"

His arms tightened around me. "Logan got a call to pick you up. I made him pick me up first."

"Yeah?"

I smiled at him, and I knew I probably looked ridiculous—wasted and dreamy—but I didn't care. I reached up and touched his chin, his very strong and hard chin with a dimple in it, and I let out a sigh.

"Thank you for coming." We were broken up, but I didn't care at that moment.

There was a lot I didn't care about, but none of that was Mason. I was all sorts of caring about him.

His eyes darkened. "You had fun tonight?"

"I was missing you, then I was dancing." I nodded, closing my eyes. "Then I became Ninja Sam."

He chuckled, the sound washing over me and warming me. "Ninja Sam, huh?"

"Yes. She comes out when she has to take care of a problem."

What the problem was, I couldn't say.

Maybe I was missing him. Maybe it was because I wanted to call him, but knew the girls wouldn't like that idea. Or maybe they would? I didn't know. Or maybe it was just because I had too much alcohol in me, and I wasn't thinking and just feeling, or no—I sat upright. My eyes opened wide.

"Sam?"

"Raelynn."

Courtney, Grace, and Heather all turned around.

"What about her?" Courtney asked.

"Who's Raelynn?" That was Heather.

"She was there."

"What?" Courtney turned fully around, her hand holding onto the back of the seat between us. "Are you sure?"

"No." Grace shook her head. "She's injured. I talked to some of the girls, and they said she was still limping and stuff."

"No." I was certain. "Well, she might still be injured, but she walked past me. I was leaving the bathroom, and she was going in."

"Did she see you?"

I frowned. "I recognized her, but I don't think she did me. Her eyes were glazed over. She was holding hands with another girl."

"Faith?"

"No. Someone else." The more I thought about it, the better I remembered. There was no limp, no hesitation. She walked as freely as I did. "I guess she's all healed up."

"But that doesn't mean anything. Walking doesn't mean she can run."

"Yeah." I felt a pang in my chest. I nodded, moving my head against Mason's chest. "You're right."

"Who is Raelynn, and who has faith?"

Grace started giggling at Heather's question.

Even Courtney was fighting back a grin as she tried to explain. "Faith is the girl who—"

"Faith is Kate, but instead of Mason, it's their cross-country team," Logan cut in.

Heather nodded. "Ah. Got it." She looked at me. "What a bitch."

"Faith didn't jump me in a bathroom."

"That's good." Heather narrowed her eyes. "For her."

"You were jumped?" Courtney asked.

I nodded. "I never did get her back."

"We did." Logan met my gaze in the rearview mirror. "We took care of her."

That pang was there again, flipping over in my stomach now.

I peered up at Mason again, letting out a soft sigh.

His arm tightened around me. He dropped his head, murmuring into my ear so no one else could hear, "You okay?"

I looked back up to him, saw the concern, and the guilt went away. I said, so softly, for only him to hear, "I missed you tonight."

He turned his head, just slightly. His lips almost touching mine, and he said quietly back, "I missed you too."

I did not want to be broken up anymore. I rested my head on his shoulder, my lips grazing his neck. "How long do we have to do this?"

His lips touched mine, just barely. "I don't think we have to anymore."

"Yeah?" My eyes found his. Hope came alive in my chest.

"Yeah." He nodded, his eyes dark with lust and love.

I felt the tingling in my body. It spread all the way to my toes and fingers. Even drunk, I could feel it. I shifted closer to him, bringing our lips in contact, just for a second. I was forgetting where we were.

"Did you fix it?" I asked.

He touched my hand, locking our fingers. "I'm trying to."

God.

I wanted that so much. Maybe too much. The need for him swam in me, intoxicating me all over again.

"That'd be wonderful."

"Sam."

"Yeah?" I sat up, straddling him and not giving one shit who was with us in that car. I was selfish in that moment, and everyone had better be looking away.

He stared right back at me, and his lips curved in a smile. "I think we're going to be okay."

"Yeah?" I matched his smile.

He nodded. "Yeah."

Screw it. I sank against him, letting my body mold to his, and my lips fused with his. Just fuck it. I couldn't stay away any longer.

Mine. That was what he'd said to that guy, and I pulled back just enough to tell him, "You're mine too."

"Always."

I nodded. "Always."

Then we were kissing again, and I didn't think anymore. I was too busy being happy.

CHAPTER FORTY-FIVE

I was stretching on the floor the next morning, getting ready to run, when I heard Mason moving on the bed. I reached for my foot and twisted so I could see him peering at me from above.

"Morning."

I should've been hung over, but I couldn't stop the pep in my voice. I was going on a run. I was itching for it. It'd been a long two weeks.

He frowned at me. "You're annoyingly chipper."

"I know." I switched feet, reaching for my other one, and laughed, shrugging.

He was right. Everything felt right. He and I would be fine. Whatever my freak out had been—and I still didn't understand it myself—something in my bones told me everything would be fine. I only had one dilemma left to deal with, and I wasn't sure what I was going to say to Faith. I didn't even know if I had to say anything. I was clueless, but I was ready.

My life wasn't going to fall apart, and now I needed to run. I just needed to feel that burn in my legs, wind against my cheeks, and the sense of freedom. It wasn't flying, but it was the closest thing I could get.

He sighed and lay back down. "It's five in the morning. We fell asleep two hours ago."

It was less than that. Logan had picked us up at one thirty, but I went home with Mason and hadn't let him sleep till an hour ago. I grinned, my body warming as I remembered straddling him. I wanted to dominate, and Ninja Sam took on a whole different meaning last night—or technically earlier this morning.

319

"Go back to sleep." I stood, bending my knees and hugging them to my chest one at a time. "I have to run. I haven't gone for two weeks."

"You haven't?"

I paused, hearing his surprise. I felt my throat thicken. "If I started, I wouldn't have stopped."

"Oh."

I grinned. "We should probably talk again."

He growled, flipped over, and buried his head in the pillow. "Yes, but not now. God, not now." The blanket moved off his back, slipping down to rest just above his ass, and I sighed.

Goddamn. That ass.

I bit my lip. I knew what he looked like from the back as he thrust inside of me. I'd watched in the mirror a few times, and I now had the urge to drag him into the bathroom.

"I'm too tired."

I laughed. "What are you talking about?"

His head was under the pillow, and his voice came out muffled. "I know what you're thinking. I can feel your thoughts, and I'm calling for a ceasefire. I'm tired, woman. Some of us are human."

Human? I mouthed that word, still grinning to myself. He was calling *me* the non-human? Him? Who could outrun and outmuscle so many football players? Who was good enough to go to the NFL? Who the coaches would go to such great lengths to keep on their team? Him?

He was the machine, but I'd take the compliment. It just added to my morning. I was already on top of the world.

I reached for the door, but paused, my eyes tracing up his back. He rolled over, his eyes meeting mine with a twinkle.

The grin tugging at the corner of his lip had my lips twitching to mirror his, and the ache between my legs blossomed into an overwhelming love for him. I could feel everything inside of me soften.

"I love you," I said softly.

"I love you back."

"We're going to be okay?"

He nodded. "We'll be fine."

My heart skipped a beat, and I felt the flutter in my stomach as I smiled back.

His words were a blanket that I wrapped around myself. I felt them as I left and started down the street.

It felt good to run, but after a five-minute sprint, I stopped.

No one else was up. No cars. I didn't see any lights in the houses. It was just me, just the street, and I breathed it in.

I closed my eyes, spread my arms wide, and tipped my head back.

I was ready to fly.

CHAPTER FORTY-SIX

"Okay," Faith grumbled as she found me on the park bench. "I'm here."

I'd called her after a couple miles. I was going to demolish this girl, but I wanted to meet with her first.

She sat down on the bench beside me, yawning, and rubbed under her eyes. "Why did you demand I meet you here? It's Saturday. You know we have a race today, don't you?"

"You and I don't."

"Yes, we do." Her yawn stopped abruptly. Her mouth flattened, and her forehead wrinkled. "We can't miss any qualifying race."

"We're going to miss one." I stood and jumped up and down. I was antsy. "You and I are going to have our own race. Right here. Right now. And this is the last one."

"What are you talking about?" She stood too, more cautious.

"You want me to help you? You want to make me motivate you?"

"Yeah, but you've been gone for two weeks. Coach said something happened."

She wanted to know what, but she wasn't asking. Good. I wouldn't have told her anyway. My hand rested on my hip. "I saw Raelynn last night."

She didn't move, but I felt her attention snap into focus. "Yeah?"

I waited, studying her, and then I saw the guilt. My lip curled. "You're such a liar. You never went to see her, did you?"

Shame filled her eyes. I saw it for a brief second before she looked away. She swallowed, and when she turned back it was gone. She'd gotten herself under control, and she raised her top lip to match mine.

"What about it? Why do you give a shit? You haven't gone to see her either. Did you talk to her last night?"

"No, but that's not my job. It's yours. You were her best friend."

"It's weird!" she yelled, throwing her arms out.

"Get over it. She's someone who loved you. She had your back against me. You don't throw people like that away. You keep them close, and you have their back too. Trust me." I felt a lump in my throat. "I've had my share of people who said they loved me, but when things got bad, they couldn't leave me fast enough. When someone's hurt, you shield them, you don't hurt them further."

Her head hung. "That's not what I did."

"It is, but you keep telling yourself whatever excuse you've thought up. That'll be there long after you chase any other good person away."

"Goddamn it!" She threw her head back, eyes blazing. "What the fuck is your problem? Why are you on my ass about this?"

"Because I'm changing too!"

I stopped, wide-eyed. I could feel the intensity in them. My blood was pumping. Everything stopped, and I felt it click.

"What?" Faith's eyebrows pinched together.

Mason had to change. He needed to find the line with me, and hold it. But I had to change too. And Faith wasn't another Kate. I had been looking at her, anticipating it, but she wasn't. She wasn't a great human being, but she wasn't going to plot against me. She was all bluff.

I was calling her on it.

"You're never going to actually hurt me, are you?"

"What?" Her head craned backward. "No. Who do you think I am?"

"People from my past."

"What?" Her eyes grew wary.

"I have been plotted against. I have been hurt. Everything you've threatened has already happened to me. I took your threats seriously." But I didn't have to anymore.

I was changing.

I was growing up.

What happened to me before wasn't going to happen again, and I could see it now. It was clearer.

"You aren't Kate, Jessica, or Lydia. You're not even my mother. You're just . . ." I looked at her again, feeling my loathing gone. Faith just looked sad now. She was a girl, her brown hair pulled up in a braid. She had a pronounced jaw, maybe a little too square for a girl, and she was thin. I would've thought she had a problem if I didn't know how strong her legs were. They were shaped and firm, like a professional runner's. But . . . she was just a girl.

All the fight I had stored for her fled. "I've been picking fights with you, haven't I?"

She closed her mouth, then lifted a shoulder, but she kept a cautious eye on me. "I've given you reason. I'm a spoiled brat, and I might tell people not to talk to you, but I'm not vindictive where I want you to actually get hurt. I just say things. My sister keeps saying my big mouth is going to get me in trouble. And you're right."

I glanced at her.

She rolled her eyes, her lips strained in annoyance. "You have made me question a couple things, and who I have in my circle is one of them. You're right. Raelynn always had my back, and I knew she loved me, but she never did anything about it. She just supported me."

"She just loved you."

"Yeah. She did." She let out a sigh. "I'll make it right with her." Her eyebrows pulled together. "You saw her last night? Where?"

"A nightclub."

"Which one?"

I shrugged. "I wasn't paying attention to much last night, but she was more drunk than I was. She walked right past me without blinking an eye."

"She doesn't pay attention. When she goes out, she purposely gets in her own head. I don't know why she does that, but she does. Always drove me crazy."

I heard the fondness and added, "She was holding hands with a girl."

Her head lifted up. "Yeah?"

I nodded.

"Good for her, if that person is *more*, you know. She better be a damned good person. Rae deserves it." She waved that off, or tried. Her hand stopped mid-wave. "She deserves more than me as a friend too."

I didn't know what to say, but I didn't think Faith cared. We stood in silence. Faith was with her thoughts, and I let her be.

After a couple minutes, she coughed and refocused. "Uh. Why did you want to meet this morning again?"

I gestured down the running path. "From here, if you follow this path until it stops, it's seventeen miles. We both skip today's race. This is ours. You and me."

"Why? I mean, you're just going to beat me."

But she started stretching again, and so did I. My body had begun to cool. I needed to warm it up again.

I grabbed for my toes. "Because this is it. This is our race. I'm going to beat you—"

"Don't get cocky or anything." She laughed.

I ignored her. "But it's up to you by how much. And after this, we're done. We're not rivals anymore. We're teammates. All the petty, catty bullshit is over. Got it?"

She paused, her eyes narrowing, and then her head bobbed up and down. "Got it."

After we finished stretching and started off, I said, "I should probably tell you something."

"What?" She grew wary again.

"I haven't run for two weeks." I smirked at her.

She groaned. "You're still such a bitch."

I didn't care, and I laughed as I pushed forward. It wasn't even thirty yards before I couldn't see her anymore, and when I got to campus, I did another bitchy thing.

I had time to go and pick up some breakfast—for one. I went back to finish it, and I ate the last crumb when she showed.

"You're such a bitch."

I handed her some water. "I have to rub it in. This is my last time, remember?"

She groaned, but took the water.

———⌐

It wouldn't have been correct to say that Faith and I stopped being rivals after that race, but it was close. We weren't friends, but there was respect for each other. And no matter how much she wanted to beat me, she never could. I always loved rubbing it in her face.

I'd run for years, but I never realized until this year how fast I was, how unique a runner I had become. I don't know if it was family genetics—Garrett was athletic, but he told me he never enjoyed running. That made me think of Analise. Had she been the one to give me this gift? Or was it more complicated? Genetics mixed with practice? Maybe I was blessed, but I'd honed it into this ability to run longer and faster than anyone else I knew.

At least until I qualified for the Olympics.

After that, I was no longer the fastest person I knew.

But I was among them.

CHAPTER FORTY-SEVEN

A year later.

I ran through the back hills near Fallen Crest, feeling the burn in my legs. I loved it, just like I always had, and I picked up my pace.

So much had happened over the last year.

Mason graduated and was drafted to the New England Patriots. His first year with them had been good, and he was happy to start a second, but he'd been restless. Logan and I had remained in California to finish school while he went to Massachusetts, and I knew it hurt. He was clear across the nation. The winter was hard, but every free moment we had, Logan and I flew out to see him. Then when it was off-season for him, he came back to live with us. But all that was done now.

Logan and I graduated last week.

I got a degree in health and wellness—yes, I'd finally picked a major. Logan was on to law school next, but for now we were back home for a couple weeks until Mason had to fly out for summer training. I was going to go with him this time. I could train wherever I was, and the Olympics were always on my mind.

Logan would join us at the end of August. He'd gotten in to University of Massachusetts School of Law in Dartmouth. We bought a huge house where all five of us could live: Mason, Logan, Nate, Taylor, and me.

Matteo had been drafted to the Los Angeles Raiders right out of school, and he was glad to stay in California, as it put him closer to his family, and closer to Grace. Those two were still together.

As for Courtney, she was headed back to Ohio for a teaching job. She'd only been there a couple weeks, but already life was boring. She wanted another dancing night with the girls.

I was all for that, and I pumped my arms harder at the thought. I kicked off with a bit more speed.

Mason and I had plans to hang out with Heather and Channing tonight. Heather wanted me to scope out a location for a second Manny's with her tomorrow, but she said tonight we'd all get fucked up, laugh till our sides split, and take our men home to have hot and heavy sex.

Sounded good to me.

I still had ten miles to go, and I approached the clearing at the top of the hill where Mason first proposed to me. We hadn't really discussed marriage since Mason had announced our engagement at his press conference—not at length anyway.

We had an understanding. Mason would wait until I felt more comfortable with the idea. As much as I tried, old scars from Analise and David's marriage ran deep in me. Or they had.

Now I was ready. More than ready.

I wanted to talk to Mason about it this summer, but I wasn't sure yet how to have the conversation. *Uh, honey? You can propose to me any day you want.* Yeah. It felt weird. Maybe I could slip him a note. I smiled to myself at how foolish that seemed as I crested the hill. The clearing opened to me, and I stopped in my tracks.

Mason stood in front of me.

He wasn't alone.

Logan, Taylor, Nate, Heather, Channing, Malinda—I scanned the group quickly. There were so many. Mark. David. Even Garrett. Sharon was there, holding my little sister, who waved, her cheeks and lips covered in chocolate. Helen was there too, looking like it was the last place she wanted to be, but she folded her hands in front of her and even managed a small smile.

Analise and James held hands, a few feet to the side and behind everyone else. My mother waved, a tentative smile on her face, and drawing in a deep breath, she stepped closer to the group. James patted her back, and she flicked a hand up to her eyes.

She was crying.

Why was my mom crying? Wait. I went back to Malinda. She was crying too. Taylor. Heather. Courtney. Grace. Even Matteo, who was holding Grace's hand. They were all blinking back tears.

I focused on Mason again. He was in front of everyone, waiting for me.

"What's going on?"

He knelt down and held up his hand. There. Right there between his finger and thumb was a ring.

I stopped breathing.

It sparkled, and it was beautiful, and it was huge, but I didn't care about any of that.

"Are you sure?" I asked hoarsely.

He laughed, his own voice raspy, and nodded. "Will you marry me, Samantha? Will you become Samantha Jacquelyn Kade?"

My throat filled, and I nodded. I couldn't stop nodding, and I couldn't stop smiling, and then I felt the tears on my cheeks, and I couldn't stop crying.

"Yes," I managed, just as he stood and swept me off my feet.

I wrapped my arms tight around him, whispering it again, just for myself. "Yes, I'll marry you."

"I love you," he whispered, carrying us a few feet away.

He set me back down, and I looked at him. "I love you too." I touched his lips. "So goddamn much."

"So goddamn much." And his lips were on mine.

EPILOGUE

Six months later.

"Tomorrow you'll become my wife," Mason murmured, lifting our hands.

We were in bed. I lay in the shelter of his arms, my head propped in the corner of his arm and chest.

"I am." I grinned up at him. "You're going to become my husband."

A soft smile crept over his face, lighting it up. "Husband."

"Wife." My grin matched his.

We were defying tradition.

We were supposed to separate, sleep in other beds, but there'd been no discussion. We both knew that wouldn't happen. And it was now close to five in the morning. The first light of the day would be showing soon, but there was no tired bone in my body. I knew there wouldn't be all day.

"Are you sure you want to marry me?"

I had settled back into his arms again, but lifted my head once more. "What do you mean?"

He shrugged, his smile gone. "I mean, are you sure? We were high school sweethearts. It'd be normal to think about being single at some point in your life. Right?" His eyes flashed and tense lines formed around his mouth.

"Mason." I shifted on the bed, propping myself to lie on my stomach. I tucked some of the sheet over my breasts, but they were pressed against his chest. I watched him. "Are *you* having second thoughts?"

Logan said their bachelor night had been epic. Maybe too epic?

At my question, the tension lines softened, and he slid his hands into my hair, cupping the sides of my face. "No. I'm just worried you might regret this one day."

"Not possible." I said those words softly, but they tore at my heart. He really thought that?

"Are you sure you're not going to regret this?" I asked, feeling my throat burning.

He laid his head back against the headboard and moved it from side to side. "Not possible."

A thrill went through me as he used my words, a loving smile on his face, and I felt my heart skip a beat. Nope. The words *regret* and *second thoughts* would never enter my vocabulary when it came to my relationship with him.

I sat up, drawing more of the sheet around me. It slipped from his waist, so I lifted a corner and spread it out over him.

He snorted, grinning. "What are you doing?"

I shrugged, holding back my own grin. "I have something to say, and I don't want to get distracted."

"Distracted?"

I nodded. "Yes. Distracted." I crossed my arms over my chest and fixed him with a sturdy look. "I want to know more about where this came from. You've never mentioned second thoughts to me before."

He reached over and caught my hands, tugging my arms back down to my lap. He slid his fingers against mine, resting our hands on his chest. "Logan said something earlier about how he got to be free and slutty. He was glad he met Taylor when he did, because he got the wild side of him out and he could be content with her for the rest of his life." He paused, swallowing. "Got me thinking. You went from Sallaway to me, and you've never been single since." His eyes flicked to mine, a haunted agony lining them. "It'd break my heart if you ever regretted us."

And that, right there, broke mine.

Feeling choked up, I could only shake my head. "You want to know what I was going to say to you tomorrow?" I murmured, hoarse around the big fat lump in my throat.

"What? No—"

But I'd already started. He was too late, and I knew this was the perfect time to say these words.

"On this day, Mason James Kade, you become my future. You are already, Mason James Kade, a huge part of my past. On this day, Mason James Kade, you are my ever-living present." I gripped his hand. "I will be side by side with you no matter where our path goes. I have walked with you. I have run with you. I have laughed with you. I have cried with you. I have supported and been supported by you. I have yelled at you, for you, and with you. I have cursed with you. I have felt pain. I have felt joy. I have felt peace. I have felt every emotion a person can experience. Some have been because of you. Some have been because of others, but it was always *with* you that I could feel what I felt. From the moment I met you, you took me in and loved me as family. We evolved. We became more, and we will continue to evolve, but there is no one else I would choose to have next to me. *Ever.*"

I had to stop. The tears were drowning my words, but he needed to hear them.

I needed to say them.

"I declare right now that I am not choosing to become Samantha Kade. I have *always* been Samantha Kade. It will be official tomorrow, but that's the only difference. That's it. I am already your wife in every sense of the word."

I took a deep breath. I had more to say, but then his lips stopped me.

He kissed me, and I felt his tears against my face.

When we parted, he rested his forehead against mine, and before I could stop him, he spoke his own words. He said them as he lifted me onto him, and he continued as he entered me.

He kept saying those words as I gasped, cried, begged, and then screamed my release, and he didn't stop whispering them until I finally fell asleep.

Just a few hours later, I stood at the end of a rose-strewn aisle, my bouquet in hand. My wedding dress had been fitted over me, and my bridesmaids were already waiting for me at the front of our little wooded paradise.

This was my wedding. This was my dream come true.

I'd gotten the family I dreamed about, but what I'd said to Mason last night was true: I always had it.

Today it was just legal. That was all.

The music changed. The volume rose, and everyone stood.

All eyes turned to me, some misty-eyed, some blurred with tears, and others smiling widely.

I walked past people from Fallen Crest Academy. I walked past people from Fallen Crest Public High School. There were others from Cain University, some from the country club, still others from the carnival. And even more from my family, biological or not. But this wasn't about them. I didn't really see them.

This was about Mason and me.

This was about me getting the happily ever after I'd always had; I just never knew it.

And then there he was. I saw the same wetness swimming in his eyes that had been there last night, but he wouldn't shed them this time. Not in front of others. That was only for me to see.

Hi," I whispered, swallowing back my own tears.

He laughed. "Hi."

Then he took my hand, and I remembered his soft plea from right before I fell asleep. *"Don't leave me. Please."*

We weren't linked by that plea. We'd been linked so long ago, and it wasn't even a request he had to make. He'd broken down his wall for me when we first fell in love. He'd taken care of me over the last years, and I knew others sometimes forgot to take care of him back, but not me. I would never forget, and just as I had this morning, I reached out and took his hand.

I glanced down at the tattoo both of us had gotten.

As we exchanged vows and professed our commitment to each other, we each stole glances down at our fingers. The tattoos were permanent, and the butterflies stood for our sanctuary. Mason's was sketched in black, whereas mine was colorful, but one at a time, we placed our rings over them.

We said "I do" and my fingers slid through his and clasped down. Forever.

"Okay." Logan raised his glass, holding a microphone in the other hand. He tapped it softly against his glass to get everyone's attention.

The room was filled with conversation and laughter, but he gave the signal, and the deejay cut the music.

"It's that time, folks." He dipped his mouth closer to the mic so his voice boomed, "Toast time." He laughed. "Say that five times fast, huh?"

A smattering of laughter came from our wedding guests.

He smirked at everyone, then turned to Mason and me. He had a twinkle in his eye.

"Aren't you guys lucky? I like you both. No, that's not true. I love you both." He laughed, glancing to where Analise and James sat. "And you guys are lucky too—that it ain't your wedding. I never did get the private jet, Dad."

James sat back, his arm resting on my mother's chair. He raised it now and motioned to his youngest son. "Anytime. Let me know."

"I will." Logan leveled him with a hard stare. "I mean it. I'm taking that jet."

James gave him a thumbs-up, appearing unconcerned.

"Dude." Nate leaned forward from the other side of Logan's empty chair. "Toast, please. Some of us are in line still."

"Chill." Logan motioned toward him. "Simmer down. Your time is coming, but now it's mine." He focused on us again, and I saw him melting already. He was softening, but with the slightly glazed look in his eye.

I wasn't sure what he was going to say. Logan was unpredictable.

Mason's hand touched mine under the table.

I had to laugh.

We were literally hanging on now.

"Talk, Logan," Mason ordered.

There was no quick retort for his brother. Logan merely rolled his shoulders back and turned to the crowd. "I think you all know how much I love my brother. I worshiped him growing up, and then I started worshiping Sam when she moved in too. You guys all know the story. Mason and I were like orphans."

People began laughing.

I did too.

Mason cracked a grin.

Logan winked at us. "Our mother cheated *constantly* on our dad, and when he decided to leave her, he left us too. Then we found out our mom wasn't even our mom, and we were really in a situation. Who was our real mom? Could it be a magical lawyer from Boston? Maybe it was our neighbor across the road the whole time. Maybe we really had a secret brother? No one knew." He kept a straight face until the end, then he began laughing. "I'm kidding. That's Nate's life story."

"Hey!"

Logan ignored him. "For real, this is a weird moment for me, because I remember when Sam and Mason first met. I was there. I think I was there for everything, except a few sex scenes. Although . . ." His grin deepened, and a dimple appeared in his right cheek. "I heard plenty of those too. That's the uncomfortable part of living together, and holy shit—we lived all over the place. The mansion. Nate's house. Mom's house."

He glanced to Helen, then turned back. "Malinda's house. The house in Cain. Shit. I'm sure I'm forgetting places, but we lived in a bunch of different spots. And no joking here, but we may have switched houses, but I never felt like I didn't have a home. You guys were my home. You guys were my family. You guys *are* my family. That's never changed, and I know it never will. Through everything, we were there for each other, and holy fuck—"

"Logan, there are children here," someone hissed.

"Oh. Sorry." He held a hand up, but didn't look away from us. Only Mason and I saw the moisture building in his eyes. He stopped, and his Adam's apple moved as he swallowed. Then he gripped the microphone with both hands. "We've been through a lot—a lot of hospital visits, a lot of middle-of-the-night phone calls, a lot of good old-fashioned schoolyard fights, and some nastier ones. Yeah." He drew in a breath, so solemn now.

I felt a tear slipping free, sliding down my cheek.

Logan saw it and gave me a soft grin. "I love you guys. And I'm so goddamn honored to have you in our family, Sam." A rueful laugh slipped out. "Despite your bloodline."

"Logan!"

He ignored James, and his voice dipped low. He said softly, "I am proud to be in our Threesome Fearsome, and I wouldn't do a damned thing to change us." He kissed the side of his fist and met it to both of ours, then rocked back on his heels.

He raised his glass. "So I'm ending this toast, because I have a feeling it's the most sober one you're going to get tonight. Please help me welcome Samantha officially into our family. You know, besides the fact that she's already our stepsister."

His grin turned wicked, and he looked back at us. "Welcome to the family, Samantha. And just so you know, you've always been one of us, whether you wanted to be or not." He raised his glass one more time, then finished it in one gulp.

Everyone drank, and Logan added, "Now I send my apologies, because you have to endure everyone else's toasts."

Nate stood up and his chair scraped backward. He held his hand out.

"Especially Nate's, but be kind. We love him."

Nate took the microphone, half scowling and half laughing. "Sit down. We all know you're going to be trying to do a second, third, and fourth toast."

Logan took the seat beside Mason and nodded. "Oh yeah. That was the censored toast. These folks don't know what they have coming later."

"Hi, everyone." Nate stepped back from the table, his drink in hand, and gazed at Mason and me for a moment. His voice grew thick as he let out an uncomfortable laugh.

"Sorry." His head dipped low, his voice was hoarse. "I'm—I knew I'd have to wrestle this thing from Logan, so I wasn't fully prepared. Now I'm standing here and staring at someone who I've considered a brother all my life, and wow." His mouth curved into a half-grin. "It's overwhelming. Man, Mase. I can't believe you got married. I mean . . ." His eyes found mine. "I knew you were the girl for Mason, but the whole journey we've taken. It's just, wow. It's a lot."

He lifted his head and looked to the crowd. "I'm not an orphan, just so everyone knows. I have some incredible parents." He pointed. "Right over there."

An older woman and man waved.

Nate cleared his throat. "Yeah. Since I came back, I haven't left your side. And we've had times, like Logan said. I was one of those hospital visits." He gestured to me. "Sam too, but we've gotten through everything, and I know I don't regret anything. I wouldn't trade anything with anybody, no matter what was promised to me. Thank you, Mason. Thank you for being my best friend growing up. Thank you for bringing me into the family. Thank you for never turning your back at some of the worst times. And thank you, Sam, for making Mason who he is today."

Logan nodded. "She did."

"Mason was an ass—"

"Children!" someone yelled.

"—not great guy," Nate continued. "And he'll say he still isn't, but he is. You've made him a better person. You made him love harder. You made him forgive harder, and the fact that he forgave even a little is a big deal. Mase was never built that way."

Mason squeezed my hand, nodding along with Nate.

"And you've made him want to build a better future with you than I think he would've if you hadn't been in the picture. I don't know what we all would've done without you. You're the glue for us. You hold everyone together, whether you realize it or not, and I thank you for that. I thank you for always being kind to me."

Another tear slid down my cheek. "It wasn't hard," I murmured. "You were kind to me too."

He grinned. "Yeah, well, sometimes I wasn't the nicest guy." He shared a look with Mason. "But we're all here now, and I think I'm kind of in shock." He clapped Mason on the shoulder, moving to Logan's shoulder too. "We grew up, guys."

Both brothers nodded.

Nate laughed. "The fact that none of us are in jail right this second speaks volumes. Thank you, Sam, for that too."

Laughter rose from the audience.

"But I really just want to say I love you both. You're family to me. I know that'll never change, and I guess, thank you for making it official." He raised his glass. "To not living in sin anymore."

He took a sip as everyone laughed again before joining his salute.

Heather stood next to me, holding her hand out. "Okay. It's time for the girls." Matteo had started to stand, but she shook her head. "Nope. It's maid of honor time."

Matteo sat.

And Nate handed the microphone to Heather.

Heather laughed into the microphone, her voice light. "Now, it's the ladies' turn." She moved the bottom of her dress over so it was more centered around her. Heather had been the most reserved about the dress. She'd confessed in the bathroom that she worried everyone would see her breasts. I'd doubled over in laughter, and I giggled again now, thinking about it.

She had looked sheepish, shrugging as she grabbed her boobs and pushed them up, adjusting.

"What? I might like to dress skimpy, but I never really show off the girls. They're for Channing only."

"No." I had touched her arm, still shaking my head. "I have no idea why that's so funny, but thank you. I worried about the dress, but everyone just agreed, and you never said anything."

"I felt bad. I think we're all just happy for you." She'd grinned. "Besides, we all look ridiculously hot in this getup." She looked down at the sheer, light green fabric flowing over the sheath beneath. "You've got style. I'll say that for you, even though Malinda fought you on it. Didn't she?"

I'd nodded, still chuckling. "Yeah." I yawned to stop laughing and wiped at a tear. "She was thinking I'd want a more formal dress, but nope. That's not me." I'd reached out and touched Heather's dress. It was a simple cut, falling just above the knee with a ruched top. The girls had picked their style. They could have spaghetti straps or sleeveless like Heather's. They all looked comfortable, but so beautiful, and the wedding was all light green and cream. I had little white lights filling the church where we got married, and the reception too. If I had to say so myself, the entire place looked beyond regal and elegant.

"Malinda started crying when she saw everything last night," I'd told her. "She said I'd been right and how dare she question me." I'd smiled, feeling Malinda's hug again. "I love her."

"You got a good one there." Heather had nodded, her flirty eyes growing serious and misty. "You're a good one, Sam. I know you think you're the lucky one, but it's not you. We're the lucky ones."

I bit my lip, my throat swelling.

"Those friends you had before, they were assholes. They lost out, completely. There's a reason Mason loves you, a reason Logan loves you like a sister and has since day one. A reason Malinda cherishes you so much. A reason Mark adores you, and not just because he's your stepbrother. They all love you because of you. You're amazing, and you have no idea how good of a person you are."

We'd stood in front of the bathroom mirror, and I turned so I was half-hidden by the tampon bin. I felt the tears flowing and couldn't do anything to stop them.

"Sam." Heather had pulled me into her arms. She'd hugged me, and while it should've been awkward because both of us had our hair done up and makeup on, it wasn't.

I'd hugged her back, whispering, "Thank you."

She was the friend I needed who'd appeared at just the right time. And there'd never be words enough for me to express my gratitude to her.

"Thank you," she'd whispered back. I'd felt her tears on my shoulder.

A moment later, I'd stepped back and fluffed her dress out. "See? Another reason my taste is spectacular. Another bride couldn't have done that." I'd smoothed my own dress.

Heather had laughed, dabbing at her eyes. "Yes, another reason."

And she was dabbing at her eyes now too, as she held the microphone. Putting her glass down, she reached for a balled-up tissue.

"I haven't even started." She laughed huskily. "I hope it's okay, Mason, but I'm going to center more on Sam."

He nodded. "Of course."

She cleared her throat, patting the side of her dress so it was smooth. "So, I have a lot of friends from Roussou and my boyfriend . . ." She gave him a soft smile, and Channing nodded from where he sat at the end of Mason's groomsmen. "He lives and works there, and he grew up there. I went to Fallen Crest, and Samantha doesn't know this because she's never stopped to think about it, but she was actually one of the first good friends I had. I grew up with Roussou people, so my Fallen Crest friends were lacking, until one day I'm sitting outside the bar my dad owned at the time, and here comes this skinny, gorgeous girl. She's all sweaty and looking at me like she's a lost puppy wondering if she can have something to eat. I think I scared you that day, but you thanked me earlier today for becoming your friend at just the right time. You don't know this . . ."

Her voice grew hoarse, and she blinked back tears. "But you did the same for me. I needed a friend too; I just didn't know it. You always say I'm the tough one, but that's not true. It's you. You're so strong, and I am beyond blessed that you chose me. Like Nate and Logan, I don't consider you a friend. You're a sister to me, and I've never had one of those. So thank you for that." She bit off the last word, unable to keep going. Her tears were blinding her.

Standing, I took the microphone from her and pulled her in for a hug. I struggled to keep my emotions in check, but that'd been the story today. I was crying one second, then laughing the next. I knew we were just starting the evening too.

Heather tucked her head into the crook of my neck and shoulder. "I'm pregnant."

"What?" I pulled back and grabbed the microphone. It hadn't caught that, but I wanted to be safe. I passed it off to Mason and looked back to Heather. "You're sure?"

She nodded. "Channing knows, but don't tell anyone. We'll announce it later. Will you be her godmother?"

Her.

I touched my chest. I was going to be a godmother. "Yes! Yes."

And we were back to hugging.

I had a feeling we'd be doing this all night long.

After we settled back in our seats, Matteo made a toast. Courtney and Grace did one together, and even Channing stood for a few words. After that, it was our parents' turn. Malinda cried the whole time, so it was really just David speaking, but when he'd finished, she grabbed a piece of paper and shoved it into his hand. He read from it, so we heard Malinda's word through him. Then it was James and Analise's turn. Everyone tensed slightly, but James only laughed.

"This would be the perfect time to get you back, Mason, but I won't," James said. His eyes filled with mirth. "I'm hoping Logan will forget the favor I promised him too, so I'm going to be the doting and proud father I always should've been when you were growing up."

And he was just that. He talked about how proud he was of Mason, how Mason was the man James aspired to become, and by the end, there wasn't a dry eye in the room. Analise took the microphone next, a tender smile on her face.

She looked exceptionally beautiful tonight, but my mother was always stunning—especially lately because she'd continued to be stable since she returned from her long hospital stay. She'd even helped me pick out my wedding dress, and advised on the decorations too. I knew she'd offered to take control of the cleanup, but that was a job in itself. Still, it meant a lot. It meant more than a lot. We weren't daughter and mother, but we were becoming friends in a way. It felt good. It felt right, and her toast was short, but very sweet.

"I have loved you since the day I met you," she said. "I have loved you when I couldn't show you. I have loved you when I was hurting you." She began crying, and so did I. "And it was because of my love for you that I sought help. I loved you every day I was in the hospital. I loved you every day I was in the residential home. I loved you the day I came home, and I have loved you every day since. I will love you every day that you'll let me, and if you choose not to, I will continue to love you even after that. I will never stop loving you, Samantha, and I am not the reason you are the amazing woman you've become, but my heart couldn't be any prouder. Like Mason has done for his father, I thank you for showing me the type of woman I should be. I love you."

I went to hug her, then moved to hug all the others.

There was more talking and celebrating after that. Helen stood up. Garrett stood up. My little sister even made a speech, and everyone melted into puddles when she waved her little hands in the air.

But then Logan announced it was time to party, and soon we were all on the dance floor.

A couple hours later, I began to wonder: Do newly wedded couples stay until the end of their receptions?

I had this idea in my head that they slunk off halfway through the night, eager for their time alone, and everyone else stayed dancing and partying until the deejay quit working. I don't know if that's the truth, but it's not what Mason and I did—not because we didn't want to be alone, but because we'd already broken the tradition of not seeing each other the night before. We not only saw each other, we slept in the same bed, and had some hot and rough sex. Oh yeah. We shattered that tradition, and we were also the last to go at the end of the party.

After the deejay finally cut the music and packed up his things, all of our friends remained in the banquet room for another hour, talking and laughing around a table. Logan held Taylor on his lap. She leaned against his chest, her eyes half closed the whole time. Nate was beside them, with Heather and Channing next to him, holding hands under the table. Matteo sat with Grace, and Courtney was beside her. Finally, with exhaustion growing, people began saying their goodnights and goodbyes.

Courtney was first to wave goodbye with tears in her eyes. She wound her little arms around me and whispered in my ear, "I wish all the blessings and happily ever afters for you, friend." She squeezed me tight one more time. "I know you guys will be fine." She kissed my forehead and waved to everyone else as she left.

Grace and Matteo were next, holding hands.

He went for the side-hug with Mason, but Mason wasn't having it. He went straight for a real hug, and the two clasped each other tight. Matteo pulled back and flicked away a tear like it was never there as he reached for Grace again. I knew she meant it when she said congratulations to me.

Heather and Channing were third in line, and we shared hugs all around. Mason was my best friend. Logan after him, but then it was Heather for sure. No girl, not even Taylor, would ever fill Heather's shoes, and this hug wasn't really a "I'm unsure how this will affect us in the future" hug, but one that said "I love you to death and call me when you wake up so we can laugh about everything all over again."

As Heather and Channing left, I knew we'd be seeing each other or talking very shortly. They were lifers with us.

Then there were five.

Nate (his date had slipped away to their hotel room for the night already), Logan and Taylor, and Mason and me.

I don't know who started it, but we all stood and moved out to the lobby. We stopped there, and I curved into Mason's side, his arm around my waist. Taylor had curled into Logan, and Nate's hands were in his pockets. Their tuxedo jackets were long gone, as were the slim black ties they'd worn, and the ends of their shirts had untucked from their pants.

Mason's eyes were tired, but alert, and his hair had been raked through so it stood up a little bit. It suited him. He could've been a CEO after an all-nighter, and one day, I was sure he would be.

I knew he would eventually tire of football. He and Logan were already talking about business ventures, starting up a tentative idea, and I had no worries about it. I was certain that eventually they would be CEOs, rivaling their father. Until then, they were going their planned routes. The NFL for Mason, and law school for Logan.

"This is it." Nate glanced around the group, a twinge of sadness in his eyes.

I wasn't sure what Nate was going to do. He'd followed Mason to Massachusetts and was working in a business there, but he'd kept quiet about his plans for the future. I had a feeling that wherever Mason was, Nate would be too.

Mason's hand tightened around my waist; I felt good and anchored, and I needed it. The tiredness was getting to me. I yawned.

Mason nodded. "This is it."

Nate looked at Logan. "I'm going up to wake my date. You'll be at the house later?"

That house was the one I'd moved into and started this whole process. James and Analise had kept their promise. They'd moved out, and it was left for us to use whenever we wanted. Everyone had stayed there this past week, but some got hotel rooms for tonight. And I knew Mason had plans for us.

We were heading to Europe for a month of backpacking. We'd stay in hostels unless they were too nasty, then we'd spend the money for a nice hotel. But we had plans to stay as grassroots as possible. I was excited about the honeymoon trip, but I knew tonight Mason was intending to take us somewhere else completely.

"Yep. We'll be there," Logan told Nate. "We'll see you later."

Nate nodded and pointed toward the elevators. "I should get up there before I can't wake her up anymore."

There was another round of hugs, but we'd see Nate tomorrow evening.

Nate was family. He'd never venture far from our side.

Logan and Taylor walked beside us out to the parking lot. Once we got to Mason's Escalade, Taylor didn't linger. She broke from Logan's side, coming to hug me and whisper, "He'll stay forever if I don't do something. Love you, sister, and I'll see you guys tomorrow for dinner."

We hugged once more, then she hugged Mason and turned to Logan. "I'll be in the car. Not too long, okay?"

He nodded, and their hands swiped as he handed off the keys.

Then there was three.

We looked at each other, and Logan blinked back a few tears. A crooked grin showed, and he sighed, "The Threesome Fearsome."

He looked at Mason, then me, and I matched his crooked grin, saying, "Always." I slipped my hand back into Mason's, but I gave him some space.

This was it. This was the final hug goodbye. In some small sense, things would be different after this. Mason was my husband.

I grinned up at him, feeling the same breathlessness I always did when he entered a room. But I also felt flutters in my chest and stomach today for the same reason Logan was trying not to tear up.

Mason was my husband now. My real family. It was him and me. Husband and wife. God, I was someone's wife. I was Mason's wife. I felt a whole new tingle at that thought. I'd never get used to it. It was all so surreal, but that was our Twosome Fearsome.

The Threesome Fearsome would remain, but it was different. Logan had always been on Mason's other side, but after this, he would stand behind us. It would be Mason and me, side by side. We'd follow our own trail, and eventually Logan would start off on his own path with Taylor.

Logan cursed. "Fuck. Why am I sad all of a sudden?"

"Logan." I opened my arms, and he moved in, hugging me tightly and burying his head in my shoulder. I smoothed a hand down his head and brought him closer.

Then he turned, and Mason gripped him in another hug. They stood together for a long time. When they stepped back, both wiped a hand over their eyes, and Mason reached for me again.

He flicked a finger up to the corner of his eye, looking away as he said, "I knew getting married would be emotional, but shit . . ."

I laced our fingers, and he took another breath and seemed to calm a little.

We waited another moment, and he looked back to his brother. He had steadied again. "I fucking love you."

Logan nodded. "Same for you." His eyes found mine. "You too."

I felt punched by what I saw there.

He was like a little boy again. There was no wall. He wasn't flirting with Taylor. There was no sarcastic joke on his tongue. His eyes weren't flashing from mischief or the need to fight. He was just simply there, staring at us like we were the two pillars he'd been leaning on the last six or seven years of his life, and we were crumbling around him.

It wasn't true.

"Logan." I reached for him with my free hand and tugged him close to us. "We're not going anywhere."

He nodded. "I know." He squeezed my hand, and the three of us formed a circle. We stood like that until Logan finally broke away.

He went to his Escalade, and I waved at Taylor inside. She waved back, her face streaming with tears. When Logan got in he leaned over, and I saw her reach for him. After a moment, he wheeled the Escalade out of the parking lot.

Then it was two.

I looked up, leaning back against my husband's chest. A smile curved my mouth. "Husband."

He looked down at me with an answering smile. "Wife."

No other words needed to be said.

I got my happily ever after one night when I parked at a gas station with two drunken friends. I just hadn't known it then.

He leaned down for a kiss, and I sighed as our lips met.

It was perfect.

ONE LAST RACE

"Kade!"

I heard my name barked out next to me, and I jerked.

"What?" I snapped my head up, irritated, but I already knew who it was and relaxed right away. I quieted my tone. "What is it, Coach?"

I half-snorted at the name. He was my coach, trainer, sadistic torturer, and grudging father figure all rolled into one. He was my Olympic trainer, and he gestured out to where the other runners had started to congregate.

"You ready?" he said.

I nodded, but I wasn't.

I was lit up like a starving dog that saw its first steak, ever. I was almost salivating, but I was distracted at the same time.

"You were supposed to sleep a full night last night." He watched me with narrowed eyes, his black jacket zipped all the way up under his jaw and whistle in hand. He dropped it, letting it fall back against his chest. "Kade. Did you—"

"Yes, yes." I waved him off. "I'll be fine. I'm ready."

Had I slept all night? No.

Would my running suffer because of it? No.

Or, I hoped not.

I scanned the rest of the runners. I'd run this race before. This was my second time at the Olympics. And I ran. That's what I did. Granted, that's what all of these people did, but it had been my life source at one point.

I knew once I walked to that starting line, everything else would leave my mind.

I was born to do this. I would be fine.

I told my trainer this, and he nodded, but I knew he didn't quite believe me.

He stepped back and pointed to the starting line. "Go and kick ass. Again."

I clipped my head in a nod. That was what I would do. When it came to running, that was all I did. I went and finished my stretching. My mind wandered off, but as I took my place at the line, I looked over and saw the reason for my scattered thoughts.

The first warning sounded.

I had good reason to daydream.

"Set!"

Mason waved from where he stood, with our daughter in his arms. We'd named her Logan Malinda Kade—we called her Maddy.

BOOM! The gun went off.

And I ran.

The end.

For more books to come, go to www.tijansbooks.com

ACKNOWLEDGEMENTS

I can't believe this. This is the last full-length novel I'll write for these characters. It seemed like so long when I wrote Fallen Crest High. I've been asked what inspired that book, and the answer always confuses me too. I just heard a song (Sail by AWOLNATION) and I sat down and outlined the entire book in three days. I had no clue what I was doing back then. I was just writing and putting chapters up for free reading. The goal was always to somehow make money writing, but I had no plan to tackle that goal. I just wrote, and then there was one time when I was at an intersection leaving my job. I was going home, and I decided to stop writing. I just couldn't put my efforts into it anymore. Financially, I had to pursue a different career and it was one that would've consumed me just as much as being a writer so...at that intersection, I quit writing. Of course, this didn't last. By the time I got home, I didn't even think about it. I think I pushed off my decision, turned on my computer, sat down, and began writing again.

Two months later—*Fallen Crest High* took off, and my life's never been the same.

I just can't believe how loved this series is. It's grown into something bigger than me. The continued love and support the Fallen Crest characters get blows me away. I feel humbled to be the writer who brought them to you, and I will miss writing these guys, but for now—they're going to be happy.

To all the readers who have loved Sam, Mason, and Logan so much that they told others about them: you guys help give life to these characters, and on behalf of them, I thank you.